DEATH BRINGS A STORKE

CRADLED IN FEAR

DEATH BRINGS A STORKE

CRADLED IN FEAR

Anita Boutell

COACHWHIP PUBLICATIONS

Greenville, Ohio

Death Brings a Storke / Cradled in Fear, by Anita Boutell
Copyright © 2016 Coachwhip Publications
No claims made on public domain material.
Death Brings a Storke published 1938.
Cradled in Fear published 1942.

ISBN 1-61646-334-1
ISBN-13 978-1-61646-334-2

CoachwhipBooks.com

CONTENTS

DANCE OF DEATH:
THE CRIME FICTION OF ANITA BOUTELL (1895-1972)
CURTIS EVANS

Introduction

Once deservingly seen as a leading player in a beguiling new troupe of sophisticated women crime writers of the 1930s and 1940s, Anita Boutell led "a wondrous whirl of a life" which included, before she published her first crime novel at the age of 43, a short-lived career in expressionist dance and short-lived marriages to three men—a popular Jazz Age playwright, a Continental playboy war hero and writer, and a prominent bibliographer—all of whom died before reaching the age of forty. The heady combination of Anita's personal beauty, social prominence, scandalous divorces, and acrimonious child custody dispute with her first husband put her name in newspapers long before she began publishing crime novels. Yet to vintage mystery fans Anita Boutell should be remembered most not for the dizzying social whirl of her admittedly rather public private life but for the delectable dance of death which she exhibits in her small but impressive body of crime fiction, published between 1938 and 1942.

Part One
"'Tis a Wondrous Whirl of a Life, My Girl"
(from "Discharged Honorably," by Sarah Williams)

Anita Boutell was born Anita Day in Newark, New Jersey on May 10, 1895, one of two daughters of businessman Waters Burrows Day and his wife Anne May (Burr) Day. Waters B. Day graduated with a Bachelor of Science degree from Wesleyan University in 1891 and the next year began working for W. F. Day & Brother, the successful catering and confectionary business of his father, Wilbur Fisk Day, and uncle, Pennington Mulford Day. The Day family ran popular ice cream gardens in several New Jersey cities, including Ocean Grove, Asbury Park, Morristown and Newark. In 1909 Waters B. Day, who by this time managed the Newark branch of the family business, was elected president of the Newark Trust Company, one of the city's most important banks.[1]

Growing up in a privileged household, young Anita Day was able to indulge her artistic interests in dance and the stage. Upon attaining adulthood she initially ran an "aesthetic dancing" studio in Philadelphia, then turned to the stage in bohemian Greenwich Village, New York, where she performed with the Greenwich Village Players, taking the role of the nymph Phoeno, for example, in *Pan and the Young Shepherd*, presented at the Greenwich Village Theater in 1918. In Greenwich Village beautiful, blue-eyed Anita met Alfred Patrick Kearney, an artistically ambitious young man who had sprung from a middle-class Columbus, Ohio, family of Irish heritage. In 1915 he left Ohio State University, where he had been enrolled as a student of medicine for three years, to move to New York. There he began writing sketches for *The Smart Set* (co-edited by H. L. Mencken) and acting with another Greenwich Village troupe, the Washington Square Players. Anita and Patrick married in January 1917, when Anita was 21 and Patrick was 23.

---

[1] Francis Bazley Lee, ed., *Genealogical and Memorial History of the State of New Jersey*, vol. 3 (New York, Lewis Historical Publishing, 1910), 1290; Henry Cooper Pitney, *A History of Morris County, New Jersey: Embracing Upwards of Two Centuries 1710-1913*, vol. 2 (New York: Lewis Historical Publishing, 1914), 433-434; Biographical Sketch, Day Family Collection, Monmouth County Historical Association, Freehold, New Jersey, http://www.monmouthhistory.org/Sections-read-94.html; Paul Goldfinger, "Days Ocean Grove Ice Cream Garden: A History Dating Back to 1876," 16 August 2014, *Blogfinger: A Digital Breeze from the Jersey Shore*, http://blogfinger.net/tag/history-of-days-ice-cream-in-ocean-grove-nj/. Genealogical data on Anita Boutell and her husbands is drawn from records found on Ancestry.com.

Two years later the couple had a daughter, whom they named Monica.[2]

An aspiring playwright, Patrick Kearney in the first years after his marriage to Anita had several one-act plays performed by the Washington Square Players, including "Tongues of Fire" and "The Great Noontide," but he did not have a major success until 1925, with the play *A Man's Man: A Comedy of Life under the "L,"* a satire of white-collar, middle-class illusions that starred Dwight Fry and Josephine Tuttle. (The play was adapted to film in 1929.) The next year Kearney authored his best-known play, a hugely successful stage adaptation of Theodore Dreiser's 'Twenties indictment of the American Dream, the novel *An American Tragedy*, which the *New York Times* enthusiastically deemed "a play to be seen." Two years later, the rising playwright, now a prominent go-to name on the Great White Way, adapted for the stage *Elmer Gantry*, Sinclair Lewis's satirical novel about American religious fundamentalism.[3]

Before Kearney achieved success as a playwright, however, his marriage with Anita had hit the rocks. Kearney obtained a divorce from his wife in 1924, citing decorated Great War veteran George

---

[2] *The Independent Press and Bloomfield Citizen*, 19 January 1917, 2; *Ohio State University Monthly* 8 (July 1916), "Pastoral Comedy Charms" (review of *Pan and the Young Shepherd*), *New York Times*, 19 March 1918; Virginia Pastor, "A Little Theater with a Big History: The Greenwich Village Theater," *Greenwich Village History*, http://gvh.aphdigital.org/exhibits/show/the greenwichvillagetheatre; "Presenting Patrick Kearney," *New York Times*, 24 October 1926.

[3] "Presenting Patrick Kearney," *New York Times*, 24 October 1926; "In Memory of Dwight Frye," *Vintage Gold*, at http://vintage-gold.livejournal.com/ 1366.html?thread=1366; "Presenting Patrick Kearney," *New York Times*, 12, 26 October 1926. In *Blood on the Stage* Amnon Kabatchnik calls Kearney's stage version of *An American Tragedy* "a cohesive step-by-step format that clearly and intelligently pictures the rise and fall of Clyde Griffiths, a victim of society, weak, confused, selfish, and ambitious." See *Blood on the Stage, 1925-1950: Milestone Plays of Crime, Mystery and Detection: An Annotated Repertoire* (Plymouth, UK: Scarecrow Press, 2010), 41.

Alexander Porterfield as co-respondent, and he was awarded custody of their daughter. The couple's acrimonious 1924 divorce was followed by a protracted custody dispute over Monica. In 1926, Kearney obtained a warrant for Anita's arrest on a charge of kidnapping after she fled from her parent's home in Glen Ridge, New Jersey, to Pennsylvania's Poconos, Monica in tow, in an attempt to prevent Kearney from taking their daughter on a long trip to Europe with his second wife. (Anita was described in the arrest warrant as "five feet four inches in height, with brown bobbed hair and blue eyes.")[4]

Part of Anita's objection to Monica's overseas sojourn may have been that Monica apparently had been scheduled to embark for Europe under the care of the Baron and Baroness von Koczian, who were friends of Kearney's. Baron Gustav von Koczian had been embroiled in his own love scandal eighteen years earlier, when, he, then "a handsome motorcar agent," had run off with, and later married, Princess Amalie zu Furstenberg, sister of Prince Max Egon zu Furstenberg, "one of the wealthiest men in Germany and a personal friend of the German Kaiser." After the couple divorced in 1917, Baron von Koczian wed actress Ossi Oswalda, "the German Mary Pickford," and became a film producer. This marriage having ended in 1925, von Koczian was on his third wife, Danish actress Elsie Fuller, in 1926, when he stepped into the acrimonious affair between Anita and her ex-husband. With Kearney trailing her in determined pursuit, the absconding Anita resurfaced with little Monica after several days; and the court to which the whole mess was handed decreed that the child would live with her maternal grandparents, with formal custody and liberal visitation rights granted to her father.[5]

---

[4] "Broadway Playwright is Hunting Hills for Child," *Indiana Gazette*, 4 June 1926, 1; "Playwright Charges Ex-Wife Kidnapped Child," *New York Times*, 6 June 1926.

[5] "Playwright Scours Mountains for His Daughter," (Harrisburg) *Evening News*, 4 June 1926, 1; "Eloping Pricess Marries Auto Agent," *New York Times*, 2 August 1908; "Custody of Child Given to Playwright," *New York Times*, 10

Kearney's second wife, an actress named Irene O'Brien, whom he wed not long after ending his marriage with Anita, divorced him in 1926. Two years later Kearney wed a twenty-year-old artist's model named Elizabeth Russell, eleven days after meeting her for the first time at a New Year's Eve party, in an extremely unorthodox ceremony arranged for the couple (who were described as "formerly . . . members of the Roman Catholic Church"), by Floyd Dell, an influential leftist author, editor and critic, and officiated over by former rabbi Lewis Browne, a prominent philosopher and lecturer. The couple honeymooned at Eugene O'Neill's home in Bermuda and the next year had a daughter, Deirdre, but this marriage, like Kearney's first two, soon deteriorated. Additionally, Kearney lost his personal fortune, estimated at a quarter of a million dollars, with the onset of the Great Depression. At the time of his death in New York City on March 28, 1933, when he was but 39 years old, Kearney was living apart from his wife and Deirdre in a furnished room at 348 East Fiftieth Street. His landlady, smelling gas coming from Kearney's fourth-floor front room, called a policeman to break down the door, whereupon they discovered Kearney dead "on the floor . . . with a gas tube in his mouth." He left no note.[6]

Anita herself married two more times. In July 1924, shortly after the dissolution of her marriage with Patrick Kearney, she wed George Alexander Porterfield, her aforementioned co-respondent in her husband's divorce suit. George Alexander Porterfield, one of three sons of attorney Charles Porterfield and his wife Katherine Knox Taylor, was born in 1892 in St. Paul, Minnesota, though in 1896, when he was four years old, the family moved to New York,

(cont.) June 1926. On Baron von Koczian's later marriages, see "Gustav von Koczian-Miskolczky (1877-1958), IMDb, at http://www.imdb.com/name/nm5588063/.

[6] "P. Kearney's Party a Surprise Wedding: Playwright and Miss Penick Married in Specially Devised Ceremony," New York Times, 13 January 1928; "Playwright Kills Himself with Gas," New York Times, 29 March 1933.

settling in the small maritime town of Northport, Long Island, home of the Edward Thompson Publishing Company, one of the most important legal publishers in the country, for whom Charles Porterfield served as managing editor for four decades. By 1908 Charles and Katherine apparently had divorced, Katherine returning with her sons to St. Paul, where as "Mrs. Charles Porterfield," an ostensible widow, she owned a comfortable Queen Anne-style boarding house. There one of her paying guests, an aspiring writer named Donald Ogden Stewart, was often visited in 1919 by another young man with considerable writing ambitions, F. Scott Fitzgerald, who at the time was working on his first novel, the epoch-making Jazz Age bestseller *This Side of Paradise*. Charles Porterfield married a second time, to Salvadora Cohen, daughter of Savannah cotton broker Octavus Cohen (and a likely relative of author and journalist Octavus Roy Cohen), and the couple resided together in Northport until Charles's death in 1936.[7] The Long Island town likely served as inspiration for the setting of Anita's final crime novel, *Cradled in Fear*, her only book set in the United States (see pp. 21-22).

Named after his paternal grandfather, a Virginian who served as an officer both in the Mexican-American War and the American Civil War, George Alexander Porterfield reflected his martial family background when, upon the outbreak of the First World War, he crossed over the border to Canada and enlisted in the Canadian Overseas Expeditionary Force. He later transferred to the British

---

[7] Frank B. Porterfield, *The Porterfields* (Roanoke, VA: Southeastern Press, 1948), 293; "The Tabb Family," *William and Mary College Quarterly Historical Magazine* 13 (October 1904): 275; *New York Times*, 14 May 1918, 4, 16 December 1936, 27; gregd3, "A Small Town Named Northport, NY," 23 September 2013, *Tuesday Night Bar Exam*, at https://gregd3.word press.com/2013/09/23/a-small-town-named-northport-ny/; John J. Koblas, *A Guide to F. Scott Fitzgerald's St. Paul* (1978; repr., St. Paul, Minnesota Historical Society Press), 45. Additional information about the Porterfields in this and the next paragraph was drawn from census, military and transportation records on the website Ancestry.com.

army, rising to the rank of Temporary Lieutenant in the Lancashire Fusiliers. After the war, the dashing, reputedly many times wounded war hero styled himself a journalist and author, though I have not been able to determine with certainty what he actually wrote. Possibly he was the Alexander Porterfield who published short stories, including one titled "The Philanderer," in *The Harper's Monthly* in 1921 and 1922 and critical essays in the *London Mercury* in 1925 and 1926. Upon becoming man and wife, the couple moved to London, but, according to Anita's divorce suit, her husband, who was dubbed a "Continental playboy" in newspapers, soon deserted her "to play about" on the French Riviera. In 1930, Anita divorced Porterfield, who died in France the next year—like Patrick Kearney he was only 39—and was buried in Paris. (I do not know the cause of the early death of Anita's second husband.) Immediately after the divorce Anita wed Henry Sherman Boutell, whom she seems to have begun seeing three years earlier, in 1927. Nine years younger than his new bride, Henry Boutell was a recent Harvard college graduate who came from a noted family that traced its ancestry back to New England in the 1630s. He was a descendant of American Founding Father Roger Sherman as well as a grandson of a former United States congressman and diplomat from Illinois, for whom he was named.[8]

The surefire combination of matrimonial discord and social prominence made Anita a source for salacious newsprint gossip in the 'Twenties and 'Thirties. Her bitter custody dispute with Kearney hit the pages of the *New York Times* and other newspapers ("Broadway Playwright is Hunting Hills for Child," "Playwright Charges Ex-Wife Kidnapped Child"), while her second divorce inspired the mocking headline, drawn from her days as a dancer, "Nimble Anita Trips to Reno, Then to Altar." Even as late

---

[8] "Nimble Anita Trips to Reno, Then to Altar," *Milwaukee Sentinel*, 26 August 1930; *The Publishers Weekly* 133 (1938), 848; St. Paul's School *Alumni Horae* 17 (Spring 1937), 23; "Henry S. Boutell Dies in Italy at 70, Ex-Minister to Portugal and Switzerland and Once Congressman from Illinois," *New York Times*, 13 March 1926.

Albuquerque, NM, *Journal*
February 3, 1935

as 1935, the magazine section of newspapers around the country, in a scandalmongering syndicated article on "millionaire playboys" who had killed themselves, included references to the first Kearney divorce and his subsequent suicide, under photos of him and Anita:

(under Patrick's photo)
HIS "AMERICAN TRAGEDY"
"Pat" Kearney, Who Ran Up His Fat Bank Balance
by Adapting for the Stage Theodore Dreiser's
Noted Novel. Kearney Got Fed Up with
Life's Vicissitudes; Slew Himself.

(under Anita's photo)
LOVE'S CASTLE CRASHED
Mrs. Patrick Kearney, No. 1, the Socially Prominent
Anita Day Porterfield. They Were Divorced.
He Sought and Found Welcome Death.[9]

With her third husband Anita Day Kearney Porterfield Boutell once again had found a partner of literary bent. Henry Sherman Boutell, a graduate of St. Paul's School and Harvard University and a son of Roger Sherman Boutell, a retired lawyer who in 1925 had founded the Tecolote Book Shop in Santa Barbara, California, in 1928 had authored *First Editions of Today and How to Tell Them*, an acknowledged classic among bibliophiles that would go through a total of four editions. The couple settled in London with Monica in November 1930, but any newfound wedded bliss for Anita was short-lived, for Henry died at the tragically young age of 26 in March 1931, after less than a year of marriage. The twice-divorced, once-widowed Anita remained with Monica in England (first in London and later in a Sussex cottage) until the outbreak of another storm in 1939—this one a catastrophic global conflagration.

---

[9] "Why Another Millionaire Playboy Preferred Oblivion to Life and Love," *Spokane Spokesman-Review*, 2 February 1935, 20.

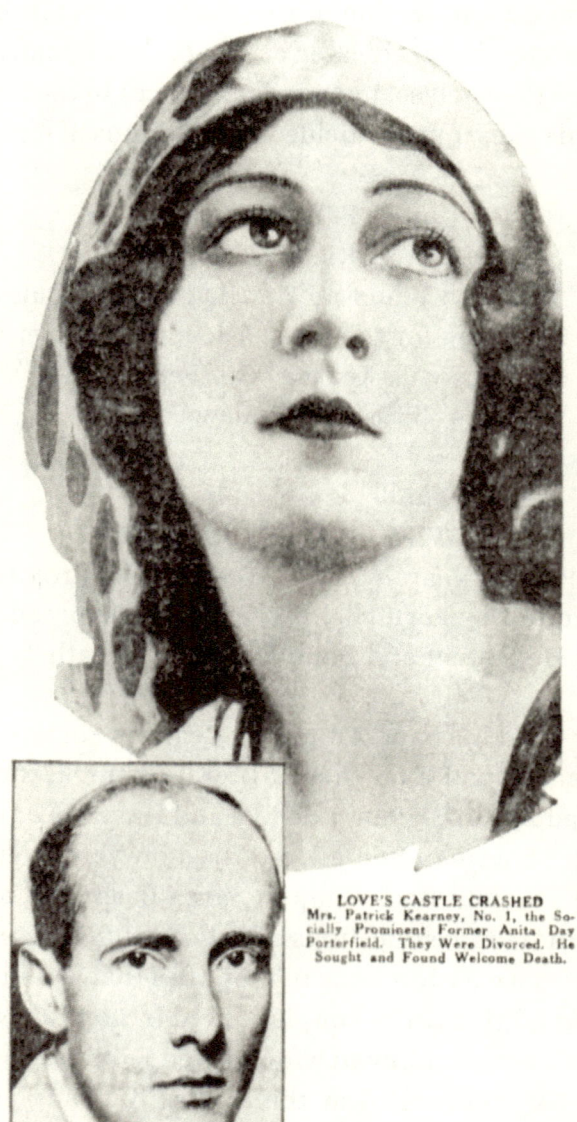

LOVE'S CASTLE CRASHED
Mrs. Patrick Kearney, No. 1, the Socially Prominent Former Anita Day Porterfield. They Were Divorced. He Sought and Found Welcome Death.

HIS "AMERICAN TRAGEDY"
"Pat" Kearney, Who Ran Up His Fat Bank Balance by Adapting for the Stage Theodore Dreiser's Noted Novel. Kearney Got Fed Up with Life's Vicissitudes; Slew Himself.

Albuquerque, NM, *Journal*
February 3, 1935

Returning to the US, the pair moved out to Santa Barbara, home of Henry's parents, with whom Anita had remained close since his death. Anita's closeness to the Boutells is suggested by the fact that she employed this surname for all her published crime novels.[10]

HENRY SHERMAN BOUTELL
Born on August 11, 1905, at Berne, Switzerland. Home address, 21 Ridge Lane, Santa Barbara, California. Prepared at St. Paul's. In college one year as undergraduate.

Henry Boutell at Harvard, probably three years before he met Anita.

Part Two
"The moon still continues her clear light to shed /
On the dance that they fearfully lead"
(transl. "Der Totantanz," Johann Wolfgang von Goethe)

In early 1938 Anita Boutell at the age of 43 published the first of her mystery novels, *Death Brings a Storke*, which she dedicated to Henry's mother, Avis, and, more enigmatically, to "Old." The seeming suddenness of Boutell's flowering as a novelist in her early forties may come as a surprise, yet the newly published author contended that she already had served a writing apprenticeship by assisting "at the birth of three novels, two plays, and uncounted short stories and articles." "Like a good wife or friend," she wryly noted of these early literary efforts on her part, "I let the male take the credit and won coyly for myself a dedication or two."

[10] *The Publishers Weekly* 133 (1938), 848; St. Paul's School *Alumni Horae* 17 (Spring 1937), 23.

Boutell's only straightforward exercise in classical detective fiction, *Death Brings a Storke* is a highly traditional English village mystery with an amateur sleuth, Doctor Archibald "Archie" Storke. When the novel opens, Archie and his wife Janey, both native Londoners, have been living in the English village of Pennerford for five years; and the locals have finally become accustomed to both their new doctor and his surname. (It was "sheer bravado," notes the author wryly, for Archie, saddled with the surname Storke, to have chosen the medical profession as his avocation.) Archie's pleasant breakfast with Janey is interrupted when he receives a call from the housekeeper at Whiteleaves, home of Andrew Herrick, informing him that Herrick has been discovered dead in his sitting room. Quickly making his way to Whiteleaves, Archie finds the unfortunate man dead in a chair, "sprawled grotesquely in striped silk pajamas and a flaunting dressing gown." A twelve gauge shotgun is lying on the floor, pointing toward the body. Herrick's left foot is slippered, while his right foot is bare. Presumably the dead man, who has a ghastly bullet wound to the head, committed suicide with the shotgun, but the compulsively inquisitive Archie has his doubts. Over conversation with the charming and empathetic Janey and investigation with Lieutenant-Colonel Roger Copeland, DSO, Chief Constable of the county, Archie discovers the shocking truth behind the affair, though not until another death has taken place. He and Janey also find time to assist a most winsome young woman—who just happens to be named Monica—through her romantic travails. (She is in love with one of the suspects.)

With *Death Brings a Storke*, Boutell devised an appealing debut for what surely must have been intended as a continuing mystery series; yet in fact the novel constituted Archie Storke's sole sleuthing flight. The author's remaining three crime novels, published between 1939 and 1942, were widely-praised standalone affairs which departed from the strict detective novel form. On the dust jacket of the first of these novels, *Tell Death to Wait*, which appeared a year after *Storke* in early 1939 and significantly was subtitled not "A Detective Story" but *A Story about a Murder*, Putnam, the publisher of all Boutell's books, announced the arrival of a major new crime fiction talent, one worthy of comparison with England's Crime Queens. "With this book," Putnam boldly declared, "Mrs. Boutell should take a front seat in that select group of mystery authors who, like Dorothy Sayers, can contrive a good plot and who at the same time provide a fine literary style and living characters."

Dedicated by Boutell to her father, *Tell Death to Wait* takes place over one cold November night and early morning at a house party at Wraith's Point, the Cotswolds country cottage of Leo (Leonora) Thane, a highly successful novelist and critic, and her much older husband, Godfrey Wellen (known as "G. W."). The guests are a married couple—Richard ("Rickey") Garnett, a fashionable Harley Street doctor, and his wife, Lady Una, daughter of the Earl of Danby—and four singles: Penelope ("Penny") Waring, Ross Fenton, Peter Druce and Nan Orr. The monstrously egocentric Leo has cuckolded G. W. multiple times since their marriage, including with two of their guests on this fateful night: Ross, an unwillingly discarded lover, and Rickey, the current one who is trying to break from her, much against her desire. Additionally Leo is writing a novel laying bare myriad slightly fictionalized details from the life of Penny, including her one-night stand with Peter, which Penny believes will ruin her engagement to another man. (His straitlaced mama will be mortified by this news.)

Everyone at the house party seemingly has reason to want Leo dead, even, perhaps, her younger, starstruck former friend Nan, who has been taken up again by Leo because she has had a successful book of poetry published. So when Leo is found dead, exactly one-fifth of the way through the novel, it does not come as a surprise to the reader. What is surprising is the course the tale takes from this point. The rest of the story is devoted to a psychological struggle between six of the guests, who insist that Leo's death was an accident, and the one remaining guest who knows that it must have been murder—and wants to report it to the police as such.

An exceedingly clever contrivance, *Tell Death to Wait* is a page-turner compulsively narrated by four different characters which most any mystery fan should feel compelled to finish in one evening. Not only does the ending deliver an emotional punch, there is as well a legitimate problem present to challenge puzzle fanciers. If the characters are not as memorable creations as those of Dorothy L. Sayers, they do indeed "live," particularly Leo, a fine etching in egoism who in her fierce unlikability is reminiscent of characters in the modern English crime novels of P. D. James.

Boutell delivered an impressive one-two artistic punch in 1939, in the late summer following the publication of *Tell Death to Wait* with that of a second highly original crime novel, *Death Has a Past*. Continuing the interesting narrative experimentation of *Wait*, *Past* is divided into five main parts, along with a prologue and epilogue. Interspersed between these sections are successive extracts from a murder confession. Reader interest in the novel is directed not to the traditional detective fiction question of whodunit, but rather to the questions of who will do it and to whom will it be done? In its book blurb Putnam again portrayed Boutell as belonging to a vanguard of authors who were carrying the mystery novel into new literary frontiers. "*Death Has a Past* is a first-rate mystery story, and it also it is something more," Putnam avowed. "Like *Rebecca*, Daphne du Maurier's famous best-seller, Mrs. Boutell's story has atmosphere and a brooding intensity. . . . the result is a most unusual story of real distinction."

Past takes place over a Monday and Tuesday at the country estate of Farthinglea during Emily's Week, an annual gathering of the female members (through ties both of blood and marriage) of the Hetherton family, over which wealthy Emily Hetherton ("Old Emily") had long presided. Old Emily is now dead, but her imperious and unlikable daughter-in-law, Claudia, who improbably inherited the family money upon the recent death of her husband, Alexander, desires to maintain the Emily's Week tradition and is forcing the other female members, all of whom for varying reasons are in need of money, to come and pay her court. It does not take long for dark passions and barely submerged recriminations to surface, and the author skillfully draws the reader onward to see just how these deadly hazards will make wreckage of human lives.

Dedicated by Boutell to her daughter Monica, who seems to have been the basis for Old Emily's appealing granddaughter, Philippa (Pippa), *Past* like *Wait* was well-received by critics in both the UK and in the US, where it went through two hardback printings by Putnam in 1939, two hardback printings by Books, Inc. in 1944 and 1945 and, finally, a paperback printing by Bantam in 1951. War soon disrupted Anita Boutell's life in England, however, and she did not publish another novel until late 1942, three years after the appearance of *Death Has a Past*, after she had settled in Santa Barbara. The previous year Howard Haycraft in his book *Murder for Pleasure: The Life and Times of the Detective Story* (1941) had bracketed Boutell (under the impression that the author was English) with Harriet Rutland, Dorothy Bowers and Anne Hocking as promising newcomers in the field of English manners mystery. Expectations were high for Boutell's new novel, a suspense tale titled *Cradled in Fear*, particularly after Putnam, comparing the novel to more mainstream bestselling fiction such as *Rebecca* and Dorothy Macardle's *The Uninvited* (1942; published in the UK in 1941 under the title *Uneasy Freehold*), listed the novel at $2.50 rather than $2.00. American reviews for *Fear* were excellent, with "a psychological thriller that will have the reader holding onto his seat" and "[readers] will find their hearts standing still in their breasts" typical testaments to the tale's palpitating impact. In the *New York Times Book Review*, *Fear* was given a long notice by novelist and reviewer Louise Maunsell Field, which is of especial interest on account of Field's observations concerning the influence of crime tales on mainstream fiction, a phenomenon Field herself did not deplore:

> Stimulated no doubt by the great popularity of the detective story, there has come a marked increase in the type of novel fairly closely related to the detective story, but making claim to somewhat more serious consideration, the type in which atmosphere and psychology are of greater importance than the puzzle as to which one of several persons is the criminal. The most recent addition to this latter group is Anita

Boutell's "Cradled in Fear". . . . It has atmosphere,
suspense, a very engaging heroine and a convincing
basis in diseased, abnormal passion. . . .[11]

For its part Putnam pronounced that *Cradled in Fear* was "a
chilling and dramatic novel of a young girl entangled in a web of
horror which ranks among the very best of psychological thrillers.
Blending the suspense of a mystery story with the polished tech-
nique of a fine novelist, it commands attention from the very first
page." Set almost entirely at a forbidding cliffside Victorian man-
sion at Prescott Point, Connecticut on Long Island Sound, *Fear*
details the perilous days that follow the marriage, after a mere
three-week courtship, of twenty-five-year-old Molly Nash to enig-
matic Sheridan "Sherry" Prescott. When the novel opens Molly has
traveled with Sherry to stay at the ancestral Prescott pile, visions
of lawfully wedded marital bliss filling her head, yet in classic fashion—*Fear* unquestionably bears resemblance to both *Rebecca* and
The Uninvited—she finds there not quite the reception she had
expected.

One would have expected that after the favorable critical reception of *Cradled in Fear* Anita Boutell might have joined the
ranks of younger women suspense writers who flourished in the
United States during the 1940s and 1950s, such as Charlotte
Armstrong (1905-1969) and Margaret Millar (1915-1994). Perhaps
Boutell was slightly ahead of her time (Millar's and Armstrong's
breakthrough novels, *The Unsuspected* and *The Iron Gates*, first
appeared in novel form in 1945), or perhaps she was disappointed
with *Fear's* sales, but, whatever the reasons, Boutell fell silent,
publishing no more fiction up to her death three decades later,
at the age of 77. Her mysteries since have remained out-of-print,
despite a brief flurry of reviews of a couple of her books on several
blogs in 2013 and 2014. Coachwhip's modern edition of Anita

---

[11] Louise Maunsell Field, "A Shivery Tale" (Review of *Cradled in Fear*), *New York Times Book Review*, 8 November 1942.

Boutell novels makes this accomplished author of charming and chilling crime fiction accessible after many decades of undeserved neglect to fans of vintage mystery. Let the dance begin again.

ANITA BOUTELL

The author of *Death Brings A Storke*, according to her own admission, is still at the beginning of her writing "career," but she adds that as an unacknowledged collaborator she has assisted at the birth of three novels, two plays, and uncounted short stories and articles. "Like a good wife or friend," she continues, "I let the male take the credit and won coyly for myself a dedication or two. As far as jobs are concerned, financial vicissitudes have led to some strange ones in the theatre and elsewhere, from the sublime in directing the movement for a production of Margaret Anglin's to selling ironers in the basement of Abraham & Straus's store in Brooklyn." More recently, Mrs. Boutell has read manuscripts and done synopses for a literary agency and for various motion picture companies. For the past few years she has been living quietly in a small cottage in Sussex, England, where this mystery was completed.

DEATH BRINGS A STORKE

TO
AVIS AND OLD

CHAPTER 1
THURSDAY 8 A.M. 9.30 A.M.

Archie Has a Corpse Instead of Breakfast

Dr. Archibald Storke, humming softly under his breath, lighted the heater and pushed wide the lattice window of the bathroom to let the steam escape. He put his head out into a world of blue and gold. It was a glorious morning and a good world. Below him in the garden Janey's late autumn flowers held their heads bravely to the sun. It was good to be alive and good especially to be alive in the country.

This morning Dr. Storke had no regret that he had foregone ambition and London to settle down in a small English village. He and Janey had made the right choice, though there had been times during those last five years when they had doubted, when the villagers had called him the "new doctor" and the "young doctor," and patients were scarce. And then his wretched, silly name? Dr. Storke smiled to himself. That was all over now; they were used to him and to his name.

His friends had said that, saddled with such a name, it was sheer bravado to become a doctor; but he, rather pleased with his *bon mot*, had replied to the colleague who rudely suggested obstetrics or deed poll, "I shall specialize in paronomasia."

He withdrew his head, lathered his face with happy care, and turned to his rack of eight razors. He hesitated.

"What day is it, Janey?"

"Thursday," Janey answered from the bedroom.

27

She had been expecting the question. Archie tried so hard to be methodical.

Adroitly Archie extracted a razor from the rack. It was another thing to be glad about, for Thursday's razor was his favorite. Still humming, he had finished his neck, his left cheek, and part of his chin before he asked the other morning question: "What time is it, my love?"

In reply Janey appeared at the bathroom door. Archie Storke stopped shaving to look at her approvingly. She was a delight, always so cool and trig, even in the early morning: well-cut tweeds with a jaunty neatness; little brogues with just the right amount of unobtrusive shine, like Janey, cheerful and experienced. For a moment she stood smiling at him. Then she consulted her wrist watch, bending her head and raising her arm with something of the earnestness of a child; she was a little near-sighted. As she lifted her head again, her ruddy hair settled round her small face in a sleek halo.

"Ducky," Archie Storke said.

Janey ignored this. "It's three minutes past eight. Hurry along, Archie, breakfast's ready."

He was putting his razor back when the telephone bell rang. Muttering, "Ten to one it's the Jenkins pest," he went to answer it.

"Dr. Storke speaking," he intoned patiently.

The voice from the other end reached him in a rush of excited, incoherent sounds. Archie Storke snatched the receiver from his ear.

"I can't understand you," he said. And then with inspiration, "Speak clearly and directly into the transmitter!"

His quotation from the telephone directory had the hoped-for effect. The rasping subsided. Gingerly he replaced the receiver.

"Yes, yes. . . . What? . . . What! . . . Good God! . . . I'll come right over. . . . At once, yes."

A flurried minute later he rushed into the dining room, straightening his tie with one hand, holding his bag with the other. Janey looked up from behind the coffee urn.

"Must you go without your breakfast, dear?"

Archie's expression answered her, he was wearing his emergency look. It was not Mrs. Jenkins then; it was something serious.

"That was Mrs. Ingles phoning from Whiteleaves. She was so rattled I couldn't understand her very well. Something's happened to Andrew Herrick: accident with a shotgun. She's afraid he's dead. I'm going right over. Keep my breakfast for me, darling." Dr. Storke was gone.

Janey finished her egg. Archie had said that when she had eaten an egg, it looked like a specimen from a collection: as if there had never been anything inside it. He had said, too, that she dealt with everything as she dealt with her morning egg; for she was tidy, thorough, and wholly without pretense.

Now, as she brushed the few crumbs of toast from the table into her cupped hand and dropped them on her plate, she began in her quiet way to meet the new fact of Andrew Herrick's death, to review what she knew of him. She knew very little but then she supposed few people knew more.

A confirmed bachelor of about fifty, Andrew Herrick had been very reticent. Archie called him standoffish and a prig. And his over-meticulous dress, his ramrod carriage, his precise way of placing his feet as he walked, all inevitably brought the words "on parade" to Janey's mind. At least, that had been her first impression, and did people know Andrew Herrick well enough to get beyond the first impression? Was there any beyond, or was that all? Andrew Herrick seemed to Janey so finished, so summed-up.

She had thought that, but now it was necessary to begin all over again. Andrew Herrick, the victim of an accident, that seemed incredible. He might have deteriorated gradually, even wax models grow old; but Janey had thought of him as going on and on until finally someone decided he ought to be replaced. Yes, she could believe that he was dead but not that he was dead because he had blundered. She simply could not imagine Andrew Herrick blundering. That was why she must begin again. Janey frowned. She was conscious of intense curiosity.

Archie's curiosity was submerged in the idea that he might still be in time, that Mrs. Ingles might be wrong. He backed his car out of the garage, swung it round with a flourish, stepped smartly on the accelerator, and took the turn out of his driveway with a skid born of long practice.

Andrew Herrick's house was only about two minutes away, as Archie took it, at the other end of the village. Pennerford was internally awake. Smoke was bustling from the chimneys of the long row of workmen's cottages, but the village street was still deserted. A woman wrapped in a shawl was scrubbing her steps, and the postman, appearing on his bicycle, saluted the Doctor.

Pennerford had never looked more cozily humdrum than it did on this morning of late October. The elm at the corner by C. HARRIS-GENERAL PROVISIONS launched into the clear, still air a couple of tawny leaves, a stately tribute to the Doctor's speed. Archie Storke rounded the corner on two wheels.

But for all his hurrying, he was too late.

His first glance at Andrew Herrick's body told him that he could never have been in time. He shut the door of the still-darkened sitting room on the hysterical housekeeper, drew back a window curtain, and turned slowly to that ghastly thing in the chair. It had nothing to do with the immaculate Andrew Herrick. It sprawled grotesquely in striped silk pajamas and a flaunting dressing gown. Archie Storke shivered. The door behind him opened to admit the bulky person of Policeman Huntley.

"Good morning, sir. Kathie Ingles sent for me. What is—"

Archie stepped aside, and Huntley made a curious noise in his throat. Huntley made an effort and met the Doctor's eyes. They were both ashamed. They both pretended brisk efficiency. Although Constable Huntley was inexperienced, he rose to the occasion with the correct gambit.

"A nasty business this, sir," he said and waited for the Doctor to reply.

Archie said nothing. He was staring intently at Andrew Herrick's right foot. The left foot had on a slipper. The right was bare. Lying on the floor with its muzzle toward the body was a twelve gauge shotgun.

"Inspector Turner should be called, and Colonel Copeland, too. Get through to them. Or wait, I'll ring the Colonel myself," he said at last.

Huntley completed his gambit.

"Won't do to touch things till the Inspector comes," he said, but the Doctor was already on his way to the telephone.

The telephone rang sharply. Lieutenant Colonel Roger Copeland, D.S.O., etc., Chief Constable of the county, who was just sitting down to a pair of admirably shirred eggs with a succulent haddock in reserve, swore softly and pulled *The Times* closer about his head. In a moment his worst fears were realized. He was interrupted by the announcement that Dr. Storke was on the phone and wished urgently to speak to him, and the Colonel knew that Archie would never disturb him at the delicate hour of breakfast without a very good reason.

The Colonel had retired from the army only to find the life of a country gentleman distressingly uneventful between meals. His excellent cook in her way, Archie Storke and Janey, "damned sensible little woman," in theirs, had done much to save him from boredom; but neither they nor his post had been able to supply just the proper ratio between alarums and victuals, which was the Colonel's idea of the perfect life.

Here at last was something turning up, but it might have waited half an hour. The Colonel went out without his breakfast and shut the front door resoundingly. An elderly black spaniel escaped the door and waddled asthmatically after him. Her name was Liz, and she was enormously fat. "Not quite fine enough," the Colonel would say apologetically. He had always outrageously overfed her.

Mongerton, where the Colonel lived, is little larger than the village of Pennerford, but its wide street lined with Georgian houses gives it an air of gracious importance. At one end of the street the Penner flows under an arched bridge of old red brick. The Colonel usually walked to the river, and then took the towpath at the lower bridge. The river and the towpath wind together between high banks crested with trees and are shut off from the fields and pasture lands beyond. He liked this way, for when at last he emerged at the lonely upper bridge by Pennerford, he always felt as if he were taking part in some forgotten military drama, leading a surprise attack on the village which seemed so secure on the higher ground.

But this morning there was no time to walk. The Colonel helped Liz into his car. It would take him about ten minutes to go from Mongerton to Pennerford, three and a half miles away. In spite of his Bentley he did not drive like Archie.

Archie Storke had spent ten weary minutes in restoring Mrs. Ingles to something approaching coherency when the Bentley flashed up the drive, and the Colonel sprang out. Archie came out on the steps to meet him.

"Well, Archie, this is a to do. Turner arrived yet?"

"Expect him any minute. Here, better leave Liz outside," he added, separating the spaniel from the Colonel's heels.

"Of course, never remember she's there," the Colonel agreed absently.

The two men went inside. Liz, shut out, ambled off on a sniffing tour of inspection.

Policeman Huntley was stationed in the hall. He saluted the Colonel and opened the sitting room door for him. The Colonel went in dutifully, but Archie did not follow. He did not feel equal to it just then. Jingling the coins in his pocket with an assumption of casualness that was wholly for Huntley's benefit, he stepped instead into the little study opposite.

In a few minutes the Colonel joined him.

"It's rather ghastly, Archie," he said. "Well, we can't do anything till Turner comes. We may as well wait here."

Archie Storke did not look up. He was standing by a small writing table. In his hand was a crumpled sheet of note paper.

"Look at this, Roger. I found it in that empty waste paper basket. This room's infernally tidy. It was as conspicuous as, well, as Friday's footprint. I had to pick it up."

The Colonel took the paper and, bending his tall body over the table, smoothed out the sheet with both hands. It was the rejected draft of a note, written in a clerklike hand devoid of all personality.

Wednesday, October 23

Dearest:

I am a miserable man tonight. I had thought to make a fortune for us all. Now there is nothing for me. Least of all can I expect forgiveness from you. Last night I lacked the courage to tell you how bad things were. I still hoped to avert disaster.

   I did not put your money in Recordians. I have lost all you entrusted to me, all John's, and all my own.

The Colonel's eyes went back once more to the beginning. In neat script the "Dearest" looked smugly and incongruously from the paper, but the rest furnished explanation enough for him.

"Accident? Hmm, I wonder? Suicide, more likely," he said.

There was a short pause.

"Yes, the right foot, that's it."

Archie Storke's remark seemed irrelevant.

The Colonel stared.

"The right foot, Archie?"

"Didn't you notice? It was bare. There was gun oil on the big toe. Fantastic!"

"You think he pushed the trigger with it, eh?"

"He must have. But why did he use a shotgun? It's awfully messy. I tell you the whole thing puzzles me." His tone now was testy.

"Why, Archie? Isn't it perfectly simple? The poor devil apparently decided suddenly, and I suppose there was no other means handy."

The Colonel could see nothing puzzling. It was all common sense. Here in the letter was Herrick's motive, and Archie himself had pointed out his method. It was so perfectly obvious. Why hunt for puzzles? Archie could be very irritating with his penchant for mysteries. The Colonel opened his mouth to nip Archie in the bud, as it were, but at that moment Inspector Turner roared up from Cambury on his motor bicycle.

After that nobody wasted time. With the briefest of good mornings and explanations they went into the sitting room, leaving Huntley still on guard in the hall.

The curtains were drawn closely over one window; at the other, they were parted slightly; and through the chink came a moted shaft of sunshine, like a spotlight picking out the high-backed oak chair and its gruesome occupant.

The Inspector crossed immediately to the windows. "We shall need more light. Was the room dark like this when you came, Dr. Storke?"

"Yes, both curtains were drawn. I opened that one to see the body, but otherwise I touched nothing. I thought Mrs. Ingles must have turned off the electric lights, but she said she didn't."

"Curtains drawn. Lights off when body found. Check with housekeeper," mumbled Inspector Turner, making an entry in his notebook.

He slipped the notebook into the pocket of his tunic and pulled wide the curtains.

The morning sunlight streamed into the farthest corners of the room, and at once the theatrical effect was dispelled. Everything became real to Archie Starke, except the tragedy. For the room which had been dim and brooding emerged bland and impersonal, like a private sitting room in a good hotel. Anyone's room, thought Archie, and no one's room. Andrew Herrick's personality seemed to have left no imprint upon his possessions, and the presence of his corpse among them seemed an alien intrusion, a monstrous impropriety.

Archie Storke was uneasy. It was all wrong, this sudden transition. He looked from the Inspector to the Colonel. They were feeling it, too: the conventional sitting room, the morning sun, that grotesque horror in the chair. The incongruity made of tragedy a red paint mockery, a cheap and ghastly Grand Guignol. It was unbearable.

The Inspector took control of the situation. It was not his business to feel things. He cleared his throat, as if to throw off a spell.

"I think, sir," he said, turning to the Colonel, "you will agree with me that accepting the letter found as showing motive, we may reject the theory of accident and accept, provisionally, of course, that of suicide. Now, the position of the body and that of the gun added to the fact that the right foot is bare would suggest that Mr. Herrick committed suicide by holding the gun by the barrel leaning forward so that it pointed up at his head, and pulling, or rather pushing, the trigger with his big toe. Likewise—"

Inspector Turner stopped abruptly. Apparently satisfied that this taste of judicial eloquence had already impressed his listeners, he advanced toward the body. When he spoke again, it was in what Archie placed as "notebook."

"Gun twelve gauge. One barrel exploded. Position compatible recoil. Muzzle toward body. Gun oil big toe. Dust for fingerprints on barrel."

Archie glanced slyly at the Colonel. The Inspector promised to be a joy. In the home circle, now, which did he use: "notebook" or rhetoric? Archie came out of this unprofitable speculation with the guilty feeling of never being serious-minded enough for county crises. The Inspector was addressing him.

"Will you make a thorough examination of the body, Doctor? Huntley will help me carry it upstairs." And going to the door, Inspector Turner beckoned the constable.

Together they lifted the blood-spattered shell of what had been the dapper Andrew Herrick. One arm in its gay silk hung stiff and, as they paced heavily to the door, jerked slightly with each step. Rigor mortis was already setting in, Archie noted.

After the two men had shuffled through the door, and their heavy tread was heard ascending the stairs, the Colonel spoke for the first time since they had come together into the sitting room.

"You weren't his doctor, were you, Archie?"

"No, I hardly knew him; only as one knows everyone in a small village; rather less. Don't think he liked me. Matter of fact he never needed a doctor, so far as I know. Although, come to think of it, I did hear him mention Sir Emmet Lucas once, a long time ago now.

He's Wimpole Street, heart. Knew him well when I was in London. Doubt if Herrick had consulted him though. Never saw any signs of it myself.

"He always seemed to me to have none of the needs that make people human. He was as regular, as bloodless, as an automaton. This, all of this, is incredible, the last thing one would have expected. Somehow that makes it much worse. If you knew how fussy, how infernally pernickety he was about his appearance—to have killed himself like this; to be willing to look like—

"And there's another thing, too: the electric lights. It's complicated enough to kill yourself with a shotgun. Why did he do it in the dark? As I was trying to tell you before, it doesn't make sense."

Archie was off again sniffing around his mystery. The Colonel hastily interposed.

"We must let his people know. Who's this John whose money he's lost?"

"John Armstrong, his nephew. That's rather the limit. Janey and I know the boy; he used to live here with Herrick. Great friend of Janey's pal, Monica Lambert. You've met her at the house."

"Hmm, yes; pretty, gray eyes?"

"That's the one. I rather think they're in love with each other. Waiting possibly till Johnny got his money. Don't know. Johnny's an orphan; his mother was Herrick's sister. She left her money in trust till Johnny should be twenty-five; appointed her brother guardian. The boy will be twenty-five in a month or so. That's another reason, I presume, for pulling this off. Herrick must have known he couldn't make good by then, and the boy has the devil of a temper; he'd have made things hot."

"Probably. Who's 'Dearest'?"

Archie Storke grinned. "There you have me, Roger. That's the prize thing I can't reconcile with Herrick." Then as police steps fell again on the stairs, he added, "I'd better go and get this business up there over with."

At the door he turned. "Oh, I almost forgot Cyril Herrick, Roger. He's the other nephew, a son of Herrick's brother. You'll have to send a wire to him. Now I come to think of it, I remember hearing the brother himself was coming over from America. He may be here now. The grieving relations thicken. Mrs. Ingles probably has Cyril's and Johnny's town addresses for you. Cheerio." But in spite of his flippancy the back of Archie's head had a get-it-over-with look as he left the room.

Turner entered it immediately.

When Archie, rather better than half an hour later, again opened the door of the sitting room, he was conscious of yet another transition. The room seemed tense now, tense with excitement. The Colonel and the Inspector stood together by the fireplace. They turned round as he came in, and the Colonel spoke.

"We must take the Doctor into our confidence, Inspector."

So they were ahead of him. Archie Storke reserved his bombshell; they might explode their first. He felt a little cheated; he had expected to startle both of them completely. Now his amazing discovery would come only as an anticlimax.

"What is it?" he asked.

The Colonel shifted his position restlessly; and when he answered, his voice sounded faintly apologetic.

"It's nothing very definite, Archie. Only that we can't account for something: the fingerprints on the gun. Turner dusted the barrel."

The Colonel flicked his fingers in the direction of the shotgun, which lay now on the table. Picked out with white powder against the purple-black of the barrel were fingerprints, and at the trigger were smudges of white.

"We merely wished to confirm our idea of how the suicide was committed, you know—"

"Matter of form," the Inspector put in, looking at the carpet.

"Yes, just that," the Colonel continued, taking a step forward. "And," he paused slightly, "we found them there as we expected, impressions of both hands. Perfect impressions." He stopped and looked expectantly at the Doctor.

Archie Storke didn't see it.

"Well, but what's odd about that? I don't see—"

For a second time the Inspector cleared his throat.

"It's just this, Dr. Storke," he explained, "if the gun in recoiling jumped to the position in which we found it, as it would have done, why are the fingerprints on the barrel so nearly perfect? They are not blurred. There are no marks of slipping."

"You must see that, Archie." The Colonel undoubtedly was excited. "It's not explicable at all. Herrick could not have held that gun barrel lightly and evenly as the prints show. He must have grasped it hard. Then, in the terrific shock of the blow, it must have been wrenched from his hands. There should have been marks of that and there aren't. Death must have been instantaneous, violent. He couldn't—it's humanly impossible—he couldn't have held on to the gun, and then tossed it from him."

Archie prepared his bombshell.

"No, he couldn't," he agreed. "He couldn't because I very much doubt if he were conscious at the time of his death. In my opinion," he added slowly, relishing his moment, "he did not die by accident or by suicide. On the contrary, Andrew Herrick has been murdered."

His bombshell was all he could have wished. Obviously their half-formed suspicion had not led them this far. The Colonel looked as he did when Archie had trapped his king and called checkmate. The Inspector looked robustly annoyed. Since neither spoke, Archie went on.

"No use looking at me like that. It's true. Murdered, I grant you, with great care, extremely cleverly; but murdered just the same. You know I told you it was all very queer, Roger."

The Colonel recovered his military dignity. He glared at Archie, as though Archie were a private at inspection whose boots were not properly blacked, and rapped out, "Explain yourself."

"I'm sorry," said Archie appeasingly. "I should have begun at the beginning. Really, I was as surprised as you when I found it out. At first I thought nothing of it, it was like the fingerprints that way. I had expected something of the sort but I got more than I had expected."

He crossed over to the oak chair which had held the body of Andrew Herrick and laid his hand for a moment on the high back where it was blood-stained and peppered with shot.

"Will you both be patient with me if I make a speech?" he asked.

Inspector Turner gravely inclined his head. Archie was determined to go him one better in exposition.

"When we saw the body, the head was resting against the back of this chair, where the force of the shot had jerked it. If the suicide had occurred as we thought, Herrick would have been doubled forward towards the muzzle as he pushed the trigger. Then the gun jumps away, and the body is hurled backward. That's all obvious, of course.

"So, I expected the mark of a contusion on the back of the head where it came in violent contact with the chair. I found the contusion, all right, but not the sort of contusion I expected to find. We'll go upstairs in a moment, and I'll show you. In the first place the contusion was over too wide an area; but more significantly, there was distinct swelling. Now swelling is caused, as you know, by the blood corpuscles rushing to the injured place to repair the damage. Conscientious things, corpuscles; but not so conscientious as all that. They don't rush about after a fellow's dead. Therefore, Andrew Herrick must have received that blow a short time before death. It was a severe blow and would have caused unconsciousness. He would have been completely knocked out. I examined the spot closely and at the roots of the hair I found several minute particles of sand.

"There it is, I'm afraid," Archie felt he was winding up rather lamely, "Herrick was apparently sandbagged and placed in the chair while unconscious; everything rigged up to look like suicide, even to the angle of the gun; and then, murdered."

He had convinced the Colonel.

"It's damnable. Foully cold-blooded." As a sporting English gentleman the Colonel was profoundly shocked.

Inspector Turner gave credit where credit was due.

"Very clever crime, sir," he said, "very clever, indeed. That accounts for the fingerprints. Thought to take off the slipper, too. Put gun oil on the big toe. Might have taken us in. Very fortunate it didn't. Hmm."

Struck with a sudden thought, he took the unfinished letter from his pocket. "I wonder if this is genuine? Well, we can identify the handwriting later. Everything in its place. Before I question the housekeeper, we had better take another look at the body."

"Quite." The Colonel silenced him somewhat impatiently. Then to Archie, "Can you say how long it is since death took place?"

"Not absolutely accurately. In my opinion, about twelve hours. There was a fire in the grate last night, and the body was close to it; nevertheless rigor mortis is well established." Archie took out his watch. "It's now twenty-five minutes to ten. I should say he was killed about ten last night; possibly as late as one."

Although this was not in its place, it was a question Inspector Turner had been going to ask. He brought out his notebook and wrote down the doctor's answer. Then he went briskly to the door.

"No one is to enter this room, Huntley. Mrs. Ingles is not to go before I have questioned her. Where is she now?"

"In the kitchen, sir."

"Tell her to wait there."

Followed by the Colonel and Archie, the Inspector started upstairs.

"We'll leave you to carry on for a bit, Turner, after we've finished up here," the Colonel remarked, pausing on the landing to look out of its long window. He was thinking wistfully of breakfast.

Archie took the hint. "Come home with me after, Roger. We'll have a spot to eat."

"Hello!" the Colonel ejaculated, still at the window. "What's Liz got there?"

Archie peered over his shoulder. Set back from the house at an angle was a garage and by the side of this a kennel. Round the kennel the spaniel was circling excitedly. Abruptly she sat down before it and threw back her head in a long howl.

"Good Lord, Mac!" Archie exclaimed. "I forgot all about him. He's the worst tempered airedale in two counties. Something's wrong, or he'd have chewed Liz to bits. I'll go and see." He ran hastily back down the stairs.

The Inspector hovered irresolutely at the top.

"Go in, Turner. We'll be with you in a moment," said the Colonel over his shoulder, as through the window he saw Archie come round the corner of the house.

"Your pantomime was graphic if not artistic," was his comment, when a few minutes later Archie rather out of breath regained the landing.

"Everything in its place," Archie answered, glancing upward to make sure the Inspector was not within earshot. Then, leaning back against the banisters, he put his hands in his pockets and said soberly, "No wonder old Liz was upset. The airedale's been strangled with his own chain. Poor Mac, he wasn't such a bad dog really, only a bit over-zealous. It seems rather wholesale to murder him, too."

"Prevented him from kicking up a row, I suppose," said the Colonel in the voice of one who admits no extraneous comment.

"Undoubtedly. But there's the rub, my dear Roger. You see, I knew the beast. Johnny brought him to our place any number of times. Mac was devoted enough to him, used to follow him about everywhere. He behaved well enough with Johnny. But no one Mac didn't know could get within ten feet of him when Herrick had him chained up. I should have thought he would have raised hell before hands could have been laid on him. He was a damned savage. No, I don't see—"

"It will bear thinking about, certainly," the Colonel rather wearily cut in, starting upstairs. As Archie still did not move he added peremptorily, "Do let's get on with this. You can hardly expect me to do any more thinking until I have had my breakfast, can you?"

Archie detached himself from the banister. With his hands still in his pockets and with an air of being far away, he followed the Colonel without a reply. When they reached the bedroom door, however, he said, "You're right. It certainly doesn't do to think on an empty stomach. It goes to your head. Just now I'd rather see a nice large cup of coffee than even the most interesting corpse."

With a sharp gesture the Colonel took hold of the door knob. Archie could be damned annoying. He turned the knob softly, and they stepped into the room.

On the bed lay Andrew Herrick covered by a sheet, covered except for one arm which Inspector Turner held by the wrist over a small table drawn up to the bed. On the table were a piece of white paper and a black ink-pad. The Inspector nodded as they came in, and lowered the dead hand until the limp fingers pressed upon the pad. Against the black they were startling white, four long curling fingers, every contour distinct.

"I won't be a minute over this, sir." Turner's full voice broke the stillness of the room.

They waited in silence while he placed the side of each finger tip at the edge of one of the ten squares he had marked on the paper and, holding the finger above the first joint, rolled it over slowly from one side to the other within its square. When he had finished, the paper held fine, clear, broad imprints. The Inspector put the paper between the leaves of his notebook and slipped his notebook into his pocket. Then he reached over and drew back the sheet.

The three men leaned over the body. With deft hands Archie lifted the shattered head.

"You will see the contusion quite clearly," he said. "It is here at the base of the skull."

When at last they left the bedroom, they were agreed upon several things. The most important was that they would, for the present at least, keep the fact of murder to themselves. That it was murder and not suicide they no longer doubted. The turned out lights, a minor point; the faked prints on the gun, made with fingers already lifeless; the swelling on the head, proving the blow to have been given before death; the grains of sand clinging to the hair, showing a sand bag used to strike the blow; all made an accumulation of evidence impossible to ignore. Finally, there was the strangled dog. For as Archie Storke somewhat flippantly remarked, "Herrick might have committed suicide, but he was never sentimental enough to take his airedale with him into the Great Beyond."

Puzzling as the whole affair was, in Turner's opinion they had one thing to go on: the strong probability that Andrew Herrick had been murdered by an intimate. There were no signs of forced entry into the house; whoever came either had a key or had been admitted by Herrick himself; for Mrs. Ingles went home at night.

Herrick was a dignified, a formal sort of man; yet he had known the murderer well enough to receive him in his pajamas and dressing-gown, when he was all ready for bed. The clothes he had worn that day were neatly folded upon a chair, and his bed was turned down but not crumpled. Apparently he had never got into it that night.

Moreover, the murderer had known of the presence of a gun in the house and had worked out the "suicide" to fit this. The careful working out of the false suicide showed a cool hand if not premeditation.

But weighing somewhat against premeditation, Archie Storke pointed out, was the strangled airedale. For although the fact that he could be strangled at all seemed one of the strongest proofs that the murder had been committed by an intimate, nevertheless wouldn't it have been much simpler, much surer, and much safer to have poisoned him if one were planning it all beforehand?

Meanwhile, there was the problem of the Colonel's breakfast, and further discussion was shelved in its favor.

Huntley was still stolidly waiting in the hall outside the sitting room door.

"Anything happen?" Turner asked him perfunctorily, while Archie, in a hurry to be off now, picked up his bag and handed the Colonel his hat.

Huntley's prompt "Yes, sir" was quite unexpected.

The Colonel stopped halfway through the front door.

"Not that it matters, sir," Huntley amended, uneasy in the limelight of the Colonel's stare. He has a proper way of looking at you, and no mistake, he commented mentally, glad to address himself again to the Inspector.

"Mr. Wilkinson, lives in Rex House, was here, sir. He came to see Mr. Herrick. I told him he couldn't see him, seeing as how he was dead. He said he was shocked, sir. And could I tell him how it happened so sudden—"

"Did you?" Turner interrupted severely.

Huntley turned a little pink about the ears.

"No details, sir. I said he'd had a mishap with a gun, sir."

"Told him everything you know, eh?"

"Oh, that's all right. It's bound to be all over the village by now, anyhow," put in Archie Storke deprecatingly.

The Inspector took no notice of him.

"Well?" he demanded.

"Well, he said he'd like to see you, sir, and could he wait for you to come down? I thought it right to give him permission, sir, and he waited in there." Huntley jerked his thumb in the direction of the study.

"Where is he now, then?"

"I don't know, sir. He didn't wait but a few minutes, sir. He came out again and said he'd go now, seeing you were all busy."

"He didn't say why he had come?"

"Only to see Mr. Herrick, sir."

"Very good, Huntley." The Inspector released his victim, took off his I-must-get-to-the-bottom-of-this manner, and said blithely, "See you later, Colonel Copeland, and you, too, sir. In the meantime I'll go over the house thoroughly and question Mrs. Ingles."

"Poor old Ingles," chanted Archie in his best Gregorian, as soon as the front door closed behind them.

Janey Keeps Coffee Hot

"Whatever else was planted for us to discover I don't believe the letter was. I'm convinced it's genuine."

The Colonel's mind, refreshed by Janey's late breakfast, was again at grips with the problem of Andrew Herrick's murder. To be sure, breakfast had not altogether halted the discussion, in which Janey had joined. For the Colonel, much to Archie's relief, had waived official reticence and signified his trust in the "damned sensible little woman" by telling her of the crime. It was, in fact, Janey, who had put her finger on the crux of the puzzle.

"It's bewildering," she had said, "because you have no glimmer of the motive. The letter Archie snooped into is a motive for suicide, but I can't see that it gives you one for murder. Why would anyone want to kill Andrew Herrick because he had made away with the money? If he were left alive, he might pay it back some time. You both say 'revenge'; but if I wanted revenge, I should choose to send him to prison myself. I just can't see that it's a reason for murdering him. There must be another."

Archie and the Colonel had suggested sudden discovery of the treacherous defalcations, fury, and murder in the heat of passion, only to feel slightly foolish when Janey reminded them that they had presented the murder to her as one coolly planned and executed. She had capped it all by saying, "And anyway whose money has been lost? As far as you know, only the 'Dearest' person's and Johnny's, and of course Johnny never did it."

At which point Archie had looked miserable, and the Colonel had said "Humm—" and Janey had been furious. She had in fact scolded them roundly. As though it wasn't bad enough for poor Johnny to have all his money stolen, let alone their being complete idiots and thinking, even for a moment, that Johnny could— It made her very cross; they had both better stop trying to be clever and go right back to their "scene of the crime." Inspector Turner probably knew who it was and all about it by now. Consequently, Archie and the Colonel had climbed obediently into the Bentley feeling somewhat subdued.

But not for long. As soon as the Bentley started down the drive, Archie, seizing upon Janey's undeniable objection to the letter as motive, had echoed Inspector Turner's suggestion that the letter might well be part of the hoax. A hoax intended to mislead the investigation along the paths of suicide, or, failing that, to supply an entirely false motive for the murder, throw suspicion on the wrong person. The Colonel thought this tortuous and over-subtle. He edged the Bentley round the tricky turn out of the Doctor's driveway before saying, "There's no reason for supposing the murderer knew of the letter's existence. You fished it out all in a wad from the waste paper basket yourself."

The Bentley cleared the gatepost and shot ahead down the road. Until they were passing the post office neither spoke again. Then Archie said, "Of course you're right about the letter, Roger. Thank you for being kind enough not to point out to me the most obvious objection to my silly idea."

"Which is—"

"Now you're being unkind and rubbing it in. But if it gives you any pleasure to hear me say it, why, simply that forgery's such a clumsy plan: in this case, sure to be detected, and no good in this case, either, unless the fact of the defalcations is true; and then, unnecessary. We were bound to find the embezzlement out as soon as we looked into the thing; and then there's our suicide motive without a doubt attached to it. No. No one but a complete moron would try a complicated forgery for the sole purpose of hurrying up that discovery."

"Precisely," said the Colonel.

But Archie appeared not to have heard him; he was tapping with idle fingers upon his crossed knee, and on his face was a benign vacant look that Janey knew well. Almost to himself he murmured, "But would he? There might be some reason. Too blooming *deus ex machina*, that letter, to my taste. Something's queer, there's a lot queer—"

The Bentley turned the corner at C. HARRIS' somewhat abruptly.

It was childish of him, the Colonel thought, to let Archie irritate him, but the fellow had the most maddening habit of proving a thing and then swinging right-about-face to question his own proof. The Colonel forced his voice into patience to ask, "My dear Archie, will you resign yourself to the lack of mystery in most things? When we've made sure the letter was written by Herrick, will you admit the not very surprising coincidence of its being in his waste paper basket? Or will you go on muttering that it's strange he wrote a letter at all during the day or evening before he was murdered? I envy you your imagination, my dear fellow."

"Sorry," answered Archie, losing his benign expression and sitting up straight. "It was not my intention to annoy. Oh, yes, if it was written by Herrick, it's all right; and I've no doubt it was. Never mind. From now on I promise to gambol my mental gambols by myself, if gambol I must. I hate to rattle you, Roger."

"Right," said the Colonel a shade testily.

Archie cast about for a not-too-abrupt change of subject.

"Wonder how old Ingles weathered the Inspector? That's the Lambert house we're passing now. You can hardly see it from the road; big place, huge grounds extending right down to the towpath. Can't see the river from the house though; too many trees. Never understand why they don't clear them. Whiteleaves used to be its dower house in the old days. There's still a path through the upper grounds which comes out into Herrick's drive."

"Oh, that reminds me," the Colonel's voice had regained its usual friendly clippedness. "I meant to ask you. Who's this Wilkinson who called while we were upstairs? I remember something vague about him, I think it was you who—"

"Oh, me, undoubtedly," answered Archie. "I'm afraid I have a tendency to make fun of the fellow. I don't like him. Comparative religions, Zoroaster, all sorts of highbrow bookishness, and a sly eye with it all."

"Was he a friend of Herrick's? They don't sound particularly congenial."

"No, not that I ever knew. Struck me a little odd, the early morning call. He's very thick with Monica's mother, Mrs. Lambert—Wilkinson is, I mean—teaching her ancient mythology under the trees. Don't look shocked. Quite innocent; but all rather silly. The Lambert's a widow; young still and a fluttering, pretty little man-trap. Spiritualistic séances are more her style, I should say, than comparative religions: my control, 'Little White Feather,' rather than Zoroaster. Our professor's smitten, I think, although perhaps he doesn't realize it."

"Doesn't seem to have any connection with Herrick."

"No; hold on, Roger, I've had an inspiration. Before the Wilkinson reign Herrick used to be there a lot; under the same trees, boutonniere, silk hanky in the breast pocket, holding a tea cup—all the symptoms of courtship present. I have it! Kitty Lambert is 'Dearest'!"

"Do you think so? Then Wilkinson—"

"Yes. Then early morning calls and Wilkinson. I wonder—"

They were still wondering when the Bentley drew up behind Archie's car which stood, with the air of having been unfairly abandoned, before the door of Whiteleaves. Liz, who had also been left behind, uncurled herself from its front seat, stretched, and wagged. The Colonel stopped to pat her, then followed Archie into the house.

Inspector Turner, who came from the sitting room as soon as he heard their voices, had all the eagerness of one bursting with information. He fairly shoved them into the little study; shut the door upon the figure of Constable Huntley, still on sentry duty in the hall; drew up three chairs into a conspiratorial circle; took out his notebook, and said, "I have managed to glean information which may be of some value, sir."

Translated from notebook into English, with comments as they were made, the information was as follows:

Taking up the facts in the order of their occurrence and beginning with the morning of the previous day, Mrs. Ingles had stated that:

She was the only servant employed by Mr. Herrick and she lived out in one of the workmen's cottages. She had been with her present master a number of years. On Wednesday, the morning before, she had come as usual at a quarter to eight, letting herself in by the kitchen door to which she had a key. As was her custom, she had put on the kettle for the morning tea; and while it was coming to a boil, she had begun tidying up: opening the curtains, emptying the used ash trays, and laying the fire in the sitting room. She also switched on the electric heater in the dining room to get that room warm for breakfast. This was her invariable morning routine. She had then taken up a cup of tea to Mr. Herrick and one to Mr. John, who had spent Tuesday night there.

Mr. Herrick had come down to breakfast at about twenty minutes past eight. He was in a hurry, for he was taking the eight-fifty train to London. He had told her he would not be back for dinner, but would have an early dinner in town, as he was not returning until the nine-fifteen. "That is the seven-thirty-three from Paddington, sir; express to Cambury. You know it, of course."

Mr. John had come down a few minutes later. He and Mr. Herrick had talked about Mr. Burford Herrick, who had arrived at Plymouth the night before. Mr. Cyril had gone to Plymouth to meet his father, and Mrs. Ingles gathered that it was to see his brother that Mr. Herrick was going to town. Mr. John had said, "I was only ten when Mother took me to America, I haven't seen Uncle Burford since."

And Mr. Herrick had answered, "Yes, I've often wondered if he would ever come back to England again."

After that, Mrs. Ingles, having served Mr. John's breakfast, left the room. She went into the kitchen for a minute or two, and then went back into the sitting room to finish her tidying. She was distressed to hear Mr. John's voice raised angrily and realized that he and Mr. Herrick were quarreling.

"She didn't want to tell me this, sir. I had to get it out of her."

"Don't put too much significance on it, Inspector. Johnny and Herrick were always having their little squabbles. They never amounted to much." This, from Archie Storke.

"Proceed," from the Colonel.

She could not hear what was being said for both the dining room and the sitting room doors were closed; but when Mr. Herrick opened the dining room door and came out into the hall, she heard Mr. John say, "Cyril better not count on it too much."

The morning post had come while they were at breakfast. She had been going to take his letters in to Mr. Herrick; but when she heard them quarreling, she had not liked to intrude. With the letters in her hand she had come out of the sitting room in order to give them to Mr. Herrick before he left. Mr. Herrick was putting on his coat and hat. She gave him the letters; and as she did so, Mr. John came into the hall from the dining room.

He looked very angry and said, "I want you to believe that I mean what I say. That is one thing you shan't interfere with. And I damn well don't intend you shall. If you try again, well, I won't be accountable, that's all." He had turned on his heel and gone back to the dining room. Mr. Herrick had said, "Control your filthy temper, John—" He had then left to catch his train.

The words were as exact as Mrs. Ingles could recall them. She thought they were almost the same, as it made her unhappy when they quarreled and she remembered it. She was fond of both Mr. John and Mr. Cyril and couldn't see why it was that Mr. John failed to get on with Mr. Herrick when Mr. Cyril got on with his uncle so well. The two cousins, she thought, were perfectly friendly with each other; for they had always been companionable enough, being, as they were, so near of an age.

Mr. John had had two more cups of coffee. Then he had gone to the garage to get out his motor car.

"There are fresh tire marks by the garage which are accounted for by Mr. Armstrong's car. Mrs. Ingles says Mr. Herrick has not had his own car out of the garage since last Sunday. What make is Mr. Armstrong's, do you know, Dr. Storke?"

"Yes, it's a Morris roadster. Johnny manages to get an incredible amount of speed out of her."

"If you say speed, it means speed." Comment from the Colonel. "Go on with Mrs. Ingles, Inspector."

Mr. John had returned to the house to telephone Miss Lambert. Mrs. Ingles was clearing away the breakfast things, passing through the hall on her way from the dining room to the kitchen, so she had heard the end of Mr. John's side of the conversation.

He had said, "I'm almost positive, Monnie. . . . It's awfully important. . . . I'll come right over now. We'll have half an hour before I have to start for London."

She was sure that was what he said. She was afraid he was talking about the quarrel he had had with Mr. Herrick. She thought Miss Lambert was the sweetest thing, but she was afraid Mr. Herrick was against the match. She couldn't see why. Mr. Cyril and Mr. John and Miss Monica had been friends for years. She had always thought it would be nice and sensible if one of them was to fall in love with Miss Monica.

"She didn't speculate on the confusion if two of them instead of one happened to do it, did she?" It was Archie Storke's question.

"No. Is that how it is, Doctor?" Inspector Turner let nothing pass.

"I don't know. It's taken a comparatively mild form with Cyril, if it has. I rather think he plays with the idea; can't resist the desire to compete, I imagine. From Mamma's point of view Cyril is the greater catch."

"Why?" This time it was the Colonel who took him up.

"The obvious reason, of course: money. Burford Herrick married a rich American. When she died, she left him her money. He's made more. Their son, that's Cyril of course, has a tidy allowance. The money Johnny should have inherited, if his uncle hadn't embezzled it and lost it, was nothing compared to what's coming to Cyril. *Ergo*, I'm sorry I interrupted the humble tale of Mrs. I. All this, if relevant at all, will keep for later."

After finishing phoning, Mr. John had started up his car. Mrs. Ingles had gone to the kitchen door to say good-by to him and ask if he were coming back that night, or should she make up the bed fresh? She always kept clean sheets ready on the guest bed in case someone came unexpectedly.

"Which is how I found the bed, sir."

Mr. John had called out to her that he was not coming back, stopped to pat Mac for a moment, climbed into the car, and driven off. She had, of course, not seen him since.

Coming to the morning of the murder: she had discovered the body when she went into the sitting room to draw the curtains. She was positive the electric lights were switched off, for the room was dim as it always was every morning. It was not until she was halfway across the room on her way to the window that she had seen Mr. Herrick. She had rushed out into the hall. She couldn't think what to do; she was struck all of a heap. She had phoned to her daughter Ruth, who worked at the manor, Mrs. Lambert's house. Ruth had said not to lose her head and to phone Dr. Storke at once, which she had done.

"The rest we know," from Archie as he threw away his cigarette.

"No, sir. Pardon me. Mrs. Ingles has made a grave blunder. I am coming to that." The Inspector was gravely corrective.

It seemed that when Mrs. Ingles came that morning, there had been an envelope in the letter box. The morning post had not yet come, and Mrs. Ingles had put the letter, obviously delivered by hand some time the night before or early that morning, into the pocket of her apron, intending to take it up to Mr. Herrick on the tray with his cup of tea. In the upset she had forgotten all about it, until putting her hand into her pocket she had felt it there. She had taken it and put it on the desk in the study. This was while the constable and Inspector Turner were arranging the body on the bed upstairs, and while the Doctor and the Colonel were waiting in the sitting room. Constable Huntley had taken possession of the morning post. The letter delivered by hand had disappeared.

Archie met the Colonel's eyes. There had only been one person in the study besides themselves that morning.

"Wilkinson?" they asked together.

"That's all I can think, sir," Inspector Turner answered.

"Now what the devil!" exclaimed Archie.

"There are one or two minor points we'd better take in their place, before we try to make anything of that," said Turner.

They were:

That both Cyril Herrick and John Armstrong had keys to Whiteleaves.

That Mrs. Ingles had found the house locked and everything as usual.

That Andrew Herrick did not possess a revolver, and that the shotgun was the only weapon in the house.

That Mrs. Ingles had unhesitatingly identified the writing on the "Dearest" letter as Mr. Herrick's.

That the morning post had contained a letter from Andrew Herrick's brokers which showed that he had been speculating heavily.

That Turner had phoned through to the London office of Dodd, Meigs, and Dodd, the brokers, and had information which made it practically certain that the confession in Herrick's letter was true.

That two telegrams had arrived in answer to those the Colonel had sent, and that Mr. Armstrong and both Mr. Burford and Mr. Cyril Herrick were on their way to Pennerford. There were no convenient trains at that hour; so they were all coming by motor, Cyril and his father in Cyril's Mercedes and Johnny in his Morris. Not to draw invidious comparisons, there was no doubt that the Mercedes would arrive first. Probably in about an hour's time.

In the meantime Inspector Turner wanted to go to the railway station and have a word with the guard to learn if Mr. Herrick had returned as planned, by the nine-fifteen the night before.

Archie Starke remembered he had patients, and that there were one or two he'd better see. And the Colonel agreed to wait at Whiteleaves until the Inspector and Archie returned.

"You'll have lunch with us, of course, Roger," said Archie, preparing to leave. "Better ring Head, or she'll break her heart over an untouched lunch. She has probably been weeping continuously over her wasted breakfast."

The Doctor tried his skid out of Herrick's drive. It worked beautifully.

It may have been that Archie Starke's patients found him somewhat unsympathetic that morning, but then fortunately none of
them was seriously ill. He had visited his pet cross, the hypo-
chondrial Mrs. Jenkins, last. She had been, of course, lengthy and
trying, so that it was nearing one o'clock when he again turned
into the Whiteleaves driveway.

The inevitable chorus to tragedy was present in a group of curious villagers on whom Policeman Huntley, removed from his post
by the sitting room door and as firmly planted between the
gateposts of the drive, kept a wary eye. The salute which he be-
stowed upon the Doctor was a masterpiece of official importance.

Archie Storke thought it all a little grim. Why was the human
race so woefully uninventive? For happiness or sorrow, the same
symbols. For a wedding or a sordid crime, the same flowers, the
same crowd, usually the same policeman. Whiteleaves might have
been the scene of a gay and brilliant party and Andrew Herrick,
suave, faultlessly groomed, moving among his guests: Andrew
Herrick, hideous, covered by a sheet, in there on his bed, murdered. Ugh! They had all been so busy, so interested, trying to find
out how, they hadn't thought much about him. Well, it was better
they didn't. As a person Andrew Herrick meant nothing to them,
thank heaven. As a problem, well—it was fascinating.

But for the first time Archie thought of the people to whom
Andrew Herrick had meant something; thought of them not as actors in an absorbing mystery drama but as individuals, bewildered,
grieved: Burford Herrick in England for the first time in many
years, what a homecoming for him! And as he swept round the
curve in the drive, Archie saw that a big yellow Mercedes was
parked now behind the Colonel's Bentley. So Cyril and his father
had arrived.

It was the Colonel who opened the door for him. They gravi-
tated naturally towards the study, and Archie sat down by the writing desk. The Colonel stood, his hands in a characteristic pose resting on the small of his back.

"They are upstairs now with Turner identifying the body," he
said.

"Oh! When did they get here?"

"A few minutes ago. The elder Herrick's taking it pretty hard. I can't tell about the other."

"Who, Cyril? Hasn't come to about it all yet, or feels it too much to show anything. Cyril's the only person whose affection for Herrick is beyond doubt. Johnny, in spite of friction, was fond of his uncle, I think; but Cyril was devoted to him. Ever since his father sent him over here to school, that was twelve or thirteen years ago when his mother died, they've been together. That was before my time in Pennerford, but I've heard of it enough. Herrick wasn't popular, you know, and Cyril was always trotted out as a proof of the old sentimentality dowagers are so fond of believing: that there is no one in the world someone does not love. It was true enough in this case."

"Why was Herrick so disliked, Archie? Any reason?"

"No. Unless his manner could be called a reason: stand-offish, a pompous sort of dummy. Always made me feel like a rude small boy. If there was a nice puddle handy when I passed him in the car, it was all I could do not to hit the puddle, splash him a little. You know the feeling. Have you ever liked anybody who made you feel like that?"

"Can't say," the Colonel answered absently. He took a restless step or two. "Seems to me they're up there longer than necessary."

"I hope Turner isn't harrowing them unduly. It's not a nice sight," said Archie.

"No. And I've got to break the news of the embezzlement on top of it."

"Perhaps they know that."

"They may. I'm taking them over to the Seven Stars. I want to make sure they're settled comfortably, and that no one will bother them. We had to send Huntley out to the gate to keep the people off."

"Yes, I saw him—I think they're coming down now, Roger."

"Will you wait here for me? I shan't be long, then we'll go back for lunch?"

"Right," said Archie.

The Colonel went to the door of the study. "We are in here, Mr. Herrick," he said.

Burford Herrick came into the room. He was a tall man but not as tall as his brother, although this impression was perhaps due to his stoop. While he was not round-shouldered exactly, he carried his body tilted a little forward from the hips. In spite of being shorter he seemed to Archie a bigger, heavier man than Andrew; bigger in every way. His personality had none of the narrow aggressiveness of Andrew's; there was room in it to move around; it was large and friendly. His well-made clothes fitted his body with comfortable looseness; the eyes behind the horn-rimmed spectacles were kind. The elusive family resemblance was there, as it was in Cyril; but Archie knew at once that in character the brothers had had nothing in common.

"This is Dr. Storke, Mr. Herrick," the Colonel said.

"Thank you for all you've done, Doctor. I should like to see you again, a little later. There are one or two things I'd like to know. Just now, it's been a severe shock." His voice, forced into control, held a faint tinge of the American intonation. He paused for a moment, and then, as though impelled to give expression to the thought that was torturing him, he said, "If I could have known that my poor brother contemplated taking his life, had he confided in me, I should have found some way to have prevented this. Do you think it was a question of money, Colonel Copeland? I could have helped him; he had only to say the word. He was always so proud." Again Burford Herrick paused before he asked, "You knew my brother, Dr. Storke?"

"Not well."

"He was very proud, very independent. He would never allow anyone to help him. You see, I'd heard, Cyril wrote me, that he'd been unfortunate lately in his investments. That is the reason I came to England. I didn't tell him, of course. I wished to make my offer of help tactfully, you understand. Yesterday he said nothing to me of any trouble, he seemed just as usual. I did not feel it was the time to mention—and now, it is too late. I cannot forgive myself."

"Don't think of it that way, Father, don't reproach yourself. How could we know?" Cyril was standing in the doorway. He crossed the room and laid his hand upon his father's sleeve. "If Colonel Copeland's ready, shall we go now?"

"I'm quite ready," said the Colonel.

"I can't stand this house!" Cyril had lost his Oxford nonchalance; he was imperative and shrill. He threw out his hands in an abrupt gesture and rushed from the room.

Archie Storke overtook him as he was climbing into the Mercedes. The big yellow car, blatant and gay, seemed to mock the white-faced boy slumped down behind its wheel. Cyril worried Archie.

"Sorry, Storke, I didn't speak to you in there—"

"Oh, that's all right. Look here, old son, you mustn't let yourself go like that."

"I mustn't? Don't you suppose I know without your advice? Do you think I need you to tell me?"

The self-starter whined viciously and suddenly was still.

"Sorry again," said Cyril. "But I don't think you understand. It's too ghastly. I can't stick it—"

"I can guess at it a little. I know, we all know, there was nothing you wouldn't have done to—"

"That's it. There's nothing I wouldn't have done. For Drew I'd—" The young voice broke with its bitterness. The big car shot forward, twinkled bright primrose yellow, vanished round the curve of the drive. Archie Storke sighed. The Colonel and Burford Herrick were getting into the Bentley. He went slowly back to the house.

In the study he sat smoking, and presently Inspector Turner came to him there.

"I want to see you, Doctor. Whew, it's been a hard morning."

"Anything special, Turner?"

"Yes. I've arranged to have the body sent to the mortuary at Cambury. I want you to be present when the police surgeon makes his examination. I'll let you know."

"All right."

"When he confirms your opinion, which I've no doubt he will, we'll have that in order. But that isn't what I wanted to tell you."

"No?"

"No. You've made a mistake, Dr. Storke."

In the Inspector's eye was to be detected a gleam of amiable triumph.

"Oh, have I? I sometimes do, you know," said Archie mildly. Whatever it was, the Inspector was prepared to enjoy it. "What sort of mistake?"

"You were wrong about the time of the murder."

"Was I?"

"Yes. The murder could not have been committed until after one."

"Oh, well, I only gave one as an approximate limit. I told you I couldn't be accurate; too many things enter in; the fire, for instance; the violence of the death. It's impossible to know definitely. Rigor mortis is very tricky. Look it up if you don't believe me. You'd get a surprise and you might be easier on us doctors:"

Inspector Turner grinned.

"You know you did rather ask for it, sir."

"Yes, yes, I suppose I did. I've been awfully cocksure about everything. Everything, that is, except the time. I thought I'd allowed for the margin of error there, but apparently I didn't."

"Not quite enough, that's all, sir." The Inspector was relenting. "I'm sure the mistake was quite natural."

"Thanks," said Archie dryly. "You haven't yet told me how you know."

"It's this way, Doctor." Inspector Turner settled himself comfortably and took out the inevitable notebook. Was it to be a long story? Archie lit another Gold Flake.

As the Inspector told it, it lasted out Archie's cigarette; but the facts were simple and few. While the Doctor was on his round, Inspector Turner had gone to the railway station to interrogate the guard. It appeared that, due to the illness of the other guard, Killick had been on continuous duty throughout the previous day and evening. He saw Andrew Herrick leave for London in the morning on the eight-fifty. He had bought a first-class return ticket. He returned on the nine-fifteen that evening, handing Killick the return half of the ticket. He was the only first-class passenger on the nine-fifteen.

Just a few minutes before eleven, when the last evening train for London was due, Killick had been surprised to see him again, waiting on the platform. Mr. Herrick had spoken to him and commented on the fact he was still on duty. Killick had explained the circumstance, and they had talked for a minute or two until the train came in. Mr. Herrick had said that, much to his annoyance, he had discovered he must return to town. Killick had presumed he meant to stay the night, "not come back and kill 'isself," as there were no more trains down, and he was carrying a small dispatch case, which Killick presumed held "'is shaving tackle and sechlike."

"I phoned Cambury, and the guard there remembers him," Inspector Turner wound up. "The eleven o'clock only goes as far as Cambury where it connects with the through London express."

"I know. And he got on the express?"

"Yes. Paddington's the next stop. There's no doubt he went all the way to London, sir."

Archie Storke resorted briefly to profanity.

"'Curiouser and curiouser,'" he ended slowly.

"You see, sir, as there are no more trains, he must have come back by motor. And putting it at the best, he couldn't have got here before half-past two. That's supposing he turned right round and came back at once, and the car was fast enough to do sixty-five miles in two hours. The eleven o'clock gets into Paddington at twelve-thirty-three."

"A fast car could do it in under two hours at that time of night; an hour and twenty minutes at a pinch. But I agree with you it isn't reasonable that he left London at once."

Archie paused to light another cigarette, then asked, "What line are you going to take? This sudden trip to town must be connected with the murder. I should think Herrick must have received a phone call, a message of some sort, which made it imperative for him to go back to London."

"It's probable, sir. Something at any rate happened between nine-thirty and eleven which decided him, though it may be only that he discovered something, something he hadn't known about before."

"Yes, you're right; there may have been no message."

"I shall attempt to discover that definitely. The trip may not be connected with the murder, but I think it is. We shall ask the Yard to investigate the London end. We must trace Mr. Herrick's movements in town. About the matter in general, Dr. Storke—"

"That's what I meant."

"Well, Colonel Copeland and I are still agreed that we must keep the matter as quiet as possible for the present. We'll adjourn the inquest and let suicide be presumed."

"You know best," said Archie, "although I don't see how you can keep it up and still make your inquiries."

"We can't indefinitely, sir. But if we can gain a little time before it is known that murder was committed, and it's spread all over the newspapers, it may make all the difference."

"Then you haven't told Mr. Herrick or Cyril the truth?"

"No. And we shan't tell Mr. Armstrong either."

"One feels they have a right to know, that's all," objected Archie uncomfortably.

"They have, sir; but unfortunately we have no choice." Inspector Turner did not sound troubled by any such delicate consideration. "You agreed with us, Doctor, in fact it was you who put it most strongly, that it appears only someone intimate with Mr. Herrick could have—"

"Yes, yes, I know," interrupted Archie, "that's quite true; I don't see how anyone else could have killed the dog. We must suspect them, I suppose, until we know. Only now we're actually doing it, I don't like it much. I know both Johnny and Cyril and I don't think either of them—" Suddenly his face lighted with relief. "Look here, Inspector, along those lines we can wash out Burford Herrick at least. He couldn't have strangled Mac. The dog had never seen him."

"That is true, Dr. Storke, but there are other facts besides the dog. Best keep an open mind. We don't know. We are sure of very little yet."

Archie Starke drooped pensively.

"I don't know that we are sure of anything," he mourned.

The Bentley crunched on the gravel outside, and in a moment the Colonel entered the study.

"Let's go at once, Archie. We don't want to keep Janey waiting for lunch," he said. "I'll be at Dr. Storke's if you want me, Inspector."

"If Mr. Armstrong comes, sir?"

"Ask him to wait and phone me. Coming, Archie?"

"Just a minute, Roger," answered Archie. He turned to the Inspector. "If you haven't taken the dog away, Turner, I'd like another look at him before you do."

"He's still out back, sir."

"I won't be a second," muttered Archie, vanishing through the door.

"Damn the dog," said the Colonel feelingly.

CHAPTER III
THURSDAY 1-4 P.M.

The Colonel Eats Creamed Chicken

It was fortunate, thought Janey, that there had been all that nice chicken left from the night before; Mary had creamed it deliciously.

"Let me give you some more," she said to the Colonel.

The Colonel passed his plate. It was evident that even murder could not impair the Colonel's appetite. He was a nice thing, but such a gourmand. Archie had eaten practically nothing. He was lighting another cigarette. He was worrying. He would worry about all this awfully. Oh dear, why had Andrew Herrick got himself murdered? It was awful but it wasn't nearly as awful as stealing Johnny's money first. Now, how were Johnny and Monica going to get married? Kitty Lambert would be pleased; she had always wanted Monnie to marry Cyril. But she wouldn't be pleased about losing her own money. Janey was quite sure Kitty was "Dearest," only she didn't like to say so. Maybe Johnny's other uncle, Burford, would make good the money. But then he was Cyril's father, and if he knew that Cyril was in love with Monica, too, and that if he made it possible for Monnie and Johnny—well, even so it was only fair. He should be made to see it that way.

"What is Burford Herrick like, Roger?" asked Janey.

"Sound fellow," answered the Colonel, beginning on an apple. "You agree, Archie?"

"I should think so. He's not at all like Andrew, Janey," said Archie.

"Not from what I've heard," agreed the Colonel. "I told him about the embezzlement, by the way."

"Did you? That was a sticky bit of work."

"Yes, but he was frightfully nice about it, though I could see the disgrace of it hit him pretty keenly."

"Naturally, even without what we know, the thing's sordid enough."

"What did he say?" questioned Janey.

"Say? Oh, that it was all due to Andrew's pride. That if he'd only told him, he could have saved him. He keeps going over that, says it's his fault his brother's dead."

"Well, hardly that. Though if it hadn't been for the money—"

"I don't believe Andrew Herrick was murdered because of the money, Archie," interrupted Janey.

"I know, Ducky, that's what you say. But there may be other people involved besides John and 'Dearest' who might have done it. So far, at any rate, it's the only reason we have."

"There must be another, darling," said Janey with calm conviction.

"My dear child—" began Archie.

"About the money," interposed the Colonel, "Burford Herrick told me he wished to make it good."

"Did he? Oh, that's fine," cried Janey.

"What he should do in the circumstances," Archie approved more quietly.

"As soon as we know how much has been taken and from whom, he will—"

"That ought to be easy. We can find that out easily, can't we?" Janey's eyes were shining with happiness. "I was so upset; now it's all right, not about the murder, of course," Janey corrected herself hastily, "but about Johnny and Monica; and Kitty Lambert, too," she added as an afterthought.

"Kitty Lambert?" echoed Archie. "Janey, you are the—the most remarkable girl."

"Well, now she's going to get her money back, I can say who she is, can't I?"

"My dear, certainly, what we want to know is why you didn't say so before."

"What more do you know, Janey?" asked the Colonel.

Janey laughed. "Nothing more, honestly, Roger. I would have told you what I thought in the end anyway. You see I'm not sure 'Dearest' is Mrs. Lambert now. I only think so."

"Anything to go by, Janey?" asked Archie.

"Only that Monica said her mother was worrying about some investment Andrew Herrick had made for her. The shares had gone up, and she wanted him to sell, and he wouldn't; something like that. I know they haven't been very friendly lately, Kitty and Andrew Herrick. She told Cuthbert Wilkinson about it, I know."

"Wilkinson?" murmured the Colonel, disposing of the last of his apple.

"And she doesn't know anything, our Janey! I'll have to teach you how to be the proper wife of a criminal investigator, Ducky. Can you tell us who delivered a letter, apparently in the dead of night, at Andrew Herrick's?"

"Of course, I can't. Don't be silly, Archie. Maybe you did, you were out."

"So I was, another Simpson baby; I never thought of it. It must have been just about the time of the murder."

"You didn't hear anything? The shot?"

"No, Roger, not I. I went past Herrick's, too."

"What about the letter?" Janey was curious.

"Mrs. Ingles found a note in the box when she came this morning. She forgot it, and then with stupid cunning she goes and puts it in the study when there's no one about. The police were upstairs at the time, and Roger and I were in another room. Later, we all go upstairs, not knowing the note's there. Then comes Wilkinson paying morning calls; waits for a time in the study, leaves in a hurry; and the mysterious letter's gone. What do you make of that?"

"I think it's very queer," said Janey.

"It's Wilkinson; that's what it is," said Archie. "Can you do a bit of guessing about that for us, angel wife?"

"No–o. But if Cuthbert Wilkinson did take it, then—"

"Then?"

"Well, it might have something to do with Kitty, that's all. He's awfully in love with her, you know. The letter might have been about the money; and when they heard about Andrew Herrick, when they knew what had happened to him, perhaps they wanted it back; so he went and got it."

"You've hit it, Janey. I bet you've hit it! I was on the track but I didn't have it right. Listen, Roger, Mrs. Lambert writes a stiff letter to Herrick. Perhaps she knows the truth, that he has deceived her; not invested her money as he said he had but put it into something else. Perhaps she doesn't. At any rate, she's worried and angry. She delivers the letter or has someone deliver it for her. Then the next morning she learns that Herrick has committed suicide. She doesn't want to be involved; she asks Wilkinson to go over right away and see if he can get hold of the letter. How's that? Another thing I've just thought of: we don't know that she didn't receive a letter from Herrick last night. The letter we found was incomplete; he had rejected that; but we don't know he didn't finish another."

"That's sound enough, Archie," agreed the Colonel. "Only Wilkinson claimed to know nothing of what had happened."

"Of course he did. That was obviously a lie. Mrs. Lambert could have known. Don't you remember, Mrs. Ingles phoned her daughter at Mrs. Lambert's before she rang me?"

"So she did," said the Colonel; "but granted Janey's right, and Mrs. Lambert wrote the letter, there's at least one important point arising from that. At what time was she or her messenger at the house?"

"Must have been after eleven when Herrick went back to London, or he would have received the letter."

"Just so, but he came back again, how or when we don't know. He was apparently alone, or if the murderer was with him, he apparently suspected nothing as he undressed. Why, in that interval, didn't he see the letter in his box if it was there by then?"

"I hadn't thought of that," Archie moiled it over for a moment or two; then he said, "There are two possible answers, neither seems reasonable: He came with the murderer, or the murderer was there waiting for him. That doesn't matter. At any rate he was sandbagged as soon as he entered the house. Then while he was unconscious, the murderer undressed him; he didn't undress himself. That doesn't seem sensible, as I can see no reason for the murderer's going to all that trouble. Why must he be in pajamas and dressing-gown? The murderer wants his foot bare in order to fake suicide, but he could accomplish that by taking off his shoe and sock.

"My other answer is that the letter was not delivered until after the murder. That again doesn't fill the bill. If the letter was, as Janey thinks, simply ticking him off about the money, surely it wasn't of such importance that it would be delivered after three in the morning."

"No, dear, of course not," said Janey. "You are overlooking the fact, it's all very confusing, that one of the maids might have taken it across this morning early. Before Mrs. Ingles came, at seven or seven-thirty."

"I don't know, Janey. A minute ago I thought you had a bull's eye. Now I'm not so sure." Archie had his benign expression again.

"He's always doing that, Roger," complained Janey, "agreeing with you one minute and—"

"I know," the Colonel spoke with feeling. "He even disagrees with himself."

Archie Storke met the two pairs of accusing eyes. "My children," he said, "I am a most aggravating creature, I realize it. Nevertheless—"

"Nevertheless, this is all hypocritical. The only thing we know with reasonable certainty is that Wilkinson stole a letter."

"The words out of my mouth, Roger. But if Wilkinson stole the letter, it seems a logical deduction that either he or Mrs. Lambert wrote it; and if he then steals it, it seems logical still to presume that, because of Herrick's death, the letter has now become dangerous to him, or dangerous to her, or dangerous to them both together."

"You sound like the House that Jack Built, Archie. It's very mixing. But isn't it the same? Isn't it just what I said?" Janey was plaintive.

"Yes, and no," answered Archie. "Up to a point I agree with you. Only I think the letter contained something much more incriminating than an innocuous request for an explanation about the money."

"Why?" asked Janey.

"Because I don't believe Wilkinson would have stolen it if it hadn't, that's why."

"Well, we'll have to see what we can get out of Wilkinson." The Colonel had the inflection of one who hopes wistfully for a change of subject.

"And that's going to be delicate going," said Archie. "You can even accuse him outright of having stolen the letter and not get any further. He has only to deny it."

"That's the snag, we can't prove it," agreed the Colonel. "However, once we're fairly sure of our ground, that 'Dearest' is Mrs. Lambert, we can tackle her. She may be easier."

"Mark my words, there's something extremely fishy about those two. Kitty Lambert's just the sort of woman to set one middle-aged admirer at another middle-aged admirer's throat, intending to enjoy the fun; and then it gets out of hand and isn't fun at all any more."

"Archie!" Janey was scandalized. "You've no right to gallop ahead with suspicions like that."

Archie Storke sent his wife a smile like a naughty child's. He reached across a corner of the table and patted her hand.

"Dear Janey," he murmured, "I won't, if you think I shouldn't. But I like suspecting Wilkinson. I don't like him, and he's so convenient; and say what you will, there has been a murder; and somebody had to do it."

"I know," said Janey unhappily, returning the pressure of her husband's fingers.

The telephone bell rang shrilly.

"I thought it was time Turner should ring us."

The Colonel rose from the table.

"Armstrong must have arrived. I must go. Thank you for a delicious lunch, Janey. Are you coming, Archie?"

"Do go and be there while they see Johnny, Archie," said Janey softly.

"Why, Janey, you funny child! Turner and I are anything but ferocious." With unaccustomed gallantry the Colonel lifted Janey's hand and brushed it lightly with his lips.

"Don't worry about Johnny, my dear," said Archie.

The Bentley was once more on its way to Whiteleaves. The afternoon sun spread clear shadow patterns of arching trees upon the yellow road. The sky above the row of workmen's cottages was still a cloudless blue. It was only three o'clock, but it seemed to Archie Storke as though several days, blue and gold like this one, had gone by since the day when he had put his head out of the bathroom window to sniff the morning and pronounce the world a good world. He settled himself further into the Bentley's front seat and sighed.

"Janey is fretting about Johnny," he said.

"Yes, she is; and I'm sorry but I also wonder why," answered the Colonel. His tone like Archie's was mildly speculative.

"I suppose we've got to go ahead with all this?"

"Of course. Does Janey know something she's not telling us, Archie, about—"

"No, I don't think so. I think she's only worrying because she's so fond of Monica and she's afraid things may work out to look bad for Johnny."

"Of course, we did tell her about the quarrel, didn't we?"

"Yes, and so—well, I think Janey's afraid you suspect Johnny."

"That all?"

"I think so. She could see where you were heading this morning."

"I have a perfectly open mind on the whole subject," denied the Colonel vigorously. "There are certain facts which we must recognize, that's all. Armstrong possesses a key to the house; though about that, it must be remembered that Herrick himself might have admitted the person who killed him. Armstrong quarreled yesterday morning with his uncle and used threatening language. It's Armstrong's money that was misappropriated. Without money he could not be sure of the girl he loves. There has been bad blood between him and his uncle for some time, and he has a violent temper."

"All true, but not much to go by. As far as keys to the house are concerned, Cyril has one, too."

"That reminds me, I meant to tell you before, at lunch, only we got sidetracked discussing the letter—"

"What?"

"I haven't time for the details now; we're almost there. But by a rare stroke of luck I managed to get what Burford Herrick and Cyril were doing last night. Got it tactfully without their knowing why I was asking."

"Good enough. How?"

"By wanting to know what they knew about Herrick's eleven o'clock trip to town. Had they seen him? Had he phoned? Had they known he was coming? Did they know why he'd come?"

"Had they and did they?"

"No. They'd left the hotel a little before seven, gone to dinner, gone on to a theater, had supper after the theater, returned to the hotel some time around one. Cyril had gone up for a drink to his father's room; then he'd gone on home to bed at his apartment. There was no message from Andrew for either of them at hotel or apartment. Burford had eaten too much rich food during the evening, he said. He'd had an attack of indigestion about an hour or two after going to bed and he'd had to ring for hot water."

"In short, if their story's true, they have perfect alibis."

"Yes. And I don't doubt it for a moment, though I'm going to have everything checked up carefully, of course."

The Bentley drew up, and the Colonel switched off the motor. Where the Mercedes had stood two hours before was a battered Morris roadster covered with dust.

"Johnny really should have his car washed once in a while," commented Archie. "It's a complete disgrace."

"Looks as though he'd been driving like the devil," said the Colonel, raising his hand to the knocker.

A new policeman let them in.

"Afternoon, Perkins," the Colonel greeted him, "where is the Inspector?"

"In the small room, sir."

The study door opened, and Turner's head appeared round it.

"We're in here, sir. Mr. Armstrong has been waiting to see you and the Doctor."

A long loose-jointed young man with tousled black hair unwound himself from a chair and stood up as they entered the room. His hands were thrust deep into the pockets of his gray flannel trousers. His thin dark face wore the suspicion of a scowl. In spite of that and of something more, instability, perhaps, it was an attractive, an arresting young face. Jack Sheppard, thought the Colonel. He's going to be stubborn, thought Archie.

"Hello, Johnny. Do you know Colonel Copeland?"

"How do you do, sir." Johnny passed his hand nervously over his untidy hair. "I'm afraid I'm rather a mess. I drove like hell and I haven't had a chance to brush up." He flashed a sudden smile, warm and disarming, at Archie and put his hand back into his pocket. His face resumed its sullen expression.

"Allow me to say you have my sympathy in all this—" The Colonel floundered a little, cleared his throat. Damn it, how was he to say the correct thing when Armstrong stood there paying no attention, looking as cross as a bear?

"Thank you," said Johnny. "I'd rather not talk about it, if you don't mind. What's happened to Drew is so—I know it's what one always says, I always thought it was awful rot, but now— Well, it doesn't seem real to me, that's all." Pain showed through the sullenness. The dark eyes were haunted.

"You got my wire?" asked the Colonel.

"Yes, I didn't get it at once. I was—I overslept this morning; my char didn't wake me. I found it when I woke up. I came as fast as I could then."

"Doesn't matter a bit." The Colonel spoke reassuringly. "Your uncle and cousin arrived some time ago, and they've done all that was necessary."

"Then you don't need me just now?" Johnny's voice was quick and eager.

Archie Starke wished it hadn't been. Why had Johnny spoken in just that tone? What was the matter? Johnny was acting all wrong. Something was awfully wrong about Johnny. He behaved as though—Archie took a mental breath; it was no use trying to fool himself. Johnny behaved as though he were afraid. Now why? He couldn't have—no, that was impossible— The Colonel was saying, "Well, yes, we do. I don't like bothering you now, but there are one or two things weed like to ask you."

"Is it necessary?"

"Rather. You see, Armstrong, in a thing like this, we must determine certain—"

"Very well, I understand. Let's get it over with as quickly as possible, that's all. I feel pretty awful. Do you mind if I smoke?"

Turner's morning circle of three chairs became four. Archie lit a Gold Flake of his own.

"Well, Turner?" asked the Colonel, shifting the responsibility.

"It's a matter of routine, Mr. Armstrong," explained Inspector Turner largely. In a delicate corner he always trusted to this magic formula. It seldom failed to cover a multitude of dodges. "In a death like this of Mr. Herrick's we are supposed to discover if we can why he killed himself. Why and how and when?"

"And where? First rule to cub reporters." Johnny was sarcastic. It needed more than rudeness to put Inspector Turner off his stride.

"Ah, it is?" he murmured blandly.

The pause he allowed to follow was flat, and again restless fingers were pushed through rumpled black hair. Then he continued imperturbably, "You want to help us, of course, Mr. Armstrong. Now let us see. We will take the things we want to know in their order. Do you know any reason why your uncle should kill himself?"

For a moment there was no answer.

"No," said Johnny at last.

Archie Storke leaned forward and flicked the ash from his cigarette carefully into the fireplace. He dared not look at Johnny. He
felt embarrassed and unhappy. Why did the young blighter lie? He
was such a bad liar, too. That "No!" Before he denied it, they hadn't
been sure he knew about the money. Now— The Inspector's voice
went on relentlessly.

"It would appear that Mr. Herrick was in difficulty about
money. Your cousin knew of it, and you did not?"

"Well, I— What's this, a cross-examination, Inspector?"

Turner had better be careful, thought Archie. It was going to
take some maneuvering to find out what he wanted and still not
give the show away. Johnny was suspicious. Was he merely shrewd
or did he know it wasn't suicide? Damn!

Turner had realized the need for caution. He was being silky.

"Not at all, Mr. Armstrong. Don't misunderstand. There is some
confusion about the matter, and we must clear it up if possible."

Johnny, too, had decided to change his tactics. "What I said
was silly. If you must, you must. Fire ahead. I'll help you if I can."

"Thank you, Mr. Armstrong. About this question of the money,
Mr. Herrick left a letter. I would like you to read it, if you will. It is
his writing, is it not?"

From his pocket Inspector Turner took the unfinished note and
handed it to Johnny. The lean fingers held it for a moment; then
slowly, reluctantly, unfolded it. Archie, watching unhappily, saw
the long body grow tense as if to brace itself, dusky red instead of
white on the mask that was Johnny's face, red seeping slowly until
it met the line of black hair. The letter was folded again quickly,
held out.

"This is not addressed to me."

"It concerns you, Mr. Armstrong, please finish reading it."

"Very well. Only I don't like this sort of thing."

Again the letter was unfolded. Johnny took a long time. Carefully, as though dragging his eyes from line to line, he read. Then
with a gesture of finality he once more held out the sheet of paper.
This time Inspector Turner took it.

"It's my uncle's handwriting," was all Johnny said.

"You did not know Mr. Herrick had—er—"

"Embezzled my money? No. That is—" Johnny hesitated.

"You suspected it?" Turner completed his sentence, and to Archie's bewilderment Johnny allowed the assumption to pass.

The Colonel intervened.

"You will be glad to know, Armstrong, that your uncle, Burford Herrick that is, has told me that he wishes to make good your loss."

But Johnny was listless.

"That's good of him," he murmured.

Inspector Turner clung stubbornly to the helm.

"And any other loss as well, was it not, sir? There's where Mr. Armstrong may be able to help us. Do you know for whom this letter was intended?"

"No, I don't." Johnny's voice was alive now and sharp.

"Ah, too bad." Turner's was gently regretful. He brought his ship hard about, took another tack. Archie Storke closed his eyes wearily for a moment, brought out and lit another Gold Flake. The interview dragged painfully on.

Turner doggedly steered his difficult course into the wind of Johnny's opposition. And slowly Turner made headway. With persistence, and at times with surprising skill, he found out what he wanted to know.

Johnny had seen his uncle last at breakfast the morning before. He declined to discuss their quarrel. It wasn't a quarrel, really, and it had nothing whatever to do with what happened; it couldn't have. He had come down to Pennerford last evening, yes, but not to see his uncle. He wanted to see Miss Lambert on a matter that was entirely personal. He had left her at ten o'clock and driven back again to London. When he got there, he had gone directly to his rooms and to bed.

"Then you can throw no light on why Mr. Herrick took the eleven o'clock train last night for London?"

"The eleven o'clock?" For an instant incredulity like a banner waved across Johnny's face. Then quickly, "No, did he?"

Archie Starke hardly listened to what followed. The thing that arrested his attention was that bewildered look on Johnny's face when Turner told him about the train. Whatever Johnny knew, and, damn it all, try not to see it as he would, Johnny knew something. Whatever it was, whatever he was hiding, he had not known about the train. That was the queer thing. Archie himself had been surprised by that same fact. He found himself wondering if after all it were a fact, if Killick had not possibly made a mistake. Perhaps it was not Andrew Herrick who went back on the eleven o'clock, but somebody else, somebody Killick had taken for Andrew: the murderer himself. By Jove! That fitted in. He must see Killick the first minute he could, go into it very carefully, and—

"That's about all, Mr. Armstrong," Inspector Turner was saying. "Thank you for being so patient. I'm sorry we had to trouble you."

"That's all right." Johnny didn't sound as though it were. "I'll go along then. Good-by, sir, I'm staying at the pub, not the Seven Stars, the Horseshoes, if you want me," he said to the Colonel. And to Archie, "Could I speak to you for a minute, Storke?"

Archie followed him into the hall.

"Nasty bit of work, that Inspector," Johnny whispered. Still in a low tone he added, "What I wanted was to ask you if Janey'd seen Monnie. . . . She hasn't? Well I'm going over there now. Monnie'll be awfully upset over this mess. I'm such a tactless ass. Monnie's always afraid I'll put my foot in it somehow or other."

Johnny started for the front door, but came back to say, "Look here, Archie Storke, may we come over for a bit this evening? Monnie and I? I'd like to talk to you. Not that there's anything particular to say, but you, well, you and Janey take the bad taste out of one's mouth. The figure's not delicate, but it's intended as a compliment."

"Come, by all means," answered Archie.

"Good. We'll be there. About nine."

The front door closed. Archie went back to the study. Inspector Turner had his comment to make.

"Difficult, very, Mr. Armstrong," he said. "Now, Dr. Storke, can you tell me—"

"Oh, Lord, Turner, you're not going to hash it over now, are you? Have mercy. I can tell you one thing, and this is for you, too,

Roger, and that is that you're making your own difficulties, some of them at any rate. You can't carry on this way. It's not feasible. You'll have to say it's murder and be done with it."

"You think Armstrong knows, Archie?" asked the Colonel.

"I don't know just how you mean that, so I don't know how to answer. But I'll say this: in spite of all Turner's care, if I'd been Johnny and I hadn't known when he started questioning me, I'd have known by the time he'd finished."

"If you'd been Johnny, yes," agreed the Colonel. "That's a very keen young man. Very keen or very—"

"Guilty," finished Inspector Turner.

"Oh, you two!" exclaimed Archie Storke, exasperated beyond patience.

He left them to it with that. He couldn't argue that Johnny's behavior hadn't offered plenty of room for speculation. It had been all wrong, worryingly wrong; but he could learn what conclusions they'd drawn from it later. Archie had only one idea now and that was to see Killick and test his own theory.

CHAPTER IV
THURSDAY 4—10 P.M.

Milk Cans and No Sugar

He found Killick on the railway platform languidly maneuvering an empty milk can.

"Afternoon, Joe," said Archie.

"Afternoon, Doctor, lovely weather we're 'aving."

"Nice and dry, yes. Good for your wife's asthma. How has she been, by the way?"

"She's nothing to complain of, sir. That last medicine you give 'er worked fine."

"Glad to hear it, Joe."

Archie Storke waited; he knew his man. The milk can completed its circle and came to rest by the group of its fellows. Killick brushed his palms together and straightened up.

"Shocking news about Mr. 'Errick, aren't it?"

"It is, Joe."

"That Inspector from Cambury was round 'ere this morning. 'E wanted to know 'ad I seen 'im."

"Oh?"

"I sez, sure I 'ave. Several times, too. 'When was the last time?' 'e asks me. 'Eleven o'clock,' I tells 'im."

"Eleven o'clock? Last night is that?"

"That's it. 'Mick,' the Inspector sez to me, 'you're the last person we knows as seen him alive and talked to 'im.' 'E's right, too, Doctor."

"How was that?"

"Like this, it was. Long about the time for the eleven o'clock, I comes out of the waiting room and 'ere on the platform I sees Mr. 'Errick. 'What, still on duty, Joe?' 'e sez. I sez—"

"But look here, Joe, it was pitch dark. How do you know for sure that it was Mr. Herrick?"

"'Ow do I know!" Killick's voice was rich with indignation. "I seen 'im, that's 'ow I know. 'E stood right under that lamp there, 'e did. 'It's most annoying,' 'e sez, 'I've just got down and I find I must return to London.' 'It's a shame,' I tells 'im, 'but the eleven o'clock's a good train,' I sez. 'E was most sociable-like last night; 'e talks to me till the train comes in."

"What was he wearing, Joe?"

"Wearing? A 'eavy coat and 'e was carrying a little case same as 'e was when 'e come down by the nine-fifteen."

"He had his case then, did he?"

"Yes, 'e 'ad it. 'E walked right by me quick. Just 'anded me 'is ticket; 'e didn't say nothing."

"Oh. You didn't speak to him then?"

"I sez, 'Good evening, sir!' No answer from 'im. I wasn't paying no particular attention but I thought 'e acted like 'e 'ad something on 'is mind."

"Why, what made you think that?"

"Well, it warn't nothing much. I 'appened to watch 'im, that's all. He walks off brisk, and when 'e gets to the road, 'e stands there for a minute like 'e was lost in thought. Then 'e goes off by the towpath. It was dark; I could just see 'im standing there."

"By the towpath?"

"Same like most evenings; it's shorter for 'im. When it's bad underfoot, then 'e don't; 'e sticks to the road. Wouldn't do to get mud on 'is shoes, it wouldn't."

"No, I dare say. Was Mr. Herrick carrying the dispatch case when he left in the morning?"

"Now you ask me, Doctor, I don't know as I can say. The eight-fifty's crowded. I don't remember seeing it in 'is 'and. Is it important, sir? Did 'e 'ave the money in it?"

"The money? What on earth are you talking about, Joe?"

Killick lowered his voice to a hoarse whisper, leaned towards Archie Storke's ear.

"The money 'e stole. Mr. Armstrong's money. Did 'e 'ave it in that case?"

"Complete nonsense, Joe. Who's been telling you fantastic tales?"

"No tales, Dr. Starke. It's the truth 'e stole the money. Tom knows it. That's why 'e killed 'isself most like."

"Out with it, Joe. What does Tom know? Who have you told this to?"

"Nobody. Nobody knows it but you and me and Tom. I don't 'old with volunteering information to the law, I don't. I answer what they asks me and nothing further."

"Yes, but what is it you know?"

"What Tom told me this morning. You listen, Dr. Storke, while I tell you. Last night long about nine o'clock Tom was coming down the path there by the allotments. 'E 'eard voices and 'e stops to find out who's talking. On the other side of the 'edge they are, sitting in a car. 'E knows the voices. It's Miss Lambert and Mr. Armstrong. Tom's curious, I don't 'old with heaves-dropping meself; but 'e waits. 'E 'ears Mr. Armstrong say as 'ow Mr. 'Errick, 'that damned swindling uncle of mine,' Tom sez 'e said, 'ad stole all 'is money. 'E's spitting mad, Mr. Armstrong is. Miss Lambert, she was trying to smooth 'im down. 'E sez 'e'll see 'is uncle and 'ave it out when the train gets in. Miss Lambert begs 'im not to. 'I'm afraid of your temper, Johnny,' she sez and starts to cry. Tom feels ashamed of 'isself and comes away. That's 'ow I come to know, Doctor."

"I see. Well, look here, Joe, this is very dangerous gossip. It won't do at all for either you or Tom Harris to repeat it. You must assure me that you won't."

"We won't, sir, it's not us as are gossiping and cadging drinks for the stories we tell in this village."

"What now?"

"It's that drunken good-for-nothing Ferris, that's who it is. Going to the Stars, then to the 'Orseshoes, 'aving drinks stood 'im as 'e'll tell 'ow 'e saw the body."

"What? Saw the body?"

"'E didn't, Doctor, 'cause 'e couldn't. But 'e sez 'e did. In a lane by the council cottages, lying in a car, with a 'at over its face. 'What time is this?' I asks 'im. 'Round about eleven-thirty,' 'e sez. 'Then it's not the body,' I tells 'im. 'Mr. 'Errick,' I sez, 'was in the train going to London at eleven-thirty.' 'I don't believe you,' 'e sez and 'as another drink. All 'e saw was somebody 'aving forty winks in 'is car, but 'e will 'ave it, it was the body."

"Ferris is a fool, everybody knows that. I wonder who he did see. Did he say what the car was like?"

"A roadster, 'e said it was. It's dark and deserted-like where they're building the cottages. Seems to me like somebody just pulled in there for a sleep."

"That's all there is to it. Well, good-by, Joe. See your wife takes that medicine I gave her regularly, won't you? And don't go gossiping or you'll land in serious trouble. I'm telling you that for your own good."

"That's right, Doctor, I won't. Good day, sir."

Archie Storke got back in his car feeling a little overwhelmed. He had heard nothing he hoped to hear and a lot he wished he hadn't. There was no doubt that it was Andrew Herrick who took that eleven o'clock to London. Archie relinquished his theory with regret. It was not till later that he got another one to take its place. At the moment he was discouraged and chagrined. He no longer fancied himself as an amateur criminal investigator. Things seemed to be piling up worse and worse against Johnny; it had been a long tiring day; tea was what he needed, tea, and to forget it all for a bit.

So it was with a groan that he saw the Bentley and Liz outside his house and with forced cordiality that he greeted the Colonel who was placidly having tea with Janey.

"'Lo, Roger. When did Turner release you?" Archie flopped wearily into his armchair.

"No sugar today, darling," he said as Janey picked up his cup and saucer.

Janey dropped the sugar back into the sugar-bowl with a little click. No sugar was usually the sign of a ruffled temper. Poor lamb, he looks tired, she thought.

"I came along here about a quarter of an hour ago," the Colonel answered. "Where did you go to in all that hurry, Archie?"

Archie had a momentary battle with his conscience, and he won. No sense telling Roger that rigmarole of Killick's.

"Oh, a patient of mine I had to see, that's all," he replied vaguely.

"Turner and I went through the papers in the writing desk. We found confirmation of all we've surmised. On one of the counterfoils in Herrick's check book was a note of a large sum deposited to his account and after the sum were the initials 'K.L.'"

"That's fairly definite then. We may substitute Kitty for 'Dearest.' Anything else of interest?"

"Not unless it's the rate at which he's been losing money. Two weeks ago he gave Cyril Herrick a check for a thousand pounds. Considering he was strapped then, that struck us as odd. What do you make of it?"

"That Cyril is the only person we know of who was paid money owed him?"

"I presume that's it. But Cyril knew Herrick was in difficulty and wrote his father to tell him so. Under those circumstances, I'm wondering why he took the money."

"He probably thought Andrew was all right. Cyril wrote his father long before that, for Burford Herrick had the letter before he left California. It takes almost three weeks to get here, and as long for a letter to get out, of course. That means Cyril would have written six weeks or more ago. Since then he may have believed the tide to have turned for his uncle."

"So when the check was offered him, he took it?"

"How can I know, Roger? I think that's the likely answer. Why don't you ask Cyril himself? More tea please, dear."

"At the moment I can't very well ask Cyril Herrick a question like that." The Colonel sounded offended. "Well, though I'm not a paying guest, I'm a damnably staying one and I'd better shove along home."

"Roger, what a ghastly pun," said Janey.

"Don't barge off in a huff, old chap," protested Archie.

The Colonel smiled down on him.

"I'm not. We're both a bit fagged out with the whole business."

"I know I am," Archie admitted. "It's like trying to reach a mountain. There it is looking large and near; and you start off for it all confident and eager and you walk and walk and never get any closer. There's the monstrous fact of the murder looming up before us, and the more we try to get at it the further off it seems."

"We'll get there in the end," said the Colonel.

"I'm not so sure," Archie answered drearily; "I feel we're walking away from it all the time, that there's only one way to get there, and we haven't found it."

"Oh, there's always more than one way to arrive at the truth. We must try the lot, that's all." The Colonel was determinedly sure of himself. "The important thing is to get a proper start, go about it methodically."

"Turner and method, eh? Well, that's where I think you're wrong. Method is not going to solve this crime, but imagination may."

"You've plenty of that, Archie, so get on with it. I'll stick to the slow and sure and I'll wager you—"

"Bet you anything you like. Listen, Roger, you won't—"

"Children, children!" entreated Janey, "don't dispute. Please! We're all much too jumpy."

"Right, angel," said Archie—then in a voice of insufferable meekness, "May I just ask the Chief Constable what his plans are?"

"Sometimes, Archibald Storke, you can be quite horrid." Janey cocked her head on one side and looked at him appraisingly.

The Colonel laughed. "Don't take him up, Janey. He's been maddening all day. Plans? I'm going to London first thing tomorrow morning to see Sir Wilfred Parker."

"The Assistant Commissioner?"

"Yes, I know him slightly. Lacking imagination, Archie, we'll have to resort to Scotland Yard."

"Forget it, Roger. I was probably talking rot. You're going to have them take up the London end?"

"We can't do without them. I want the alibis checked up, and Andrew Herrick's movements traced: what he did and whom he saw on Wednesday, and most particularly what happened after he reached Paddington at twelve-thirty Wednesday night."

"That's vitally important. If we can discover that—"

"Well, we'll set the machinery of the Yard in motion. Now I must go. Thanks again, Janey; your creamed chicken is something to remember, and breakfast and tea."

"Will you look in tomorrow night?" Archie asked.

"If I'm not too late. Don't trouble to see me out."

But Archie collected himself in sections from his enormous chair and for another minute or two the murmur of their voices came to Janey from the hall. A door closed, there was the quick purr of an engine, the receding sound of wheels upon the drive, and then Archie: "Janey, what time is it?"

"Almost ten minutes to six, dear."

"Blast it! Fine office hours I keep, twenty minutes late. Why didn't you tell me?"

He reappeared briefly in the doorway and was gone again. Janey sat on in a darkening room, staring at the fire, wondering—

They had finished dinner. Archie had picked up the book he'd been reading Janey had lighted her after-dinner-coffee cigarette. The room gathered closer to them in an intimate cozy silence, an evening just like all other evenings.

Archie's book hit the table with a sharp little crash.

"Damn it, it's no use!"

"You can't read?"

"No, I just go on and on moiling this wretched business over in my mind, not getting anywhere. I've got to find out. I'll have no peace until I do."

"I know, darling. You can't bear things you can't explain."

"No, I can't. There's always an explanation, a solution. Until I find it, I'm uneasy, all disintegrated, don't you see? I wish I weren't like that."

"It's the scientific mind, I suppose."

"Yes, just vulgar curiosity. What are we going to do?"

"Find out, that's all."

"The way you say it, Janey! It's not going to be easy."

"Perhaps not. But after all, Roger and Inspector Turner are—"

"Professionals? Or finding out?"

"Both."

"Turner's a professional, if you will; that is, he's trained in such things; Roger's not. As for their finding out—Ducky, you won't think me silly, will you? It's not conceit really. It's, well, it's instinct. I don't think they're going to."

"Why, Archie?"

"I said it was instinct, so it's hard to put into words. I have a feeling about this crime. I know I'm being vague. But there's something very queer about it. It's not normal. What I'm trying to say is that there's no motive, no meaning; and there's so much that is curious."

"There must be a motive."

"Of course, but not the way we're looking. You said yourself Andrew Herrick wasn't murdered because he turned crook. You know yourself how weak Roger's 'revenge because of the money' is. Then take another far-fetched theory: We didn't know Andrew Herrick well, but we knew his background. Where will you find his 'mysterious past'? He didn't have any."

"No. It's even harder to believe in a 'dark stranger from foreign parts bent on settling an old score.'"

"Well, there we are back to the meaninglessness of the thing. Why did anyone murder Andrew Herrick? What is there to gain?"

"Nothing that one can see. I suppose it's revenge for some reason, after all."

"It's not good enough. No, there's something very queer, something we haven't begun to catch a glimpse of, something routine investigation is likely never to see. That's why I think Turner and Roger will fail."

"And the things you call curious?"

"The tidiness, the untidiness, the eleven o'clock trip to town, and the secret no-one-knows-when-or-how return again."

"They'll be able to find that out. He had to come back by motor, and someone must have seen the car."

"What car? Whose car? We haven't the foggiest notion."

"Not yet. But the detectives should find it easy to trace Andrew Herrick after he got to London, and then they'll discover why he went and how he got back. He wasn't trying to help his murderer by sneaking about unseen. He didn't know he was being murdered."

"That's true; he made no secret of his going to London. He talked to Killick about it." Archie paused to stare dreamily at the tip of Janey's shoe. "Talked to Killick," he repeated absently. "What's more," he went on abruptly, "there's this business of the dispatch case. It may have no connection with the murder, as I admit the eleven o'clock may not have either. However that may be, they are linked with each other: the dispatch case and the trip, I mean. Killick's not sure whether the case went to town on the eight-fifty in the morning. He thinks not, but he is sure it came to Pennerford on the nine-fifteen and went back on the eleven. Herrick was carrying it both times, but it's not at Whiteleaves now. Therefore, some time after midnight on Wednesday he went somewhere and left the case."

"Papers of some sort in it, of course."

"What else? He brings them down with him in the evening, looks them over, and, because of what he finds, he rushes off back to London again."

"He can't even wait till morning."

"No, it's so urgent he must see to it at once. See whoever it is that gave them to him at once."

"He does see that person, and then—"

"And then he's found murdered."

There was a minute or two during which Archie and Janey examined their jerry-built hypothesis. Janey found it unsteady.

"The trouble with that is: doesn't it rather call for the 'mysterious stranger' who couldn't have done it because he couldn't have planned the fake suicide?"

"Not necessarily, no. It needn't have been a stranger to Whiteleaves Herrick went to see."

"But we know all who aren't, and it couldn't be any of them. Take them in order, Archie."

"All right, Wilkinson."

"I think it's preposterous to suspect Wilkinson."

"That's not the point."

"I know. I just said what I thought. Anyhow, Andrew Herrick didn't see Wilkinson Wednesday night in London."

"Are you sure?"

"Yes, because Wilkinson was at the Lamberts' Wednesday night. He stayed until after eleven."

"He could still take his car and be in London by one."

"Now do you think that's reasonable yourself? If it were Wilkinson Andrew Herrick wanted to see and they were both at Pennerford, why would they—"

"Don't go on; it's too idiotic. The same thing washes out Kitty Lambert."

"Surely you're not mad enough to think—"

"Well, no, I only toy with it a little. I can't see her planning or executing the actual murder but I do think perhaps she— All right, Ducky, don't snort at me. Who's next? Cyril? Well, Cyril was with his father all evening, and they didn't see Andrew."

"If what they say is true, they could have just managed to see him in the half hour between the time his train got in, at twelve-thirty, and one when they got back to the hotel. It might be hard to check up on them for such a short interval."

"All right. But it's not hard to check up, as you call it, on whether they went to bed. If they were in bed in London, they weren't here in Pennerford murdering Andrew."

"I'm worried about Cyril, by the way, Janey. He's frightfully cut up."

"There you go! You're too illogical. One minute you're twisting the tail of improbability to include Cyril, the next you're sympathizing with him because you know how much he cared."

"Oh, well, we were going over everybody. I know we ought to suspect someone intimate with Andrew; and yet the whole trouble is that as suspects none of them are any good. Let's finish, now we're started."

"Johnny?"

"Yes, Johnny."

"He was seeing Monica."

"I know. He told Turner so."

"And then he went back to London."

"Started back at ten, yes."

"And went to his rooms and bed when he got there."

"Janey, what's the use? Both you and I know that he hasn't the ghost of an alibi. These rooms of his; there's never a soul about, no doorman, caretaker, nothing; walk ups. There's not a soul to prove when he got home or whether he stayed after he got there. And to make matters worse he'd a legitimate grievance against his uncle and he hasn't been too discreet about it. Everyone knows they didn't get on even before this money thing happened. To cap it all, he goes and lies to Turner."

"Did he?"

"Like a trooper. Bungled it, what's more. Janey, I didn't want to face it but I had to. Johnny's hiding something. And it's not only that; he's afraid, terribly afraid."

"Poor Johnny. He never did it, Archie. Does he know you know?"

"What? That he's afraid? I can't tell. Isn't it about time they turned up?"

"Yes, it's a little after nine now. I don't want to be talking about it when they come. I won't be able to switch myself off and be natural. I feel queerly disloyal."

"I've felt that way myself off and on all day. As a problem which is jolly and fun to solve, this leaves much to be desired. We'll try to talk about something else. What did Sylvia have to say in her letter this morning? Weren't you reading one from her when I came in for breakfast—the second breakfast?"

"Yes. Oh, nothing much. George has gone away somewhere for a week and she—"

There was the noise of a car outside. The knocker rapped sharply. After a moment came footsteps in the passage, and then voices.

"Here they are," said Janey.

Mary, smug in white apron and cap, opened the door softly and stepped aside.

"Miss Lambert and Mr. Armstrong."

"Janey, angel, I meant to get over before and couldn't. Hello, Archie Storke."

But for all her show of naturalness Monica's gray eyes were large and wistful and had dark shadows. At the corners of her delicately rouged mouth were tired, tense little lines. She was a slim girl who moved with unconscious grace.

Johnny, grotesquely tall in the lamplight of the low-ceilinged room, his black hair still ruffled, made no attempt at deception. He stood there, scorning Monica's pretense, defiant.

"Good evening," he said simply and sat down. His long hands hung limply between his knees.

Janey looked at him, and with a distracted gesture of her head tossed back her heavy hair.

Monica, perched on the arm of Janey's chair, her face half in shadow, said gaily, "Janey's upsetting her halo again, Archie Storke. That means she's worried. It's you, Johnny, you're so impossibly glum."

"Glum? Am I? I'm sorry."

"Have a whisky and soda, Johnny?" asked Archie.

"I will, thanks. Forgive me, Janey, if I'm not very merry and bright. I—"

"Merry and bright? Oh, my dear, you're—you're—" Monica faltered, caught her breath in a little gulp, buried her face suddenly in Janey's hair, and burst into tears.

There was an incredulous moment filled only with the sound of her sobbing. Then Johnny sprang to his feet.

"Monnie, Monnie, darling, don't cry. What's the matter, darling, what have I done? Janey—"

"It's all right, Johnny. Monnie dear, please stop crying. Tell us what's wrong."

"It's—it's— Oh, I'm terribly ashamed to make a scene. I didn't know I was going to; but it's so awful. Please, please, Janey, make

Johnny tell us. Archie, you know it's better, you make him. Johnny, dearest, please—"

"There's nothing to tell, Monnie. There's nothing wrong." Johnny's face was stiff with misery. He lit a cigarette with hands that trembled.

Monica jerked upright suddenly. She was angry, but her eyes were hurt.

"Very well. I've made a fool of myself, that's all. Please all forgive me. May I have one of your cigarettes, Janey? Thanks."

No one knew what to say.

"How about a little bridge?" suggested Archie lamely.

Janey took her courage in both hands. She plunged recklessly, "Johnny, I've no right to interfere, unless loving you and Monnie gives me the right. I don't suppose it does. And I don't know what the trouble is, but you can't expect us not to see how unhappy and worried you are. Perhaps, if you'd tell us, we could help. You do trust us, don't you, Johnny? Why, we all know you never—" She caught the warning in Archie's eyes and stopped.

"Why don't you finish your sentence, Janey?" Johnny's tone was listless. "You might as well. I'm not a complete fool— Everyone will know sooner or later. You suspect it now, don't you, Monnie? That that's why you—"

"Suspect? Oh, what, Johnny, what—" Monnie's mouth was like a red wound in her white face.

"That Drew didn't commit suicide—"

"Johnny, for God's sake!" cried Archie sharply.

"You must know what that precious Inspector of yours thinks. Did you suppose after the cross-examination he gave me I wouldn't know, too? Good Lord, it was obvious."

"Is it true, Archie?" Monica whispered, and then at his slow answering nod her chin lifted. She swung quickly towards Johnny, and now there was determination and courage in her voice.

"Johnny, dearest, listen to me. Your uncle's been murdered— Well, I know *you* didn't do it but I *do* know you're hiding something. You may be suspected. There's only one way to save yourself from that. You must tell the truth." Her voice softened, pleaded with him. "I love you, Johnny, it's the last time I'll ask you—won't you tell us?"

There was a tortured silence; then Johnny said levelly, coldly, "You imagine it all, Monnie. I am hiding nothing. There is nothing to tell."

"Oh." Slowly, very slowly, she turned away from him and stood quite still. "If you loved me, you wouldn't lie to me. Apparently you don't trust us. Well, that settles it. What is it a girl always says in circumstances like this?—'We have both made a mistake.' That's it, isn't it?"

"Monnie! You don't mean it, do you, Monnie?"

"Yes, I do. I think the Storkes have had about enough of us for one evening. Will you take me home? Good night, Janey, I'm sorry about the dramatics and I won't say anything about the—the other thing, Archie. Good-by."

Johnny said nothing. He just followed Monica from the room. The front door opened, closed—

For a long time neither Janey nor Archie spoke. At last, "Poor children," murmured Janey.

"Yes, pathetic little devils— Janey, what do you think?"

"I don't know, Archie. I simply don't know. I don't believe Johnny did it; I don't think he could, but—"

"Oh, Lord, what a mess it all is—what a ghastly mess. Let's turn in, Janey, shall we?"

CHAPTER V
FRIDAY MORNING TO FRIDAY NIGHT

Bread Returns Upon the Waters

The next morning Archie drove into Cambury for the post-mortem. He was not in the best of moods. The weather had broken, and, pinned to the leaden sky, a thick rain hung down like long strands of gray wool.

"Damned wet wool," qualified Archie dismally, for he had slept badly. It would never do to let this thing get a hold on him; ruin his good night's sleep. Why should he care who murdered Andrew Herrick? It was no concern of his.

Of course, there was Johnny and Monica. But if Johnny hadn't done it, that was all right. They couldn't prove he had if he hadn't, could they? And anyhow they had nothing against Johnny, had Turner and Roger, not much anyway. It was worrying, certainly, that Johnny should behave so—well, so suspiciously, but that probably meant nothing, nothing at all. As for looking at it all as a problem, as a mental exercise, that was all right, only he mustn't let it bother him.

By the time he reached the police station in Cambury, he was impatient but resigned.

"Confound me for a curious meddlesome idiot," he muttered, dexterously righting a skid. "There's nothing for it. If I can get to the bottom of it, I must. And that's that."

He mounted the steps of the police station with the important air of a self-appointed martyr. Archie had entirely forgotten that it was Inspector Turner's job to solve murders.

The post-mortem was painstaking and thorough. They found nothing new, and Archie was bored.

Yes, yes, he was in complete agreement with Dr. Storke. Yes, a severe blow, cruel blow; some blunt instrument. Sand to be found, here at the roots of the hair. Ah, a sandbag undoubtedly. Struck before death, he would say emphatically; from the condition of the contusion, he would say positively acquired before death. Lower part of the face completely destroyed. Several molars left intact here in the upper jaw; not pleasant, no, very deplorable, very deplorable.

The police surgeon was pompous and verbose.

At last Archie was released, then captured again by Inspector Turner.

"You've finished, sir? Good. Would it be too much trouble to ask you to run me over to Pennerford if you're going back?"

"Not at all, Turner. Too wet for the motor-bike?"

"I thought if you'd take me, I'd come back by train."

"Righto. Hop in then."

It is probable that Inspector Turner did not enjoy that ride. He talked not at all, but whether this was due to Archie's driving would be hard to say. Be it as it may, it was not until the speedometer dropped to a placid fifteen that Turner spoke, "I've been over that house with a fine-toothed comb," he said.

"Did you find anything?"

"No. Only this." The Inspector fished in his pocket and produced a brown furry object. He held it up by one corner: a driving glove, very old and worn. Across the back of two fingers the fur was matted together in a thin streak.

"Blood," said Inspector Turner briefly.

"Where did you find it?"

"Behind the tea cannister on the kitchen shelf."

"It's not Herrick's?"

"Does it look as though it was, sir? The mate's not to be found among his things."

"No, he wouldn't own anything as old and ratty as that. What are you doing with it?"

"Taking it with me to Mrs. Ingles'. Will you drop me there, sir?"

"I'll come along," said Archie.

They stopped before one of the workmen's cottages, and Turner rapped on the door. Mrs. Ingles opened it.

"Oh, it's the Inspector. Good morning, sir. And the Doctor, too. Won't you step in out of the rain?"

They had to bend their heads under the low doorway, but the tiny room was warm with a generous fire and bright with flowers standing in a neat row of pots on the window sill. Mrs. Ingles bustled about in a flurry of hospitality.

"Will you take a seat, sir? You'll find that a comfortable chair. Can I make you some tea? It's a miserable morning. I didn't go to Whiteleaves, sir, because I thought—"

"That's right, Mrs. Ingles. Won't you sit down yourself? Don't trouble about tea, thank you. I only wanted to ask you one or two things."

"But, perhaps, the Doctor would like—"

"No tea for me, Mrs. Ingles, I must go right along as soon as the Inspector is ready for me to take him. He mustn't be long; my patients will be wondering what's happened to me."

"I won't keep you a minute, Dr. Storke." Inspector Turner moved his chair slightly so that he faced the housekeeper. "About these things I wanted to know—" He paused as though to collect his thoughts, and then said inconsequentially, "Oh, before I forget, I found this at the house. Do you happen to know whose it is?" He put the fur glove carelessly upon the table. "I'd like to give it back, if you do."

"Why, that's the other one of Mr. John's rabbits. He calls them his rabbits, you know, sir. He sets such a store by those old gloves, he does. It's right lucky you found it for him. I thought he hadn't only lost one."

"Well, isn't that fortunate? Did you find one, too?"

"Yes, right in the middle of my kitchen floor. I put it back of the tea cannister for safe keeping and clean forgot all about it. I haven't seen Mr. John. Anyhow, it wouldn't have been any use to him without this one."

"No, but if he was attached to—his rabbits, did you say? That's good." Inspector Turner laughed genially. "I like old things best myself. Well, if he's so attached to them, he'll be glad to have them back. I wonder how long they've been lost?"

"Oh, not long, sir. I remember seeing him wearing them only the other day."

"When was that?"

"He waved them at me so comical like. I went to the kitchen door to say good-by. It's as I told you, sir, he's always been that fond of me. 'Toodle-loo,' he calls out and waves the—"

"When was that did you say?"

"Day before yesterday, the same day that Mr. Herrick—such a shock to me that was, I can't throw it off at all, at all— You know, Doctor, my nerves are all of a dither like; I just keep seeing him sitting there in that chair; I didn't get no sleep last night, thinking about it."

"Naturally. It was a terrible experience for you, Mrs. Ingles."

"Oh, terrible. I said to Ruthie—"

"Perhaps Dr. Storke can give you something to brace you up, Mrs. Ingles. Now just one or two questions, if you'd be so kind—"

"Oh, certainly, sir."

"You were at Mr. Herrick's all day Wednesday?"

"Yes, sir."

"No one came?"

"Only the tradesmen, sir."

"Not Mr. John or—"

"Oh, no, Mr. John went back as I told you. He went to London."

"You left Whiteleaves when?"

"When?"

"What time did you go home?"

"Not until going on eight. You see I had extra cleaning to do; I was kept late and thought I'd cook myself a bit of dinner there so's to save getting it home; this stove's that slow—"

"I'm sure you're a good cook, Mrs. Ingles. Well, and the next morning, that's when you found Mr. John's glove?"

"Yes. When I opened the door, I seen it lying there. I puts it on the shelf, so's I won't forget. Then when the kettle's on, I went into the sitting room and—"

"You mustn't think about that any more than you can help, must she, Doctor? I won't worry you further just now, Mrs. Ingles." Inspector Turner rose, picking up the glove from the table.

"It's no trouble, sir, I'm glad to oblige. You'll see that Mr. John gets his gloves, won't you? The one I found will be back of the tea cannister in the kitchen. If you're going there, perhaps you'd get it. Good day, Doctor. Good day, sir. I hope the weather'll clear." The cottage door shut behind them.

They drove off in a silence that was to Archie ominous. He broke it at last to say, "And Ingles never noticed that it was the same glove."

"No, I didn't expect that she would."

"Damn it all, Turner, you got that out of her by a trick."

"We must get at the truth, sir."

"Yes, but what does it amount to, all this, this—"

"Evidence? Quite a bit, don't you agree?"

"Just what?"

"Come, Dr. Storke! Mr. Armstrong has said that he was not in that house after he left on Wednesday morning until we saw him there yesterday, Thursday afternoon. Yet his glove is picked up from the floor early Thursday morning. The glove has blood on it. From eight o'clock until ten Mr. Armstrong claims to have been with Miss Lambert. A man named Harris, I've discovered, heard them talking together some time around nine, before the train got in. Mr. Armstrong was threatening to go to the house and see his uncle. If he didn't then, how did his glove come to be dropped on the kitchen floor Wednesday night? You can't answer that, Dr. Storke. The thing's beginning to look bad."

"I know, Turner. Nevertheless, I know Johnny Armstrong couldn't—"

"You can't know it, Doctor. You can't go against evidence."

"Purely circumstantial, Turner. There's an explanation."

"Then Mr. Armstrong should be willing to give it. Innocent or not, lies are a mistake."

"I thoroughly agree to that. How about these other things? The missing letter, for instance? You have no explanation for them as yet?"

"No, I intended to ask for your help. If you don't believe Mr. Armstrong guilty—"

"You're going to use that to get round me, are you?"

"No. Well, only in a measure, sir. Believe me, I don't want to make a mistake any more than you want me to. There's a lot that needs clearing up still, I know. What I wondered was would you be willing to see Mrs. Lambert?"

"Why me?"

"I can't very well go myself, Dr. Storke. Colonel Copeland feels we must gain as much time as possible before the press gets to know about the murder. Whoever did this was fencing for time; the suicide fake shows that."

"Surely, the purpose was to avoid detection."

"Primarily, yes. But if we can, for a little, make the murderer believe his hoax has succeeded—"

"We've gone all over this before. You mean that because of keeping it dark you can't go yourself and question Mrs. Lambert?"

Inspector Turner smiled somewhat ruefully. "That's it. I learned my lesson yesterday when I tried it out with Mr. Armstrong. There will be nothing suspicious in your going to see her, if you will."

"What do you want me to do?"

"Get her to admit that she's 'Dearest.' Find out what you can of her relationship with Mr. Herrick. Discover if she wrote the letter that's missing. Did she ask Mr. Wilkinson to get it back? You know, the whole bag of tricks."

"Rather a tall order. I don't like the job, Turner."

"I quite understand that, sir, but if you—"

"Don't argue with me. I see there's nothing for it. I'll go. This afternoon about tea time, will that do?"

"Splendidly, sir."

"Ducky," moaned Archie, shaking great drops of rain from his hat, "what I need is a good stiff drink. And I'm going to have it. What time is it? Must I go straight to the office?"

"No," answered Janey, "you've plenty of time. It's only a little after five. Was it too bad?"

"Awful, simply awful." Archie headed for the dining room.

"The decanter's on the table in the study. There's a nice fire there, and I thought you'd want—"

"Wonderful woman." Archie changed his direction. "You think of everything. Come on with me while I have it. I desire to unburden myself."

The whisky rilled pleasantly into Archie's tumbler, siphon spurted, and jolly little silver bubbles rose winking in the firelight. Archie took a long swallow. "Ahhh, that's better."

His armchair swallowed him, then, complete with tumbler. Janey sat cross-legged on the shaggy bear rug. It was soft and warm from the fire, Archie's knees were visible; she leaned back against them. His hand stroked her hair.

"How about a drink for yourself, dear?"

"I don't think I want one just now. Aren't you going to tell me about it?"

"Oh, Lord, yes. It was sticky, distinctly sticky. She's a poisonous creature. Really, Janey, she is: wiles and pretty flutterings and soft cooings. She does coo, you know she does. Whoof, how I hate women like that!"

"Yes. Well, you're rather unreasonable about Kitty, darling. What happened?"

"Oh, I got her to admit it in the end. She produced a blush for me. Can you blush to order? I've always wanted to know how."

"Archie, please! Begin at the beginning."

"All right, my love. At approximately four o'clock I bade farewell to my adored wife and staggered forth into the rain. My trusty motor awaited me. First switching on the ignition, I pressed the self-starter. Happiness, it worked! The accelerator pedal was beneath my foot, I—"

"Archie, don't tease." Janey's voice changed from exasperation into tentative suspicion. "Was that a very strong whisky?"

Archie laughed. "No, darling. I'll be good. I felt too comfortable to be serious. I've been so tired and cross. I want to tell you about it, as a matter of fact. I didn't think I was going to see her alone at first. Wilkinson was there when I arrived. I thought of course the blighter would stay to tea, but he didn't."

"Did you see Monnie?"

"Yes. Cyril was there."

"Oh."

"I was coming to that. Monnie and Cyril were sitting on the window seat; you know, the thing in the recess. They had their heads very much together when I came in. The Lambert and the Wilkinson were over by the fire. I upset the arrangement; I've never felt more *de trop*. Presently Wilkinson shoved off; and Monnie and Cyril made some silly excuse and got themselves out of the room."

"Damn." Janey did not often swear, but she put feeling into it when she did. "I was so afraid of that, Cyril's always around just waiting for something like this to happen. And he's attractive, and Kitty is always urging him on Monnie. I wish they hadn't quarreled."

"Johnny and Monica? I thought Monnie was a bit abrupt about that."

"So do I. But she loves Johnny. I'm sure she does, terribly. And he hurt her."

"Oh, he behaved badly, yes. But all the same I feel she should have trusted him a little more. He must have some good reason for lying, and we none of us know what it is, yet."

"Archie, I'm worrying because I think Johnny believed, when Monnie threw him over like that, that it was because she thought he wouldn't lie unless—"

"That's the trouble."

"But I'm sure she doesn't think Johnny did it, not for an instant. That's why she can't understand his lying and why she's so hurt. But she shouldn't encourage Cyril, just the same."

"I didn't like it, no. Kitty went on about it, too. Trying to enlist my sympathy and get at yours through me, I suppose. She knows you influence Monica."

"What did she say?"

"Dear Cyril and dear Monnie, such naughty, charming children. Didn't I think so? Always together. Years, this has been going on. But could anything be nicer? And dear Cyril's father; Monnie had met him, they'd liked each other so much, *ad nauseam*. Not a mention of poor old Johnny."

"You showed her the 'Dearest' letter?"

"Didn't I! She tried bluff, larded with flattery to wiggle out of that. I got nowhere until I mentioned that 'dear Cyril's father' was so anxious to redeem the money. Then she manufactured that pretty blush of hers. She couldn't understand why Mr. Herrick had begun the letter so—so affectionately. That was why she hesitated in saying it was intended for her, but she supposed the poor man was not quite himself. And he knew it was the last letter he would ever write, didn't he? He had shown his feelings; and she had never dreamed; they had been only good friends. You can imagine how it went."

"Easily. But why was it sticky then?"

"Because Kitty Lambert is dodging, Janey. Why, I don't know. She wasn't one bit surprised to hear her money was gone. My impression is she's known that, or at any rate suspected it, for a considerable time. She says she received no letter from Andrew the evening he died. There she's telling the truth, I believe. I floundered around about the stolen letter and Wilkinson, but I'm no good at that sort of thing. If Turner sends me to do his dirty work, he'll have to take the consequences if I fizzle it. I came out flat-footed and asked her in the end."

"Had she written it? Did she take it over and then ask Cuthbert Wilkinson to get it back, as I guessed?"

"I don't know. She denied it. But if she's not lying, she's very uneasy about something. In her own way she's acting rather like Johnny."

"You mean, she's afraid?"

"That's my impression. I think she wrote the letter. When Roger gives up this flabby idea of his and lets murder out of the bag, then Kitty will talk; that is, unless telling the truth is even more dangerous than lying. She'll save herself in any case, if she can."

"Kitty would. If you're right and she's involved Wilkinson in this awful business—"

"By Jove, yes. I become almost sorry for him— We don't get anywhere, do we? A day of sleuthing on my own, and I begin to appreciate the practice of medicine. It's not as disagreeable by a long way, and one's mistakes don't often have the same chance of exposure. I was scornful of Roger and old Turner yesterday; now I pine for their support."

"Roger's dropping in tonight if he's not too late."

"Sturdy and complacent, corseted with Scotland Yard; that will be our Roger. Have I time for another drink?"

"Archibald Starke, do you never look at your own watch?"

"Not when I have yours. Lord, no, I haven't." Archie shifted Janey's head from his knees to the chair and got up. "Wear your nice red dress for me tonight, will you, darling?"

Janey wore her red dress, a delightful dress with round velvet buttons on its tight bodice and velvet bands on its long full skirt. And at nine o'clock, Liz at his heels, Roger came, sleek and well fed as usual but for all that just a little harassed.

The truth was Lieutenant Colonel Roger Copeland, D.S.O., was not altogether happy.

That was not Scotland Yard's fault. They had rushed about and done things. This was, perhaps, a poor way to describe a quiet, matter-of-fact efficiency. But when at six o'clock various neat reports had been spread out before the Colonel, he felt nothing short of rushing about could possibly have produced them. No, that was not the reason the Colonel was unhappy. He had wanted the reports. And it was only after he had read them and was comfortably smoking in his first class carriage on the way back to Mongerton, that he realized that he was vaguely unsettled.

Was it because a certain rather rude young man had rumpled black hair and unhappy eyes? The Colonel stoutly denied this. A somehow appealing young beggar who was, after all, a murderer? The Colonel heard himself say, "I don't believe it!" And yet there was the report. For now that his suspicions were rapidly, too rapidly, turning into facts, the Colonel made the discovery that he had never really had them. He had not believed in his suspicions himself. In the light of damning, cumulative evidence the Colonel veered illogically to Janey's calm "Johnny could never have done it, Roger." Nevertheless, he was a chief constable, and murder was murder.

And when he got home there was Turner and the glove. So it was that Lieutenant Colonel Roger Copeland came to Archie and Janey looking harassed.

"Hello, Roger, we were hoping you'd turn up." Archie slid off his chair and rose hospitably. "Have that chair. May I give you a drink? You look tired, old chap."

"I am rather. Good evening, Janey, what a charming frock; I haven't seen you wear it before. No drink for me just now, Archie."

"You'll have some coffee? I've been keeping it hot for you." Janey crouched by the fire and lifted the coffee pot from the hearth. "Ouch," she exclaimed and put it down again. "Lend me your hanky, Archie, the handle's hot."

The Colonel supplied his and took the steaming cup Janey held up for him. He also took Archie's armchair. Liz, with a slow wheeze like a punctured tire, deflated herself at his feet. The Colonel sipped:

"You're a most thoughtful person, Mrs. Starke," he said.

"Play me a game of chess, Roger? Or are you too tired? Perhaps you'd rather talk."

"I'd much rather play chess but I've something to tell you both."

"Ah, Scotland Yard crashed through, did they?"

"I had the reports by six o'clock."

"And, what, Roger?"

Janey fixed anxious soft eyes on his face. There was nothing vague about the Colonel's feeling now. He was acutely miserable. It was going to be hard to tell Janey.

"Bad news, I'm afraid. You see—" The Colonel hesitated and cleared his throat.

"Go on, Roger. It's Johnny again, I suppose," said Archie. "Janey knows about Turner's finding his glove."

"Yes. Please tell me. You see, I still don't believe Johnny murdered Andrew Herrick. And the more we learn, even though it's against him, the nearer we'll be to the truth, won't we? And the truth will clear him, I'm sure it will."

"You're extremely loyal, Janey. It makes it very difficult for me."

"I don't want you to feel that." Janey was earnest. "It's different for you. You don't know Johnny, and you have only facts to go by." The ardor faded from Janey's voice; suddenly she sounded unsure. "And if the time comes when the facts prove— Only you will be sure, won't you, Roger?"

"As sure as it's possible to be. I shall wait until I'm absolutely convinced, that I assure you, before I do anything."

"Inspector Turner?"

"He must abide by my judgment."

"That's good," said Janey, disposing of the Inspector.

She was conscious, so to speak, of bread returning upon the waters. It was a distinct advantage to have well-fed a chief constable. In this Janey was unfair. It was not Janey's food but Janey herself; secretly the Colonel adored her.

"Fire ahead. Let's have the reports, all of them." Archie reached for his cigarettes.

"I saw Sir Wilfred Parker and explained matters. He detailed an inspector to investigate the London end. A most intelligent chap by the name of Nokes. He went himself to Gray's Hotel where Burford Herrick is staying, then to Cyril's apartment, and last to Armstrong's.

"I'd better take it in order, as Turner says. The report from Gray's is that at about three in the afternoon a gentleman called to see Mr. Herrick. His name was sent up, Mr. Andrew Herrick, and he went up to Burford Herrick's sitting room. He stayed until almost five, when he left the hotel. By the way, there's a report on what Andrew did most of Wednesday, I'll give you that later. This is Burford Herrick now. Shortly before seven Burford and Cyril went out; Cyril had apparently been there all afternoon. They returned to Gray's late that night, a little after one o'clock. We will get from them what they did in that interval, just where it was they dined, what theater they went to, and where they had supper; and verify all that, if we can, later. It's not very important, as it's long before the time of the murder.

"When they came in at one, Cyril went up to his father's room for fifteen minutes or so, and then he left. He said good night to the night porter as he went out.

"Between two-thirty and three Burford rang his bell. When it was answered, he asked for some hot water to be brought him and explained that he was suffering from an acute attack of indigestion.

"The next morning Cyril Herrick called. He appeared agitated. Almost immediately afterwards both he and Burford went out; that was to come down here, of course. That places Burford. There had been no phone calls whatever for him during the evening or night, and no one inquired at the hotel for him."

"It's just as he told us, in other words."

"Precisely, yes. And so is Cyril's. The night hall porter saw him come in at one-thirty. He took him up in the elevator to his floor. Cyril did not go out again."

"Is the hall porter on duty in the entrance hall all night?"

"So he told the inspector."

"No visitors came for Cyril? Any phone calls?"

"No one came there. The telephone's a private line, but Cyril wasn't there to get a message, in any case."

"No, not until one-thirty. Where does Cyril keep the Mercedes?"

"In a lockup garage near his apartment. If you're thinking of that, he could take it out late at night and return it again in the early hours of the morning without risking much chance of being seen. But first he would have to evade the night porter at the flat."

"I wasn't thinking of it as in any way a probability. I am only attempting to test all the possibilities which arise, no matter how unlikely they are. This finishes the alibis of Burford Herrick and Cyril then. What is your verdict, Roger?"

"Taking Burford Herrick first; his alibi is cast iron. We know that he was in the hotel from one o'clock till the next morning when he received news of Andrew's death. He could not, therefore, have had any hand in it. But though he had absolutely no motive that we know of for committing the murder, and though the whole impression he gives one is against the likelihood of his having done so, nevertheless, I was struck, as no doubt you were, too, by the fact that his arrival in England coincided so neatly with the crime. Therefore, although I judged the two occurrences to have no connection, I was not convinced that they had none until now.

"Taking nothing for granted, I admit still the *possibility* of Burford's having seen Andrew Wednesday night between the arrival of the train at twelve-thirty-three and one o'clock when Burford and Cyril returned to Gray's. We have not proved what they were doing during that half hour; we have only their word for it. But as Burford has lied about nothing else, and as he must be innocent of the murder, the presumption is that he is telling the truth throughout. Is it not?"

"Oh, quite; Cyril?"

"You've implied, though not very seriously, I take it, Archie, that Cyril's alibi might be found to have a flaw. Again I'll grant you the *possibility* of Cyril's having somehow managed to leave his apartment unobserved, taken out his car, met Andrew in London somewhere, driven him down to Pennerford, murdered him, driven back again, put away his car, and returned still unseen to his apartment—this, only if the hall porter is inaccurate in his statement to the inspector; if either he were not continuously at his post in the entrance hall all night or, being there, had dropped asleep. Stretching things to admit all this, we still have no motive. It was you who first told me of Cyril's real affection for his uncle. That seems an established fact which we cannot ignore. Coupled with no imaginable reason for Cyril to desire Andrew's death, any suspicion of his being guilty falls below the line of probability."

"Lord, yes, miles below. That's the baffling thing about all this. As I said to Janey—"

"To Janey! You're always saying it. You've said it to me any number of times."

"Sorry I'm repetitive. But as I see the problem, that is the rub. We've no one who fits the role of murderer, though perhaps— However, grousing about the difficulties doesn't help us. Do you think Johnny and his curious behavior fill the bill? Let's have the latest specimen. Buck up, Janey," added Archie gently.

"I'm all right," stated Janey. "I've been waiting for Roger to tell us."

The Colonel's voice was kind, but there was a hint of grimness in it, too, as he said, "Armstrong did not return his car to the garage until six o'clock Thursday morning."

"Six o'clock!" Archie and Janey echoed together like a well-trained response in a melodrama.

In spite of himself the Colonel smiled. Then he answered seriously. "Yes, six. He left here, by his story, at ten o'clock to go sixty-five miles, straight to his rooms and to bed. He should have been in by one o'clock at the latest, and yet it was six when he got to the garage."

"How do you know?" Archie asked the question.

Janey sat silent, twisting round and round one of the velvet buttons on her gay red dress.

"Because he was seen. Armstrong keeps the Morris in a large garage which closes at one in the morning. Car owners are supplied with keys to enable them to put their cars away if they are later than that.

"At six o'clock Thursday morning one of the mechanics came earlier than usual to do some work for which he was being paid extra. As he turned the corner of the street leading to the garage, he saw a man close and lock the double doors of the garage and he recognized him as Armstrong. Armstrong did not see him, apparently, and immediately walked off, going in the opposite direction towards his rooms which are three blocks away. The mechanic reached the garage and found the Morris, as he expected, the last car in. He had to move it in order to reach the car he was at work upon and, when he did so, he found the radiator hot."

When the Colonel had finished, it was a long minute or two before Archie said, unscrewing the top of his fountain pen, "That opens the way for a number of unpleasant speculations. I need a notebook like Turner's."

He dove into his pocket and after some fumbling emerged with his prescription pad. He wrote busily while the Colonel decided dismally that Janey's button had been extremely well sewed. It came off suddenly just as Archie handed him the sheet of paper.

J.A.

Leaves Pennerford 10:00 P.M.   65 miles
Arrives London 12:30–1:00 A.M.   2½ to 3 hrs.
Meets A. H.   ?   O.K.
Arrives Pennerford with A.H 3:30—4:00   ditto

Commits   ?

Leaves Pennerford 4:00–4:30   Time too short,
Arrives London 6:00   but possible.

     (Also, why: go to London to meet A.H. at 1:00 A.M. there, when from 9:15 P.M. till 10:00 P.M. they were both in Pennerford?)

Does not leave Pennerford 10:00 P.M.
(Ferris sees man in car with hat over face. J.A. ? 11:30)
Goes to Whiteleaves and waits for—
          or
Comes to Whiteleaves after—
A.H.'s return 2:00 A.M. (?)   Time still a difficulty.
  how?   earliest possible   A.H. in fast car could
  when?   reach Pennerford by
     3:30 A.M. (?)   2:00 A.M., if met at
    latest possible for   Paddington to return
    J.A. to manage   immediately. 4:00 A.M.
Commit murder—½ hr. at   outside limit of J.A.'s
  least necessary   leaving Pennerford.
Leave Pennerford 4:00
Arrive London 6:00
      More likely:
A.H. return Pennerford 2:45–3:00 A.M.
J.A. leave Pennerford 3:30
J.A. arrive London 6:00

Janey gave an exclamation of annoyance that was, in the circumstances, a little unreasonable, got up, and, leaning over the back
of the armchair, read with him what Archie had written.

When they had finished, Janey made no comment. She went
back to her seat by the fire.

"That about covers it," said the Colonel. Then, "Let me have a
prescription blank. I'll give you Andrew Herrick's day in London.
The time-table arrangement will serve beautifully."

A.H. Wednesday.

Left Pennerford 8:50 A.M.	10:18 Arrived Paddington
Arrived office of Dodd, Meigs, and Dodd at approximately	10:45
They say he stayed slightly more than an hour, so— left there about	12:00 M.
Arrived at his club shortly after 12:00, say	12:15 P.M.
Lunched, etc., and left	2:30
Called at bank, collected pass-book	2:40
Arrived Gray's	3:00
Left Gray's just before	5:00
Hiatus of 2½ hours	
Left Paddington	7:33
Arrived Pennerford	9:15
Left Pennerford	11:00
Arrived Paddington	12:33 A.M. (Thursday)
Left London ⎫ Arrived Pennerford ⎭	?
Hiatus of 7½ hours	
Found dead	7:50 A.M. (Thursday)

Archie studied the Colonel's neat table. "Hmm," he said, "Andrew seems to have been most accommodating up to a point. No
trace of him between Gray's Hotel and the train?"

"No. Not yet."

"He picked up the dispatch case in that period."

"So he did—"

"And whenever the blinking dispatch case appears, appears also a hiatus as you've called it. He had the dispatch case when he left Pennerford on the eleven o'clock. He reaches Paddington, and again you lose track of him. In that nice, large, generous hiatus, twelve-thirty-three to seven-fifty, he got himself murdered. Well—"

"Scotland Yard are working hard on those two intervals. Particularly the latter, of course. We should pick up the trail again, though it may be slow work. A porter remembers Andrew getting out of the twelve-thirty-three. He offered to carry the mysterious dispatch case, as a matter of fact. Andrew did not take a taxi in the station; the porter saw him leave on foot. That means patience, trying all the cab stands near by. We may get it quickly; we may not get it at all, for he may not have taken a cab. But surely we shall be successful at least in picking up the car that brought him down here. And we may strike it lucky."

"Find him between five and seven in the evening, and you've found him between twelve-thirty and seven in the morning. And incidentally you've found the murderer as well. That's my opinion."

Janey did not seem to be interested in any of this. "Roger," she asked, "what are you doing about Johnny?"

"Nothing yet, Janey." Then as she shook her head, "Oh, I see what you mean. The license number of his car has been telephoned to the police stations between here and London, inquiries will be made as to whether it was observed at any point along the road Wednesday night or early Thursday morning. If it has been seen, it may be good news about Johnny yet, you know. He may have been miles away from Pennerford at the time of the murder."

Janey shook her head again. "No, I'm afraid not. If he was, there would be no reason for him to lie. All the same, I'm as sure as ever that he didn't do it. Isn't it obvious to you both what the matter is? Johnny is shielding someone."

"But who?" demanded Archie.

Janey was indifferent to this difficulty.

"I don't know," she said vaguely. "Someone— You say 'the time of the murder,' Roger, but you don't know when that was."

"From the condition of the body," Archie answered for him, "I should place it as early as possible. It's hardly reasonable to suppose Andrew reached Pennerford again much before two-thirty, or three. He was killed, then, between two-thirty and three-thirty."

"But an hour's such a long time," wailed Janey, "and sometimes you even give the limits as two to four, and that's two hours. I wish you knew."

"So do we," said the Colonel fervently. Janey drooped, so he added briskly, "I must get home and turn in. The inquest's tomorrow at eleven. But Turner told you, didn't he, Archie?"

"Yes. He said you were only going to have formal evidence of identification taken and ask for an adjournment. That right?"

"That's it. We can hardly let it go through as suicide and we're not ready for anything else. The adjournment will cause talk, but we can't keep the fact quiet much longer, anyhow. I'll see you there, then. Come along, Liz. Good night, Janey, get a good rest and stop worrying if you can. You take other people's troubles too much to heart."

With which parting platitude the Colonel went away, not a bit happier than he had come.

CHAPTER VI

No Food at the Inquest

Throughout the proceedings of the Coroner's Court, Archie's imagination was giving him trouble.

That faculty, belittled by the Colonel, had been much cozened and encouraged by its owner. This morning he wondered if, like an only child, he hadn't rather spoilt it. Certainly, it refused to behave. It performed acrobatics of the most fantastic order, contorting an idea it had found first into this shape then into that, a mad idea, much better left alone. Commanded sternly to be good, it began in its waywardness to distort reality. The scene around Archie no longer reached him as a whole. Broken up and unrelated, it came to him disguised in a series of wholly dreamlike impressions.

The faces of the eleven jurymen, so many letters spelling in a uniform line of type "becoming gravity." Only, thought Archie, unable to stop himself from counting, they were four letters short of that, and weren't they somehow conscious of their deficiency? Anyhow, they were doomed in their solemn importance to disappointment. There would be no verdict for them to deliver, no need to weigh each word spoken with ludicrous care: Mrs. Ingles deposing to finding the body; Burford Herrick giving formal evidence of identification; Cyril giving it all over again. When Turner asked for that adjournment, what would their faces spell then? Eleven faces, eleven letters, "speculation." That had it.

Yes, the whole thing had been a mistaken farce. How much further might they all not have been if Roger had not insisted upon secrecy; had been content to discard the cover of suicide; let the truth come out. Now there would be speculation, rumor. What was to be gained? In the end murder must out. That redheaded reporter over there ready to write up the short account of a suicide; after the adjournment, free to hint at something else, theorize— After this morning, even Roger's credulous murderer would suspect his hoax had not succeeded. Cyril had finished his evidence, that would be Turner's cue.

The Inspector rose to his feet. His full voice caressed stilted formal phrases, "requested that."

Archie's glance, directed idly towards the jury, was arrested by a sudden movement of Cyril. With his father he was seated near the jurymen, and, as the import of Turner's speech became clear, he turned his head quickly and whispered to Burford. His profile was directly in the line of Archie's eyes; and with a curious clairvoyance that was part of his mood that morning, Archie knew what it was that he had said. Of course, he had merely read Cyril's lips. It happened sometimes that one found oneself able to do that for a word or two: in the old days at the cinema, for instance. But it had had a sense of the uncanny just the same. The words had been so plain Archie had the sensation of having overheard them—all but the last, that he failed to catch. Cyril had said "I knew it," and one more word. Was it "too"? Archie thought it must have been. Not that it mattered, except for the fun of it, for the feeling of power it gave, what the missing word was. For that, he would have liked to have been sure of it as well. "I knew it, too."

So Cyril, like Johnny, hadn't believed in the suicide. Well, who would? Not one who had known Andrew intimately. Archie himself, who had known him so slightly, had questioned it, felt it to be out of character. Not so much the act itself—Andrew might have been goaded to that—but the method, the hideous, grotesque, damn it, the undignified method.

Burford had frowned slightly when Cyril spoke, but he had not answered. They had undoubtedly been discussing it, and Cyril had been emphatic in his objection, while Burford, who after all had seen little of his brother for many years, had perhaps accepted what seemed on the surface an unquestionable fact. Now that he knew it was not—for Turner's asking for an adjournment could only mean that the police themselves were in doubt—what would he do? From his impression of the man Archie was sure that Burford would not rest until he knew the truth.

When he did, when he knew that his brother had not killed himself but had been murdered, he would devote himself, his wealth, everything to the one end: the discovery of his brother's murderer. He would see it simply as a matter of duty. Archie was as convinced of this as if he had known Burford Herrick all his life, for among other things Archie prided himself on being an accurate judge of character. And although he had put Burford down as "tolerant, kindly, just," he had also added "determined." And with "determined" went the footnote: "ruthless." Yes, if he were roused, Burford could be ruthless.

All this, thought Archie Storke, with only the data of a five minutes' conversation; a habit of his, one of those leaps-without-a-springboard that he was inclined to make, the sort of thing Janey and the Colonel deplored.

However, he would seem this time to have been justified; for the inquest having been adjourned for three weeks and the burial permit signed by the coroner, the proceedings were over; and waiting outside for Archie was Burford Herrick.

"Dr. Storke, I have delayed in the hope of seeing you. Could you spare me a few minutes?"

"Most certainly," answered Archie with the feeling of clairvoyance still at work. He knew this was about to happen. Burford would try to pump him, and that would be awkward. If only he would be content to wait, the police would have to tell him the truth. Why must he fasten on him? Particularly when Archie wanted to work over that mad idea which had come to him during the inquest, wanted to see if he could make anything out of it. Archie was irritated, he did not wish to talk to Burford Herrick just then.

"Where would you suggest going, Doctor? Some place where we shan't be disturbed."

"Why not my car, Mr. Herrick? If you will drive back with me—"

"That will be excellent, thank you. One minute, my son is waiting. I'll just tell him to go along without me."

Burford crossed the pavement to where a little further down the Mercedes waited beside the curb.

Cyril nodded, put his car in gear, turned it about in the full width of the broad street, and, as he passed them, raised his hat to the Doctor. The inquest had been a strain; Archie saw that he looked drawn and tired. Poor Cyril, he was, after all, the only one to feel grief; not quite that, perhaps the others, Burford and Johnny, felt it, too, but not as the dominant emotion. With Burford it was the disgrace that counted most; with Johnny it was fear. But to Cyril, Andrew's death meant loss, loss of a person he loved. Out of the welter of conjecture one thing, Archie knew, stood clear: Cyril's absolute devotion to his uncle. Yes, it was too bad.

"Dr. Starke—"

Archie swung round.

"You're ready? I'm sorry, Mr. Herrick, I was 'lost in me thoughts,' as Joe Killick says. My car's just down there."

Burford fell into step beside him, but he did not speak. Archie felt the need of making conversation.

"Joe, the railway guard, whom I quoted just now, is quite one of our local characters. He's the possessor of an enviable gift, the ability to drink without the trouble of swallowing. To see him with a pint of bitter is a treat. Up goes the tankard, out of gear goes the trachea, down goes the bitter, and on the bar is the tankard empty, one graceful and beautiful gesture. But he tells me he can only do eight and a half pints with safety. At the ninth he sings 'The Return of the Swallow.' I respect his limitation and admire his choice of ballad. Appropriate, is it not?"

Burford was not amused, and Archie felt tactless and flat. Oh, Lord, it was no use, one could hardly expect the fellow to be entertained, to think about anything except—

"Here we are. Will you scramble in somehow, Mr. Herrick?"

Burford compressed his large body into the compass of Archie's small car. Archie resolved to drive slowly and let Burford do his worst. Somehow he must manage to evade those inevitable questions. It was Turner's and Roger's business. Until they permitted it, he mustn't let the cat out of the bag. He suffered from a sense of guilt whenever he remembered that he had broken his promise and told Monica the truth. It was most unethical. But Burford took the bull by the horns—Archie seemed to think in animals—with a grip that was totally unexpected. He neither hedged nor pumped, he simply stated, "You are being most considerate in giving me this opportunity to talk with you, Dr. Storke."

"Not at all," murmured Archie, resisting the lure of the accelerator pedal and the pursuit of that fugitive idea of his. He mustn't be absent-minded, he must concentrate on what Burford was saying.

"I will not make it difficult for you by asking you to give me any information. I quite realize that you can't, that you are not in a position to do so. Let us say it's a matter of trust, that you've been told for the present to hold back, to say nothing of what you know. That is if I am right and there is something—"

Archie did not answer. What was there to say? No reply, he knew, was tantamount to an affirmative, but a denial was impossible, for later— Archie turned his head, and for the fraction of a second their eyes met. Burford's were still kind, behind their thick lenses, magnified and soft, but they were mercilessly steady.

"I should not have said that. You have every reason to resent my assuming anything of the sort. Only—I am in great distress, Doctor. Until this morning I had accepted what I thought to be the—the circumstances of my brother's death. Now I am forced to think that I have not been told everything, that there has been something discovered—well, that puts the matter perhaps in some doubt?"

There was a pause. Archie spent it silently cursing Lieutenant Colonel Roger Copeland, and all his works. This was what he'd let him in for. Why couldn't the fellow go to the police?

As though he had heard him, Burford went on, "Naturally, if there is any doubt, I feel it should not have been concealed from me. I feel that I have the right to know. It is intolerable to think that the police have held anything back. You understand that, don't you? It is what makes going to them so very awkward. I thought perhaps I might be wrong, there might be some other explanation for the adjournment than the one I dread. In my difficulty I came to you. I hoped you might be able to set my mind at rest. Good God, Dr. Storke, if there is something even more horrible, if my poor brother did not take his own life, but— It's incredible, incredible! Who could wish him harm? In his misfortune he used money that did not belong to him. But a crime so brutal, so—I do not believe it is possible."

Archie saw Burford's hand resting on the door of the car close spasmodically, slowly relax. Long fingers against the black wood, every contour distinct. Irresistibly he was reminded of the dead man's fingers, rigid, pressed to the black pad. The hands were identical. Yes, in the bone structure was the family resemblance, the Herrick mold. But how different they were, Andrew and Burford, for all that. Their aura, thought Archie, hating the word, wasn't the same. One lost the resemblance in that, it became non-existent.

"No. Any such suspicion must be wrong. I am letting my thoughts run away with me. If my brother did not commit suicide, then his death must have been an accident. Perhaps, it is this the police must determine. Forgive me, Doctor, I did not mean to let myself go. I have no right to burden you. It's the doubt that's breaking me. I realized quite suddenly this morning, after the Inspector spoke, that I have doubted from the first. It is unthinkable that Andrew should choose so disfiguring a means to death. I often criticized him for his vanity, he was always too overly particular about appearances—"

The village street of Pennerford was a haven to Archie. Never had the road from Cambury seemed so long. He hadn't known what to say, what to do; and all the time to make it worse there was that idea of his, that wholly preposterous idea, nagging him, driving him distracted. He must get home to his armchair and think it out. He said, "I am sorry not to have been able to help, Mr. Herrick. I understand how you feel. Why don't you go to Colonel Copeland?"

"I shall. But you have helped, just by listening to me so patiently."

"Where do you want me to drop you? At the Seven Stars?"

"Anywhere will do. I don't want to impose further on your good nature by taking you out of your way. A walk will do me good."

"Nonsense, Mr. Herrick. It's a matter of a few minutes at the most. You must let me take you."

"You've been most kind, Dr. Starke. I was planning, as a matter of fact, to spend the time before lunch at Whiteleaves."

"I go directly by there, so it's no trouble at all."

"You do? Then if you will—"

There was another pause. Archie felt more confidences were imminent. What was there about him, he wondered, that made people tell him things? He certainly hadn't encouraged Burford, quite the reverse, and yet— He must have a porous sort of personality, rather like a large sponge. People were always using him to mop up their thoughts. And Burford was so stiff about it, too, not the sort of man who was used to confiding, the very rarity made him sound unnatural, almost pompous.

"Pennerford is an attractive village. We have nothing like the English village in America. I have been homesick for England in late years. I pulled up stakes over there. I wanted to come home, to settle down somewhere in the country, but now—"

"It's been a very sad homecoming for you."

"Yes. It's quite spoiled England for me. I no longer want to stay. Later, perhaps, I'll return but for the present I may go back to California or travel for a time. I haven't decided. I am closing Whiteleaves; I could never live there. I don't imagine it would even be possible to rent it now to strangers. In a few years when people have forgotten— It's a pleasant little house. It would be a pity to let it stand vacant, houses deteriorate if they're not lived in."

"They do, yes. England has too many jerry-built monstrosities now, it would be almost immoral to leave Whiteleaves deserted. But practical details must be painful for you. Is there anything I can do to help?"

"Thank you, no. Unless— It's painful for me, Doctor. A person dies, and there still are all the things belonging to him. One always feel that they should have gone, too, books, clothes— I want to give my brother's suits and things to someone who will use them. I wonder if you could tell me of a charity, some place where I could send them? That is the reason I'm going to Whiteleaves this morning. I told the housekeeper I would come and look things over and have the clothes taken away. I want her to shut the house at once. After the funeral I shall go back to London. I don't want to come down again."

"If you are giving the personal belongings away, Janey, my wife that is, would be awfully glad of them. She has all sorts of deserving people she's always taking care of. I'll stop with you now, if you like, and we can get it over with at once together. I can bundle them all into the back of my car. You won't have to worry about them again."

"I should be most grateful if you would. But isn't it asking too much? I could have them sent somehow to your wife."

Archie hesitated for a moment, sympathy was warring with his desire to get home to his armchair and his idea— But it was a beastly business for Burford. If he could make it easier—

"I've nothing I must do just now. It'd be much simpler if I stopped with you, and carried them away. Pennerford doesn't boast a delivery van."

"My son could take them in his car, if—"

"I'd like to do it."

Archie became stubborn. Burford really wanted to get it over with the easiest way. What was the use of arguing about it? They swung into the Whiteleaves driveway in silence.

For the first time since the tragedy, the house stood deserted and empty: no Huntley, no Turner, no Colonel. Did they know Burford was going to raid the place? Apparently not, but it could make no difference. Certainly Burford had every right to close the house and take Andrew's personal things. Besides, the clothes had all been gone over with, as Turner put it, a fine-toothed comb. There was nothing more to be learned from them. Still Turner might be annoyed. Burford Herrick had certainly no consciousness of doing anything out of the way. He stood on the doorstep, feeling in his large overcoat pocket for the key. He transferred a key ring laden with keys to his left hand, and reaching again into his pocket brought out a single key.

"This is it," he said. "Cyril gave it to me this morning."

He turned the lock, and they entered the hall. The house seemed ominously still, as though brooding upon the dark crime which had robbed it of its right of privacy, to peaceful, uneventful days.

The door of the sitting room stood open. Burford passed it with averted head. Archie paused for an instant to glance inside. The room had been put to rights. It was as "infernally tidy" now as the rest of the house had always been. Save for a spattering of small dark stains on the light wallpaper near the fireplace, it was no longer, as Archie had felt it, the incongruous setting for a Grand Guignol. The high-backed oak chair was gone. Archie remembered that Turner had taken it away. Poor Turner, he had hunted so patiently for fingerprints, but Mrs. Ingles was too careful a duster, and the murderer, too careful a murderer to go without his gloves. Driving gloves, very old and backed with fur, that was what Turner thought. The chair had held no prints, and the gun, only the dead man's own; yes, a fairly careful crime, taking it all and all.

Burford had stopped at the foot of the stairs.

"There will be nothing for us to do down here. I shall leave the furniture as it is, even the books. The house will rent later the more easily for being furnished. It's only the personal things I wish to dispose of. Will you go first, Doctor? I have only been here once. I asked Mrs. Ingles to put them into the guest room. Do you know which that is? I'd rather not go again into my brother's room after the other morning. You will think me absurdly sensitive, morbid about it all, but I—"

Burford broke off, afraid of the emotion which had crept into his careful voice, fighting, Archie knew, against the memory of what he had seen lying there on that bed upstairs.

Was it necessary for him to force himself to do all this? Why not close up the house just as it was? But then that wasn't in character: Burford was imaginative and sensitive, but he was also practical and businesslike. If he left all those clothes of Andrew's to the moths, undoubtedly he would reproach himself, think it wasteful.

Archie supposed this fell under the heading of duty, and Burford would insist on seeing it through.

"Can't Mrs. Ingles or I take care of this for you, Mr. Herrick? If you do not wish to keep anything yourself—"

"No, no," Burford answered almost impatiently. "I cannot ask anyone else to take the responsibility. I must tend to it myself. There might be something I would not care to let strangers have, some memento Andrew left. I feel I owe to him to do at least this."

So they went upstairs, and Archie, leading the way, turned directly down the corridor to the guest room.

"This will be it," he said.

Burford opened the door.

Heaped upon the bed were clothes: brown suits, gray suits, blue suits, overcoats, hats. In a mute line, ready as if to step forward like their dead owner, on parade, stood a company of shoes: brown, black, pointed, shiny patent leathers, sturdy smart brogues, and, marshaling these, a little apart, a pair of riding boots. Chairs and the top of the dressing table were covered by piles of linen. A pyramid of gay handkerchiefs blazed upon the window sill. The two men halted overwhelmed. Then Burford turned to Archie and for the first time he smiled.

"Really, Dr. Storke, did you ever see so many clothes? You can't possibly get them all into your car. And where will you put them when you do get home?"

"I think I can manage," Archie answered a tinge dubiously. "Let's try anyway."

"You're being much too good. Then I'll just go through them first, although it's probably a foolish precaution of mine. Andrew was curiously unsentimental. Among all his papers, which Colonel Copeland handed over to me, there was nothing that did not relate to business; and everything else that could be considered personal, I asked the housekeeper to collect together here. Yet you see there isn't a photograph, a trinket of any sort, only clothes." Burford sighed.

Even in death with all that had been most intimate to him spread out before them, Andrew remained impersonal, unreal, only a wax model, as Janey had said, a wax model that someone had hated enough to kill.

Burford moved toward the laden bed. He picked up a brown coat from the top of the pile and slid his fingers quickly into the pockets, found them empty, and tossed it to one side. A blue serge, a gray flannel, a Harris tweed, another serge, a dinner jacket followed the brown coat. Archie would have liked to tell Burford to save himself the trouble; he knew all the pockets were empty, for Turner had already been exploring and had found nothing. He checked a restless motion of protest. But Burford, as if he too realized the complete fatuity of it all, abruptly put down the overcoat he was holding and said:

"This is sheer scrupulosity on my part. Andrew never left even a match box in his pockets; he was too careful of his clothes for that. He used to scold me when we were boys for ruining the hang of my coats. I won't bother about the rest. Shall we carry them down to your car, Doctor?"

Burford gathered a pile into his arms; Archie made a swoop at the bed. How proud and priceless Janey's poor would look bravely arrayed on a Sunday in Andrew Herrick's faultless tailoring. And then Archie had a twinge of uneasiness. What would Janey say to all this? Hadn't he been rather tactless? Suddenly what they were doing struck Archie as being grotesque, somehow monstrous. Even Burford's action became unnatural, open to question. Still, if the fellow wanted to finish with it all, close up the house, not return again, wasn't it just what he would do? Didn't it have, after all, to be done?

Up the stairs, down again, several times they went. The floor, the back seat of Archie's car was brimming; a trouser leg hung appallingly out; Archie tucked it in. At last they stood in a room trim now as to empty bed, empty chairs. Only on the window sill blazed the pile of bright silk handkerchiefs, and in a corner on the floor lay a cardboard box filled with bottles.

"What are those?" asked Archie.

Going over, he lifted the box from the floor and set it, too, on the window sill. "The contents, apparently, of Mr. Herrick's medicine closet," he muttered, answering his own question.

There was the clink of bottle against bottle as Archie examined the labels. This at least, he felt, was his own province. He had never been able to resist peeping into medicine closets. The things sane people dosed themselves with! Here there was nothing out of the way. He had been right. Andrew had, it seemed, never needed a doctor. Only the ordinary things: aspirin, iodine, a small bottle of fruit salts, shaving stick; hmm, yes, a familiar bottle with a red triangle, "works while you sleep"; a bottle with no label at all; ah, here was something he'd never seen. Archie extracted a white tube, "Citroneige. Pour la beauté des mains." How vain Andrew had been, stuff to whiten his hands! There was a jar of beauty cream, too. All at once he realized that he was prying. He turned swiftly, terribly embarrassed. How could he do such a thing? Let his outrageous curiosity—

But Burford appeared not to have noticed. He was leaning against the doorjamb, passing his fingers wearily across his lips, his thoughts far away from Archie and his lapse in taste. Archie took courage again.

"What do you want to do with these bottles, Mr. Herrick? Shall I take them away, too? It's never safe to leave medicine about."

For a moment Burford seemed not to have heard him; his mouth was set in a straight line of pain; he came to himself almost with a jerk.

"This has been an unpleasant task. I'm glad it's over with. The medicine? Oh, yes, certainly, much better take it away."

So Archie gathered up the cardboard box with its "Citroneige," and together they left the room.

The silk handkerchiefs, forgotten, flaunted their colors gaily upon the window sill, the frivolous survivors of all that had been Andrew Herrick's. The house became once more deserted and very still.

Road Maps and Nightcaps

Archie stood by his car. From the back protruded a wuzzle of cloth arms and legs. Janey stood on the front steps and slowly took it in.

"The hunter home from the hills," said Archie gesticulating. "A fine bag, my love. The pheasant of tweed, the partridge of cheviot, the blue jay of serge, the—the—well, what do you think of it?"

Janey murmured something. Her face expressed many things. Disapproval was among them.

"What did you say, Ducky?"

"I said *outré, outré* simply."

"Don't scold me, Janey. Maybe I shouldn't have taken them but I've gone and done it now. And think how splendid Bill Hicks will look, and that Mills boy, buttoned fatly into Savile Row!"

Janey's lips twitched. She turned her head.

"That's a darling," exclaimed Archie, relieved. "Help me to stagger in with them. Can't Mary lend a hand?"

"Yes. I'll call her. We'll put them in the big cupboard, it's practically empty."

"That's the thing, but look snappy. We must finish before lunch. I'm retiring into the silences immediately lunch is over. Mustn't be disturbed. I've some extensive thinking to do."

"All right, dear. But Archie, how did you—"

"Burford Herrick gave 'em to me; he didn't want 'em; doesn't like to be reminded. That cardboard box's medicine. I'll put it in the office."

Janey bustled, Archie bustled, Mary of the white apron and cap bustled. They got Andrew's clothes put away. Archie bolted his lunch and sought his armchair; now at last for his idea.

That preposterous idea seemed during the morning to have crystallized and to have become much less preposterous. He resolved to deal with it fairly, apply method to it, view it in the light of all that was known. All the facts and all the queries, he'd better put them down in black and white, make some sort of outline. His prescription pad wouldn't do for that, it wasn't large enough. Archie fetched a pad of paper from Janey's desk and arranged an ash tray, a box of matches, and his Gold Flakes on a table by his chair. He sat down and took out his fountain pen. He felt rather as though he were taking an examination. Now, what to head it?

Bewildering Aspects of the Crime

I. The dog.
  A. Why killed?
    1. Bark at shot.
    2. Sense death—howl   } Thus giving alarm.
  B. By whom?
    1. A stranger: Impossible unless I have overlooked something.
    2. Someone well-known to dog: Strong probability.
  Remark: Consider more fully.

II. The turned-out lights.
  A. The murderer was ingenious and careful in his suicide fake:
    1. Wore gloves.
    2. Chose high-backed chair to explain contusion of head.
    3. Selected a time when A.H.'s money troubles would supply a motive.
    4. May even have known of the letter in the waste paper basket or put it there, etc. But—
  B. He forgot the lights: Had A. H. committed suicide he would have had the lights on, since it would be most difficult and unnatural to do so in the dark.

C. Why were they off?

Remark: Did he neglect to think of this when he thought of so much else? Or did someone turn them off afterwards? Did someone come in later? If so, who?

The deliverer of the letter? Hardly. In that case would he or she have left the letter in the box?

Johnny?

III. The letter delivered by hand.
   A. What was it about?
   B. What time was it put in A.H.'s box?
      1. After the murder? If before, would not A.H. have seen it?
   C. Who wrote it?
      1. Kitty Lambert?
      2. Wilkinson?
   D. Why has it disappeared?
   E. Has it any direct connection with the murder?

IV. The man Ferris saw in the roadster.
   A. 11:30 Wednesday night. There was a bright moon, but it was cold and gusty—not a night to choose to sleep out of doors. Then:
   B. What was he doing?
   C. Did it have any bearing on what happened later?
   D. Was it Johnny?
   E. Wilkinson has a roadster.
   F. Car was in lane back of Lamberts' where they are building council cottages.
   G. Sand there for making cement. Sand used for sandbag?

V. The dispatch case.
   A. What, if any, is its connection with the murder?
      1. Easy to pick up A.H.'s movements except when he collects or leaves case.
      2. It is linked with the 11:00 trip to London.
   B. What was in it?
   C. Where is it now?

VI. The trips to and from London.
    A. The 11:00: Its purpose?
    B. The final return to Pennerford.
        1. When made?
        2. No trace as yet of car; but A.H. was alive, since death occurred at Whiteleaves.
        3. Was it voluntary? Willingly with the murderer? Or alone in car hired by himself? Or was he brought by force and perhaps already unconscious?

VII. Persons

	Motive	Opportunity	Alibis	Remarks
A. Johnny	Hatred and Revenge	Plenty	None	Lying, acting suspiciously
B. Cyril	?	?	Good	but just possible for him to sneak out after 1:30 unseen by porter.
C. Burford	?	None	Cast iron	
D. Kitty Lambert as accessory to:	Secret entanglement? Revenge because cheated?	Plenty	None	They could both have left their houses unseen, and gone to Whiteleaves at any time. Suspicious actions regarding letter.
E. Wilkinson	To free Kitty? Jealousy?	Plenty	None	
F. *Unknown*	?	?	?	Owner of dispatch case? Man in car?

In the ash tray the little pile of cigarette stubs mounted. Down labyrinthine ways Archie pursued his fugitive idea. In the corner of its logical conclusion he brought it to bay at last. And stood gaping at it appalled. It was an idea, that! Once more he reached for his outline— Well, it explained a lot. It was reasonable. Oh, yes, damnably reasonable. But how could he think? He was mad. It couldn't be right. What had he better do?

Archie lit a final Gold Flake and leaned back closing his eyes. One thing was sure. He mustn't tell a soul. If he were wrong—he had no vestige of real proof as yet—he'd have accused somebody who— It was unthinkable. But if he were right, that was the danger, of course. However, if no one suspected what he thought, it was safe enough for a time. That was it; let things drift; see what developed.

"Mum's the word," said Archie aloud. He got up from his armchair, emptied the ash tray into the fire, and opened the door. "Janey," he bellowed, "come talk to me, I've finished thinking."

The small clock on the desk pointed to twenty-five minutes to seven. Archie scrawled his signature across the bottom of a prescription. Lord, there'd been a lot of patients this evening. Was there anyone else waiting?

The querulous voice at his elbow droned on, "And it do get me something awful in the nights, Doctor. I've had it before but never so bad. This time it's something cruel, why—"

"You are to take this every night before you go to bed. Have it made up at once." Archie tapped the old-fashioned round bell on his desk impatiently. "Call in, in a day or two and let me know how you are. I'm sure this medicine will give you relief."

Mary came promptly in answer to the bell. Removing patients was one of the things she did best. She stood holding open the door.

Archie rose and resolutely extended his hand. "Good evening, Miss Uglow. Come again, say on Wednesday evening, and let me know how it goes."

Mary closed the door again.

"Any more, Mary?" he asked.

"Yes, one more, sir. Ruth Ingles is waiting to see you."

"Oh, all right. Show her in. And tell Mrs. Storke I haven't forgotten we're dining with Colonel Copeland. I'll be right up to dress as soon as I've finished Ruth."

Ruth was nervous. She sat in the chair by Archie's desk, twisting the handle of her garish blue purse into a tight spiral. She looked, too, as if she had been crying.

"Well, Ruth," Archie prompted encouragingly, "what can I do for you? You look unhappy, child, what's the trouble?"

Tears and words came with a rush.

"Oh, Doctor, I'm in such trouble. I'm—I'm afraid I'm going to have a baby. And Mrs. Lambert, she's given me notice and—and—"

Gulping noises took the place of speech. Archie waited. Silence, he knew, was the discourager of tears. The gulping noises grew further apart, dwindled into little sniffs. Ruth fumbled in her bag; her handkerchief had a large purple butterfly in one corner.

"That's better, Ruth." Archie saw that the blue bag still yawned open. "Go ahead, powder your nose like a good girl. Now, sit up and tell me all about it. It's Bill Simpson, isn't it?"

"Yes. You know Bill and me; we've been walking out together three years. All the time I've been working at the manor. I haven't ever had another boy. We've been saving up, him and me, to get married. But it's been a long time. Seems like we'd never get ahead, what with him having to help his mother, all them young brothers and sisters. Well, you know, we got tired of waiting and—it happened. What am I going to do, Doctor?"

"You're going to get married to Bill, Ruth. We'll fix things up somehow. You've saved a little, haven't you? And isn't Bill working now at the garage in Mongerton?"

"Yes, but I could have gone on at the manor a long while still, couldn't I? And it would have helped. It's not fair, Mrs. Lambert giving me notice like this. She knows I'm a steady girl and wouldn't— Well, it's different, isn't it? Being only Bill, and us having always planned to get married? Could you speak to Miss Monica for me, Doctor? Could you see Mrs. Lambert and ask her please to let me stay?"

"I don't know, Ruth. I'll try. The thing to do is for you to get married, and if you really can't manage— When did Mrs. Lambert give you notice? Did she do it because she knew about the baby or for some other reason? I must know there's nothing you've done if I'm to try to persuade her to keep you on. I don't know that I should. It's not my business to interfere, you see."

"Oh, please, Dr. Storke! No, I haven't done nothing. She gave me notice today, it's my night off, and she said she wouldn't have me coming in late any more. She said I was always too late nights, and it was a disgrace. Then—then, she said I could go when my month was up." Ruth's voice grew bitter. She turned her head away. "It's not fair coming from her," she muttered slyly, angry.

Archie didn't like her tone. He spoke sharply.

"What do you mean by what you've just said? Because you're in trouble doesn't excuse insinuations of that sort."

Ruth swung round defiantly. Her cheeks were red with anger. Before Archie could stop her, resentment broke through.

"What right's she got, Doctor, being so fussy and strict? It isn't like she was stiff and dried up herself and didn't take a bit of fun like the rest of us. She ought to know how it is. 'Out with a man, sneaking in late, disgraceful!' she says. And why not, I want to know? I do my work just the same. Why should she bother? She knows Bill and me's going to get married. Let her give me notice then. I don't care. I got a clean conscience that's better than what she's got. The blood of no man's on my head, and won't never be either. Driven to kill himself, that's what he was, because of her. Didn't I see her that night he did it, running along the path going over there to him? And here's Mother and me both out of work, and—"

"Ruth, stop!" shouted Archie.

In the suspended stillness which followed, the little clock on the office desk could be heard ticking fussily. Archie picked it up absently, wound it, put it back again. He felt fed up to the teeth with it all. He would be late for dinner, have to dress in a rush, but he couldn't let it go like this. He couldn't whoof away responsibility. If things would persist in taking him into their confidence—

"I wonder if you realize what you're saying, Ruth? The seriousness of it, I mean. That you must never make accusations of this sort lightly or out of anger? Now I want to know just what the truth is. And then I want you to give me your sacred promise that you will never, under any circumstances, mention it again; that is, unless you are asked to do so by either myself or the police."

"The police? Oh, Dr. Storke, I didn't mean to—"

"Yes, I thought you didn't realize. You hadn't stopped to think, had you, what harm such talk can do? Now look here, I think you're a good girl, although you've behaved very badly about this, and I'll continue to try to help you; but you must tell me the absolute truth."

"I'll tell you the truth, Doctor. Honest I will. I haven't lied. I lost my temper, but what I said's true."

"All right. We mustn't waste any more time. I'm going to be late to dinner as it is. Suppose you just answer my questions. That will be quickest."

"Yes, Doctor."

"Are you quite sure that it was on Wednesday night that you saw Mrs. Lambert?"

"Yes, sir. Mr. Wilkinson came to dinner. He stayed so long I couldn't get out. I promised to meet Bill and I was crazy with having to wait. I was scared to try it till Mrs. Lambert went up to her room."

"You weren't supposed to be out, then?"

"No. But I had to see Bill about—"

"I see. What time did Mr. Wilkinson leave?"

"It was going on twelve."

"And did Mrs. Lambert go upstairs then?"

"No, that was the nuisance. She never went up at all. I hung about for an hour, then I just had to chance it. I thought Bill wouldn't wait, but when Bill promises anything he—"

"What time did you go out?"

"I couldn't say exactly, Dr. Storke. It was awful late, nearly one o'clock."

"And you saw Mrs. Lambert where?"

"Running along the path. You know, the path that goes through the grounds there and comes out on Mr. Herrick's drive. We was talking by the bushes, near the gate. There's a gate where you come out into the drive. She, Mrs. Lambert, came running along. All in a hurry, she was. Never saw us at all, she didn't. The gate caught, and she says, 'damn, damn,' just like that, like she couldn't get it open quick enough. I was afraid to stay any longer; I was scared she might catch me when she came back, so I went for the house right off."

"What time was that?"

"I don't know. You see, I daren't light a light. I just went up the servants' stairs and got undressed in the dark; it must have been two, maybe even later."

"And you are absolutely positive that it was Mrs. Lambert you saw? No one else?"

"Oh, no, Doctor. There was a bright moon. It was cloudy early, but there was a moon then. We saw her plain, Bill and me. She would have seen us only we was sort of behind the bushes, and she was in such a hurry."

"Did you hear a shot, Ruth? Think now."

"No, sir."

"Not at any time? You stayed there by those bushes?"

"Yes, sir. No, Bill and me didn't hear it. It was awful windy, but if Mr. Herrick'd done it while we were there, I think we'd have heard it."

"You don't know when Mrs. Lambert came back to the house? You didn't hear her come in?"

"No, Doctor. I was that tired, I went straight off to sleep, not as I'd have heard her if I hadn't."

"Well, that's all, Ruth. You must trot along. Don't worry about things, we'll fix it up right away for you to get married. Pull up your socks like a good sensible girl; Mrs. Lambert hasn't treated you badly. You shouldn't stay out till all hours; you know yourself it's wrong. Besides, it's very bad for you. You must take care of yourself now. I want you to come in next Saturday, a week from tonight—it's your night off you said, didn't you—and let me look you over. In the meantime I'll see what I can do. I'll speak to Miss Monica, and to Mrs. Lambert if I see her. And remember, not a word of this to anyone. See that Bill doesn't talk about it, either. You will be in serious trouble, both of you, if you do."

"Yes, Dr. Storke. Thank you, Doctor—"

The office clock said ten past seven.

"Uncle's buttons! But I shall be late," moaned Archie.

And there was no rest for the "weary-of-Andrew-Herrick's-murder" to be had at the Colonel's, either. Oh, they had a superb dinner and played bridge with an attractive young widow, who lived up the street, as the fourth. That was all right. But when the car had called for her, and she had been driven away, and just as Archie was dodging for the hall and his coat, the Colonel buttonholed him with, "Look here, Archie, if Janey isn't too tired, I want you to stay a moment longer—"

"I don't know about Janey, old chap, but I'm whacked."

"What is it, Roger? Have you more news?" asked Janey. "Of course Archie'll stay. I don't mind waiting a bit. But may I sit right here in this comfortable chair and read? I've been dying to read this for ages. I didn't know you had it." Janey held up a book in a bright green jacket. "Do let me. Take Archie into your study for a final drink."

"If you'd rather, Janey, that's what we'll do. Archie can tell you the gist of it later." The Colonel failed to hide his relief.

Behind his back Janey closed one eye impishly at Archie. She knew perfectly well that the Colonel wanted to get out of telling her himself. Therefore, she also knew that this latest news must concern Johnny. She hid her curiosity tactfully behind the green book. She would have to be patient for half an hour or so, that was all.

Spread out on the table in the Colonel's study was a large road map.

"I had a phone call from Inspector Nokes at the Yard this afternoon," explained the Colonel. "They've succeeded in tracing Armstrong's car. You'll have a whisky, Archie? I have brandy here if you prefer."

"No. Whisky for me please."

The Colonel took a decanter from a small corner cupboard and poured out the drinks.

"They've been rather lucky over it," he continued, squirting the soda into the glasses. He handed a glass to Archie and carried his to the table where he set it down by the map.

"Come over here and look at this."

Archie bent over the map obediently. With the point of a pencil the Colonel indicated a small round dot.

"Yattendon, you know the village, Archie? It's eight miles north of Cambury."

"I've been through there several times."

"Yes. Well, about half a mile outside of Yattendon in the small hours of Thursday morning, half past three to be precise, a policeman on a bicycle passed a young man walking towards Yattendon. He was carrying a petrol tin. The policeman— Don't ask me what he was doing bicycling along the road at that hour. The explanation's immaterial. That's where the luck comes in. Anyhow, the policeman gave the man a 'good evening,' to which he got no response. Around the next bend in the road he came upon the stranded car. Prompted partly by curiosity, partly by something furtive in the young man's manner, he flashed his bull's eye on the license plate, YK60316. He dismounted and examined the license disk at the side, found it in order, and went on again. However, he made a note of the license number. When the number was posted at his station, he, of course, reported the occurrence."

"Wonderful police force," murmured Archie. "And then?"

"There's a small filling station on the outskirts of Yattendon. The man in charge lives in a cottage next door to it. He says that at about twenty to four he was awakened by a knock, and a young man, answering Armstrong's description, asked him for petrol. The filling man was naturally annoyed at being routed out of bed at that hour, but he filled the tin and was somewhat cheered by a generous tip. So now we know one reason Armstrong didn't put his car away in his London garage until six o'clock."

"We do," Archie agreed, "and it's pretty damnable. Let's have a good look at this map."

The Bath Road does not run through Pennerford. The village is connected with it by a road three quarters of a mile in length which runs at a right angle. At Cambury on the Bath Road a turn branches north leading to Yattendon and hence by Henley, Beaconsfield, and Uxbridge into London. This route is slightly longer than the direct one of the Bath Road through Reading and Maidenhead. From Pennerford to Yattendon is fifteen miles. From Yattendon to London is approximately fifty.

The Colonel's pencil traced the route: Pennerford to Cambury, Cambury to Yattendon.

"At half past three Armstrong ran out of gas. He had gone fifteen miles. He must have left Pennerford about thee o'clock. It would be four by the time he was filled up again. That makes fifty miles in two hours, when he reaches his garage."

"But what was he doing in Yattendon? It's out of his way. Why not the Bath Road into town?"

"You know the probable answer, Archie, even if you don't like it."

"Panic? He was afraid he'd be traced if he went the direct way?"

"Don't you think that's it? I figure that he knew he would run out of petrol. He hoped to find an inconspicuous place, somewhere we wouldn't be looking for him."

"Hard luck about that petrol." Archie took a long pull at his whisky and soda. "Wonder how he came to run out?"

"Another answer you know and don't like, eh? He'd already been back to London once that night."

"Oh, that's your theory. He left Pennerford at ten as he says. Met Andrew in London after his train got in at half past twelve. Drove him back to Pennerford, murdered him, and left again at three. I pointed out to you before that the time's a difficulty to that. There's hardly enough of it."

"It could just be done. The roads are clear then, and it's quite easy to average thirty miles an hour. Let me remind you that you pointed out the incredible amount of speed Armstrong manages to get out of his Morris. I quote you exactly."

"Oh, hell, it's all very distressing," was Archie's complaint to that.

They stood looking down at the map for a moment in silence. The Colonel picked up his empty glass. "Have another spot before you go, Archie?"

"No, thanks—"

"You realize, don't you, just how strong a case of circumstantial evidence there is against Johnny Armstrong?"

"Yes."

"Turner wants to make the arrest. I am uneasy about it, though, in spite of all this."

"You may make a mistake if you do arrest Johnny, Roger. You're safe enough to let it drift for a bit; the boy can't bolt. Wait and see what turns up. Has Turner questioned him again? He's still in Pennerford, isn't he?"

"He's staying until after the funeral on Monday. Yes, Turner saw him late this afternoon; confronted him with the glove; told him we'd discovered he'd been lying; told him we knew it was murder; did his best to frighten him into talking, but he got nothing out of him. Armstrong knew it was useless to invent a new story; he simply refused to give any explanation at all. I believe he said we could arrest him if we chose but we couldn't make him tell us anything."

"I've seen Johnny in that there's-nothing-to-tell mood. He can be as stubborn as a mule and twice as foolish. God knows, I'm beginning to wish we knew the truth, no matter what it is."

"Do you still think him innocent?"

"I don't know what I think. Only— Will you hold Turner back for a bit?"

"I wish I could feel sure that's best. I can't."

"There's more to come. You haven't heard about an interesting interview I had this evening. Ruth Ingles, the parlormaid at Mrs. Lambert's, came to see me."

Archie retold Ruth's story. It may have lacked some of its color in his rendering, but the essentials were there.

"A new kind of creditors' meeting," said the Colonel, when he had finished.

"A Kitty Lambert-Johnny combination? Don't forget the Wilkinson-Lambert. Well, it's got me. I'm damned if I know what it's all about."

Which, as Archie meant it, was quite true.

He didn't. Janey had the Yattendon business before they reached their door.

"I must see Monica," was what she said.

CHAPTER VIII
SUNDAY AFTERNOON

Archie and the Colonel Take to Drink

It was Sunday afternoon. The Colonel and Archie were calling on Mrs. Lambert. That is to say, Ruth had shown them into the spacious drawing room, taken up their names, returned to answer that Madam would be charmed to see them, would they kindly wait. That was twenty minutes ago. They waited. Archie fidgeted, the Colonel turned over the pages of the *Sketch*.

"She might just as well see us now," he murmured to a full-page brunette. "Jolly pretty girl, that. Just as well. I shall sit here until she does."

"'On and off for days and days,'" acquiesced Archie. "My poor Roger, my heart bleeds for you. You sit there blown with confidence. Wait!"

"What I intend to do, wait."

"That's not my meaning. I said 'wait.' I meant beware."

"Don't be tiresome, Archie."

"Why not? I have to entertain myself somehow, you've the only magazine. And it's all very well for you to be superior; you don't know what you're up against. I've tackled her before, remember. I was in need of strong drink when I'd finished. Oh, yes. What's more I didn't want to come this afternoon, anyhow. She will weep. I predict she will weep."

"What does it matter what she does or does not do? She may count herself lucky that I came and not Turner. Let me tell you, Archie, I'm—"

Footsteps sounded. The Colonel appeared engrossed in his *Sketch*.

They passed, and Archie strolled aimlessly to the window. He stood looking out over the wide lawn. Stretching across it and disappearing round some trees was the path leading to Whiteleaves. Another path at right angles led away down the slope to the river.

Suddenly Archie stiffened. A man had come from somewhere in the house and was hurrying away from it along the river path. Archie side-stepped behind a curtain.

"Well, well. The worthy Wilkinson."

"Eh?"

Archie came back to his chair.

"Wilkinson, our beloved dark horse, out there streaking it down to the river: a complete get-away via the towpath. Very shy these days: always present, seldom seen. The vigil's over, Roger. She'll be along now."

"So he's been with her all the time we've been waiting. Isn't that the very devil? That's just what I wanted to forestall."

"Too bad. They'll have fixed it up nicely between them. Kitty will be thoroughly primed in what to say, but she's not prepared for what we know. So bluff, my lad, and let not blush nor tear deter you. Hush! My lady comes."

The door opened, and Kitty Lambert wafted herself into the room.

The Colonel, rising to his feet, saw a small fair woman, undeniably pretty still, whose soft gray frock and fluffy hair conspired to a girlishness that only the eyes, wide and blue as they were, betrayed.

A white hand fluttered forward impulsively.

"Dear Dr. Storke, how charming of you! And at last you've relented and brought Colonel Copeland to see me."

The Colonel received a full smile and a half blush.

"I've wanted to meet you for such a long time and now I know you'll forgive me for keeping you waiting and stay for tea with me. Sundays are so dull. I had a mite of a headache, oh, it's quite gone now, so I slipped upstairs to lie down for a moment. I fell asleep

and I hadn't quite finished dressing when you came. You will forgive me, won't you? Oh, please sit down, both of you."

Kitty Lambert sank delicately into a little heap in one corner of
the large couch and patted the place beside her invitingly.

The Colonel found himself there. Archie was right; he hadn't
realized how awful it was going to be. How in the name of social
decency was he to begin? He'd come prepared to ask stern questions about a murder, and here she was, pretending it was all a
delightful tea party, a delicious treat! Although she knew perfectly
well, of course, why they were there. It was her weapon, this
social-use-and-wont pretense; she would make it as awkward for
him as she could. Turner wouldn't have been susceptible to this
sort of difficulty. Why hadn't he sent Turner?

The Colonel attempted to catch Archie's eye. He needed solace
and courage. But Archie had forsaken him. He was chatting easily
with Kitty Lambert, talking about Monica. They appeared to have
forgotten him. The Colonel became indignant. He was not to be
beaten by such obvious means. In a moment one of them would
have to include him, and then he was determined to have no beating about the bush. Since he was not allowed to approach things
gently, he would simply bang right out with it. Better in the end
anyway. The Colonel braced himself grimly to await no more than
the first conversational pause.

Out of the corner of his eye Archie saw the Colonel's mustache
bristle. Kitty was in for it now! She was prattling on and on ani-
matedly. Wasn't she hiding apprehension underneath all this
brightness? She couldn't keep this steady tick tick of soft chatter
going indefinitely, babbling against time— She was showing signs
of running down.

"Yes, Monica went over to your wife's this afternoon; you must
have missed her. I suspect she had a confidence to make. Girls
never confide in their mothers these days, do they? But we mothers know without it; we can sense our children's happiness. And
Cyril is a dear boy. But I mustn't bore you men talking over my
little girl, must I? When things are near to one's heart, one for-
gets, doesn't one? Do you enjoy our country here, Colonel? Isn't it

dull for you? You have been used to wider activities. But there, I suppose you shoot and fish, and the Penner is one of the best trout streams in England; it brings all sorts of people here. We had a charming army man, very keen on fishing, staying at the Seven Stars last year. I wonder if you would know him? A Captain Maitland. His regiment was the—oh, dear, I'm afraid I've forgotten."

Even after all that, the breath Kitty took barely stirred the soft ruffles at her throat. But her blue eyes fled the Colonel's face and with furtive haste seemed to search in the familiar objects around her a refuge. A postponement, another subject— They came to rest on a huge bowl of russet chrysanthemums, her lips parted—

She was too late. The Colonel was in. And in, Archie saw, at his regimental best.

"Captain Maitland? No, ma'am, I have not his acquaintance. And now if you will permit me—" The Colonel cleared his throat, squared his shoulders, made sure of his seat.

He's sitting the couch as if it were a horse, thought Archie. Parade inspection. Oh, good old army. Attention, Kitty! Lord, I mustn't laugh! Archie coughed.

The Colonel turned for a second to glare at him, then, "Mrs. Lambert, our visit must be considered as—er—official. Deuced awkward, but we have our duty to do. We are dealing with murder."

This time Kitty's breath was audible in a little gasp. She put one hand to her throat as though to catch it back, then let it out again in one soft word.

"Murder—"

Oh, the Colonel had startled her, all right, Archie saw. Startled her by the suddenness of his pounce. But there was no surprise there, no incredulity. She'd known it wasn't suicide. How? Just as everyone must be suspecting it by now unless they were damn fools? Or because—

Archie had thought her frightened, apprehensive, as long ago as Friday, the day after the murder was discovered, when he'd seen her and questioned her; just as frightened then, as she was now. And at that time she shouldn't have known anything. Unless—

The Colonel was carrying on remorselessly.

They were facing each other now. The Colonel erect, defying the softness of the couch; Kitty drawn back even further into her corner, looking younger and more childlike than Archie had ever seen her even when she was trying hard. Her eyes, a shade too widely held, perhaps, met the Colonel's with bland inquiry.

Archie noted and knew defeat. One gasp, that was all they would get. Kitty was entrenched behind her feminine defenses, detestable little general that she was. Archie felt reluctant admiration. He couldn't stick the woman, but she had them licked before they'd really started. We might as well go home before the tears, damn it, he told himself, bringing his attention with impatience back to what the Colonel was saying.

". . . . evidence that leaves no doubt at all."

"You mean facts prove? But you know, Colonel Copeland—you'll think me only a silly woman—but, you know, it's been given me lately to see so far beyond mere facts. Dear Mr. Wilkinson, he's shown me how wrong we are to trust in the material world. He says the belief in the evidence of our senses has—has fettered mankind and prevented us seeing the higher truth. We can be so wrong in interpreting facts. He's seen that over and over, he says; like the world looking flat, you know. And so he believes we should be guided by our inner light of truth. He has taught me to trust in that, and so I know you are wrong, Colonel Copeland. Oh, you're so nice, I know you think you're right. But, but I know dear Andrew couldn't have been murdered. We have to *deserve* murder, to attract it to us by our own wickedness before it comes to us. Only things come to us that we will to come. Yes, I know what you are going to say. Please, please don't. Andrew was wrong to take the money. But we must make allowances for those still bound to a lower plane, not liberated from earthy things, the vanities of the flesh. Poor, poor Andrew. If he had only lived just a little longer, if only my influence had been greater—I wanted so much to help him—but, you see, we were never very close to each other."

Kitty's hands performed a pretty gesture of resignation. She smiled a pitying sweet smile. She patted the Colonel's arm, a wise mother quieting an explosive child.

The Colonel's mustache bristled alarmingly; his face turned peony red.

Archie decided to intervene. Poor Roger, he was out of his depth; he would only splutter. The brutal attack now:

"A long tale of nonsense! Still, just like a sensible tail, it carries a sting in its end."

Archie's voice cut across at her even more sharply than he had intended.

She swung towards him quickly as though to snap. "What do you mean, Dr. Storke?" And her tone was soft, softer and more unbearably sweet.

"Just this: You want us to think you didn't know Herrick well, and yet you went to his house at two in the morning, Thursday morning. Why?"

"Oh, how did— How dare you insinuate!"

This time there was no doubt the blush was genuine. It spread slowly from the soft ruffles at her throat to the pretty line of her hair; a painful blush, unhappy to see. Archie was ashamed. From attack forced to defense.

"My dear Mrs. Lambert, please. I didn't mean— Nothing like that. We never thought—" Archie floundered miserably.

Denying his own ignominious past, the Colonel looked upon him with momentary contempt.

"You have misunderstood Dr. Storke's intention. It was—er— somewhat tactlessly put. We wish an explanation, ma'am, that is all."

"Explanation? But—but there's nothing to explain. I didn't—" Kitty Lambert halted on the brink of denial, fell back on defiance.

"You have no right to question me like this. I'm sure you haven't. You come to my house, and I see you, and—and then you are rude to me. I must ask you to go, now, at once!"

Very surprisingly the Colonel did not move except to put his hand with kind gentleness over both hers where they twisted together in her lap.

"Listen for a moment," he said. "Your maid saw you go through the gate to Whiteleaves. It was late, very late, about two o'clock.

She did not see you return, for she did not want you to see her and she came at once back here. Mr. Herrick was killed soon after. That is the position. Don't you think it would be better to explain? You are right, we can't force you to; but for your own sake?"

The tears came as Archie had expected, but with them came words which he had not.

"Yes, I did go. I was fri—worried; I was worried. I wrote a letter, just a letter, about—about my money, that's all. I took it over; I was going to leave it but I didn't. I didn't. I brought it back again. I didn't go in; I didn't do anything. I just came right back because I saw the lights of the car. It was coming up the drive. I didn't want them to see me, whoever it was. I don't know who it was. When I saw the lights, I ran home. That's all, really it is. It's the truth. You do believe it is, don't you?"

For a moment tear-drenched eyes were raised to the unhappy Colonel's face, then disappeared behind a gray chiffon handkerchief. The Colonel and Archie were treated to a crown of fair curls.

Muffled by chiffon came the command, "Go. Go away. You've been horrid, perfectly horrid. Go away."

They went.

"Monica, dear, how nice of you to come over," said Janey, uncurling herself from her chair by the fire.

"Sit here, child. Are you sure you'd rather have the bear?" she asked, as Monica, with a shake of her head, sank down on the hearth rug and crossed her legs under her.

Janey re-curled herself and looked down at the head by her knees.

"I don't know how you do it. I've seen you sit for hours like a funny little female tailor. I should ache all over. You must be double-jointed or something."

"No, it's only practice. I can't help it now it's become a habit. It's very convenient for trays in bed, that's how it started. I like breakfast in bed, don't you, Janey?"

"Yes, but I've forgotten what they're like; Archie has to get off every morning."

"Oh, I know, darling." Monica put her hands flat on the floor behind her and, leaning back on them, looked at Janey with such candid admiration in her eyes that Janey was embarrassed.

"Nonsense. I like getting up."

"That's just it. That's what I mean. That's what makes you so grand, Janey. You really like doing things you do for Archie, and for all of us. You just naturally are the perfect wife."

"Monnie, how grim! It makes me sound too appalling: my lap always covered with socks that I'm mending with a sweet smile, I suppose."

"You can't mend socks with a smile, dear idiot. And you know I didn't mean anything like that. It's only that you wouldn't fail anyone you love. You wouldn't even try not to. You just naturally couldn't. You're not all mixed up with silly pride. And—and things that get hurt and make you say things and do things, like me. Oh, Janey, I'm such an awful fool; I've been so horrid. Oh, Janey, say something. Make me feel better, Janey."

In her earnestness Monica had risen to her knees and knelt now between Janey and the fire, like a frantic little penitent.

Janey smiled and pushed her gently down.

"Be a tailor again, dear, and have a cigarette, and let's get down to it. Why are you lashing yourself?"

"That's not like you, Janey. You know why I feel so rotten. You heard what I said when Johnny—"

"Yes. I think you were unkind. It wasn't like you, either, Monica. But I know why you did it. You were hurt."

"Hurt! Of course I was hurt. So would you be hurt. Doesn't he trust me?" Monica's voice rose shrill for a moment. Then she said with something of flat despair, "Just the same I shouldn't have let that matter. Johnny needed me. He needs me. I know he does and I failed him, made him think I wasn't loyal." Her voice rose again to vehement protest. "And I am loyal, Janey. No matter what, no matter—I am loyal."

There was a shocked little silence. Then Janey said slowly, "Monica, dear, you're torturing yourself. And you're loyal, only I don't think you are quite loyal enough. Oh, it's not that I think you don't love Johnny—" She threw this in against Monica's movement of protest, then went on weighing her words, slowly as before.

"It's— Well, it's nothing to do with loving exactly. Perhaps loving makes it harder to see. It's just that Johnny couldn't—" Janey took a little breath and ended firmly, "He couldn't murder."

Her last word hung in the stillness that followed like a dread summons to action and to fear. Janey rose to meet it, to dispel its terror.

"He could kill someone. I know that. I know he has a violent temper, just as well as you do. But, Monnie, think—think how it was done. All planned: horrid, fiendish. That's impossible for Johnny. Isn't it? Isn't it, Monica?"

"Yes, Janey, yes. That's what's been so awful. I couldn't believe, I never really believed— But it's all been so queer. Why is Johnny lying? That's not like him, either, is it? Janey, I'm so afraid." Monica reached out and took hold of Janey's fingers, clung to them.

"I know, dear, I know," soothed Janey.

"And he does know something. You could see he does, you and Archie, both of you. I knew you thought so the other night. And if it's all right, why won't he tell us?"

"I don't know. But I think the reason is he's shielding someone. That was what it was at first, I think. Now it's that and something more."

"More?"

"Yes, I think, perhaps, he feels he'll only make matters worse by talking now."

"Oh, Janey, have the police—"

"Yes, dear, they have. Look here, Monnie, don't look like that. It will be all right. Archie doesn't believe Johnny did it. And Roger listens to Archie. Trust Archie, he's really— Well, he really is awfully clever."

The deprecating pride in Janey's voice brought a smile back to Monica's face. When she looked up again, her eyes were steady and sure.

"Thanks, darling. And you are a perfect wife. And a perfect friend, too. I'll tell you one reason I've been such a frantic frightened nit wit over all this. It doesn't matter now for apparently the police have found out anyway. Johnny was here in Pennerford late Wednesday night. At least, I'm sure he was. He was waiting to see me again."

"Again, dear? You were talking to him in the car, weren't you?"

"Yes, but I had to go back in. You know, Mother is—she is— Oh, damn it all, Janey, Mother is very unfair about Johnny. I like Cyril and all that. And I suppose he's more reliable in a way than Johnny; but I don't love him. I wish sometimes I did; it would make life much simpler. You don't know what Mother's like. She's so soft and helpless: violets, chaise longue, smelling salts, so positively archaic. But when it comes to getting her own way, she's a steam roller! Really, she is. She just comes along so darn slowly you think you've got lots of time, and then she just methodically rolls over you. And there you are quite flat. It's grim; you don't know how grim it is." Monica laughed, but her laugh had a hint of panic.

Janey tossed back her hair and brought her feet from where they had been curled beneath her to hit the floor with a decisive little stamp.

"Monica, sometimes you make me feel cross. I'd like to shake you. Why don't you fight? There are some things you can't let people interfere with. Let's talk sense. It's Cyril's money, isn't it?"

"Ye-es. I suppose that's what it really is. Of course, Mother doesn't say—"

"No. She wouldn't. But, my God, *money!*"

"Janey! I've never heard you swear before. It's—it's exhilarating. Up School!"

"All right, Monnie, that's better. But you're not going to make me change the subject. You came and asked for it and you're going to have it—flat. First, about the money, does it matter to you?"

"Good Lord, no. Janey, surely you don't think—"

"I only wanted to be sure. Now we have it. The problem's quite simple. You love Johnny, and the money doesn't matter. All we have to do is get Johnny out of this mess, and everything's all right. Right?"

"Right."

"Well, the best way is to face everything that's bad about it and work back to what isn't from there. That isn't very clear, but I know what I mean."

"I do, too, Janey. You're a brick."

Monica scrambled to her feet and looked at her watch. "Wow! It's later than I thought, I'm due home. I'll tell you everything I know, it's not much. Then I must run."

The need for haste established, Monica lit a cigarette and sat down again. The early autumn dusk was seeping into the room, and the fire-light glowed on her pale face, made of her black hair a charcoal shadow. Her wide red mouth was beautiful. Something stabbed in Janey. Monica was lovely: so lovely and so pitifully young. She must make things right. Archie must do something.

"You see, Janey," Monica said, "I had seen Johnny earlier. That was around nine o'clock. He was furious, in one of his black moods. He'd found out that day in London, found out for certain, that Andrew Herrick had lost his money. What made it so bad was that we'd been counting on it to, well, to defy Mother. We'd been up against both of them, really. Cyril was Andrew's candidate, too. There'd never been any question that Cyril was his uncle's favorite. Ever since they were little, Johnny's been discriminated against. If Cyril wanted anything, Andrew saw he had it. And that went for wanting me, too. What we wanted, Johnny and I, didn't seem to matter to either Mother or Mr. Herrick. They couldn't do anything about it, of course, as long as Johnny got his money. We had to wait until he was twenty-five. We've been waiting two years now and we were on the last lap, in a month and nine days he'll be—" Monica gave a little gulp and then went on resolutely, "So you see when Johnny found out, he was desperate. He was so mad he couldn't even be reasonable. He said he was sure Drew had lost the money on purpose to give Cyril a clear field. He worked himself on from that and accused Mother of being in the plot, too. I tried to make him laugh. Usually when he's being absurd, he knows it underneath, and you can make him laugh at himself, and then he's all right. But it was no use. What he wasn't going to do to Drew when the train got in wasn't funny. I was frightened, really frightened.

I cried. That's the thing I try after the laughing doesn't work. Even it didn't do much good, only enough good to make him promise not to see Mr. Herrick then. I had to get back to the house because I didn't want Mother after me. She didn't know I was seeing Johnny. I was still afraid of what he'd do, and we'd left things all up in the air. It was a mess, Janey, no matter what you say. Money doesn't matter, but no money at all, does."

"Poor Monnie, yes, I know. Go on."

"Well, the end was I promised to come back. Johnny promised to wait. I told him I didn't know how long I'd be. Cuthbert Wilkinson was at the house; he'd been to dinner, and I didn't know when he'd go; and until he did, and Mother went up to bed, I couldn't get out. He stayed and stayed. I was frantic. It was cold, and I kept thinking of Johnny out there, working himself up, getting madder and madder, perhaps not waiting, perhaps going to Whiteleaves. Oh, it was a hell of an evening.

"At about half past eleven I went upstairs. Mother thought I'd gone to bed. I couldn't see the car from my window because Johnny didn't dare leave it in front of the house, and he'd gone up the road somewhere. I couldn't get out possibly without Mother knowing. About midnight Cuthbert went. Heaven knows what they'd been hashing about all that time. Slimy object, he's dosing Mother with the most poisonous rot. Do you like him?"

"No. But I think he's harmless."

"There's where you're wrong, Janey. He's not harmless—no more harmless than a nice, belly-smooth, crawling, poisonous snake. He gives me the creeps. Anyhow, when he went, I thought, 'At last!' But Mother didn't come up. She didn't come up for ages. I could hear her walking around down there every time I sneaked out onto the landing. I could see the light from the open door when I leaned over the banisters. I hadn't a chance in a million to slip by. It was after two before she finally came upstairs. I gave her a few minutes, and then I pussy-footed it down and out the front door. I was afraid Johnny wouldn't be there, it was so terribly late."

"What time was it exactly, Monica, do you know?"

"Twenty minutes past two. Johnny wasn't there."

"Is that all?"

"Yes, that's all," answered Monica, but she didn't move; and Janey knew there was something more, something still to be said, the last nail to be driven in that black case against Johnny.

"Let's have it, Monica," she commanded firmly. "Let's face the whole thing. You saw something. What was it?"

Monica threw her cigarette, burned down now to its very end, with a gesture of curious and desperate finality into the heart of the fire. She turned and faced Janey squarely.

"Yes, I saw something, and you'd better tell Archie. Tell him all of this. You said, 'let's know the worst and work back to the best,' didn't you? Well, the worst is I saw a car come out of the drive to Whiteleaves. And it was a roadster; it looked awfully like the Morris. I—I'm afraid it was Johnny. Janey, I'm sure it was. Oh, what are we going to do?"

"Do, Monica darling? Tell Archie and trust him, and keep on remembering the truth. That's the main thing not to forget: That we *know* Johnny didn't do it. Hold on to that, dear."

"I will. How I wish I hadn't been so awful. Johnny won't see me; he's all stiff and proud. If only I hadn't been so foul, perhaps I could have made him talk to us. If he only would— Well, sweet, I'm really going now. Thanks so terribly."

Monica had stooped swiftly and kissed Janey. The front door closed, and Janey was alone. She sat quite still staring into the fire. At last she stirred and with both hands at her temples pushed back her heavy hair. She was suddenly very, very tired. And where was Archie? He was late for tea.

When Archie came, the Colonel and Liz were with him.

Janey prepared to hide her disappointment. She had wanted Archie to be alone. She had been very reassuring to Monica but she seemed to have used up all her own certainty in the process. Now she felt she needed Archie to give it back to her again. This way she might not see him alone until dinner time. Then she remembered it was Sunday, no patients. All the same, she just didn't feel like the Colonel, not at the moment.

Their voices reached her from the hallway raised boisterously. They had, as a matter of fact, quite recovered, and were in high spirits.

"'When shall we three meet again?'" declaimed Archie, striking an attitude against the doorjamb. "Oh, there's Liz. That's four, not three. Come in, Liz, come in, my good dog."

Liz was already in and making a quick line for the fire. The Colonel followed looking somewhat sheepish.

"And how's Janey? How's my own dear love?" Archie demanded, going on with cheerful *non sequitur*, "'But at my back I always hear, Time's winged chariot hurrying near . . . The grave's a fine and private place, But none, I think, do there embrace.' Ha! that's so, isn't it, my love? And now tea, tea for the troops. The noble troops' tea!"

"Sit down, Roger. I've rung, Archie, tea's coming." Janey sounded very much out of key. She smiled at them both, hoping to smooth it over.

"You know." Archie pointed an accusing finger at her. "You always know. Yes, we have imbibed. By God, we needed it. Or didn't we, Roger?"

"We did. Janey, we went to see Mrs. Lambert. She—"

"Ho, that female woman! That octopus of virtue and soft vice!" Archie's hands sketched a shape in the air, and Janey laughed, happy and all at once no longer tired and uneasy. Archie made everything seem good.

Mary came in with tea.

And after tea, things got more settled down. Archie stopped quoting, and they began to tell her about Kitty Lambert.

"She got Roger down in the first round," Archie exulted.

"But nothing like the knock-out blow you took in the second," roared the Colonel.

And then they both started to talk at once, tripping over each other, laughing like two schoolboys delighted with some unique naughtiness.

"You should have seen. Roger's face when she patted him. She did: she patted him, Janey! Nice doggy; he looked as if he'd swallowed a fishhook."

"I did, did I? Well, when you pulled your gaff, you squirmed. You must have swallowed the fish!"

"I don't want to crush your boyish spirits," said Janey, "but just what are you being so pleased about? Do you know?"

"Now, isn't that unkind." Archie mourned graphically.

"Do you want us to be serious, Janey?" The Colonel's good manners reproached him.

"It's all right, Roger." Janey was reassuring. "But I've had Monica here. So— Oh, it's hard to see anything funny in it, that's all."

And as though her words were a signal, a bell ringing at the end of play hour, they were all at once grave, too grave.

She got it all: their bewilderment, their doubts. Mrs. Lambert, they told her, had told the truth. But only, they thought, part of the truth. She had admitted going to Whiteleaves, but only when she knew they knew. She said she hadn't left the letter. Somehow, they didn't quite believe that. She'd seen a car. That they did believe. But when she saw it—if, as she said, when she first got there, or later—they couldn't tell. She'd said the letter was only about her money; that the Colonel was inclined to doubt, and Archie stoutly pronounced it a lie.

"Wilkinson," said Archie, "looms. He definitely looms. The moose—I wish it were meese—the regal moose, horns locked, battle over shrinking doe. I think she's a moose, too, but doe sounds better. That is my theory."

"It's handsome and does you credit," said Janey. "And you may be right. You're probably right. But does it mean anything? Has it anything to do with all this?"

"God knows. But—" Archie snapped his fingers suddenly. "But I've thought of a way to make sure. There's no use your asking me, my children, 'cause I shan't tell you. The office calls."

"Archie, Archie," wailed Janey as he made for the door. "It's Sunday. You don't have office hours on Sunday!"

Archie's head reappeared briefly round the door.

"I know it, Ducky, but I have a patient in there all the same: Bill Simpson, Ruth's young man. He's not on at the garage on Sunday afternoons, so I said I'd see him. Sorry, I won't be long."

In spite of that, it was three quarters of an hour later, when Archie strolled back into the study, across to where his decanter waited for him. He poured out a whisky and squirted soda from the siphon into his glass. He brought it to the fire and sat down. Janey lowered her book.

"The Colonel and Liz have departed, I see," said Archie, watching the bubbles as they rose slowly through the amber liquid.

"A half hour ago," answered Janey. "What ever kept you so long? Or is it professional confidence?"

"No, my dear. Only the sorrows of a young man trying to get ahead." He sang, "'For a mechanic's lot is not a happy one.'"

"Are they going to get married?"

"Yes. That will be all right. He's quite keen. I gather it's Ruth who wanted to wait till they'd saved more money. She had a good job, till it went west, and didn't want to leave it quite yet. No, he's not a reluctant bridegroom at all. His only grouse seems to be his job. He doesn't like the uncertain hours. I told him he should be a doctor, and then he'd find out what uncertain hours really meant. He was not to be consoled."

Archie chuckled reminiscently. "He'd missed a Mae West picture Wednesday night and consequently life was black. He told me all about it in great detail. 'Here was I,' he said, 'all ready to leave, just in time to get to the show, and along comes a blooming chauffeur with a blooming hired Daimler and a blooming slow flat that he's too blooming lazy to fix himself'; those weren't his adjectives, incidentally. Anyhow, he had to mend the puncture and so lost Mae West. And after that the poor devil had a long, cold vigil waiting for Ruth. All very sad."

"Sad waste of your time, I'd say," said Janey with unaccustomed tartness.

"You think so? Because I'd—" The telephone ringing interrupted him with shrill imperativeness.

Grumbling, "Ten to one the Jenkins pest!" Archie went to answer.

He had no takers. Mrs. Jenkins it was.

CHAPTER IX
MONDAY

"Orphan-Like" Lunch and Whyte Ladye Tea

It was Monday morning Archie Storke, whistling with discordant preoccupation, lighted the heater and threw wide the bathroom window to let the steam escape. He looked out on a world of gray. Below him Janey's autumn flowers hung heads heavy with the night's rain. Seen through the mist, the trees on the ridge had lost the gayety of their bright, individual colors and glowed, subdued, a smoky orange. Archie stopped whistling, shut the window, and turned to his rack of eight razors.

"Janey," he called.

Janey came to the bathroom door and stood smiling at him. "It's Monday," she said. But Monday's razor was already poised before the shaving mirror and, as she spoke, rasped softly downwards from Archie's right ear.

"I know it," came from the left side of Archie's mouth. "I was only pretending. I wanted to look at you, Ducky."

"But you're not looking at me; you're shaving."

"I know it. You're there to be looked at though, so it's all right."

"Archie, silly," said Janey as though she didn't think it was. Then, "Is anything the matter?"

"Hell, yes!" The words had a soft vehemence. He stopped shaving, turned to lean back against the wash basin, and stared at her.

"Everything's wrong. I'm worried, I'm all balled up. Everything has gone cock-eyed. Nothing's the same. Damn it all, I even know

150

what day it is, ever since that beastly thing happened I've known. It's awful."

"Darling!" Janey laughed. "Darling, that can't be so dreadful. You were always complaining because you never knew."

"Jeannette Storke, that won't do! It's not a nice pretense like mine. It's a cheat. You know damn well that everything's getting spoiled. Where's our nice, happy, each-day-the-same life gone? Where? Into a mess. Moil, moil, moil. Always thinking, always stewing: Was it this? Was it that? Why? How? Who? To hell with it I say!"

Archie glared, then added with hopeful matter-of-factness, "May Andrew Herrick sizzle. May he well and truly sizzle."

"Archie!" Janey made shocked protest.

"Well, why not? 'What's Hecuba to me'—er, I mean, 'him, or he to Hecuba, That he should weep—' I didn't know the man, hardly, anyhow. He wasn't a friend of ours. God Almighty, it isn't as if we cared! Yet here we are, you and I, Janey, all mixed up in this—this bloody murder. And all because I was curious. Curious? I'm a tiresome meddling moron that's what I am. I'm quitting."

Archie turned on his heel and presented a defiant back.

There was silence while, with over-carefulness, Archie relathered his face.

Archie shaved his left cheek, his neck, his lip. Janey waited motionless in the doorway. Archie turned on the hot water and soused, reached blindly for his towel, hid his face in its folds. Janey was still there. It was no use.

"Sorry," the towel mumbled. "Sorry, Ducky. Forgive?"

Janey left the doorway, came to put her arms around him. The towel fell into the wet washbasin. They kissed, long.

"My sweet," said Archie. "I am a pig, a petulant pig. You're quite right, I can't quit now. I know I can't."

"Monica and Johnny," said Janey.

"Yes, Monica and Johnny. And, if you must know, I—"

"You've got to find out for yourself. That's what you were going to say, wasn't it? You may hate it but you can't help it, either. You can't rest with things you don't understand."

"No. I never could."

"Well, it's all right. Try to stop fretting. You'll find out. Darling, look at the time; you're going to be late."

"Yes, I'll hurry. But, Janey—" Archie stopped her, put his hands on her shoulders, and turned her to him. He looked down into the steady eyes raised to his in quiet confidence.

"Janey, you frighten me terribly sometimes. You believe so awfully in me. It scares me cold. What if I failed you?"

"You won't, dear. But if you did, it wouldn't make any difference. So there's nothing to be scared of, nothing."

"Hurry up," she called back. Her heels clattered on the stairs, and as Archie picked up his tie, he heard her happy "Good morning, Mary. The Doctor'll be down in a moment."

Just like all mornings, after all. Unconsciously Archie squared his shoulders. That was that. No more drifting, no more delaying, no more letting distrust of himself stop him. Get down to it. The sooner it was over, the sooner they could forget it.

"I shall find out." It was a vow to himself, to Janey.

Archie went downstairs to breakfast.

Andrew Herrick's funeral took place that morning at eleven.

Archie had announced firmly that he was much too busy to go. Janey, who had no excuse and an uncomfortable social conscience, went alone. She found it very trying, even worse than she had feared.

The weather was still overcast, grass wet and sodden after the heavy rain. They stood round the open grave, the rich full voice of the Vicar reading, lingered on the syllables to give to each its awful slow solemnity. While the trees above them dripped, dripped as if to punctuate each pause with mournful tiny sound. Janey tried not to hear, tried not to see the others' faces: Cyril Herrick with his father beside him; over there, standing apart, Johnny; Mrs. Lambert, Monica, Mrs. Ingles, Cuthbert Wilkinson.

The voice went on and on. The old churchyard with its heavy trees, the open grave, the broken group they made, all seemed to Janey to be etched in immobility, dreadful and permanent. Against her will, lines remembered spaced themselves with measured throb:

> And now my heart is as a broken fount,
> Wherein tear-drippings stagnate, split down ever
> From the dank thoughts that shiver
> Upon the sighful branches of my mind.

Ugh! Janey shivered.

A drop, larger than any before, hit the crown of her hat with a plop that was audible and somehow indecent and almost farcical. She raised her eyes to find herself looking into Johnny's. He had shifted his position slightly, as though to make sure of this. Across the space which separated them, only the length of that sharp brown gap in the green grass, an untidy mound of earth, he was gazing at her with an intentness which seemed to plead. Janey hoped her eyes had answered, for after a moment he looked away.

I'll manage to speak to him as soon as this is over, if it's ever over, Janey said to herself, changing her weight from one very wet foot to the other.

And then finally it was over. They began to move away in broken twos and threes. The Herricks lingered behind to speak with the Vicar. Monica made an unsuccessful attempt to hang back; but was shepherded neatly between her mother and the inner light of Mr. Wilkinson. So, with even her ankles looking rebellious, she was marched decorously away.

By the lich-gate Johnny was waiting. He slipped his hand under her elbow, and Janey's bag, which had been held in the crook of her arm, tilted. Janey caught it and tucked it against her other side.

"Hello, Johnny—"

"Hello, Janey, may I walk some of the way home with you?"

"I'd love it, of course you may."

They paced silently side by side. Their feet, her little brogues small beside his, came down in rhythm on the glistening brown leaves of the walk: right, left, right, left. They turned in step and took the footpath through the fields. The unbroken rhythm their feet made began to hypnotize Janey. It became very important that she should not lose step, that she should place each foot just so, level with Johnny's, timed exactly. It became more important than speech. Speech might spoil this perfection. Right, left, right, left. All at once they were at the stile. They stopped, the spell broken, and immediately Janey felt angry with both of them. They must talk. It was terribly important.

"Johnny—"

"Janey Storke, I must talk to you. I've got to talk to you. You're the only one I can talk to. Thank God, it is you. Monica—" Johnny stopped abruptly, his brown fist beat twice against the post of the stile, then dropped to his side. "I'm crazy about Monica, and you know I am. So why I should feel an ass— Hell, it's hard to—to—"

"Johnny, you needn't. I know; you don't have to."

"I love her like the devil. She can drive me nuts sometimes, make me so mad. Janey, it's sickening; we're always fighting. There's no sense to it. Take the other night."

"Monica's sick at herself over that, Johnny. She said—"

"Oh, is she? Is it all right? Didn't she mean it?"

Johnny's wide smile flashed out. He pushed his fingers through his black hair and grinned down again at Janey. He was completely happy.

"That's fine. Everything's oke. Janey, you're a lifesaver. Everything's hunky-dory." But at something in Janey's eyes, he added, "Well, almost."

There was a not-so-happy little silence.

Then Johnny said soberly, "Sure, I know. I'm in a hell of a jam, I haven't forgotten that. But it's different, a whole lot different, now I know Monica doesn't think I did it."

"She's never thought that, Johnny. You misunderstood. It's all rather complicated. I'd rather she told you herself. None of us thought it. That is, Archie and I know—"

"Yes, you and Archie. Thanks, Janey, but the police are on the other side. I've got a damn fine team on mine, though; I just want you to know I know it, and I'm damned grateful. Don't know what

I've done to deserve it. I've been a particularly bright ass over this."
Johnny finished with reminiscent contempt.

Janey did not deny that.

"What do you think I ought to do?"

"How can I say, Johnny, when I don't know what the problem is?"

"You can't. I'd like to tell you the whole thing, Janey. If you
weren't married to Archie, and Archie weren't hand and glove with
the law, I would. But as it is, it wouldn't be fair. I can't tell you and
ask you not to tell them. And as I can't decide whether I ought to
tell them or not, it all comes to the same thing, I don't know and I
can't ask advice."

"Johnny, don't you think," said Janey slowly, "that it's better to
tell the truth? Things usually get straightened out quicker that way?"

"Usually, yes. I'm probably a sanguine fool but what I'm hoping
is that they'll get fixed without my having to talk. You see, someone else is involved."

"But, Johnny, hasn't it occurred to you, you're probably being
quixotic for nothing? The someone else is probably as innocent as
you are?"

"That may be. You realize, Janey, or don't you, that my talking
won't clear me. When I realized that, there didn't seem much use
my shooting off my mouth in any case. When they arrest me—"

"Johnny, they won't!"

"Yes, I think they're going to, Janey. Well, when they do, I shall
get me a good lawyer and let him do the deciding for me. Poor devil,
I feel sorry for him. There's one of the prettiest little cases against
me that ever was. If I didn't know I hadn't murdered Drew, it would
make me sure I had, if you know what I mean. Cheer up, Janey."
Johnny suddenly swooped and, picking her up bodily, set her on
top of the stile, steadying her with hands still at her waist.

"How's your faith? You've a clever husband, Janey. You know
it, and I know it. On a thing like this I'd back him against the local
law any day. You can tell him that from me. Tell him I'm backing
him with everything I've got. And that's the sober truth. Everything I've got, while I've got it."

Johnny let go Janey's waist, took a pace or two backward, put his right hand to his temple.

"Madam, we who stand in the shadow of the gibbet, salute you."

He wheeled, broke into a long loose-jointed lope which carried him away, over the footpath, round a clump of trees, out of sight.

Like Monica, absurdly young, pitiful.

Janey climbed down the other side of the stile and went home to see about lunch.

The lunch which had had Janey's attention was delicious for Monday; even startlingly original in not being that noon a distant relative of Sunday roast. Its orphan-like charm should have merited appreciation; it got none. Archie was abstracted: his fork rose and fell; but no light entered his eyes; no comment rose to his lips.

He was perhaps a little irritated as well. Certainly it was to be seen his morning had not been a success. Janey tried, not very subtly and not at all satisfactorily, to pump him. He grunted several times which meant "stop worrying me," and once he muttered, more to himself than in answer to her, "Wash out. That theory's gone west." After this Janey gave it up, and they finished in silence. It was as he was pushing back his chair that Archie snapped out of his preoccupation and said with alarming suddenness, "Get your things on."

"My things?" quavered Janey, for he had made her jump.

"Your things, girl, your coat, your hat. We're going out."

"Are we?"

"Come along, look lively. I'll get the car. Don't you be forever getting ready." Archie had started for the door. As he went out of it, he threw an explanation over his shoulder, "Blow the cobwebs out of my brain if nothing else."

Janey qualified once more for Monica's title of perfect wife. She was ready in not more than seven minutes after that. Which, considering all the "last things" she had to do, she felt was pretty darn good. Archie seemed to find seven minutes far from a record.

"Ten minutes to put on a hat and coat," he grumbled as she got in beside him. "What do you women find to do?"

"I was only five minutes," said Janey righteously indignant.

Which is the way it goes even in the most perfect of marriages: what men put on, women take off, and vice versa. In fifteen minutes they had forgotten all about it, which is also the way it goes if you are lucky, and the marriage is perfect.

The day, too, had decided to let bygones be bygones. The morning's gray sky was now a pale blue with fast-scurrying white clouds. The trees on the ridge once more flamed with authentic autumn color. Archie had put down the top. He was stubborn in his refusal to buy a closed car. "When I am genuinely middle-aged, mentally, morally, and physically, then I shall come to it, not before," he always said.

Today Janey was glad. She exulted in the wind against her face. A wisp of hair escaped from under her rakish small hat and whipped across her nose. She tucked it back and slid further down behind the windshield, her legs straight, feet against the floor board.

"Going to talk at all?" she asked as the car took the road towards Basingstoke.

"Shall we? This is nice, isn't it?" answered Archie. Another quarter of a mile flew past in companionable silence before he added, "What do you want to talk about?"

"Oh, I don't know," lied Janey.

Archie took one hand off the steering wheel and patted her knee.

"Yes, you do. For one track minds, give me the female. There's all this; it's jolly and lovely, just look at those trees. What more can you want? You should be content; you've got me and the trees and a peaceful forty miles an hour, but is it enough? No. You want to talk about murder."

"We-ell." Janey tried to hover between affirmation and denial.

"Come on, then. It's spoiled now anyway. I'll talk about the blasted thing. But I warn you," he amended with the air of a stubborn child, "I shan't say much."

Janey was hurt, her lips set in an unbecoming little line. Then she turned her head to look at him. She saw only his profile, his eyes were busy with the road before him. But he hadn't the expression she had expected to see. It was, as a matter of fact, very different.

She could not put a name to it exactly, but it caused her lips to curve again and her hand to reach out until it rested for a moment on his arm.

"That's all right, Archie. I didn't know. We've been talking about this together right along, and I didn't realize that you—that you didn't want to tell me about it any more. It doesn't matter."

Archie still kept his eyes on the road, but his voice when he spoke was a caress and a blessing.

"My sweet, I adore you. Do you know how unique you are? You are delectable *and* you are discreet. A glandular combination hitherto unknown to science. And, Ducky, I trust you utterly. You should know that. No, Janey, you mustn't think for one moment I don't want to tell you what I'm thinking because you're you. That makes me want to, dreadfully, just to prove how wrong you are. It's never that. It's something I don't believe you can guess."

Janey laughed and turned a face merry with teasing up to his.

"I can't? That just shows your conceit. It's easy. I can get it in one."

Archie smiled down at her. "I'll give you three," he offered.

"I don't need three guesses, thank you. You won't tell me now because you aren't sure you're right. And if you aren't, you're too vain to let anybody know it, even me."

Archie turned a little pink about the ears. "Loathsome female," he said. "If you have no respect for your lord and master, you should spare him that dreadful knowledge. Am I to have no mystery?"

"Oh, I'm not always sure. Sometimes—"

"Hurrah for that! Once a year I am permitted to slightly baffle. That cheers me enormously. I suppose that's a good married-male average."

"Don't be silly," said Janey somewhat irrelevantly. A moment later she remembered her duty. "Archie, you've passed the thirty mark."

The speedometer needle dropped to thirty, crept up again to thirty-four, and stayed there.

"Let's have tea here, shall we?" Archie suggested.

"Here in Basingstoke?" Janey sounded surprised. "If you want to; but it's early. We could drive through and go on back the other way, we'd be in plenty of time for tea at home."

"We could. We'll go home the other way in any case, but let's tea here. I feel like tea out."

"All right," agreed Janey good-naturedly.

Somewhat over an hour later Janey's good nature had worn very thin. It had distinct bare patches at the elbows. The elbows had, with the aid of hand and wrist, been supporting Janey's chin on and off between cigarettes for a sufficiently long period to wear down anything. Before her was a depressingly cold tea. The charms of Ye Whyte Ladye revealed themselves as thin also, thin and bogus.

"Drat Archie, what can he be doing all this time!" Janey viciously struck a match for her sixth cigarette and fixed her eyes on the door. In desperate boredom she went back to what Archie had told her about Turner. Perhaps she could find a clue to Archie's activities in that. Passed in review, however, it seemed shabbier in possibilities than before.

Turner had seen Wilkinson. He had denied everything: taking the letter, a problematical quarrel with Herrick. Nothing there, or if there was, she couldn't find it. Of course his denial was in a way damning, but it didn't seem to get them any further.

Turner had seen Cyril and his father, too, but only to inform them that it was murder. Nothing new there. Archie had said he was quite sure Burford Herrick suspected it when the inquest was adjourned. Roger had been slightly ridiculous, Janey had always thought, trying to keep that back. Of course it had saved them publicity. A blank there, then.

What more? Oh, yes, Scotland Yard was still busy trying to trace Andrew between the time he left Gray's and the train down; also—and this time seemed the one that really mattered—after he got to Paddington again at half past twelve. But Archie said they'd had no luck so far. No, it simply couldn't have anything to do with Turner. Unless—that was it, right under her nose all the time! Why had Archie had to see Turner at all that morning? Why was it so important he couldn't come to the funeral? For a moment Janey was elated, then she collapsed like a pricked balloon. What was the good of seeing that, when she still didn't know what Archie had seen Turner about. Drat!

And yet, hidden in something Archie had told her was an indication; but Janey, missing its significance, had forgotten all about it.

She stubbed out her cigarette in the ash tray which was of so genteel a size that it was already over-full. If Archie didn't come soon, she'd— She heard the door open and raised her eyes without hope. But it was Archie, after all, and he looked cheerfully unrepentant.

"Did you have a nice tea, dear?" he asked.

It was fortunate Monica was not present to hear what Janey said, it might have disillusioned her.

Janet Prescribes Scones for Nerves

Janey pushed her chair back from the dining-room table so she could sit sideways and cross her knees. It was depressing, eating lunch alone. She sighed and reached for the porcelain box holding her cigarettes. She lit one, took a puff or two, then rang the bell. Mary appeared at once.

"You may clear the table, Mary; I've finished."

"But you've eaten hardly anything. Didn't I get the curry right this time?" Mary was aggrieved.

Janey hastened to mollify. "The curry was perfect, Mary, nice and dry, just the way it should be. It was the best you've ever done. I just wasn't hungry."

Mary looked relieved, but she still hovered. The cheese dish, which she had picked up, remained suspended in mid-air a few inches from Janey's nose.

"What is it, Mary? Did you want to ask me something?"

"Yes, madam. I wondered if it would be all right if I went out this afternoon instead of tomorrow?"

Janey's unhappy notion that a domestic crisis was impending evaporated. "Why, yes, I think so, I shall be in."

"Thank you, madam." The cheese dish descended on a tray where salt and pepper hastily joined it. "There aren't many dishes this noon, and I can catch the two o'clock bus."

"All right, Mary." Janey got up. "Switch the telephone over to the study before you go out, so I can take any calls that come for the Doctor."

Janey went upstairs to the bedroom to fetch her book. She would have to give up her idea of a walk, but it didn't matter, and perhaps Archie might phone her from London. She tucked her book under her arm and crossed to the dressing table to powder her nose. She knew she wasn't being very fair to be so annoyed with Archie. After all, she'd told him it was all right; and if he wanted to be mysterious, surely he had the right; it would be horrid if he felt he hadn't, if he thought she always wanted to pry into his mind But I can't help being curious, she said to herself in justification.

The telephone started ringing as she reached the top of the stairs. At the bottom she almost collided with Mary hurrying from the kitchen. "These tiresome extensions," muttered Janey. "Where's it ringing?"

"I've switched it over, madam. It's the study. Shall I—"

"No, run along and get off. I'll take it."

Janey ran down the passage, dodged through the study and round Archie's big chair, paused for a second to catch her breath, lifted the receiver, and said, "Dr. Storke's residence."

When she heard the voice at the other end, she hooked one foot about the leg of the telephone stool and drew it to her. She sat down, and her face settled into resigned impatience. At intervals she said, "Yes, Mrs. Jenkins. . . . I'm very sorry, Mrs. Jenkins. . . . But, as I've told you, the Doctor had to go to London, so he can't . . . . That's too bad, perhaps you had better send for Dr. Hill . . . Yes, I understand. . . . Yes, but he is taking Dr. Storke's emergency calls today. . . . Oh, isn't it? Yes, yes, I'll tell him as soon as he comes in. . . . Not until evening I'm afraid. . . . Yes. . . . Yes. . . . Good-by."

"Fool!" hissed Janey as soon as the receiver was safely in place. Bored and somehow uneasy, she went to the window and stood looking out at the garden. She hoped there wouldn't be a frost; the dahlias were lovely this year. She especially liked her new singles, they were more lovely than the big decoratives, less vulgar. Those yellows, clear, but with just a hint of green, they— Behind her the telephone rang again. "It's going to be one of those afternoons," she said aloud.

This time she sat down before she answered, "Dr. Storke's residence."

To her surprise it was not a patient. The voice said, "This is Inspector Turner speaking. Is Dr. Storke in?"

"No, he's not." Then, in the hope of satisfying perhaps a little of her curiosity, Janey added hurriedly, "This is Mrs. Storke, Inspector. Can I help you?"

"Oh, good afternoon, Mrs. Storke," said the telephone politely. It went on doubtfully, "Thank you. I wanted to speak to the Doctor. Do you know when he'll be in?"

"Not until just before dinner; he's gone to London."

"London?" Turner sounded disconcerted. There was a short pause.

"I don't want to wait till then."

Turner's voice suddenly altered as though he had made up his mind. "It's about the dog, Mrs. Storke."

"The dog?" said Janey, bewildered.

"Mr. Herrick's airedale, ma'am."

"Oh, Mac. What about—"

"I want to bury him. If the Doctor doesn't want him again, I'd like to get him buried. We haven't any proper place to keep him, and he's— That is, it's very inconvenient, if you see what I mean, ma'am."

"Yes, I see, of course." Janey answered hastily. "But I don't understand what Dr. Storke has to do with it."

"He had us dig him up yesterday. He was doing a P.M. on him yesterday morning."

"Oh, yes, of course," said Janey again. So that was what Archie was busy about during the funeral!

"Do you think," insisted Turner's voice, "the Doctor's through with him? He left without seeing me, and so I don't know. I'd like to get that dog buried."

Janey dragged her attention back from profitless speculation.

"Naturally, Inspector. Of course, I can't say for certain whether the Doctor has finished but I should think he had. I should think it would be all right."

"Thank you, Mrs. Storke. Will you let the Doctor know for me when he comes back?"

"Yes," said Janey, and then she couldn't resist adding, "If it isn't all right, you could dig him up again, couldn't you?"

The telephone muttered something indistinct and unquestionably impolite, then recovered itself, "Er—yes. Thank you. Good-by."

Janey was smiling as she replaced the receiver. Poor Turner, obviously she wasn't the only one Archie annoyed and mystified.

She had been reading in peace for perhaps half an hour when the doorbell rang. She put down her book in horror. What if it was the Vicar? Mary was out; she'd have to go to the door herself, and then she'd be caught. She took slight comfort when she remembered it wasn't the first of the month. He wouldn't be bringing the parish magazine, so perhaps it wasn't; anyhow, she'd have to go.

She braced herself as she opened the door, fixing a mechanical smile of welcome which changed to surprise and pleasure. Monica and Johnny stood there together, and they looked happy and eager.

"Hello, Janey," they said in unison.

"Come in," said Janey, holding the door wide. "Oh, I am so glad to see you. I was afraid it was the Vicar, and Mary's out, and I hadn't a prayer to escape."

"We came to see you and Archie," said Monica following Janey down the passage.

"Isn't Archie here? We hoped we'd be lucky and catch you both," explained Johnny, ducking his head expertly under the low beam at the angle of the study door.

"He's in London," answered Janey for the third time that afternoon. "We'll have to sit in here, so's I can take any calls that come."

"I like the study." Monica sat down on the window seat, put one leg under her, and swung the other gently back and forth. She gave the impression of waiting impatiently for something to begin. Johnny lounged beside her and put his hand into the pocket of his tweed coat.

"Cigarette, Monnie?" Janey held out her box. "Johnny?"

"I'd rather smoke my pipe if you don't mind." Johnny brought it and his pouch out of his pocket. He began to fill the bowl. Janey watched him. Wasn't it odd the curious absorbed concentration all men gave to doing that? Monica glanced at him, her impatience seemed to come to a head.

"Janey, we came over to see you because we wanted to tell you and Archie all about— We have decided— Johnny do stop fiddling!"

The last shred of tobacco arranged to his satisfaction, Johnny put his pipe in his mouth and struck a match. Over its flame he smiled slowly at Monica. "Just a minute, till I get this going." The match moved over the bowl in small ritualistic circles. Smoke appeared, thin, blue, at last thick and white. Johnny took his pipe from his mouth and said, "All right. Let's go."

"It's this way—" began Monica.

"We were talking it over—" started Johnny. They both stopped and looked at each other. "Who's going to tell this?" Johnny demanded of her. "Because if we both do, it's going to be damned confusing."

"You'd better," decided Monica. "I'll keep still, it's your story. Only for heaven's sake get on with it."

"Mayn't I kiss you first?" Johnny teased her. Monica wrinkled her nose at him.

"Yes, do; that would be nice," encouraged Janey resting her head against the back of Archie's tall chair. "Why are you in such a rush, Monica?"

Johnny pretended to misunderstand.

"That's sweet of you!" He grinned, and got up as if to come over to where Janey was sitting. Janey flushed.

"Johnny, don't tease."

Monica laughed. "Now you know how I felt. Sit down, idiot."

Johnny sat down and, resting his elbows on his knees, leaned forward, his pipe held between both hands. He looked over at Janey. His expression was all at once sober and businesslike.

"Well, Janey, we had a long talk this morning. After seeing you yesterday, I decided not to go back to London until I'd talked things over with Monnie. I was going back; Cyril and Uncle Burford left yesterday afternoon, by the way."

"Yes. Archie told me."

"Anyhow, the upshot of our talk was we decided to come and tell you the whole story."

"There isn't really much you don't know already," interrupted Monica.

"No." Johnny agreed. "I had no idea how much you've both known. It makes all my stewing about whether to talk awfully pointless."

"But just the same, we thought—" Monica caught herself up. "Go on, Johnny, I'm sorry. Really, I won't—"

"We thought that perhaps there might be something in the full details to give us an idea. At any rate it wouldn't do any harm to try."

"No," agreed Janey. "I'm sorry Archie isn't here, I'm not very good at seeing things. I remember well, though, so perhaps it doesn't matter."

"No, just as good your telling him. As you know, I was waiting for Monica to come back again on Wednesday night. She'd said she would get out somehow but she couldn't say how long she'd be. I was mad as all hell and I wanted to do things about it. I knew Drew was coming back on the nine-fifteen and I could just go to Whiteleaves and have it out with him. Not that that was any good, but I wanted to get it off my chest. I would have gone, too, only I'd promised Monnie I wouldn't, at any rate, till I'd seen her again.

"Well, I waited and waited and I began to cool off. I began to think it had been a good thing I hadn't seen Drew earlier after all. No telling what I might have done when I was in such a filthy temper. I'd parked my car round by the new council cottages. Couldn't stay outside Monnie's house and I knew Monica would look for me there all right. I smoked a good many cigarettes. It was cold, so I got out the rug and wrapped it round me. And then— Well, I'd had an awful day in town rushing here and there getting the dope on the money and I was all in. Being so mad hadn't helped either. I went to sleep, sound asleep; slept like a log.

"When I woke up, I turned on the dashboard light. It was a quarter to two. It was no use waiting for Monnie any longer, that was obvious. Something had happened to prevent her getting out before, and naturally she wouldn't come now. I was cold and stiff and fed up. I decided to buzz off to town as fast as I could. But as I stepped on the self-starter, I happened to look at the petrol gauge and saw I was low on petrol. That was a curse. There'd be no pumps open until almost into London. I lit a cigarette and wondered what to do. Then I remembered I could cadge a tin from Drew's garage. He always keeps—kept a couple of full tins. The only thing bothering me was could I get it without waking him. I decided I could. The bedroom he used is at the side of the house; he wouldn't be likely to hear the car.

"I backed her up and drove there. As I came round the bend in the driveway, my lights shone on the front of the house, and I almost jumped out of my seat—"

"It was Mother," broke in Monica as though she wanted to help Johnny.

"Yes, it was Mrs. Lambert. I couldn't mistake her, my lights caught her full for a second. As soon as they touched her, she ran away from the house and disappeared into the shrubbery."

"Where the gate is to our path, you know, Janey." Again Monica interrupted. Johnny turned rather miserably to her, but she gave him a smile which seemed to choose once and for all between her loyalties.

"That was why Johnny wouldn't explain to us. I—I think it was damn wonderful of him," she ended, defying in advance his protest.

"Oh, come, Monnie, what else could anybody do?"

Monica tilted her chin at him. "I don't care. Lots of people would have done something else if they'd been on your spot. Wouldn't they Janey?" Without waiting for a reply she rushed on, "And I only got it out of him by accident. I told him I'd seen the car and that I knew Mother was about, and he thought I'd seen the car go in, not leaving, and that I'd actually seen Mother. And he started to tell me that he knew Mother couldn't have—" Monica stopped in full spate, and said in a lowered voice, "She couldn't have, you both know that, don't you?"

"Of course, Monica," said Janey.

"Don't be an ass, darling," said Johnny.

"No; but she was up to something. Do you know what I think? Mother was very pally with Mr. Herrick at one time, when she let him have the money to invest. And then Mr. Wilkinson came along. Mother's fallen hard for all that rot of his. She thinks he's wonderful. And you wouldn't think he could, but I believe he's really madly in love with Mother. I haven't been able to make out whether he knows he is.

"Anyhow, I think he found out for Mother about her money and got himself all stirred up in righteous indignation. Of course he'd been jealous, and I think she was flattered by it and didn't try to calm him down as she should have done. Then I think she got frightened and wrote a letter or something to warn Mr. Herrick and ask him not to see 'Wilky-Pilky.' Have you ever thought that could be the explanation?"

"No," lied Janey, "but it sounds very reasonable. I should think that's what happened."

"I'm sure that's it," said Monica satisfied. "Go on, Johnny, you were where you were coming up the drive."

"Yes. I was flummoxed, as I said before; but the house seemed all dark so I kept on going. If Drew was up, I'd have to see him, that was all. I drove on round the house to the back where the garage is. I shut off the engine and began calling softly, 'Mac! Mac!' I wanted him to hear my voice so he wouldn't start barking. I got out and went towards his kennel. Then I sort of felt something was wrong. I'd expected to hear the rattle of his chain as he got up, I suppose. There wasn't a sound. I stooped down and put my hand inside. I had on my heavy driving gloves, but the minute I touched his head I knew something had happened to him. I squatted on my heels and struck a match. Then I saw the poor brute. Hell, it was awful."

Johnny took a deep breath, looked at his pipe as if in surprise to find it had gone out, and a little silence settled for a moment. A moment in which Janey saw all too unbearably that stiff, poor, hairy figure, the gilt of chain about its throat, a tongue lolling.

"Well? Then, Johnny—"

"Then, Janey, I was scared stiff. I wanted to beat it. I didn't know why I was scared cold but I was. I wanted nothing in the world so much as to beat the hell out of there. But I knew I couldn't. I knew I had to go inside. So I did. I got my key out of my pocket somehow and I unlocked the kitchen door. I switched on the light. God knows what I expected to see, but there wasn't a thing. Everything was all right. I just stood there. I was telling myself everything was oke and I could go away now; arguing with myself because of course I knew I had to go on until I found what there was to find.

"After I'd kicked myself for being a coward long enough, I opened the door, and as soon as I could see down the passage, I saw there was a light under the sitting room door, just a crack of light because the door was closed. I'm telling you that passage seemed miles long, and it took me years to go down it. At last I got there and got my hand on the knob, and then I felt I couldn't get the door open fast enough. I sort of jumped on it and flung it open.

"Then I saw Drew. He— No matter, let's skip that. I lost my head. I don't know what I did exactly. I must have taken off one of my gloves 'cause I remember picking it up. I must have dropped it again somehow because the police found it. Turner showed it to me. I know I turned off the reading lamp. I had some idea it would be better if the room were dark so I wouldn't have to see—so no one could see, as though it made any difference. God, I've been seeing it all over and over again. I can't stop seeing it!" Johnny covered his face with his hands, his long fingers were tense. Ashamed, he ran them in his characteristic gesture through his tumbled hair. "Sorry, girls, to let myself go all emotional on you."

The telephone rang sharply. Janey said, "Just a moment," glad of the interruption.

"Hello."

"Hello? Is it you, Janey?" came the Colonel's voice.

"Yes. How are you, Roger?"

"All right, thank you. Is Archie there?"

The Colonel sounded hurried and urgent.

"No, I'm sorry; he's in town."

"London? Damn it all, is he? Do you know where I could reach him?"

"No, I'm sorry; I don't know where he was going."

"Blast! Damned unfortunate! If he should phone you— No, that's no good."

"If he phones, I'll ask him to call you," volunteered Janey, realizing that Roger must want Archie badly to be so abrupt.

"Thanks, no use, Janey. I've got to go to London myself right away. I wanted Archie to come along." Then, suddenly conscious of having treated Janey in a somewhat barrack-room manner, the Colonel began to apologize.

"Roger, nonsense, not at all. . . . Good-by."

Janey went back to the big chair. Monica and Johnny were sitting very close together on the window seat; they smiled at her.

"Well, children, is that all the story?"

"That's all," answered Johnny. "Except for how I came to be so late getting back to London. And that's short and simple, especially simple. I forgot to take the petrol."

"I don't wonder. Poor Johnny, it must have been ghastly for you."

"I forgot the petrol and I grew panicky, too. I remembered all the wild things I'd said to Monica and I remembered the hell-awful row Drew and I had during breakfast. Self-preservation began to function. I realized I was in a spot. Somehow it never occurred to me that Drew might have killed himself. I don't know why. I thought I'd be clever. I tried to cut over a back way onto the other road, get to London by Beaconsfield and Uxbridge. I couldn't have done anything more stupid or anything that looked worse. I see that now, but I wasn't thinking any too clearly then. And to cap it all, I got lost."

"Lost? How in the world?"

"Between Mongerton and Wantage. Those footling little roads twist and turn, at night it's hopelessly confusing. Everything went wrong that could go wrong. I got a puncture somewhere at the end of nowhere. I hadn't a flash and I had the devil of a time changing wheels. At last I got to Yattendon, or nearly there; then I ran out of petrol. Walking to find a garage I could awaken, what do I have to do but pass a policeman! When that happened, I decided I was sunk for sure. And how right I was."

"But, Johnny, you haven't been arrested yet," consoled Monica. Janey felt this was such cold comfort it needed hasty wrapping up.

"Come on," she said quickly. "Let's go out to the kitchen and make tea. It's early yet, but we can bake some scones."

"That's a swell idea," agreed Johnny with enthusiasm. He linked his arm through Monica's and pulled her to her feet. Janey hurried out ahead to give him time for the kiss he'd mentioned.

Three quarters of an hour later Janey was just taking the scones from the oven when a bell rang dimly. She set the baking pan down on the kitchen table.

"Good heavens!" she exclaimed. "The telephone! I'd forgotten all about it. Go ahead you two. Don't let the scones get cold."

It was Archie this time.

"Hello, Ducky, is Roger with you by any chance? I've phoned his place; he's not there."

"No, he isn't," Janey answered with an understandable feeling of repetition. "He phoned you himself about an hour ago. He was going to London and wanted you to go with him."

"God's buttons," said Archie. "Do you know what he wanted?"

"No, he didn't say."

"Say where he was going?"

"No."

"Damn. I must reach him."

"That's too bad, Archie, is it important?"

"Terribly. Never mind, I think I can find him. I'll try his club, or perhaps he's gone to Scotland Yard. Sorry, Ducky, I must ring off, I'm in a hell of a hurry."

"Wait, wait a minute. Archie, what have you been doing? Will you be home for dinner?"

"Reading *Punches*, my love. And you'd better expect me when you see me. I love you, good-by."

There was a click of finality.

"Drat that man!" said Janey to an empty wire.

CHAPTER XI
TUESDAY 5.30-6.30

Again Nothing is Eaten

The taxi drew up with a jerk. Archie sprang out and fumbled in his pocket for change. His face was crumpled with anxiety, it had lost all trace of its accustomed expression of impish humor. As a matter of fact, Archie felt uncomfortably queasy; he was nervous. He hadn't felt like this for years, not since that awful day at school: he'd just been made a prefect and he had— "Lord," breathed Archie to himself as memory returned.

Standing there on the London pavement, he was for the moment once again that far-off boy, saw again in vivid detail the shabby cluttered study, the head master's face. Whew! was it going to be as bad as that? Roger was going to be furious. I'm in for an awful wigging, summed up Archie. Mentally he squared his shoulders, straightened his tie.

To the uniform by the front entrance Archie said, "I am Dr. Storke. I phoned the Yard. Inspector Nokes expects me."

"Yes, sir. I was told to watch out for you. He's in the building now."

Archie was escorted to an elevator. "Take this gentleman to the second floor, Harry."

The elevator shot upwards, sucked to a sickening stop, the door clanged open. Archie approached the policeman standing in the corridor.

"I am Dr. Storke."

"I have orders to admit you as soon as you arrived, sir." The policeman moved to one of the doors, opened it, announced, "Dr. Storke," and stood aside for Archie to enter.

The room had several people in it, but the first thing Archie saw was Roger's broad back. Another man, also with his back turned, stood beside the Colonel. They were looking down at something which was hidden from Archie by their positions.

As Archie stepped forward, they moved apart; and Archie saw what it was.

"God! Cyril," Archie exclaimed.

The Colonel turned a stern face upon him.

"Yes, Cyril. And he's dead."

"Dead!" Archie took another step forward. "Roger, let me explain. I didn't expect this. I—"

The Colonel silenced him curtly.

"If you have any explanations, they can wait; no importance. Inspector Nokes, Dr. Storke."

The large square man beside the Colonel shook Archie's hand. "Suicide, as you'll see, Doctor. Take a look for yourself. Give you the circumstances presently. Fred," he said to a man with a camera, "you finished?"

Archie went reluctantly and stood looking down at Cyril's body: in the right temple, a round black hole; on the rug near the outflung hand, a revolver; Cyril. Poor bloody little bastard, and he'd said, I'd do anything for Drew. He'd dared to say that! Archie knew he was guilty, but Archie could feel only overwhelming pity.

He heard Inspector Nokes' quiet official voice. "You've got the prints, Williams? Right, then you can clear out. As you go out, tell the men they can take the body and send Monroe in."

The room began to empty. The policeman appeared in the doorway.

"Monroe, get a hold of Mr. Herrick yet?"

"Yes, sir. They said at Gray's they thought he'd come in. I left a message he was to come here, sir."

"All right. That'll be all for now. Stay outside in the corridor and you can let Mr. Herrick in when he comes."

Monroe disappeared, and there were two different policemen in the doorway. They carried a long narrow wicker basket.

Archie moved out of their way. Going out, they had difficulty maneuvering the basket through the corridor door because the tiny entrance hall was at right angles to it.

"Take it down the service elevator."

Inspector Nokes came back into the room. "We try not to upset the management more than we can help. High-class apartments like these, a thing like this doesn't do them any good. Now, sir," turning to Archie, "I expect you'd like to hear all about it."

"Yes, I should," Archie answered, feeling more and more like a miserable small boy brought before a kind but firm master. "But first—" Archie caught himself, he had almost said "sir," "but first, before you begin, I'd like to explain why I—I phoned the Yard to—"

Inspector Nokes cut him short, impatiently polite.

"That's quite understandable, Doctor, quite all right. You've been in on the case from the start; only too glad to have you."

"Of course, Storke." The Colonel's use of his last name made it all more dreadfully official than ever. Archie felt useless and superfluous. "But—" he muttered.

"Glad you located me," finished the Colonel.

"Won't you sit down, sir?" suggested Inspector Nokes with more than a hint of impatience in his quiet voice. "We may just have time before Mr. Herrick gets here. Don't look forward to the job of breaking it to him," he added in parenthesis.

That was so, Herrick would be here shortly. Archie sat down. "Let's have it," he said.

Inspector Nokes marshaled his facts in orderly array. He began where he should: at the beginning.

"As you know, sir, we have been trying to trace Mr. Andrew Herrick's movements after the twelve-thirty-three train. We had no luck until yesterday. Yesterday evening one of my men reported that he had got hold of a taxi driver who thought he might have seen Mr. Herrick. I had the man in for questioning. His story was that while cruising through one of the quiet squares near Paddington station, he noticed a long foreign sports car parked by the curb. The time was approximately twelve-forty. A man was sitting at the wheel, and another man came walking from the corner and joined him. He thought the second man was carrying a small bag. We got a description of the car from him. It sounded as though it might be Cyril Herrick's Mercedes. To tell the truth I didn't think much of it, too vague by a long way. However, it doesn't do to let anything go, so I detailed one of my men to interview young Mr. Herrick. He saw him early this morning and reported back to me. He had formed the impression that Mr. Herrick was nervous and uneasy, unduly so. This made me wonder if there might be something in it, after all."

Archie moved restlessly in his chair, and Inspector Nokes paused, expecting him to speak. When he didn't, the Inspector went on, "I came over here, saw the man who's on the door now, and got the night porter's address from him. I questioned the night porter myself. Eventually I got him to admit that he had dozed off for a short time early Thursday morning. That opened the possibility that young Herrick, after coming in at one-thirty, could have left here again without being seen, taken out his car, and met his uncle again somewhere." Inspector Nokes interrupted himself to turn to the Colonel.

"Undoubtedly he had arranged to do this when he met Herrick for the first time near Paddington."

"Yes, that is fairly obvious," agreed the Colonel.

"After I'd broken the alibi, I decided to question Cyril Herrick more fully. I also arranged that the taxi driver should be brought along to see if he could identify the car. I telephoned Colonel Copeland; it was not rightly our case, and I wanted him present. Mind you, we had very little so far."

"Very little," put in the Colonel. "Extraordinary his nerve should have broken like that. Doesn't it surprise you, Archie?"

Archie did not trouble to answer, he was impatient for Nokes to finish. "Go on, Inspector," he urged.

"Colonel Copeland picked me up at Scotland Yard, and we came right over here chancing to find Mr. Herrick in. We were in luck, for the porter said he'd been in all afternoon. We came up, rang, and when after a time we'd had no answer, I sent for the porter to open the door. You know what we found."

"Show Dr. Storke the letter, Nokes. That explains the whole thing, Archie," said the Colonel with an air of melancholy satisfaction."

"Another letter?" Archie was surprised. "Good Lord, this case rustles with them."

"Well, this one is the last; it closes the case." Inspector Nokes took an envelope from his pocket and handed it across to Archie.

"We found it under the newspaper in the grate. The fire had been laid fresh over it. You'll see there has been an attempt to burn it."

Archie turned the scorched envelope over in his hands. At one corner the paper had been charred away.

"Cyril must have received it Wednesday morning, thrown it on the fire, and thought it had been burned, as he meant it to be." The Colonel always liked to dot his "i's" and cross his "t's."

"Lucky for us, it's been warmish, and he hasn't had a fire since he got back from Pennerford yesterday, or it would have been." Inspector Nokes shook his head almost sadly. "Amazing how careless the average murderer is, we see it time and time again."

"Yes, careless, yet careful in spots," Archie half agreed.

"Look at the postmark, Archie. Pennerford, Tuesday night. You recognize the writing, of course?"

"Andrew Herrick's. The letter—"

"Read it, man. That gives the whole thing."

Archie drew it out. Writing covered both sides of the single sheet. The crisp heavy paper was discolored only on the back. One top corner and the bottom corner that, when folded in the envelope, had lain over it, were burned away.

White
Tues

Cyril:

I have reason to suppose y

did not deposit the thousand pounds as I

told you to do. You must be mad. It was

my only chance to tide things over. If you
did not, your father will find out we have
been speculating with his money. Let me remind you that as he put his English interests in my hands I must account to him. You
have used his money just as I have. If you
think by covering yourself with my check
you are going to put the blame entirely on
me, you are much mistaken. You have forgotten, have you not, that I hold absolute
proof of one occasion at least upon which you
allowed the cleverness of your penmanship t
overcome your discretion. You father i
likely to be lenient with you over th
I shall not hesitate to tell him i
becomes necessary.

Archie's mouth was grim. He turned the sheet over and read on.

I get the papers tomorrow. I
y have no opportunity to look them
r before returning to Pennerford. Nor
all I probably be able to see you without Burford being present. If it is as I
think, and you have double crossed me, I
shall return to London by the eleven o'
clock tomorrow night. You are to meet me.
Perhaps you have an explanation. If you
have not, I shall be forced to think of
my own safety. Mere speculation pales beside forgery, my dear nephew. If I am
forced to draw the comparison, I shall
benefit thereby.
Think it over.
Yours,
Andrew Herrick.

When he had come to the end, Archie did not at once give up the letter. He remained frowning at Andrew Herrick's neat, clerklike writing, that writing so devoid of character, so noncommittal. The first time he had ever seen it was on another letter: a letter that the Colonel had been so sure was proof that Andrew Herrick had committed suicide. And it hadn't been suicide, it had been murder. This letter, it was foul. Archie folded it, slipped it back in its envelope.

"The swine," he said to no one in particular.

"Eh?" grunted the Colonel. "Oh, I see. You mean the letter. I heartily agree. He must have been a nasty bit of work. Still, Archie, you must admit that doesn't excuse what Cyril did."

"No. No, nothing could do that, of course."

"And you told me Cyril was devoted to his uncle!"

"He was. There is no doubt of that, none."

"Nice way he had of showing it," scoffed the Colonel, jolted off his balance into vulgar sarcasm.

"Look here, Roger, you've got me all wrong. You're both going to be very angry with me when I tell you how criminally lax I've been. I should have prevented this from happening."

"Nonsense," barked the Colonel. "For my part I confess I feel a certain amount of relief. Perhaps it doesn't say much for me as an officer of the law, but I can't help being glad the boy took this way out."

"Between us, so am I. Saved us the expense of the trial. And what's more, you can never be sure of a conviction." Inspector Nokes was firm, yet soothing.

Archie felt better. A good man that: the very way he sat, squarely upright in his chair, showed confidence in himself. All the same, I am sorry for him, thought Archie. Herrick would be there any minute now. That was going to be sticky for the Inspector, for all of them. Archie fought down an ignoble impulse towards flight. He didn't want to face Herrick when he was told. What would he do when he knew? God! it was hellish. Cyril dead. Perhaps, if Cyril'd lived, there might have been a chance he'd have got off. Well, it was too late now to think about that.

They heard the outer door open, and Monroe's voice saying, "They are in there, sir. Will you please go in?" In a louder tone he announced, "Mr. Burford Herrick."

Automatically they rose to their feet and turned to face the doorway.

Herrick paused on the threshold. For a moment he stood supporting himself with one hand against the doorjamb. He looked drawn and dreadfully tired and years older. The light from the lamp they had turned on glinted across his heavy horned-rimmed glasses. His stoop was more pronounced; in every line of his figure was grief and utter despair.

"My son—" he faltered. "What has happened to my son?"

"Mr. Herrick," Inspector Nokes crossed the room to him, "Mr. Herrick, you must try to pull yourself together."

"Yes, yes. Yes, I must." He walked unsteadily into the circle of light. Inspector Nokes pulled forward a chair.

As though he had become conscious of them for the first time, Burford murmured their names, "Colonel Copeland—Dr. Storke."

The Colonel cleared his throat, forced speech from it. "Mr. Herrick, this is hard for us. It is terrible for you."

"What— What has— God, man! Can't you speak?"

"Your son is dead, Mr. Herrick. He shot himself this afternoon."

"No. No. It can't be! That's impossible." Burford looked wildly from one to the other in frantic eagerness. Then he covered his face with his hands. His voice came broken and almost inaudible, "Cyril dead! Suicide! I—I can't believe it—"

"*I don't.*" Archie spoke suddenly into the stillness. And after he had spoken there was stillness again. It was as though he had not spoken, as though no one could believe that he had.

And, curiously, it was Burford who said at last, "You don't? What are you saying? What do you mean?"

"I mean that he was murdered."

"Doctor, are you mad? Do you know what you are saying? You must be mad. Murdered? Who would murder Cyril?"

Archie sprang to his feet.

"You. You, *Andrew* Herrick!"

A chair crashed over.

"Watch him, Nokes!" cried Archie.

There was a short scuffle by the door. Then stillness, save for the sharp sound of rapid breathing.

Archie felt weak at the knees. His chair was right behind him, he sat down. He had moved only to his feet, but his heart was pounding as though he had been running.

Slowly he raised his eyes to the face of the man pinioned in Nokes' strong grip.

As their eyes met, the prisoner said, "You are mad." Again Archie was accused.

"No use, Herrick," Archie answered him very gently, "no use. I have proof."

After a little pause he added even more gently, "I saw Sir Emmet Lucas today and he told me the name of the man I needed for proof, a Mr. Hunter-Smith, your dentist, Herrick. I have seen him—so you see it is all up."

With a sudden movement that took Nokes by surprise, Herrick freed himself and took two sharp paces nearer to Archie.

The stooping figure straightened, heels came together with precision. He swept from his eyes the horn-rimmed spectacles. All at once Andrew Herrick stood before them, erect, on parade, debonair, suave.

"My congratulations, Dr. Storke, and my mistake. I took you for a nonentity."

Archie rose again to his feet. They faced each other across a short space of floor.

"Let me congratulate you in return," answered Archie softly. "You are a superb actor. What a pity that you are a murderer as well. Your Burford was the finest bit of character acting I have ever seen."

Andrew Herrick bowed, accepted the compliment.

"Tell me one thing. I should like to know: Was he like that?"

"Burford? No. Had he been, I should not have found it necessary to kill him. Good-by, Dr. Storke. In you I have found one man whom I can thoroughly respect."

Andrew Herrick held out his hand. To his own surprise Archie found that he had taken it.

Whatever Andrew Herrick might be, he was a good loser.

Whisky and Sodas for All

Janey, Monica, and Johnny sat round the bridge table playing Storke three-handed contract. A weird game, which aptly symbolized its inventor's mental habits. The rules, like Archie, leaped imaginatively over obstacles to land somehow on their feet.

Tonight the febrile excitements of Storke contract were welcome. The three of them had resorted to it as to a drug, worn out with the suspense and impatience of waiting for Archie. All of fifteen minutes had gone by without Janey's looking at the clock. Johnny had called three no trumps. He went down one, and Janey sat back in triumph.

Monica picked up the cards to deal for Johnny's dummy.

"If only Archie had told you more about it when he telephoned," she said for the eleventh time.

"He should be here any moment now," answered Janey. "If you had got together on your clubs, you'd have made it."

"Monica, why on earth did you lead that heart?" Johnny joined in the post-mortem.

Monica began to deal. "Not concentrating, I'm afraid."

Janey looked across the table.

"How are you now, Johnny? Feeling better?"

"I'm all right now, really." He smiled at her. "You girls have been swell. Coming like that, it was a hell of a shock. I was fond of old Cyril. The whole thing's so damn sordid. I hate that. No matter how you look at it—"

"I know," said Janey. "But there is a side to it that isn't sordid—that is, I don't mean that exactly, only that in spite of all that's sad and shameful, you and Monica are safe now. And I can't be really sorry when I am so glad for you."

"That's how I feel." Monica spoke eagerly. She did not try to hide the happiness in her voice. "I've been so sick with fear for Johnny, and now that's over, oh, I could just shout and sing. I'm not ashamed, not the least bit. I might even sing 'Trees.'"

"Don't you dare." It was good to hear Johnny laugh again. In an unctuous tenor he sang, "'Upon whose bo-som snow has lain; Who in-ti-mate-ly lives with rain'— Holy Cat! Shades of the B.B.C.! It's your bid, Janey."

"One spade," complied Janey in a doubtful, informative tone.

A car drew up outside.

"Archie!" Janey jumped up.

"At last!" exclaimed Johnny.

"Here, let's get the bridge table out of the way," said Monica.

Janey ran to the front door and flung it open.

"Hello, Ducky! Did you think we'd never come?" Archie kissed her.

"It's my fault, Janey," apologized the Colonel over Archie's shoulder.

"Of course it is, she knows that," said Archie. "She knows you by now, Roger. Of course he wouldn't leave town before he had his dinner. Come on in. Who's here, darling?" Archie lowered his voice to ask.

"Monica and Johnny. You don't mind, do you? They've been so anxious—"

Archie went straight to the sitting-room door. "Hello, children. I'm glad you're here."

Janey followed with the Colonel, who crossed the room and held out his hand to Johnny.

"My boy." Barriers of restraint were down. The Colonel was almost emotional. "Will you forgive me?"

"Nothing to forgive, sir," mumbled Johnny, acutely embarrassed.

Janey rushed in upon a self-conscious pause, took it up by the scruff of its neck, as it were, and shook it.

"Why are we all standing up, like this? Roger, Archie, I thought you might like some sandwiches; they're over there by the decanter. We'd all like a drink, I know. Johnny, will you get them, please?"

As usual Janey was successful, for presently they were all quietly grouped round the fire: the plate of sandwiches handy to the Colonel's elbow, Johnny's pipe well alight, and Archie comfortable on the small of his back in his big chair Never happy unless he could get his feet higher than his head, his present position was perfect. A straight upward line of legs to feet braced against the side of the mantelpiece, Archie sighed in contentment.

"Delicious sandwiches, Janey," said the Colonel. He looked at Archie and frowned. "Your husband has been worse than usual."

"He's cross at me because I wouldn't spoil my dinner by explanations." Archie was not at all contrite. "You'd think after keeping me in London against my will, the least he could do was let me eat in peace."

"But, Archie, you are going to tell us, aren't you?" Janey was plaintive.

"You bet your sweet life I am, Ducky. Do you think—" Archie peered over his knees at her. "Do you think I'm lazy or too modest, perhaps? Well, hardly. I've been dying to hear someone say 'Master, tell us all.'"

"If that's all you're waiting for, I'll say it," offered Monica.

"Master, for the love of Mike!" Johnny reached out a long arm and stabbed Archie's knee with the stem of his pipe.

"Ouch, damn you!" said Archie, then, "Now that you've all urged me so prettily, do you want it all or only the high spots? On second thought," he decided, "I shall give you the whole dose whether you want it or not."

"Archie," Janey started excitedly, "how did you—"

Archie raised a hand at her. "Out of order. As our dear Turner would say, 'everything in its place.' Look here, it's no good your all shooting extraneous questions at me. I intend to lecture. Anyone who finds the lecture dull may hold up his hand and be excused."

"You have the floor, Archie." The Colonel flicked a crumb from his last sandwich into the fire and sat back prepared to listen.

"We'll take it in order. In divisions, as it were," Archie began. "First of them is why: motive. Roger knows all this because he had a long telephone powwow with Nokes just before we left the club. Andrew Herrick is too whole-hog a gambler not to know when he's lost. He made a full confession, so we don't have to speculate. So, motive: Your uncle Burford, Johnny, was, it would appear, a severe, autocratic man, an extremely overstuffed, stuffed shirt—" Archie interrupted the beginning of his own lecture as a thought struck him, "Johnny, how was it *you* didn't twig?"

"I know, it seems amazing that I didn't," answered Johnny. "But I couldn't have remembered Burford. I hadn't seen him since I was ten, and then I saw him only once or twice. Besides, it never occurred to me to question. Why should it? Cyril's father, I thought of him like that much more than as my uncle, well, his father was coming to England; and then there he was with Cyril saying 'my Father this and Father that.' And he was so different from Drew. Oh, he looked like him, but he wasn't at all like him otherwise. Even now I can't make him into Drew, if you know what I mean. What's more, they avoided me all the time. Of course I thought that was because they thought that I'd—"

"I see," said Archie. "Where was I? Oh, yes. Well, Burford was a stern, unforgiving sort of cuss. And he picked a bad time to come to England. Andrew and Cyril had been speculating with his money; they'd lost heavily; with Burford on his way they had no time to recoup. Something desperate had to be done. Before he could discover the defalcations, they must act. He was already annoyed with them both, perhaps even suspicious; for he had no patience with Cyril's extravagances and had written several times threatening to cut Cyril out of his will. Cyril was certain, after the last letter, that he had done so. He had also refused to help Andrew. That was the situation. Simply to kill Burford was no solution. Cyril, who, as you all know, was thoroughly spoiled, faced poverty; Andrew, prison for embezzlement.

"With daring and brilliance, Andrew seized the one way out. No one had seen Burford. There was only Johnny, and he was safe enough, as facts have proved. Why should they not kill Burford, and Andrew, posing as Burford, get control of Burford's money? In this last Burford had played into their hands by pulling up stakes, and putting everything into negotiable securities, with the idea of settling down over here. There was a strong family resemblance. And here was the really brilliant psychological stroke: Would anyone question Burford's identity when there was his own son vouching for its genuineness? State a thing boldly enough, and people unconsciously accept it."

"You're right there. That's what did it," murmured the Colonel.

Archie settled lower in his chair before he continued.

"So they planned the suicide hoax. In the guise of father and son they would be asked to identify the body. Andrew did not even lie when he said, 'that is my brother.' Cyril? Perhaps it's harder to understand Cyril. But Andrew had been much closer to him than his father, who was like an unsympathetic stranger. Cyril was educated here, and in all those formative years it was his uncle's influence that shaped him. We all knew what 'Drew' meant to the boy."

Archie sighed and thought again of Cyril's white, unhappy face behind the wheel of the gaudy yellow car, that first day outside Whiteleaves.

"Well?" Janey probed.

"Well, that finishes the first division, why: the motive. Next is how: the method. *I* come into this." Archie stopped to beam at them complacently.

"You do preen, don't you, dear?" Janey remarked with wifely tolerance.

"Let him. He deserves to," pronounced the Colonel handsomely.

"Thanks for those kind words, Roger. I stopped really because I was trying to think just how to go on. Perhaps it'd be more exciting, for the lecture's getting on the dull side, if I give it to you as I discovered it."

"That's just it," broke out Janey, "I can't see how you did."

"The clues were all there, Ducky. Under all our noses. The first one, I admit, meant more perhaps to me than it would to the rest of you. That was because it had to do a little with what Janey so rudely calls my vanity. It was a time clue.

"Roger asked me how long Andrew Herrick had been dead, and I put it between twelve and fifteen hours. With a leaning towards the first. In other words, he had been killed between ten and one o'clock. And I thought nearer ten than one. It was, of course, impossible to be accurate. There had been a fire in the grate, and the body was near it. Moreover, when death has been violent, rigor mortis sets in more quickly, and— Sorry," Archie broke off as he caught a glimpse of Monica's face, "you won't want the medical details. At any rate, when Turner came to me in glee and told me the death couldn't have taken place before two-thirty and was probably even later, I mentally rebelled. I was damn puzzled and I hate to be wrong. But I told myself I must be wrong this time. I consoled myself with the knowledge that under the circumstances it was almost impossible to be sure, even within the limits I'd given. But the doubt stuck, just the same.

"My second clue was the dog. And that, my dear pupils, was the most important clue of the lot. Look at it: The dog was not strangled because he was fierce; a chained dog can harm no one. He was not strangled because he would bark. The objection to this is obvious. If the murderer were a stranger, the dog would have barked before it was possible to silence him. More, it would have been well-nigh impossible to do the strangling. If the murderer were known to the dog, the dog would not bark at all.

"There is the superstition that a dog will howl when there is death. I dismissed this as too fantastic to be the reason. There was also the possibility that suddenly occurred to me halfway through the case that Wilkinson might have doped the dog some hours before killing him: while Andrew was still in London, that is. Even this didn't seem to make much sense because if the dog were successfully doped, which he would have to be to enable Wilkinson to strangle him, why should Wilkinson trouble to kill him at all? Let a doped dog lie, why not? However, to make sure, I did a post-mortem. And was Turner annoyed!" Archie chuckled reminiscently.

"So there was left only one logical and imperative reason for the dog's death. The dog was not strangled before the murder, but *after the murder was done.* For a dog cannot be deceived by clever acting. Mac would have known; he would have recognized his master."

For a few moments Archie was silent. Johnny got up and wandered restlessly from chair to table and back again, then once more came to sit down.

"My third clue," Archie resumed abruptly, "Joe Killick gave me. I'd gone to the station to talk with him because it had suddenly come to me that perhaps it was not Andrew Herrick who went back on the eleven o'clock train to London, but the murderer masquerading as Andrew. I was wrong; Joe Killick put it beyond all doubt that it was Andrew himself. The platform is dimly lighted, but Herrick stood directly under a lamp and chatted with Joe. How very out of character was this unusual affability on Herrick's part did not strike me at the time. But I was to remember it later, remember it as odd and contrast it as well with his previous behavior when he arrived for the first time that night from London on the nine-fifteen. Then he had brushed past Killick without speaking, merely handing him his ticket. Only, in spite of his apparent haste, to stand hesitatingly in the road below, as Joe put it, 'lost in 'is thoughts.' Then he hurried away down the towpath. Both when he got off the nine-fifteen and when he took the eleven o'clock back to London, he was carrying the dispatch case. Joe could not remember seeing it when Andrew went up in the morning. That, for my third clue. It's coming clear to you now, of course."

"Clear as mud," protested Johnny. "I still don't see—"

"Nor do I," Janey joined with him. "Archie, please explain—"

Archie held up a professorial hand. "Order. I am doing this my way. And it's dry work, too. Get me another whisky and soda, will you, Johnny?" He turned to Janey. "If it still isn't clear when I've finished, I shall be surprised at you. However, when I've finished, but not before, I'll allow questions, if any." Archie leaned forward and took the glass Johnny was holding out to him. He took a long swallow.

"My fourth clue was a bit of luck. Or rather, it was more magical than lucky. It happened to me at the inquest. I was very tired that morning, I'd slept badly. And I was bored to boot. My mind was in that kind of blank state that comes sometimes when you're very tired. I was looking across the room at Cyril and Burford. I still think of him as Burford, you know, it's odd. Cyril leaned over and said something, and I found to my utter amazement that I knew what he'd said. I'd simply read his lips; can't do it once in a hundred times. Cyril said, obviously apropos of the fact that the police weren't allowing a verdict of suicide, 'I knew it,' and one other word I thought at the time was 'too.' 'I knew it, too.' Much later it came to me in a flash what that last word had really been. Cyril had said, 'I knew it, Drew.' When I got that, it was as though a spotlight had been turned on my first encounter with Cyril, making it stand out horribly clear. I remembered the exact words he had said to me then. Right after he had seen the body, it was. He was terribly shaken. I think what he had conspired to do became real to him for the first time then. In the shock of realization, he spoke the truth. It was all there by implication, only I didn't take it literally enough. Quite literally, I failed to see it.

"The— Where am I, Janey? What's the right number?"

Thank heaven, that was more like Archie. Janey didn't care much for Archie in this cock-sure mood. She smiled at him as she supplied it.

"Five."

"That's right. My fifth clue was a bottle with a red triangle from Andrew Herrick's medicine chest: a bottle of Milton. And Milton is used for cleaning false teeth. I looked for a toothbrush, there was none. That was all wrong because although the jaw of the corpse was badly shattered, several molars were intact, and it was obvious also that there had been teeth, real ones. Certainly dentures and denture brush were conspicuously absent.

"A conversation with Bill Simpson put me on to my last clue. Perhaps it isn't strictly accurate to call it a clue. It supplied me with an idea of how to prove what I already suspected."

"Bill Simpson, Ruth's beloved?" asked Monica, surprised.

"The same. And I heard it all because of that young man's passion for Mae West, which goes to show her uses are varied, to say the least. He told me that a hired Daimler over from Basingstoke had come to the garage at Mongerton to have a flat tire fixed. The time was a little before eight Wednesday night, the night of the murder. I heard this on Sunday evening."

"Oh," Janey exclaimed, enlightened. "That's why we went to Basingstoke yesterday afternoon. That's why you left me all that time at that awful tea place!"

"That's why, Ducky. I had to wait for the chauffeur to come in. But when he did, he gave me what I wanted. I was satisfied that the man who arrived at six-twenty-eight from London and who hired the car to take him over to Mongerton was Andrew himself."

"But look here, Archie," the Colonel was angry. "If you knew then, you had no excuse not to tell me."

"Don't, Roger. Please don't rub it in. I know now I should have told you; chanced my arm that you would believe me. But you must remember I would have been asking you to believe something pretty preposterous. The whole crime was bizarre to say the least. It worked because, in spite of that, it was built on a sound psychological basis. The whole strength lay in the father-son combination, as I've said. I was wrong to wait but I wanted proof. I had no real proof until I could locate Hunter-Smith, Andrew Herrick's dentist."

"I see that." Although the Colonel conceded the point, he was still stern. "If you had spoken sooner—"

"Shut up, Roger. Can't you see how I feel? You all think I'm so pleased with myself, don't you? You're all of you wrong. I'm as bitter as hell. I blame myself more than any of you can blame me. If I hadn't been so, well, let's give it Janey's word, and be done with it, if I hadn't been so vain that I wanted to be absolutely sure, Cyril would be alive now."

"Archie, Archie, dear, don't—" Janey begged.

"My dear chap—" The Colonel was pink with shame at his want of tact. No one knew quite what to say.

Archie pulled himself together. "I tried my damnedest to reach you, Roger. As soon as I heard from Janey, I tried your club. The asses thought you would be back, so I waited. Then as soon as I phoned the Yard and learned you were at Cyril's apartment, I came at once."

"I know you did, Archie. You are wrong to attach blame to yourself."

"And I did my damnedest, too," Archie went on stubbornly with his justification. "My damned-allness to make you and Nokes listen to me. But you would keep pushing me aside. And then I gave up. I knew Andrew Herrick would be there any moment, I had no time to explain, no time to make you believe me. Also I decided there was more chance to break through Herrick's guard if it was sprung on him. If I told Nokes, he would be bound to caution him. I wasn't hampered by legal niceties. Lord, but I was scared, all the same! Never have I had such cold feet."

Again there was a pause. Archie was remembering that ignoble moment; that shameful impulse to run away. Then he remembered something else.

"Janey, my dear, Nokes is a wonder, a man in a million. The most remarkable thing in this whole affair is Nokes; the way he caught on, not a chance to prepare himself. I just bellowed at him out of the blue. He didn't hesitate for even the fraction of a second. He must have the quickest reaction time on record. Wonder what it is?" Archie mused in scientific curiosity.

Janey rose to stir the fire. "Well, I'm glad it's all over," she said. No one took her hint.

"Archie," Monica questioned, "will you tell me if I've got this right? Burford came down on the nine-fifteen, not Andrew."

"Yes, Andrew gave him his own return ticket and described how to reach the house by the towpath. That was why Killick saw Burford hesitate. He was making sure of his way."

"But," Johnny objected. "Wasn't it risky? What if Killick had seen it wasn't Andrew?"

"Yes, that was tricky. But they were banking again on their principle. It's used all the time in conjuring tricks. Simply, one sees what one expects to see: Killick expected Herrick back on that train. The ticket was the return half of the one he had sold Andrew Herrick that morning. The platform is dark, the brothers were of the same size and general appearance. Andrew seldom spoke; he was very stand-offish. The chance was Burford would behave just as Andrew usually did. It was a risk they had to take, and Andrew made surer of it by establishing in Killick's mind, while waiting for the eleven o'clock, that he had just come down on the nine-fifteen."

"While really he had gone from Gray's to Waterloo, and caught the five-thirty to Basingstoke," contributed the Colonel.

"And taken the car to Mongerton and walked to Pennerford by the towpath. He'd never be seen in the dark this time of year and he could get right into Whiteleaves by the back way, and be waiting there!" Monica was so delighted with herself that no one had the heart to point out that she was being obvious.

"All that is clear in Herrick's confession." The Colonel decided it was his turn. "Burford wanted to go over the accounts with Andrew. So Andrew proposed that he come down to Whiteleaves as there were papers there they would need. Once there, Andrew persuaded him to stay the night, suggested they would be more comfortable in pajamas and dressing gowns and offered to lend his brother a pair of his. As soon as Burford had fallen into the trap, Andrew hit him on the back of the head with a sand-bag. He made it out of a sock, imagine! Hm-m-m, very neat, though. There was the poor devil, stunned, and all fixed to be made into the corpse of Andrew Herrick."

"Meantime in London," Archie took it up again, "Cyril was establishing a false alibi for a man who was already dead."

"It's all clear to me now except one thing," the Colonel said.

Thank God for that, thought Janey. Perhaps after it they will all go home. She found she was terribly tired, and poor Archie must be dead.

"What's that, Roger?" Archie was saying patiently. "Andrew Herrick's letter to Cyril."

"My dear man, haven't you spotted that? Why, it's very repetition gives it dead away. Remember the first letter we found? What was it? A reason for Andrew Herrick's suicide, that wasn't suicide but murder. We find a second letter: the same plot once more, for, what is it: a reason for Cyril's suicide, that isn't suicide but murder. Both planted for us to find."

"But the envelope was postmarked Pennerford the evening before the murder, Tuesday, that is. Do you mean to tell me Herrick had planned to murder Cyril as well, as long ago as that?"

"No, my dear ass, of course not. Andrew had no intention of murdering Cyril. He only did it when he was forced to out of self-preservation. The boy would crack up under your questioning, and Herrick had to silence him. When necessity came, that was simple enough. Crudely: to call upon his unsuspecting 'son'; to slip Cyril's revolver from the drawer where he knew it was kept; to walk close to Cyril—and it was all over; horribly, hideously easy. But I wonder if at the last moment Cyril knew . . . if there was a look? It had been easy, but it broke Andrew. For as much as he could care, he cared for Cyril. As a matter of fact I believe that is the reason he put up no fight to save himself afterwards. Can't you see what must have happened?"

"Yes, I do now," answered Roger.

"Of course, Andrew wrote a letter to Cyril Tuesday night. I imagine it to have been intended to show what good terms they were on. So, if in case the suicide hoax failed, Cyril would have it to show the police should he come under suspicion of having murdered his uncle. Andrew simply made use of the envelope. He was very quick to seize lucky breaks. He must have seen it lying about somewhere in the apartment; and after he'd killed Cyril, the idea, not a new one, came to him. Right then in Cyril's apartment with Cyril lying dead at his feet, Andrew sat down and wrote a different letter. Then, because it would look too utterly bogus if he left it openly for us to find, he scorches it a bit, and voila! the reason Cyril killed himself."

Johnny got to his feet and stretched. "This has got me beat," he said. "I never knew Drew was so clever. Thank God, you were cleverer still, Archie Storke. There's nothing adequate to say, so I won't try."

He held out his hand to Monica, and when she took it, pulled her up. "We must be getting along, the two of us."

Janey went to the front door with them. Monica kissed her. "Bless you," she said and went before Johnny out into the cold darkness. Johnny lingered a moment. Suddenly he stooped and brushed Janey's cheek with his lips. "Poor Drew. You understand, Janey. Good night, God bless."

And they were gone, down the path.

The Colonel went, too; and Janey and Archie were alone.

There was nothing to moil about any more; back to their happy every-day-the-same, nothing-ever-happens peace.

Arm in arm they went up to bed.

Cradled in Fear

Anita Boutell

Author of "Death Has a Past"

Original cover image courtesy Curtis Evans

CRADLED IN FEAR

TO
B.C.

CHAPTER ONE

A gust of wind, clammy with the nearness of the sea, caught at her coat, swirled the mist, and set to creaking the old wooden sign on its rusty hinges. Then there was only the mist, cold and sticky and salt to her lips. The red light on the rear of the train disappearing down the track seemed to take with it all that was known and safe.

Molly shivered, and for a moment the old desolation and the old fear came back to her. She was lonely and lost again as she had been before he came—alone in a hostile world where even inanimate objects wore the shape of inimicality: the drained-pale emptiness of vast stations in the dawn, the menacing black of trees against the sky in the dark of a country road, an overturned chair, an old sign that creaked in the wind. . . .

In the dim light of the platform's lantern the faded letters blurred, ran together, and took form again: PRESCOTT POINT. Those letters, those two words, were to mean home to her. Strange and unfamiliar now, from this moment on they were to be the symbol of all journey's end—waited for, longed for. Faded letters on an old board, they were an affirmation of faith, a promise of safety. She wasn't Molly Nash. She was Molly *Prescott*, she need never be alone or frightened or wandering any more. She belonged, this was home. Inside her glove she felt the new, strange pressure of her wedding ring. Only this afternoon, a few hours—tomorrow, next day, in a week, she wouldn't feel it there any more. It would be part of her hand, of her, she would be used to it by then.

It was bitterly cold. The red light of the train was a tiny bright speck retreating into the blackness. It swung, changed shape, and was gone: the train had rounded a curve. The sound of its going came back to them, growing fainter until it, too, merged with the sounds of the night, the wind, the creak of the sign. . . .

"It's cold, darling," Molly said.

He didn't answer, and, looking up at him, she knew all at once that he was angry.

"They haven't sent the car. Good God, do they expect us to walk! They must have had my telegram."

They, thought Molly. They. Who are *they?*

And with the intrusion of that word came again the little sneaking fear, the mere ghost of a dread: memories of words said; the implication of things unknown to her; of explanations made that still did not bring the saving weight of reality. Was it all a lie?

Above her head the old wooden sign creaked again in the wind. Molly raised her eyes. No, it was true, it was there, it was real. PRESCOTT POINT—once that had been among the explanations, as insubstantial and unreal: it was now a concrete thing of sense and sight. Why should she doubt? Why must she always question happiness? She loved him, wasn't that enough?

She slid her arm through his, and for a moment pressed her cheek against the rough tweed of his coat. Its harshness was reassuring, masculine and dependable. She wasn't alone, he was there. She loved him. She was his wife.

"Stay here, Molly," he said.

And all at once she was alone on the dark platform, in the mist that tasted of the sea, and the wind and the desolate blackness.

He had gone, and she was alone. Only a few steps away, just into the little wooden station— Oh, why must she feel this way? Why must she see him and touch him to believe? Was it because it was new that it became so easily unreal—needing for its security the concrete evidence of her senses? That was mad. It couldn't go on like that. She had been battered and lost and frightened. Now, she'd become a coward. A coward to happiness, that was what it was. She'd lost faith that there could ever be anything else but desperate necessity and a bleak 'going on with it' courage. That was the reason for her terror and desolation. She must learn security, as a child learns a lesson, by having it repeated over and over. Then she could see him go, and go with him in imagination, and not be alone.

Molly laughed out loud, and the wind took the sound away as though it were something shameful, being humanly small. And the thought that had made her laugh struggled against the darkness and the cold and the vast stretching emptiness of the night: She was like a dog. Because when you went away a dog couldn't know you'd come back. She suffered like that—each time was a final time, each casual absence a desertion.

There had been other moments like this. There was that time in Chicago just after he'd told her he loved her. She'd been happy, utterly happy and safe. And then he'd gone away. She'd almost said, "Let me come, too," and he was only going for cigarettes because the hotel didn't have his kind. But she'd sat there at that table with all the brightness and chatter, desperate again, alone and frightened, until he returned. Why she'd even asked the waiter, because suddenly in her terror it had become a lie—an excuse. And the waiter's, "We don't have them," had come like a reprieve from doubt. She'd been ashamed—she was ashamed now.

Why must she doubt? Why, oh why? When she knew two things with certainty: that she loved him and that he loved her. They were the only two things that could matter. They were all that were needed. Why weren't they enough? Why couldn't she make them enough? This ridiculous terror was like a test of faith—she'd meet it, and she'd never tell him until it was over.

It was bitterly cold. Molly wrapped her coat closer around her and began to walk up and down. He'd said, "You must have a warm coat, darling, a fur one." And she'd said, "Mink?" and they'd laughed. And then she'd said, "I'll settle for rabbit, I've never had a fur coat," and he'd stopped laughing. Oh, he was sweet. . . . And then he'd forgotten. He did forget things, little unimportant things.

Suddenly he was there beside her again.

"I'm cross," he said. "It's a hell of a home-coming."

He caught hold of her arm. "Never, mind, Molly. Come along. Thank God, there's a taxi of sorts."

He swung her into step beside him, and together they bent their heads against the wind.

"You can taste the sea," Molly said.

"We're lucky. Fred Kirkwood happened to meet this train. He's—"

"What?"

The wind took the rest of his words and swirled them away, forgotten.

They rounded the corner of the station.

The headlights of the aged car made a luminous smudge upon the mist, livid and death white. Then with another gust of wind the mist was gone, and for a moment there was clean, shaking light in which, out of the night, objects showed—a baggage truck, its handle rigidly upright like a cross, a bit of road, an abandoned crate—jigging a little in the light quivering with the vibration of the running engine.

In summer it wouldn't be like this. There'd be a crowd of cars: station wagons, and children with brown scratched legs, and women in gay print dresses, and men getting off the train, their city newspapers under their arms—laughter and noise.

But perhaps—Molly's thoughts stood still, and she felt Sherry's hand on her arm urging her forward. Perhaps, even in summer, there'd be only the Prescotts: herself and Sherry. But there'd be, oh there was sure to be! a morning-glory vine on the station and geraniums and white pebbles spelling PRESCOTT POINT....

Unconsciously, Molly turned her head, looking backward into the mist.

"Come on, Molly," Sherry said.

He wrenched the door of the car open.

"Lucky for you I come down to the 7:04, seeing you ain't been met." The driver's voice was drawling and old. "So you're back, are you, Sherry?" Something sharp like malice ran through the slowness. "Abby said, 'This time'll be it.' Shucks, I knowed you'd be back."

"Get in, Molly," Sherry's hand was tight on her arm; and inside there was dank, stale coldness without the astringent smell of the sea.

"It even smells old," Molly said.

"It'll get us there."

Sherry's tone was like the slam of a door, cutting her off, leaving her outside. He was angry—terribly angry. And something else—what? She didn't understand. How could she help when she didn't understand? She knew so little—nothing. Only that over and over again she loved him.

"Darling—" she said.

Beyond the misted dirty window Fred was a dim bulk of hunched overcoat and cap, noncommittal and menacing: This time'll be it. I knew you'd come back. This time'll be it I knew you'd—come—back, this time'll be it I—knew— The words accelerated, bounced and jerked and tumbled together with the jolting of the car.

Molly shut her eyes. The road was old, too.

In the dankness Sherry was there, then, leaning across her, his breath warm on her cold cheek.

"Molly," he said. "Molly—"

His arm went around her, awkwardly with the jerking car. Molly's hat slid over one eye. They bounced and lurched together drunkenly. Then his kiss came, hard and firm on her lips, and by some magic the rough motion of the car was stilled, translated into swaying rhythm on which they moved, easily, in a swinging peace.

"What ruts!" Molly said.

"S'sh, darling. Kiss me."

But this time the peace had gone, although the car moved swiftly and smoothly now. We're on a highway, Molly thought, diluting with this trivial fact an uneasy wonder that came somehow through the hard softness of his lips on hers. What was wrong with his kiss? There was passion and love and need of her. And something too urgent, desperate, like a farewell— She moved her lips under his, trying to communicate a reassurance, a promise, against what she did not know.

ANITA BOUTELL

"I love you, Sherry," she said.

"Love me? God! If you knew how I love you."

"Are we nearly there? (*Home*. . . . What a lovely word to own for the first time!) Sherry, are we almost home?"

"Through the village. A few more miles."

A few more miles, and a few more hours, and then it would happen. She was frightened. But was there any other fear, warm and exciting and dear like this? In the cold, leather-smelling dimness of the car, he was there, close beside her. And yet he was strange still, and apart. Just loving couldn't change that. But in a few hours he could never be strange or apart again. That was the miracle. No matter what might happen afterward, that stayed true. In a sudden welling of happiness, Molly thought: I love words. Old-fashioned simple words. It's my wedding night. I'm going home. I'm happy.

"The—our house, is it big, Sherry?"

"Yes."

"With servants and everything?"

"Three of 'em."

Servants—of course! That was who "they" were. How silly she'd been. No wonder Sherry'd been angry when they didn't send his car. She pressed her face against the window.

"Oh look, Sherry, we're going through the village. We've just passed a church. A nice white wooden one. I'm so excited, I can hardly wait. How far now?"

"A mile and a half, out to the end of the Point. The water—" he stopped.

"What? Is it right there?"

"Yes, at the foot of the cliff."

"And you can hear the sea all the time, like living on a ship? Darling, why don't you talk? Why won't you tell me all about it?"

"You'll see it, Molly."

The car turned off the highway. There were pines; and in shifting mist skeletons of trees, leaning and twisted; and then no trees at all. The wind had a sharper sound and into the stale dankness of the car came a colder sense of the sea's nearness.

"Molly— Promise me something?"

"Anything, Sherry dear."

"Just one thing. Promise you'll always remember I love you. I love you, Molly. Remember, I love you."

Remember? When it was only beginning. When it wasn't the end? Remember?

"Promise me?"

"I promise, Sherry."

"Darling—" Sherry took her hand in a queer formal gesture. And it was as though that moment of lonely intimacy together there in the darkness was one of lights and strangers, his hand extended in crowded greeting or farewell.

"Darling, there are things I should have said and now there is no time—"

"All our lives, Sherry!"

"I want you to know the one important thing. I'm not much good with words, so it's hard— But here's all that matters. I don't love lightly, Molly. You're it for me—the beginning and end."

Again Molly put her cheek against the harsh tweed of his coat.

"Thank you, Sherry. What more can I need to know, ever or ever?"

"You'll never doubt that. No matter what happens. That's your promise to me, Molly."

"My sacred promise."

This was their true marriage vow: This instant with her hand tight in his, in darkness and musty cold, with the wind's sound and the knowledge of the sea.

"Be happy," Molly said. "Oh, be happy, Sherry!"

"Happy?" His voice found the word strange. "Happy through you, Molly—some time, some day."

He lifted his hand from hers and leaned forward, looking past Fred's hulked shoulder along the mist-torn road.

"We're there," he said. And then, so low it seemed she could not have heard him speak, "I had to come back, I had to know—"

Gravel crunched beneath the wheels, and under the string-shrill crescendo of the wind came the muffled drumbeat of the sea.

CHAPTER TWO

The car slammed to a stop.

Molly caught her breath. The impact of the thought, We're there, seemed to have arrested everything—the mechanism of the car, the quiet process of her own breathing. She sat rigidly still: an arrival come to a wayside halt in space, her fingers hard against the wedding ring beneath her glove, a traveler ready with her only passport at the frontier of an unknown land.

Sherry didn't speak but, reaching across her, swung open the car door.

Molly got slowly out. She raised her head and looked, and the welcoming gracious shape of her imagining fell in ruins. . . .

The house was hideous. It sprawled a contorted bulk, rearing above her fantastic turrets, angles, against the paler darkness of the sky.

"Ornery looking, ain't it?"

The voice spoke oraclelike, and Molly turned, startled.

Near as she was, Fred presented still the hunched impersonal mass of overcoat and cap.

He's like a speaking dummy, Molly thought, only his hands holding the wheel are real.

He did not look at her, and, as he spoke again, Molly was sharply conscious of the tableau made: Sherry behind her, stooping forward to drag from the car the last and heaviest of the bags; herself standing by the lowered window of the front seat, her head twisted in surprise; the stuffed, clothy hulk of Fred behind the

206

wheel; and as a backdrop the house, a menace of wooden gesticu-
lation—shrugging a turret shoulder there, cocking a dormer eyebrow here, pointing, writhing, in a frozen expression of some monstrous threat.

"Ornery," Fred's voice had again its hidden malice. "But no
more ornery than the folks that's lived in it. Take Sherry. He's easy
riled. Closer than a clam, too, same as all the Prescotts—won't tell
a body nothing. But shucks, it don't bother us none, we find out.
Prescotts sorta belong to us folks up to the village. They've been
here, and we've been there, so long's there's been recalling here-
abouts. Married him, hain't ya?"

She could hear the sea plainly now.

"Yes," said Molly.

She turned again, facing the house squarely, her head thrown
back a little in defiance. What if it wasn't as she'd imagined it?
What if it was somehow frightening—witch-castle and strange? She
was cold and tired and it was night. In the morning— It was home,
that was what mattered. Only why wasn't there a light, not one in
all those windows?

It's a dead house, thought Molly suddenly. A dead house for
home. . . .

"Thanks, Fred." Sherry beside her thrust a bill over the top of
the half-lowered window. "Here you are."

Fred's hand left the wheel, reaching as if to take it, and then
abruptly he put the car in gear.

"Congratulations, Sherry," malice crept into the open. Fred
chuckled, and for the first time he turned his head toward Molly.
"You're back with more than usual, ain't ya?" The car began to
move. "You keep it. For a wedding present."

The engine raced, and with a scrunch of gravel Fred had gone.

For an instant Sherry stood motionless, his arm still raised,
holding the money out as if now he offered it to the dark and violent night. Then he opened his fingers, and the wind snatched it
away and whirled it into the blackness.

"Damn him," Sherry said.

Molly caught at her hat, ducking her head into the wind.

"I don't like him, either. He's—" She stopped. Fred didn't matter.

"Let's get out of this," Sherry leaned down to pick up the bags.

He has to bend right over, Molly thought, he's so terribly tall. And immediately the happiness was back, warm and sharp inside her.

Sherry straightened. "You told him?"

"Of course— He asked me."

"Let's get out of this." Sherry said again.

They started across the wide gravel driveway toward the dark house.

"There isn't a light, not one."

"Yes there are." Sherry laughed, and in the sound of it happiness went and Molly was left once more abandoned and alone.

"Sherry darling, please—"

"Lots of them, blazing away. Welcome Home. You can't see them, that's all."

"Darling, please. Tell me what's wrong."

"Wrong, at Prescott Point? Nothing, ever. Close the shutters, draw the curtains, don't show a light. Shut out the storm. Be snug and warm and safe. You'll see."

They climbed the steps onto the broad wooden porch. Sherry dumped the bags by the front door and caught her by the shoulders. His voice changed. He said softly:

"Love me, Molly, and let me love you, that's all."

Suddenly he stooped and swung her up into his arms. He took a step or two for balance and then stood, his legs braced, facing the closed, inscrutable door. His laughter rang out gay and hard into the wind and the night, and Molly heard the beat of the sea like the beat of his heart.

"Put me down," she said. "Darling, put me down, I can feel your heart thumping."

"Because I picked you up? You're a feather, darling, that's not it. Come on, we're going to do this right. Bride over the threshold. Ring the bell, Molly, I've no hands."

"This is fun." Molly was happy. "A little nearer, Sherry, I can't see it."

"It's there somewhere—right about where your hand is. Don't tell me I've got to put you down and light a match? That would be an anti—"

"I've found it!" Molly gave the bell a long push and flung her arm in triumph around Sherry's neck. Sherry rocked back on his heels.

"Look out," he said, "you almost had me over."

Molly began to giggle.

"Don't do that. If you get me laughing I'll drop you sure. You feel silly as hell, Molly, like a baby donkey engine."

Sherry began to shake, too.

The door opened.

Sherry stopped laughing. . . .

Light streamed out and warmth and a sense of shelter startlingly sudden, as though in some fairy tale a cold black rock had slit apart to show a magic garden beyond. And it had the tidy magic of a fairy tale, for at first Molly saw no one. The door seemed to have opened by itself, obedient to the exigencies of the exact, inevitable moment.

Molly felt Sherry's arms tighten around her. He took two long steps and placed her carefully on her feet beside him. For an instant he retained his hold on her arm, then he dropped it and turned:

"Good evening, Nona," he said.

Still with her hand on the knob of the door was an elderly woman so nondescript, so humanly erased, that the spectacles she wore were more concrete than she was.

She's like a ghost in glasses, Molly thought.

And the idea of herself giving household orders to a pair of steel-rimmed spectacles made Molly smile. Hastily she turned it into a greeting thrown shyly in Nona's direction, but Nona, in a disembodied way, completely ignored her:

"Your bags, Mr. Sherry?" she said.

"They're right here on the porch," Sherry went back out the front door, "I'll bring them in, they're heavy."

A little dashed, Molly walked slowly across the cluttered, old-fashioned hall. It was stuffy and somehow depressing. Later on perhaps, Sherry would let her change the furniture and paint the woodwork white. . . .

At the foot of the stairs she stopped, waiting. Sherry hadn't followed her. He was still standing just inside the door holding the bags.

"Which room is it to be?" he said to Nona.

"Don't ask me, it's no concern of mine." Nona's thin thread of a voice robbed her words of any offense, leaving them merely the indifferent statement of a fact.

Sherry dropped the bags.

"Just a minute, Molly." Sherry moved abruptly to a door at the left of the hall. "Come along in here, will you, for a second?"

He opened the door for her and Molly went past him into the room. She heard him snap on the light and close the door. It was a small room and cold with the accumulated chill of rooms seldom used.

"Sherry dear," Molly began, "something must have happened to your telegram, that's all."

She knew he was upset again. What could she say to make things better? She took a step or two farther into the room.

"It doesn't matter a bit. Since there isn't a bedroom ready for us, let's choose the one we like best together, it'll be fun. Maybe I mean the one *I* like best. It's such a big house I'm a little overwhelmed." Molly laughed; she felt nervous and shy. "But I'm full of plans already, I—"

She turned around eagerly.

She was alone. She had been talking to herself. The room was empty.

"Damn," said Molly.

She sat down abruptly on a gilt chair, glad of the warm little surge of rebellion that arrived to cover her old sense of desertion. Why did Sherry disappear in this maddening way? He hadn't come in with her at all; he must have gone when he shut the door. And if she was to be dumped unceremoniously somewhere, why must it be the front parlor? Molly crossed her legs and folded her hands in the attitude of resigned belligerency usually associated with dentists' waiting rooms, while her cross words spaced themselves in her mind with an emphasis that was nearly as satisfactory as out-loud speech. One thing was definite, she was certainly going to change this room, it was absolutely impossible. . . .

Molly glared angrily at a Roger's Group placed in the exact center of a spindly-legged table, and then very slowly her lips curved. She hadn't seen one of those for years and years. It wasn't the same as her great-grandmother'd had—

She got up and went over to the table. Behind her the door opened.

"Sherry," Molly cried, forgetting, "you've got a Roger's Group!"

It was Nona.

"I'm to show you your room, Miss," Nona said.

"Oh—" Molly pushed away a disappointed hurt. Where was Sherry? "Of course. I'll come right away. I'm—" she hesitated. Nona'd said 'Miss,' perhaps she really didn't know; Sherry was so absent-minded sometimes—

"I'm *Mrs.* Prescott."

Molly finished with subdued pride and smiled determinedly at the steel-rimmed spectacles. But again Nona ignored her and, with a gesture queerly theatrical, turned in the doorway without a word and went swiftly toward the stairs.

Molly stopped to pick up her handbag from the gilt chair.

She had a feeling of confusion and of haunting familiarity. The strange happenings; 'Curiouser and Curiouser'; Nona the Ghost; all this was like something remembered. . . .

And suddenly she was there, thrown back into her childhood, a sleepy little girl nodding over her book in the wings. A little girl whose only reality had to be found among the trappings of make-believe, whose dearest dream of imagination was only another child's everyday world. *Alice in Wonderland* mixed itself with the Ghost scene in *Hamlet* and for an instant, the cold, forbidding little parlor was filled with memories: words declaimed in dawn rehearsal hours of how many towns, station and theater all she knew—how many years!

"Exit the Ghost. 'It will not speak, then will I follow it,'" she muttered to herself.

She caught up with Nona at the turn of the stairs.

Nona threw open the door of the bedroom.

"This is it," she said and stepped aside, adding in her toneless, lesson-reading voice:

"I'm to tell you that dinner is ready and you're to come right down, please, as soon as you've dressed for it."

"Yes," murmured Molly, a little surprised.

Obviously, life at Prescott Point had its customs and graces, including changing for dinner; and even on this first night Sherry would not alter them. But Molly was glad. It was what she'd longed for: to have every day the same, pleasant and secure, so that she might look and see the years and the days and the hours like a quiet road stretching ahead.

"Thank you, Nona, I'll hurry," she said.

She went in and shut the door behind her.

The room was very large. Her bag had been brought up, it was there on the floor by the foot of a narrow single bed, and at first Molly did not realize what was wrong. Then, when she did, she walked quickly away from it to the middle of the room and stood still, her eyes tight closed.

A single bed. . . .

Everything was going wrong, one thing after another, strange and wrong. But she mustn't feel like this, she couldn't afford to. Not when she loved Sherry, when they were going to be so happy together, not when she'd promised him never to doubt again—

"I won't look at it yet," she whispered, "not yet. I'm not ready to look again yet."

She was fighting the small sense of panic rising within her as she would a mortal enemy. She knew that on the issue of this moment, absurd and ignominious as it was, everything depended. It was ignoble and painfully ridiculous, but here truly was her test of faith. By it, irretrievably, her promise to Sherry was won or lost.

And so, standing there in the middle of the enormous room, she fought with her hurt, her humiliation, and her growing bewilderment. It was a struggle all the more valiant because the cause of it was shamingly without dignity, and in itself an object so humdrum, so accustomed a thing, that at the moment of entering the room she had accepted it without question. Cold and empty and tired and very near tears, she told herself that it was funny—really awfully funny. . . .

At last she was ready. She opened her eyes.

It was there—undeniably and unalterably there, symbol of the loneliness she feared and thought behind her for ever: A narrow single bed, alone and convent-like, severe with a white spread, looking lost and out of place with the heavy ornate furniture and the vast room. It had, too, an air of having just arrived, like a very young girl at a very big party. It wasn't at home; it had never been there before. Its implication, as it had first come to her, was monstrous, but—

Molly shook her head. She understood so well what she was doing. She knew the quick treachery in her old anticipation of disillusionment until now, automatically, she cringed—always expecting even from happiness or love a blow to fall.

"You're a fool," said Molly out loud.

What a fuss over nothing when the explanation was of course so simple! You'd think from the way she went on that she thought of nothing except— Molly felt herself blushing.

She went over to the bed and, picking up her suitcase, put it down defiantly on the starched white cover.

"That for you," she said.

She began hurriedly to dress.

For once, everything went miraculously smoothly and well. Her only dinner dress, which fortunately she had packed in her bag and not in the trunk that wouldn't come until morning, shook out with hardly a wrinkle; she found her slippers and stockings, her powder and odds and ends, exactly where she first looked for them; and even her hair fell becomingly into place with the first touch of the comb. It was a charmed dressing, and in five minutes she was finished.

As she poised her powder puff for that last, unnecessary, ritualistic pat to the tip of the nose without which no woman will leave a mirror, Molly smiled at herself. She was completely happy again, serene with her explanation.

This room wasn't hers, and theirs wasn't ready. This was a guest room with a bathroom and all, and so she'd been given it just to dress in tonight. Under that white spread on that narrow lonely bed there weren't any sheets. She didn't need to look, she knew they weren't there. She had been incredibly silly, just because she'd been expecting it to be her room and Sherry's and she'd tried down there in the parlor to imagine what it'd be like—

This was the end. She was never going to doubt again. She would learn happiness and love and security. This was her house and Sherry's. She had come home at last.

Downstairs Sherry was waiting for her. . . .

Molly put off the light and left the room.

She went along to the stairs and started down.

Sherry would be waiting in the hall. He'd be looking up, and when he saw her he'd smile. She would see him now in just a moment, as soon as she reached the turning—

But Sherry wasn't there. The hall below was bright and empty.

For an instant vivid to her senses, Molly stood poised, feeling again through the stillness of the house the throb of the sea like a pulse beating, alone alive in the absolute silence. The house felt empty, as though it had died leaving its lights burning; and for that instant once more Molly was afraid. Her expectation had been so sharp, her picture of Sherry waiting for her so real, that it came to her as a shock almost of incredulity that he wasn't there—emptying the house in stillness, stranding her posed on the turn of the stair, an actress making her entrance upon a deserted stage.

She ran down the rest of the stairs and hesitated again, her hand on the newel post, as she looked from one to the other of the two closed doors. Her head turned to the one on the right, for the other was the parlor and Sherry wouldn't be in there. . . .

Then, all at once, she understood. With happy, sudden-found clarity, she saw it all as something planned, arranged by Sherry with tact and care. This wedding evening was to form a pattern of accepted happiness, a mold into which the future could be poured. Not unique and momentous because it was the first, but same and unimportant when it was to be one with all the evenings to follow.

Mold and pattern, she must be careful, she must make the right entrance now.

So, quietly, casually, she would open that door: A Wife come down to dinner—looking forward to her cocktail, her coffee after dinner, and the friendly hours together in front of the fire, until, flushed with warmth and sleepy content, it was time to go up to bed.

Love and security, a husband and a home—child's need and woman's longing: this was her unimaginable dream come true.

Molly put out her hand and opened the door.

Seated one on either side of the bright log fire were two women. One was gray and sparse and pinched; one was round and soft and rosy. The severe woman was knitting, and on the soft spread lap of the other lay a cat, blinking and turning his head in sensuous ecstasy under the caress of the slow-moving white fingers.

Knitting and a cat and a fire, two elderly women fixed and at home. From the first cold moment Molly knew that they belonged.

Sherry came out of the shadows into the lamplight and firelight. He was in his dinner jacket, and in his hand was a cocktail just as Molly had pictured him. His eyes flickered toward her and hastily away.

Remember I love you, remember. No matter what happens, remember— Molly sent the memory of his words up like a prayer; and in that moment of disillusionment and pain the prayer was answered. At the moment of greatest doubt, Molly ceased to doubt.

"Here I am, Sherry," she said quietly.

It was a challenge and a promise.

He looked at her then, and for the briefest instant his eyes accepted hers. He put down his cocktail glass.

"Aunt Clytie and Aunt Helen," he said, "this is Molly."

The gray, knitting woman inclined her head, and the small ticking sound of her steel needles did not alter.

But the stroking fingers of the rosy woman were suddenly still, and she said softly:

"My dear—"

CHAPTER THREE

"How do you do," said Molly.

Her words were inanely formal, but her voice was steady and clear as it had been when she spoke to Sherry, and she was glad of that.

She came into the room and very quietly closed the door behind her. She shut it upon her happiness as upon a child's bright toy, loaned to her for a time but never hers to keep. She saw it lost without surprise, and she knew that she had never believed it hers.

Many things fell into place in that moment for Molly, things Sherry had said and left unsaid, explanations made that did not explain—so many things that later she must take out of her memory, look at, and try to understand. But there was no time for them now. Now she could be conscious only that her hand was shaking as she took her cocktail from Sherry, and that everything in her was needed for the momentous effort of moving and smiling and speaking. . . .

Two elderly women, domestic by the fireside— Molly knew them at once for enemies. Reason had only Sherry's evasiveness to tell her so, but instinct ran far ahead of that. It took its impetus, not from the shock of finding them there, mistresses of the house she had thought was to have been hers—her home and Sherry's. It went beyond that; even beyond the heart-stopping strangeness of Sherry's silence about them—although this did give to instinct its odd shove. For if they were only what they appeared to be; if there were nothing hidden and dark of which they were somehow a part; why had Sherry held back all knowledge of them from her, letting her create from his omission a lie for truth?

So many things— In the whirling confusion of her thoughts Molly found one thing firm and still: her lack of surprise.

She had always known something was wrong. It had been there, crouching behind her happiness, waiting for recognition: like a fawning animal creeping on its belly nearer and nearer. Until from the time she had come into this house it had been close beside her, under her hand to touch—only she would not look and see it there.

She must push it aside, she must go on smiling and talking and moving: refusing its presence as the bright closed room refused the night, and made muted the alien sound of wind and wave.

Somehow she did it. And out from the dream unreality of those first few minutes emerged the edges, the sharp shape of reality again. Color poured back into a scene that had been gray as dreams are gray with color known. She saw the taut red of her dress, the moon-yellow of the cocktail she held, and felt against her fingers the curved coldness of her glass. Her senses stood sentinel once more before a world that was real; she raised her glass and drank.

Nona came then, and at the end of the room double doors were pulled wide.

And now in the dining room, Molly could no longer hear the beat of the sea. But the sea was there, sensed without sound, as it was in every room of that house. And here it was symbolized, declared as a sacred statue declares a faith, in the polished shell among the china of the hanging corner cupboard. A large, dappled shell, and inside it would be softly pink like an ear, and listening through the shell's ear one could hear forever the hollow roar of the sea.

"A house like a ship," Molly had said that to Sherry. . . . It seemed a long time ago, something hunted for remembrance. . . .

The severe gray woman that was Aunt Clytie sat at one end of the polished table, and the soft rosy one that was Helen sat at the other. Across from Molly as though he, too, were but a stranger in this house—a guest like herself, not intimate to its life—sat Sherry.

Through the flowers Molly could see his bent head; his fair hair, the color and sheen of gilt faded almost to silver around old mirrors, gleamed in the candlelight. But he did not raise his head or look at her.

'The Prince was very young and very charming'—

Sherry had sung that once laughing, excusing away some slight arbitrariness, and, teasing back, defying him, she had thought the song his—that it fitted him.

For he'd had a faint and courteous arrogance—a touch of mystery, of questions not to be asked, royalty's prerogative of reserve, a sort of spiritual incognito that was Sherry's own.

She'd been a little afraid, a little lonely and shy of trespassing, but she'd loved it in him, too. Now?—that was gone. A Prince without a kingdom, who would not meet her eyes.

Did they, in spite of herself, accuse him, Molly wondered? Now, when his need of her made her his equal; brought her, no more lonely and lost than he, to share together his strange and disinherited exile? What, if he would only look, could there be to show in her eyes but her love and the sustaining understanding which, comes when one outcast discovers another?

We could be an army, Molly thought. Together. Fight and regain the lost kingdom. Invincible then—if he would only look at her, seal and accept the allegiance she offered.

But since that brief moment in the living room his eyes had fled hers. Had he brought her this far, pledged her against doubt, only to desert her?

""'Tis deeply sworn,'" Molly intoned silently, haunted still by Hamlet's ghost. "Act three, scene two, and not the ghost," she added, correcting herself with meticulous self-conscious humor.

The Player King and far more apt. . . . But was there a hint of warning; did she, like the Player Queen, protest too much? What was it she was prepared to fight, for Sherry, and alone if necessary? It was something evil, that was all she knew. It had no face or form, but it was there in that house, a palpable presence, as the beat of the sea was there.

Against that evil, tangible yet unknown, Molly had taken up arms. And it made no difference that Sherry had lied to her, even that he was prepared, perhaps, to desert her: the compelling urge to her loyalty was still there.

Molly, shy and ill-equipped, useless in her own defense, was for others a born crusader.

"So be it," she said, while her lips formed different words, sedate and meaningless, to throw across the bright expanse of polished table.

She had taken up arms, yet she did not, at that moment, feel very brave. Reality had returned, bringing with it an acute awareness of herself: the toll her shyness always paid at the barrier of any new encounter—made exorbitant tonight, raised by the circumstances, to an agony of self-consciousness. But she was gallant and skillful; and long-accustomed necessity had shown her ways to lull and circumvent embarrassment, taught her the soothing trick of concentration upon external things. She counted the eyelets of men's shoes, the buttons on a dress—the flowers in a bowl upon a polished dining table. . . .

Tonight, more than ever before, she had had to find refuge in this: and at long last dessert was reached.

"Thank you," she said to Nona, and gazed down at the strange pink mass placed before her. It was raspberry fool, she decided, and of course the raspberries must be canned, unless—

Still clinging to distraction, Molly became absorbed, peering with a scientist's intentness at the released-from-the-mass raspberry near the edge of her plate. It looked smug and new. "Birdseye" were wonderful, it was probably— She became aware of an expectant silence.

"I'm sorry, I—" Molly forced her eyes round to Clytie's agate gray ones. "Oh. No, I'm afraid I haven't read it, Miss—" Molly hesitated, "Miss Prescott."

"My name is Clytemnestra," Clytie said suddenly and with a kind of grim distaste. "Cly-tem-nes-tra."

From the other end of the table came, surprisingly, a shocking, small sound.

Helen snickered.

Startled, Molly jerked round.

Sherry's head was still bent above his plate, and on Helen's face was no expression at all. It was as bland and soft, as innocently pink-and-white, as ever.

I've begun hearing things, Molly thought a little wildly.

There had been something weirdly disjointed, mildly mad, about the whole horrible dinner.

Clytie paid absolutely no attention.

"Helen and Clytemnestra," she went on, and now she had a sort of ferocious finality. "Have you," she demanded suddenly, "have you never studied Greek mythology in school?"

"Gr-Greek mythology?" This was too crazily unexpected. In the end, Molly's bewildered mind balked and refused the jump.

"Well I—that is, I—" she floundered, guiltily fixed in the glare Clytie turned on her. "You see—"

"No matter." Abruptly Clytie became gracious. She smiled. Her smile was by a long way the worst of all. "It's of no importance— Only if you had," this last was cryptic, "you'd have known, that's all."

Clytie returned to her raspberry fool.

Known? Known what? Anger stronger than her shyness took hold of Molly: all at once she had had enough of things unexplained. She had opened her lips to speak when Helen sighed. It wasn't a loud sigh, only the gentlest suggestion of one, but for some reason it was very arresting.

"Oh dear—" Helen said, and smiled at her.

This smile was different—so different it might have been designed to contrast with Clytie's. Tentative and slyly gay, it seemed to promise something. Yet it was deprecatory, too; there was a kind of 'I would if I could' about it.

Molly smiled back. She might be my friend, Molly thought; and then with a flash of insight—if she weren't so frightened. She's as frightened as I am. Of Clytie? Her own sister! That was absurd. But had there ever been two women more unlike? It was hard to believe that they were sisters— More, that they were— I've got it! Molly cried triumphantly.

Memory came flooding back: Leda and the Swan, two eggs, Castor and Pollux, Helen and Clytemnestra. Good God, they're twins! cried Molly, and raised startled eyes.

Sherry spoke suddenly:

"People call this the house of Gemini," he said, and his words had, somehow, an ominous ring.

Then, at last, he looked at her: a blank, hard stare she didn't understand, but that made her queerly ashamed. Her heart gave a sick, out-from-under thud, and she knew that she was blushing.

"Yes, yes, indeed," said Helen softly, "it is all most appropriate. Clytie and I were born in June. Twins under the heavenly sign of the Twins. You see, my dear?"

"Yes, I see," said Molly.

But whether she saw or not, it didn't matter. For, conscious only of a wracking inward struggle, she was, just then, beyond all caring. It had all been too much. Now disaster in the form of a ludicrous mental picture threatened to overthrow her. The idea of a swan as Clytie's papa was, quite simply, the last straw.

Molly fought madly with a nervous, irresistible desire to giggle. . . .

Her victory was ignominious. She choked on her raspberry fool.

Politely solicitous, Sherry came round the table and thumped her on the back.

There was little comfort in that.

There was little comfort in anything. Certainly not in the hours which followed dinner. The wind had risen again: Molly could hear it scurrying out there in the darkness, keening plaintively like a banished thing. On the hearth the log fire burned brightly; the soft lamplight winked in the darting, shining steel of Clytie's knitting needles; over the cat's black fur Helen's white fingers spread and curled, stroking; and the slow blue drift of smoke from Sherry's pipe was sucked swirling, gray and away, under the lampshade.

Shutters closed tight, curtains drawn, out there in the cold and wind you couldn't see a light. . . . What was it Sherry'd said? "Be snug and safe inside—you'll see."

Snug and safe. The room was much too warm. Safe—

"Stop shivering, you fool," Molly said to herself fiercely.

And the talk went on. . . . Polite impersonal talk, the makeshift conversation of strangers—but Molly knew it now for what it was: the battle's opening maneuver. Subtly, and oh so blandly, she was being robbed of her strongest defense: her right to be there.

They were doing it with words: words to parry intimacy, to negate reality—the held-within-her, tremendous reality of that morning. She saw again with vivid clearness, as though transposed over the soft lamplight and the cluttered coziness of the old-fashioned room, the stark glare of unshaded lights, the battered emptiness, the discouraged palm, the magistrate needing a shave—the scene, sordid and dear, of her marriage to Sherry.

How can they ignore it? Molly thought. How can they!

And yet it was just that that they were so busily doing. Making conversation, pretending it wasn't there, with her brand-new wedding ring a shiny blatancy upon her finger, positively shouting—look, look!

In a moment of wild impulse, Molly wanted to hold it aloft, point to it in exaggerated mime, wave it under their noses—

She found that she had covered it carefully with her other fingers.

She thought of them as "They," although from the first shocked moment when she had seen them seated one on each side of the fire as they sat now, exactly as now—gray knitting and black cat—it was Clytie who directed operations, Helen who followed.

And like a good general, Clytie was being painstakingly wary. Not only did she make as-if-it-weren't Molly's marriage to Sherry, she went further. Never once during those two slow hours did she permit a hint of curiosity about Molly herself. There were no family-like probings, no questions—nothing. Until, around about ten o'clock, Molly felt that she had indeed been very successfully obliterated—gradually but ruthlessly faded-out as a recognizable human entity. Erect and small in her stiff chair, she told herself that soon, if she became any dimmer, she herself would have to start hunting about for herself.

Sherry did nothing to help. His long legs stuck out in front of him, his eyes fixed on the ceiling, he was as remote and unconcerned as the moon.

"Oh Gosh!" Molly whispered, childishly near tears.

And endlessly Clytie went on talking. . . .

"—so I told him that it was not to happen again. I would *not* have mixed tulips in the front borders. 'Obadiah,' I said" (the biblical person was, obviously, the gardener), "'once and for all, you have got to keep the bulbs straight. Every spring that hideous mixture of colors is an affront to my eyes.'"

"But I thought," interrupted Helen very softly, "that flowers couldn't clash. Colors in nature—"

"Bosh," Clytie gave her sister a withering glance and dropped her eyes once again to her knitting, "tulips can."

"Yes. Yes, I suppose so," Helen murmured and sent Molly, now that Clytie wasn't looking, another one of her conspiratorial little smiles.

Sherry spoke.

"I honestly believe," he was coldly meditative, "her precious garden is the only thing in the world that Clytie gives a damn about. So help me, the only thing."

"Sherry dear," Helen's protest came quickly but as softly as before, "you really mustn't say things like that."

"Why shouldn't he?" Clytie was acid. "Sherman's right, it's perfectly true. I like to make things grow—things I can *control*."

"Oh, good God!" Sherry sat up. "How much longer does this have to go on? Haven't we had enough? You'd think—" Sherry broke off. He leaned back again and closed his eyes. "O. K. let it ride." His voice was resigned. "Have it your own way—both of you. You will, anyhow."

There was a pause: a heaving, tossing sort of pause. Molly sat very still, clinging to one small word. Sherry'd said 'we'—he hadn't deserted her after all. Perhaps. . . .

Sherry was speaking again.

"But you needn't rush to Clytie's defense, Helen. I'm on her side. A garden's got it all over a cat. That damned black monstrosity of yours makes me—"

"Sherman!" Clytie's voice was like the snap of a lion tamer's whip.

Sherry laughed.

"That's right. Twin hearts that beat as one, quick to defend and cherish— Watch them, Molly. By God, their team work never fails!"

Sherry got to his feet. He bowed first to Clytie, then to Helen.

"I'm sorry. I apologize abjectly."

Helen chuckled, tilting back her head to laugh up at him. The firelight caught her soft white curls, turning them almost golden, and for an instant the illusion stayed: she looked very young—a mischievous child, confiding and gay. She caught hold of Sherry's hand and, pulling him down toward her, whispered something to him.

"Tut, tut!" Sherry was gay, too. "Now Nell, don't be naughty," he said.

And they laughed again together—two children in a roomful of grownups.

Molly caught her lip between her teeth. Something heavy and cold sat down with a plop inside of her just where she needed to breathe, and she was horribly afraid she might really be going to cry. In the middle of all this that was so queer, so hatefully *wrong* somehow— On top of everything else, did she have to go and get jealous!

"Don't be cross, please," said Helen gently.

She said it to Clytie, but it was at Molly that she smiled; leaning past Sherry's turned back to send once more across the room the secret message of her shy, forbidden, friendliness.

Molly's answering smile was stiff. Right then she wished most fervently that Helen wouldn't do it. What was the use of surreptitious sympathy? And sharing it like this was worse, it only made Molly out a coward, just as Helen was. For she is afraid, thought Molly, with conviction. And at that moment, Clytie's open hostility seemed to Molly a clean and almost wholesome thing, pleasanter far to take. Until—at that precise instant, Clytie raised her head.

She stared full at Molly.

The impact was uncanny and disintegrating in the extreme. Molly felt naked, as if she had been undressed in public: she had that shamed and guilty sensation which comes from being mentally overheard. She was in no doubt whatever that Clytie had listened in to every word she'd thought. Molly changed her mind: Helen's stealthy partisanship became a refuge of safety. Molly turned tail and plunged in. . . .

But what Clytie said was mild enough. She had put down her knitting to stare at Molly, now she picked it up again.

"'Cross'?" she repeated. "What a ridiculous word, Helen, for a grown woman to use. Of course, I'm not cross.

"Sherry didn't mean it, Clytie." Helen spoke of Sherry as if he were a child to be explained. "He was only teasing us."

"He was extremely rude." Clytie pronounced judgment. "I see no excuse for that."

"God give me patience!" Sherry said. He was suddenly angry again. "You'd think I was ten years old. I tell you we're going to have it out this time, once and for all."

Helen put her hand on his sleeve.

"Yes, dear, we'll talk."

Sherry shook off her hand. He took a step nearer Clytie.

"I came back, didn't I? Running away—I'm through with that. We're going to settle it, do you hear? And now there's Molly—"

"Control yourself, Sherman," Clytie said.

"Please, please, Sherry dear," Helen's voice was as soft and slow as ever, "don't get excited. You know what will happen if you do."

Sherry put his hands to his head.

"I'm not afraid," he said with a kind of still wonder. "Can't you see, I'm not afraid any more?"

"We need," said Clytie coolly as if nothing had happened, "another log for the fire. Sherman, will you fetch it, please."

Molly jumped up.

"Let me go, too. I could carry—"

"In such a pretty evening dress?" Helen murmured. "My dear, it would be a shame."

Clytie merely turned her head.

Molly sat down.

Surprisingly, Sherry grinned at her. Under cover of his turned back he waggled a triumphant thumb; he seemed very cocky all of a sudden and pleased with himself.

He vanished through the hall door.

There was another silence.

It was a silence simply because no one spoke, for it was filled with sound; a nightmare pattern of small repeated sounds, recurring over and over: The wind moaned, the fire snapped, the needles clicked, the cat purred, the ormolu clock on the mantel ticked—

The clock said five minutes to eleven. She had been in this house a little over three hours, that was all. It wasn't even late. Down there in New York the theaters were getting out, people would be—

Clytie was looking at her again.

"It's late," said Clytie. "I think you should go to bed."

"Clytie!" Helen's face flushed scarlet in the firelight. "How could you!"

"I see no point in beating about the bush." Clytie was imperturbably concise. "We must talk to our nephew . . . . alone."

Helen made a fluttery, beseeching little gesture: "So—so awfully impolite— My dear, I don't know what you must think of us."

Molly stood up. Her cheeks were burning.

"No, please. I—I understand. I should have gone. I'll go right away, I—"

"Before Sherman comes back. That will be best."

"Yes, of course." Molly's absurd bow was a little girl's, dismissed from class.

"Good night, Miss Prescott. Good night, Miss—"

"Ah, no—" Helen was very gentle, "you must call us both by our first names." She smiled again, a warm, sweet smile. "Good night, my dear—"

"Good night," Molly said.

And then she was out in the cold empty hall; and, as she turned her head, once more for a split second she saw them there, one on each side of the fire, gray knitting and black cat, as if fixed forever in unalterable repetition—like a motion picture whose first scene, even as you leave the theater, begins again upon the screen.

Over the rustle of her dress and the sound of her hurrying footsteps a phrase floated out to her, and, monstrously detached from the rest, as if they alone had power to reach her, she heard the words:

"Poor child—"

It couldn't be, for that was mad and impossible. And she must be wrong—for the voice was Clytie's.

CHAPTER FOUR

Molly opened the bedroom door.

There were sheets, after all, on the narrow single bed, and the bed had been turned down. Laid out on it was her new, her very precious, nightgown.

Molly sat down and contemplated all this. . . .

Her wedding nightgown, bought only that morning in New York—it represented her contribution, spendthrift and lovely, her only trousseau, her 'dot.' Reckless and very happy, she had taken all the money she had and gone out to buy it: hoping the salesgirl wouldn't see her excitement, wouldn't know that it was the first time in all her life that she had ever bought so luxurious, so fragile a thing. She had felt that, in this one garment at least, she was the equal of the rich and the glamorous; she might have nothing more, in all else be shabby and poor, but in that she had all there was to have, there wasn't any more—it was a nightgown to be desired by a queen.

And there it was, laid out on the narrow single bed. And in her purse was exactly three dollars, all the money she had left in the world.

"Oh well—" Molly said.

She got up and then sat down again and put her head in her hands. The tune of an old song was running through her mind, wryly she identified it:

> 'A strange romance, with no kisses,
> 'A strange romance, my girl, this is'—

I must think, Molly determined.

She had come back to this room only because she had not known where else to go; she still had not conceded it might be meant to be hers. She had clung to the explanation she had given herself before dinner, in spite of all that had followed, deceiving herself. Then she had come back and found it like this—made ready for the night, made ready for her.

Someone—Nona?—had unpacked her bag; her things were on the dressing table, neatly arranged. And there was no need to look in the closet, the suit she had worn was gone from the chair. She was—she hunted for the word and accepted it—she was installed. There could be no more doubt about that; no longer any hope that it had not been planned and intended from the first. All evening they had ignored her marriage to Sherry; this was simply pretense carried logically through into action.

Yet recognizing it, and saying it, and knowing it was true, didn't make it better or one bit less frightening and strange. They didn't want her to be married to Sherry. Why? That was what mattered. Why?

But that 'why' brought fear in, because there could be no answer that did not make it worse. And Sherry? Wondering and loving him, and not understanding about him, that was the worst of all. . . . But of course he would come for her and talk to her. And perhaps, in spite of everything, there was a reason—a perfectly ordinary reason that wasn't frightening—only she hadn't been able to think of it by herself. She would stay up and dressed, and wait for Sherry to come.

The big gloomy room was cold. Molly hunched herself farther down into her chair. This was, surely, the oddest of all wedding nights. If it hadn't been for her foreboding, her prescience of evil, she might have found some bolstering of spirit, at least a temporary refuge, in the tart humor of that. There were some things, certain aspects of it all, which were, she supposed, really funny. But the sense of evil, the chill of something too much like fear, lay dank and heavy upon her flimsy shelter of self-laughter. Molly could find no haven there.

She began with resolution to think things out, to hunt among her memories of Sherry for some clue, some hint that might lead her to the truth; taking her memories up one by one, turning them over and over. . . .

But her thoughts were wayward, remembering the suddenness of a smile; a crowded city street and his hand upon her arm; a shaft of sunlight in a room when he had gone; how—that first time, his fingers cupped under her chin—he had lifted her face to his kiss, arranging with a sort of trancelike precision the perfect meeting of their lips. Remembering that tonight—

"Oh no!" Molly whispered.

For memory had made immediate again the sweet urge of her senses, summoned the warm and dear excitement of a few hours ago, only by its very potency to show all that tonight was to have held fastidious and tender, intruded upon—spoiled.

Oh no! Even when Sherry came for her, even when he took her away out of this room—they couldn't! Not tonight, in this house where they weren't really alone. It was hateful. Oh, they *couldn't* start love that way! She would tell Sherry so, she would explain as soon as he came— Sherry would understand. . . .

And she'd stay here in this room tonight. Because if she went when they loved each other so much, wanted each other so urgently— Oh, why had they come! Why had he brought her here? So soon, so awfully right away? Before they had even—

"Damn it all!" cried Molly, and told herself for a few, realistic, letting-off-steam moments, just exactly what it wasn't even before.

It did her good and made her feel slightly grubby and more human and less tied up with vague forebodings and with mysteries—comfortably let her down a peg, from self-appointed heroine to exasperated little girl. Then, pleasantly diminished, Molly took her mind firmly by the hand and led it back and told it sternly to begin all over at the beginning again.

Because she simply had to know. No matter how she might have been dramatizing things, Sherry was in trouble, and something was really dreadfully wrong. . . .

But it was no use. Once more her memories showed her only her love and the poignant quickness of her desire, which, try as she might to pull it down, make it matter-of-fact and physical, still broke away with a shy and soaring wonder. Curled tighter in her hard chair, very cold and very tired and very desolate, Molly gave it up.

And then, all at once, for no reason that she knew, she began to think about her father.

It wasn't the normal mental jump that a daughter feeling lost and in need of help might have been expected to make, for theirs had never been the ordinary father and daughter relationship. He was dead now, and in life he had been scarcely less removed. She had never turned to him. Disembodied and vague, he had circumvented reality as a blind man skirts an obstacle in his path. Molly's share in his life had been, she thought now, very much like that of a blind man's faithful dog—guiding him past the ugly stumbling blocks of responsibility, around the sharp corners of the practical. And in those long growing-up years she had had many a barked shin, often been bruised and battered, but he had not suffered. She had seen to that.

When his dwindling fame set them upon the weary road to theatrical obscurity, it was Molly who counted the milestones as they passed, he saw not a one. Wrapped in the tattered remnants of what once-had-been, he believed himself still glitteringly clad. The faery sun of his world-of-make-believe shone as warmly down upon the end of that journey as ever it had shone before the journey began.

Magnificent in his own eyes to the last, his shoddy descent became a "mission"; the cheap hotels, the dirty "opera houses," the tank towns—all the hardship, the sordid, grueling degradation, was but a slight inconvenience willingly endured for his high calling. He was keeping the theater alive, bringing to the starved, movie-fed people throughout the land, the vital bread of great and living drama.

"The road," he would say in his rich, Sir Henry Irving-Sir Martin Harvey voice, "the road is the artery through which flows the life blood of the theater. Remember that, daughter—always remember that. We have work to do. Noble work. When petty difficulties beset us, let us not complain."

And so, seeing it clearly, detesting it but cherishing him, Molly went on. And year by year as cold reality crept insistently nearer and nearer he wrapped ever more tightly around him the warm protecting garment of his dreams. Until at the last, oblivious even of human contacts, he moved in remote serenity, his escape from the world complete.

Molly's mind, traveling back, found no bitterness, remembering. Retrospect could not create pain from the loss of something she had never known. Dispassionately she appraised it and found its worth: If she had never been a child—if loving had always meant guarding and protecting and fighting—she was the readier now. And somewhere in all this was there a hidden significance, a reason for remembering only instinct knew? It was back—back even further if it was there. . . .

Her father had not always been as she remembered him, an escapist and a failure. Once he had been practical and shrewd—a highly successful actor-manager.

Winnowing by sheer business acumen the maximum element of chance from every enterprise he touched, his name had become a by-word among his contemporaries. 'Standing-room Stanley' they called him. And as success followed success, magic in the annals of Broadway, the legend grew that with his brains and his wife's beauty, Stan Nash could never go wrong.

That was long ago now, when Molly was very little. And out of that time only one thing had remained unchanged, constant to success and failure: he had always been loved. 'A great guy'—that was his epitaph, and it was enough.

Of her mother in that far-away time, memory came hauntingly only through the passageways of sense—the rustling sound of silk, the bitter tang of medicine, a whiff of scent, or the touch of cool fingers upon her hot cheek.

She could not say, this or that was what Mother liked, or thought, or did; another's loving reminiscence had not painted for her the picture of a mother she never knew. She had been deprived of that, for from the day of her mother's death her father had not spoken her mother's name until the day of his.

Molly heard it then, so faint it was no more than breath taking form: "Alison". . . .

The last time and the first.

"Your father blames himself for her death, Molly," "Uncle Ned" had said. "That's what it is."

The words came back to her; and the scene, vivid across the years, returned as it had before, over and over again, to enact itself once more.

Molly shut her eyes, but she knew there was no escape; she had to go on remembering it now through to the end: The bowl of crackers and milk on the marble-topped table; the beating hum of the electric fan whirling round and round on the hot white ceiling; the weight of her thick braid against the nape of her neck—that braid that she hated because it made her "old-fashioned" and in one more way different from other girls; and opposite her, "Uncle Ned," his genial face, close-shaved and with the faint sheen some actors' faces have, puckered by the effort to be understood which afflicts those unused to children.

"Blaming himself—that's what's wrong. It wasn't his fault. Six years and he can't forget, not for a minute. It ought to be getting easier, but he won't let it. He goes on thinking: 'If only I'd made sure.' Over and over like that. He never says anything, but that's what he's doing. I know."

"Yes," Molly'd said. And the hard thud, thud of her heart had begun because she was going to find out now how her mother had died, because Uncle Ned thought she knew. And she felt she might be going to be sick because she wanted him to go on and she wanted him to stop.

"You were just a little tike, Molly, then, maybe three, and your mother hated leaving you nights in the hotels. 'Ned,' she'd say to me, 'you can't trust those chamber-maids to look after her right.' 'Well, Alison,' I'd say, 'Little Extra sure takes some looking after.' That's what the company all called you—Little Extra. You certainly were a cute kid, full of the devil."

"Spoiled, I guess," Molly'd said.

"Sure. We all made too much fuss of you; Alison was forever having to scold us for it. A sweeter woman never drew breath than your mother, Molly. Tell the truth, I was kind of in love with her, like a lot of other guys. We were none of us good enough for her— she'd picked the only one that was. Still I couldn't help wanting to go on being near her. I'd turn down good parts—leads—season after season, just so's I wouldn't have to leave the company—Stan and Alison. You didn't know I was that much of a sentimental damn fool, did you, Molly?"

"No, Uncle Ned," Molly'd said: thinking, I'd better stop him now. It's going to be horrible. I've always known it was something horrible—but oh, please, hurry, hurry! Please, please hurry—

"Yes, just an old softie. Off I'd go on the road with them again. And all the time she'd be worrying about leaving you nights when she had to come to the theater. She'd worry about it the whole time we were gone. . . .

"That year— Well, I've always thought she got Stan to do *Song at Twilight* only on account of it. *Twilight* isn't much of a play, but she was crazy about it. And why? Simply because she wasn't on after the beginning of the third act. She'd whip her make-up off and be back in the hotel with you twenty minutes before the last curtain. Night after night, the whole run, she'd do it. Every night, except that one night—

"We never knew why she decided to wait. There must have been some reason. I don't suppose it was even important. She sent her dresser—old Sally Barnes it was—back to stay with you instead. We'd made a long hop, and Alison was all in like the rest of us, I guess. She must have lain down on the couch in her dressing room and fallen dead asleep. Then the smoke—

"You see, it all happened so quickly, Molly. That old Warren House went up like kindling. No panic, thank God. If it hadn't happened when it did—but the audience thought the play was over. We dropped the Asbestos on them and they went out like lambs before most of them even knew anything was wrong. Backstage it was already blazing— God! I wake up sometimes still and—

"There wasn't any time. It was over, like that. In the confusion we all thought Alison had gone. She always had, night after night . . . always. We never thought that this would be the one night. And they said she'd gone, 'Pop' and Crane, the stage manager, they said they'd seen her leave. Believing they'd seen what they were used to seeing. We never knew—not until we got back to the hotel and found she wasn't there, we never knew— It wasn't your father's fault, Molly. It wasn't his fault."

(It was almost over now, soon she could stop remembering. . . .)

"She burned to death—"

"Lass! Didn't you know?"

"My mother burned to death. Oh—Oh please, *please* stop!" Molly'd said.

And then she'd been sick, very sick all alone in the "Ladies." And afterward "Uncle Ned" had been awfully kind and they'd talked and talked.

"You're getting to be a big girl now, Molly."

"Almost nine and a half—"

"A big girl. That's why I'm asking your help. Don't you see, we've got to do something for him? Stan's washed-up if we don't. He's got to stop blaming himself—I've seen a look on his face sometimes. A terrible, still sort of look. Like—like a man haunted."

Like a man haunted—

Molly's thoughts stopped. Memory checked, and for a long, empty second everything waited, arrested.

Then, suddenly, she knew.

She got up and, going over to the window, pulled aside the heavy curtain. Leaning her forehead against the cold glass, she stood staring out into the blackness.

That was the reason she'd remembered. That was her clue. Her father and Sherry. The same look, like a man haunted. She'd seen it on Sherry's face. They were alike. Of course they were alike! Wasn't that why she had accepted the strange in Sherry without question? Was it the same all the way through? Her father haunted because he couldn't forget, blaming himself; and Sherry haunted, never forgetting, because guilt— But not his! Molly cried, no more than my father's was his. I know. It's the same—the same all the way through.

Could it be? So neat like that? Her mother . . . . His . . . . Something that happened, perhaps—horrible, bad to remember— Could it be, even to that, the same?

It was true that Sherry would never speak of his mother. She was dead, long ago, that was all Molly knew. Once, only once, Sherry had spoken of her. A sentence or so and then he had stopped—suddenly—as though inside himself he had come to a guarded place beyond which he dared not go. . . .

There was another thing, too. Something else he would not talk about. An ordinary kind of thing that ought not to matter. But it also had its sentry, for when he came to it he would stop in just that queer, quick way. That had happened several times. It had happened again, only tonight— What was it? Molly knew, but she could not remember now.

She was so terribly tired: drained of everything, memory and thought. Even her body was hollow, an emptied mold, oddly light. Only her forehead pressing against the windowpane seemed to belong to her, sentient and real. On an absurd impulse—almost as if to reassure herself—she brought up her hands, flattened them, too, hard against the glass and felt, with curious satisfaction, the cold strike into her palms. She wondered when before in all her life she had ever been so tired.

"Tired . . . tired . . . tired . . ." Molly said. And somewhere out in the blackness the rhythm of her words began to beat, grow, and merge: until once more into her consciousness came, insistent and slow, the deep sucking throb of the sea.

Molly turned and went back to her chair.

She would wait, without thinking. Simply wait, quiet and tired, for Sherry to come.

"Quiet and tired, wait. . . . Quiet and tired, wait. . . ." They were nice together, soothing up-and-down. . . . Timed to her breathing, rise and fall, nice words together. . . . Quiet and tired, wait. . . .

It was late when Molly woke up; her watch on the dressing table said twenty minutes past two. The room was very cold; and under her feet, all around her, she could feel the house's stillness.

Twenty minutes past two—

And Sherry had never come.

CHAPTER FIVE

Molly swam out of sleep slowly. It was morning the room was filled with a flat gray light, but Molly knew that it wasn't early. The house was as still as when, last night, she wakened stiff and cold in her big chair. But now it was the stillness of emptiness, not of sleep. And the chill gray light was that of a dark winter's day, the dull aftermath of last night's storm. It was nine o'clock at least, Molly decided.

She raised herself on one elbow and reached out for her watch on the bedside table. It wasn't there. She could make it out in the distance lying beside her powder bowl. Twice around the deck would make a mile, Molly thought: in daylight, without its cornered shadows, the enormous room was even more forbiddingly vast. Lazily half-awake, she wished she had not forgotten her watch, because to know the time seemed the right point at which to begin thinking about it all again. And much as she didn't want to begin, she knew that she must—and she knew that she would. But not now, she thought, not for a little longer. . . .

Holding on to sleepiness, she closed her eyes once more, moving her arm beneath the pillow to cup her head. Her fingers closed about the crumpled wad of her handkerchief. And suddenly it was on her—the half-fear, the bewilderment, the pain of last night. You have to admit the nighttime into the day, Molly thought, no matter how you may try to keep it out.

She had ended by crying herself to sleep; although when first she had wakened, painfully huddled in the big chair, she had felt safe from feeling—too mercifully dazed and groggy with weariness for anything to matter then. Even the sharp hurt that Sherry had not come could not prod her into feeling. Not even that! No, when hurt awareness had returned, it had been through a little, foolish thing, childish to matter, treacherous only because it was, after all, so unimportant that she had not guarded herself against its smallness. Absurd, perfectly absurd—

Molly sat up and looked down at herself. Over her breasts where soft lace and chiffon should have begun was the plain, uncompromising edge of a pink rayon slip. Absurd? . . .

Molly smiled ruefully. "But I'm still glad I didn't wear the nightgown," she whispered defiantly.

For—when she had believed herself safe, at that very last minute when nothing more could possibly matter, at the very moment of putting loveliness over her head—Molly had rebelled. Very sleepily she had taken her nightgown off again and with fumbling patience had folded it carefully and laid it away all by itself in the big bottom drawer. Rather like a burial, Molly had thought, as she placed once more among its folds the little hunk of perfumed cotton—a bunch of flowers for its grave.

Then, because the trunk hadn't come, and because she was very cold, and because, after all, she had to wear something—she had put her pink rayon slip back on and climbed into bed.

Her wedding night. A pink rayon slip and a narrow single bed. . . .

And here it was morning and she didn't know the time or why the house was so still. And she had to begin again with the worrying and the wondering and the being hurt. And trying to be flippant about it wasn't any good, no good at all.

"Oh, where is everybody? What's going on around here?" cried Molly suddenly ridiculously afraid.

She heard the footsteps then, soft and very slow. They stopped and there was a knock on her door.

"C-come in," Molly said.

The door opened. There was a pause, a faint clatter, and Nona carrying a breakfast tray came into the room. She advanced to the side of Molly's bed, stopped, and thrust the tray with a desperate sort of gesture straight out in front of her.

"One, two, three," counted Nona under her breath. "*Now!*"

There was a belligerent little click and four short legs sprang suddenly into position from under the tray's belly.

Molly jumped, conscious of a wave of irritation. She had been scared to death. And of what? The Ghost with a gadget of a breakfast tray!

"Good morning, Nona," she said.

Nona plumped the tray down across Molly's knees and straightened. She was panting a little, apparently the leg trick wasn't easy, and as she breathed something about her produced a diminutive creaking. She pushed her spectacles home on her nose.

"If you didn't come down by now, I was to bring you up your breakfast," she said.

"I'm so sorry," Molly tried another of her useless smiles, "is it awfully late?"

"Quarter of ten," said Nona. She made it sound like a quarter to three.

"Oh, dear," murmured Molly, "I must have overslept."

This was not strictly the truth. In fact it might even qualify as a "lie by implication": Molly, like most theatrical people, seldom got up before eleven.

Nona sniffed.

"I daresay it's only what you've been used to. Folks come just two sorts: Church-going-Godlies or Lie-abed-Sundays."

Of course! Today was Sunday, Molly had forgotten that.

"Then the others?"

"Gone to church."

"Oh. Has my—" Molly took a bite of toast for courage, "did my husband go, too?"

"*Mister* Sherry went." Nona's italics were corrosive. "He's got to drive 'em. Obadiah didn't ought, he's deaf as a post."

"I see. . . . So that's why," expanded Molly, enlightened, "the car didn't come for us last night."

"No it wasn't." A tone less flat than Nona's might have been called gloating. "I didn't say he didn't. I said he didn't ought.

Obadiah's mighty proud of his driving. Riled as a hornet he was when he got told he wasn't to go."

So that was that: even the car had been planned. . . .

Molly remembered something— "But isn't it awfully early for church, ten o'clock?"

"Not when you figure on a good hour to get there. They've got to go all the way to Pohassett."

"Then that nice white church in the village?—"

"Congregational. They're Episcopalians, so it won't do. . . . Stuff and nonsense!" Nona sniffed again. "If God's everywhere as they say He is, then He's one place same's the other. That's common sense."

This seemed unanswerable. There was a pause.

For a Ghost, Nona's views appeared strangely materialistic. Even agnostic—that 'if' of hers, for instance. All together, what with one thing and another, Nona was rapidly emerging from her Ghost-like cocoon, growing moment by moment more aggressively solid. Molly was not at all sure the nebulousness wasn't better, what was coming out of it was so uncomfortably bristly. From Ghost to Porcupine, Molly thought, catching back her smile in the nick of time: she had realized it was no use trying to put a converted version of it over on Nona. What chance had secondhand smiles when even mint-condition ones didn't work?

"If you're only going to peck at your breakfast," Nona said in an after-all-my-trouble sort of voice, "I'd as lief take it away."

"Oh no, but I'm not. It's lovely, thank you. I was—" Molly cast hastily about for something propitiatory, "I was fascinated by this tray. It's awfully ingenious, isn't it?"

Wonderfully, this came off: Nona lowered her quills.

"It is right smart at that," she said, mollified. "Mr. Malcolm thought it up." Now her flat voice had an unmistakable overtone of pride. "Real clever, he was, with his hands. Even when he was only a little shaver he was forever making trick notions you could work. His 'inventions' he called 'em."

Behind the spectacles Nona's eyes had a reminiscent, far-away look, and something unaccustomed was happening to her mouth. Molly recognized it with amazement: Nona was smiling.

"Mind you," she conceded, "they weren't all sensible like that tray there, lots of 'em were plumb foolish—magic tricks and 'illusions,' truck like that. But then, you'd hardly expect different— Taking it by and large, he was a rare one, Mr. Malcolm."

"He was Sherry's father, wasn't he?" asked Molly—softly so as not to break the spell. "And he became an engineer."

"He became famous," corrected Nona simply, but she was not thinking about that. She was busy still, remembering the little boy who made things; for while she went on, it was absently: "Traipsing all over creation, he'd go, building those bridges and dams of his. Into all sorts of outlandish places where it isn't fit for a white man to be, swamps and fever— Ah well, it's always the clever and good ones who get taken first in this world," Nona finished—not sadly, only saying it because it was the way that story always ended, her mind left behind in the magic of younger, happier years, the little smile still on her lips.

"I know. My husband told me," Molly said, daring the words again; inserting shyly under cover of the spell her dear, forbidden claim.

But deftly as she had done it, unobtrusively and gently spoken, those two words had even now their disruptive force. In the short quiet which followed her voice, they seemed to fling themselves like twin rockets into the air, to burst in a bright signal of danger.

The smile left Nona's lips.

"I'll take the tray now, Miss, if you've finished," she said. Her tone was once more level and dead. The Ghost had come back.

Submissively, Molly lowered her coffee cup. She had risked this, called punishment down upon herself, there was nothing to be done. Silently, she folded her napkin and put it by the side of her saucer.

Nona stooped over and picked up the tray.

Her footsteps went away, soft but purposeful. Molly leaned back on the pillows and closed her eyes, listening expectantly. Yes, there it was, the footsteps had stopped.

"One—two—three," counted Molly into the pause. And, from out in the hall, on the three it came—the sharp little click: the legs were safely back under the tray again.

"Right smart, at that," muttered Molly ruefully. She sat up. "Oh, right, right smart!"

She was angry, trapped and rebellious, her loyalty and love submerged under a mounting sense of outraged exasperation. It was too much—really it was! They were screwy, the whole lot of them. Plain screwy. The whole setup was screwy. And so was she— never asking a thing, marrying like that, trusting, getting herself into this. The faster she got out of it, the better. Sherry didn't want her. And what if he did? She was going. Right now, while the going was good.

She got out of bed and began feverishly to dress.

Running away—that had a horrid sound. That wasn't what she was doing. She was *going* away, and that was only sensible and wise. She would pack her suitcase and take it with her. She'd leave a note and her trunk could be sent on after her, later. She must hurry, it was a long way to walk.

Afraid? Cowardly? Breaking her promise? None of that was true either. *Her* promise? When had Sherry kept his? And she wasn't afraid, she was simply not standing for all this. Why on earth should she?

Molly lifted her suitcase out of the closet.

They were all mad in this house. This hideous, dreadful house. Evil. She'd felt it here, from the very first moment, too strong to hide. Sherry needed her. . . . What nonsense, a strong, grown-up man! Yes, but not in terror. In some old, hidden terror only a little boy. . . . And she'd been going to find out what it was. Save him, take it away by knowing, make him sure and happy—a man as he was meant to be. She'd been going to do this. Always the little crusader, never admitting the fight was too large. Wonderful. So brave.

'EVIL. At Home. R.S.V.P.' . . . . Romantic tommyrot. 'Come and Do Battle'—why she hadn't been even invited!

Molly opened the drawer and took out her nightgown. The perfumed hunk of cotton had worked beautifully, it had a delicate, lovely smell. She laid it gently in her suitcase.

No, go away quickly. *Run away*—call it by its name, what did it matter? Leave Sherry— Oh all right, *desert* him, it made no difference. Anyway get over him, and do that quickly, too. Find a real,

live, honest-to-God husband, if she must have one. What use to
any girl were lost little boys who didn't— *Love?* That had nothing
whatever to do with it.

She'd have to get out of the hose and down the long drive without being seen. She'd look awfully foolish if anyone saw her—

> The bride of a night
>> Was seen in full flight.
> Wife only in name,
>> She runs just the same—
>> Poor dame.

Would Nona smile at that? No, she'd merely be ghostily grati-
fied at work well done. She'd congratulate herself. 'Right smart,'
she'd say. 'Right smart'—

Molly's hand poised above her comb and brush hesitated uncertainly. There was bitterness in the thought of Nona's smug satisfaction. The rout of an unwanted Lie-abed-Sunday.

Sunday! There'd be awfully few trains. She must hurry, get away
from here at once—

Molly grabbed her comb and brush, stuffed them into her suitcase, and put on her hat. She was ready.

She picked up her purse, and for a moment panic, a cold sense
of defeat, stopped her dead still, looking down at the bag in her
hands. Three dollars and fifty-six cents. She couldn't buy a ticket
to New York with that—it wasn't enough, not nearly enough. Three
dollars in the world! But that mustn't stop her, that wasn't anything really. She'd manage somehow. She'd been broke and frightened about money often and often. That was an old familiar terror, one she knew—not like this other. She was only a little afraid
of it any more. She'd get out of it somehow, she always had.

Perhaps it would be better not to go to the station, just to stay
on the highway and hitch-hike her way back to New York. A three-
dollar ticket wouldn't take her very far; and, if she had to wait a
long time at the station for a train, Sherry would come and—

But what if he didn't? What if Sherry never came after her at all?

"Oh damn, damn, damn!" Molly sat down on the rumpled bed and put her face in her hands.

What was the use? She knew she'd been counting on that all along. It was even worse than that— She'd known all along she'd never go. She couldn't— She was scared to death and part of her wanted to go most awfully. . . . But she couldn't.

And now she had to unpack all those things. . . . There was only one consolation: it was a cold, foul day, and it would have been a dreadfully long way to walk. . . .

She opened her suitcase and very slowly lifted out her comb and brush.

CHAPTER SIX

She went out then; buttoning up her coat as she went down the stairs, turning up her collar around her ears. The hall was empty, the doors closed, the house hollow-silent.

She crossed the wide gravel driveway and turned, lifting her chin a little as she had done last night, bracing herself in preparation.

"Oh—" Molly breathed.

Daylight had not improved the house nor taken away its menace. Menace was there still, although now, morning-seen, it was, perhaps, no more than the impact upon shuddering sensibility of so much sheer ugliness. The house was the finality of hideousness; the ultimate flowering of gimcrackery; the supreme exemplar of First-Term Grover-Cleveland Ghastly.

It reared while it sprawled, its posture uncertain. Dun-brown colored clapboards, utility-plain, gushed over like a middle-aged spinster, in simpering curlicues; against the rigid bosom of the house, porches and balconies tittered coyly—an architectural expression of false curls and tight stays. Stained glass broke out here and there; it should have had an iron dog or a stag on its front lawn, but it hadn't. They might have redeemed it slightly, made a forlorn attempt at the 'period' and 'quaint.'

"I wonder if you would call it American Gothic?" Molly speculated, trying out the flavor of that. But somehow it didn't help. There didn't seem to be anything which ever could—

"Wow!" ended Molly out loud.

She gave a final shudder, thrust her hands in the pockets of her coat, and walked on. She was thinking that if only she could see it merely as ludicrously hideous, laugh at it and hate it, it would be all right. But the trouble was that under its absurd ugliness there was something more, something witch-castle and cruel she had seen last night by darkness and that lived on still by day. Malice and sly evil, twistedly unkind—something that was not quite sane.

'The House of Gemini,' she remembered Sherry's tone as he had said those words. Yes, familiar and everyday as it should have been to him, Sherry felt it, too. . . .

The house was very large and so confusing in its construction that Molly, exploring, failed to identify her windows. At one side, sheltered by a windbreak of firs and scrubs, was Clytie's garden: a winter-grim design of crushed sea-shell paths; circles and squares of hard brown earth; the bare, fragile twigs of rose bushes. Behind it lay the garage. The big double doors were open and an old man pottered about inside. He gave Molly an incurious glance and turned away.

"Good morning," Molly said, and added, "Obadiah"; but he did not look up again or answer her. He hadn't heard her, of course. It was stupid of her to forget: Nona had told her he was deaf. Strolling on, Molly wondered without much interest how Clytie managed to talk to him. It was obvious that she did, there was that long story last night about tulips. . . .

She came around another clump of low firs, and there suddenly, stretching before her, was the sea.

Molly caught her breath. She had not been thinking about it, and the sudden sight of it so near, so vast and gray and cold, startled her. It was like stepping out suddenly upon the deck of a ship. Water was all around her, a flat, reaching-out-forever distance of icy grayness.

She had said 'a house like a ship,' but she had not known, until then, how apt the description had been. She was standing now at the back of the house, and it was as though she stood on the forward deck of a liner. Behind her towered the 'bridge' of the house, while the high point of land on which the house was built thrust itself like a prow sharply into the sea. And, exactly as it should to carry out the impression in minute detail, the level deck of lawn ended in railings round the bow, for there were white posts with thick white chains outlining the prow-shaped edge of the sheer cliff.

Thoroughly pleased with the perfectness of her comparison Molly walked nearer, only to stop after a few steps in disappointed surprise.

The unbroken, evenly spaced curve of the line of white posts had altered before her eyes: one of the posts had moved suddenly back out of place as she went forward: and there was now a strange little nick in the faultless outline of the cliff's prow. It was disfiguring and startlingly unexpected, for—due to some trick of perspective, or simply from the angle at which she had been standing—it had been, up until then, hidden from her.

And it was with somewhat the sensation of having been cheated that Molly saw, as once more she walked nearer, that a narrow fissure broke back into the clean contour of the cliff. Although shallow in length and at its apex hardly wider than the span of a man's arms, it was as abrupt and sharply cut as if it had been gouged out with a knife. Faithfully guarding it, a white post fell back out of line, the white chains drawing a V-shaped nick as they followed in and out again.

"Oh dear, what a shame!" Molly said to herself. She was foolishly disappointed.

She began to retrace her steps. . . .

She did it automatically, for like a great many people whose formative years have been lonely ones, Molly was still an inveterate player of secret games, bringing with her into the cramped reality of grown-up life some of the magic escape of childhood. And, worried and unhappy as she was that morning, she nevertheless could not leave her game until she had put back together again an illusion which had been more than usually perfect. Watching the white post, she continued to walk backward.

She found it unexpectedly difficult—the recalcitrant post stayed stubbornly out of place—and it was only after a good deal of maneuvering that she discovered the exact spot at which it would merge into line with its fellows. But at last she had it; if she stood absolutely still the prow's curve was flawless. Once more, it was gloriously like a ship.

"Man the fo'c'sle!" Molly shouted. (Her nautical terminology might be shaky, but her shout, at least, was safe—Obadiah couldn't hear her.)

Skirting the offending gouge, she ran across the lawn and, feeling a little foolish by then, fetched up against the foremost post and looked down.

The illusion held: the cliff dropped clean and straight into the sea, and the white line of surf breaking against the rock gave, as she looked, the sensation of forward motion, the curling-away movement of waves against the gentle, forward thrust of a ship's bow.

Molly sighed, satisfied. She tucked her numb fingers under her crossed arms and, leaning on the post, gazed out over the sluggish expanse of oily gray sea—sullenly calm after last night's storm.

She stood like that a long time. It was raw and bitterly cold, but she was hardly conscious of it. Her game was finished, and her mind had begun again its weary trudge over the events of the night before. Moisture caught up light little strands of hair, lifting them out of the smooth fall of her long sleek bob and twisting them into tendrils. Every now and then she put up her hand and absently smoothed them back into place.

She made a picture that Manet might have painted as she stood there, the subtle and lovely monochrome of her coloring blending into the colder monochrome of sea and sky. Molly had real beauty, but it was the beauty of delicate harmony, not of contrast—elusive and impossible to make true with words. You could not say her hair was either blond or brown for it was neither, just hair-colored hair, but what it was, didn't matter—it was the whole, lovely going-together of hair, skin, and eyes; the sweet use of one perfect tone, shaded and blended, that made color unimportant and contrast crude.

To the careless and imperceptive who never looked a second time, Molly was mousily pretty and that was all. But to the attentive who looked again, she was loveliness itself: the enchantment of one perfect, repeated phrase, eludingly fascinating—always a little beyond the grasp—and at the same time, contentedly satisfying and complete. Under this spell of tantalization and peace, those who saw Molly at all became helpless—slaves bearing homage. Between worship and indifference there was no middle ground.

To Molly herself the result was unfortunate either way—the indifference annoyed her and the worship bored her. She would much have preferred an ordinary sort of good looks, a workable mean between the two extremes of dull bunny and unattainable goddess. And the worst of it was, there was no rule for predicting which it would be: truck drivers and hard-boiled magnates jibbered while attenuated aesthetes remained cold. It was all very trying and difficult—

Sherry had been the one exception. Alone among the rest of mankind he had taken Molly straight, standing unique and calm upon that comfortable, but deserted, middle ground. It had been the first thing she had noticed about him, and it had been an enormous relief. To him, she had been just like any other girl; and if he thought her beautiful now it was because he loved her, not like the others who loved her because they thought she was beautiful. It might be only a question of cart before horse, but it made all the difference. And perhaps the start of Molly's falling in love with Sherry was simply that—when she found he had his horse, like his heart, in the right place.

Molly smiled. Her mind had taken a pleasant little detour, and for a moment she allowed it the luxury of feeling warm and friendly toward Sherry again. Then she frowned and told herself for the hundredth time that there was nothing, absolutely nothing, which could excuse last night. He hadn't given her any explanation. He hadn't said he was sorry or told her he loved her. He hadn't come to see her at all— And that was unforgivable!

Damn it, what did he think she was? You couldn't go about producing twin aunts like rabbits out of a hat and say nothing about it. You couldn't park a wife all by herself in a room on her wedding night and never come near her at all—not even to say, 'Bung-o.' You couldn't—

Molly stopped spluttering and took a deep breath. It was no use, she couldn't make her anger convincing, even to herself. Her bewilderment and hurt went too deep. It seemed to her, then, that Sherry had left her nothing. Nothing except what she, herself, had given to him: her promise that she would never doubt his love. A promise he knew would be difficult to keep, else he need not have asked it of her; that might become, even yet, more and more difficult. . . .

Suddenly, with clear cold certainty, Molly knew that there would be no explanations.

That was what her promise had meant. The conditions had been made, the contract drawn up— She had to take it blind, on faith alone. Somewhere there was something that made that necessary. Somewhere in the dark confusion of the explanation she would never have was a necessity that made her act of faith vitally important. She saw, all at once, that she was like a person acting under sealed orders—responsible, monstrously trusted.

Molly pushed back her hair.

Oh yes, it was like that. Her dispassionate mind, working free and apart from emotion, told her so, compellingly; relentlessly divided for her the important from the unimportant; commanding her to stand true. If only, seeing the issue clearly, she could rise level to it! If only she could stop being so humanly hurt—

She turned, and Sherry was coming toward her across the frozen lawn. He stopped short of her, waiting, as though he had gone as far as he would; and suddenly, destroying thought, anger leaped inside her and became real.

She left the post and walked up to him.

"Hello," Molly said.

He did not answer, and for a long moment they stood motionless staring at each other, as if they flung their intimacy down as a challenge between them, like two duelists with the glove at their feet.

"You're back from church, I see." Her voice was icy-sweet.

He caught hold of her arm, roughly.

"Don't do that!"

"Do what?"

"Go so near the, edge of the cliff."

"Oh—" She had thought he meant the way she had spoken to him, but now she realized that that had had no importance for him: he appeared barely conscious of it, absorbed in some emotion she did not understand.

"You're not to do it again, do you hear? It's dangerous."

"Nonsense—" Tears stung Molly's eyes, she jerked her arm away. "It's perfectly safe, you're being absurd."

He caught hold of her again, by the shoulders this time, his fingers hard even through her heavy coat. "Molly, you—"

"Let go of me! I'll do as I please. Who do you think you are to—"

"I thought I was your husband."

"*Husband!*" The sneer in Molly's voice was venomous. She heard it with horror. "You're a fine—"

"Go on, Molly, say it. Say it." The words came at her with horrible, slow gentleness. He shook her lightly. "Go ahead, say it. Let's have the truth at last."

"You're—" The unforgivable yawned before her. She stopped on a sharp little breath that was almost a sob. "You—you can't order me about that way. . . ."

It sounded lame and inadequate.

"How dare you speak to me like that!" she added fiercely, back on safe ground again.

Sherry dropped his hands from her shoulders. The emotion which had first moved him was gone, he was only very angry. He stepped back a pace or two and looked down at her, raising one eyebrow appraisingly. His voice was sleek silk.

"For the matter of that, my dear, your own tone left much to be desired."

So he had heard her, after all.

"Sherry, I—"

What could she say to make it stop? They were quarreling and it was horrible. The first time— But there was always a first time, Molly thought. She began to throw words, any words, into the humming emptiness between them.

"Listen, Sherry— Oh, this is absolutely silly! A fuss over nothing. I'm sorry, but how was I to know how you felt? It's perfectly safe—solid rock, and I was only standing there. Really darling, do be reasonable. Naturally I went, it's fun. Look—don't you see? It's so complete. The house is the bridge and here's the deck with the railings and all. It's a shame about the nick but I've found a place where it doesn't show and—"

"'Nick'?"

"Yes. But you can get it to disappear—optical illusion or something. Come along, I'll—"

"Good God! And you have the nerve to ask me to be reasonable! Pardon me, if I point out that you aren't making sense."

There was a thoroughly horrid little pause.

"Sense," Molly said then very quietly; "probably I'm not. And you can hardly be blamed if you don't understand what I was saying, I hardly knew what it was, myself. But you *can* be blamed for not understanding all that mattered about it. And that is that I was trying to be friendly and love you and forget all this mess."

Molly stopped, waiting. She felt with a sort of proud-of-herself outrage that she had gone far enough, done far more than her share.

She raised her eyes expectantly. Sherry's eyebrow crept imperceptibly higher and that was all. Above a blank steady gaze he flaunted it at her; and for a disruptive moment the sensation of laughter filled her: for an amazing second she thought they might both be going to giggle.

She rallied hastily.

"Sherry, whatever is the matter with you! What a fantastic thing to quarrel about when—" She stopped again.

"When there is so much else— Was that what you were going to say?"

"No— Yes, perhaps it was. After all, last night—Sherry, you don't understand."

"Well, go on. How about last night? It strikes me you didn't give me much chance to do any understanding. You were sore. That's all right, I don't blame you. But sore or not, doesn't let you behave as if I were the villain in a melodrama. For the love of Mike, what do you think we're playing at, East Lynne?"

"Sherry, please. I simply don't know what you're talking about. Now it's you that's not making sense."

"Come off that, Molly! Damn it all, how did you expect me to feel when you do a thing like that? We've been terribly in love with each other, sure, but I've always been under the delusion that we happened to be friends as well."

"Friends?" Molly stumbled. "We are—aren't we?"

She couldn't get any further. She felt paralyzed by her bewilderment, powerless to sort out from all the words and thoughts whirling around in her mind ones coherent which would serve. The tables had been inexplicably turned and now she was accused. What had she done? Somewhere, somehow, there was a crazy misunderstanding, and she had to speak and break through it, and in the confusion she couldn't find words to begin. "Friends—" she said again.

"Yes, friends." Sherry's voice was crisp with hurt. "That's what I don't get. No matter what your provocation, I still can't see you pulling such a cheap, mid-Victorian trick. It makes me want to go Victorian, too, and say 'women are all the same.'"

"Sherry!" Molly cried, urging just that moment's respite where thoughts and words would come together, "Sherry, will you please shut up for just one second?"

"I'll do better." Sherry dropped his eyebrow into place and smiled. "I'm sorry I blew up. Come along in, and let's forget it."

"Darling, I've hurt you, but won't you see I don't—"

"Forget it, Molly, it's all right. I'm sorry I shot off my mouth, it's hardly the sort of thing one likes to be . . . gauche about. I only wanted to assure you that it isn't at all necessary. I understand. When and if you feel differently, you've only to let me know. And now, for God's sake, forget it."

He took her arm on that, turning her toward the house, but there was no magic or comradeship in his touch. It was all like some maddening, bad dream where ordinary, familiar words had lost power and meaning; where they could be said over and over again and not be understood.

Molly lost her head. She whirled free of Sherry and executed a weird little dance, waving her arms and jumping up and down. Baffled and goaded to exasperation, her voice rose perilously near a scream.

"Stupid!" she shouted. "Stupid, stupid, stupid! Will you get it through your head I don't know what you're talking about? I don't know what I've done. I don't know *anything!*"

"Sherman—Sher-man—"

The call came, imperious and thin, through the dank, cold air.

"That's Clytie," muttered Sherry. Authority was menacing them, and his tone became urgent with distress. "Molly, for heaven's sake—"

"I don't care. You've got to listen—"

Clytie appeared at the corner of the house, beckoning.

"Lu-nch—"

"Not now, Molly. For heaven's sake pull yourself together." Sherry turned, "Coming—" he called.

"Why won't you give me a chance?" whispered Molly, wildly. "All that I want is a chance to tell you—"

Sherry took her arm again, very firmly.

"Stop it, we can't have a scene here. Stop it, Molly, and come along. I don't know what in the world's seized you. I've told you it's all right, what more do you want? I've been a fool, and you haven't done anything. So for the last time, let's forget it."

What was the use? Words were just no damned good.

"Oh my God," said Molly fervently. "I give up."

They walked toward the house in silence.

CHAPTER SEVEN

And it was at this point that long, strange day might properly be said to have begun. Its quality was tangible and definite. Molly walked into Strangeness and Longness just as sensibly as she walked into the house. Not that it lost for one moment its identity with Sunday—it could have been no other day in the week. In fact, its very strangeness and longness heightened its Sundayhood, until it became the distilled essence of all grim Sundays ever endured or ever to be endured.

It had everything: the claustrophobia, the empty, cotton-wool-in-the-stomach feeling, of lonely Sundays in big cities; the fixed smile over gallant desperation of country-house Sundays when, under its stultifying spell, brilliant 'lions' became bores, and 'best friends,' distant strangers; even the last horror—that disastrous super-concentration upon one's own physical processes, the false-alarm desire to leave the room again, the nervous something-to-do longing for mealtime coupled with the immense, stuffed loathing for food.

It had all these and something more, an added dreadfulness all of its own.

For 'They' were still 'doing it.' . . .

And the remarkable thing about that, Molly thought, was not that they were going on doing it, but that it had ever occurred to them in the first place that it could be done. It wouldn't have, to most people. And that was the secret. Once it did occur to you, it was easy. You simply Ignored and went on Ignoring. What was to stop you? Particularly, if you did your Ignoring in a really big way:

(Clytie said, "I trust you were comfortable last night."

And Helen said, "Did you have enough blankets, my dear?"

And they both said, "I hope you slept well." Helen's hope was trimmed with a smile and another my dear, Clytie's was bare.)

And after that, all during the long strange day, Molly found herself saying over and over:

"'Would it swing if I swung it? Would it swing if I swung it?'"

She even tried it as a muted aside to Sherry, forgetting that he wouldn't, of course, know what it meant.

She didn't know, herself, why the Ignoring reminded her so irresistibly of that old family joke, but it did. . . . She must have been about seven, and she had been taken to lunch at a house very much like this. Low over the dining-room table only a foot above their seated heads—there had been a chandelier. One of those inverted affairs of stained glass like a vast rubber suction cup at the end of a stick. It had purple grapes and apples and flowers all mixed up, and it fascinated Molly. Most fascinating of all, was the way it hung there, such a long way from the ceiling and so near to her. An object of ceiling-heaven splendor come down among them, heavy and gloriously crashable. Its long brass tube, that had once held gas, was carved like a chain; it looked rigid and pliable, both. Speculation started, became an overwhelming desire to know; until, dessert reached, Molly, desperate, her shyness forgotten, had burst out, rudely pointing:

"Tell me! Tell me, please— Would it swing, if I swung it?"

"*Will it be ignored, if we ignore it?*"

The answer to both those questions was, Yes. And while, for her, lacking their audacity, the chandelier must remain forever a lost opportunity, the moral, nevertheless, held good:

If it occurs to you to try the impossible, nine times out of ten it will work.

And in their hands, this, unhappily, was no tenth time. . . .

As for the rest— There were the meals. Sunday dinner: soup and roast chicken, mashed potatoes, creamed onions, and salad and apple pie and black coffee and cheese *and* (thank God!) peppermints.

Tea: toasted crackers and cucumber sandwiches and cupcakes and other sandwiches and other crackers *but* no peppermints. Supper: cold meat, hot biscuits, a blur, *then* (double thank God!) the peppermints again. There was bridge and Russian Bank and polite talk and Kaltenborn and more bridge and more polite talk and this and that and waiting and hoping— And never once, through it all, alone with Sherry.

The bridge began at half-past two and went on until tea time. Clytie's game was precise and steady, Helen's brilliant and a little reckless—both played with complete absorption. They were obviously keen, and this caused small rifts of comfort to break through the dank cloud of not-being-wanted which hung over Molly. If she was unwelcome as a niece-in-law, she at least had her value as a fourth at bridge.

The best and brightest rift came as they were settling up. A disastrous gamble of Helen's had put Molly forty-five cents down, and in the most casual and natural fashion in the world Sherry had taken it from his pocket and handed it over to Clytie.

"It's all in the family," he said.

And for that one, bright, happy moment, Molly felt that she belonged. Forty-five cents had made her the complete wife at last.

What was more, Clytie had, just as casually, accepted it!

And then Nona had come in with the tea, and the firelight had been bright on silver and china, and just for that one lovely moment strangeness and longness lifted and things didn't seem too bad.

She had even felt hope just then that after tea was over there would be naps, or letters, or Sundayish chores, which might take them away and leave her alone with Sherry. The miasma of the morning's bewilderment had cleared, the power of coherent speech had returned to her, and through three stiff rubbers finessing and bidding and keeping track of trumps she had been planning what she would say to him. She'd begin, as all good Clarifiers do begin, with, "Now please don't interrupt . . ."

It was, after all, an absurd situation. One of those things that have to happen in movies or the plot couldn't go on, but that never happen in real life. One of those fantastic 'misunderstandings' that have to lean clean over backward to balance at all, and that would cease to exist the instant either the celluloid hero or heroine gathered wit enough to utter a single sensible word. She had always had such impatient scorn for them, always wanted to shout from her seat in the darkened theater the words that would clear it all up, and to hell with the plot!—if the scenario writers couldn't get along without that particular piffle, they could stew in their own ink. Because real human beings didn't behave like that, she'd said.

And yet that morning—standing on the cold lawn, wanting to see each other, wanting to kiss each other, with so many things desperately wanting to be said to each other—Sherry and she had done exactly that. They'd had a movie-misunderstanding. Good God! if they weren't careful they'd be doing the next thing soon: they'd be trying to 'disillusion' each other. Who knew? perhaps this sort of thing grew on one. . . .

And if she had any courage she wouldn't be waiting on that after-tea-time hope. She would speak up right away and say, 'Sherry, I must see you.' She'd say, 'There is something we have to talk over.' And, very politely, 'I'm sure your aunts will excuse us.' There ought to be the right moment for her to say that any instant now.

But somehow neither the moment nor her courage ever came.

Then tea was over.

Clytie got up from her chair. She went across to the long, cluttered table at one end of the room and picked up a small parcel which had been lying by her knitting bag. She turned round and, for almost the first time that day, addressed Molly directly. It was quite plain, however, that she did so out of no sudden impulse of friendliness, but merely because Molly, as a new audience, had proved irresistible.

"I've broken my own record this week," she announced. "I've knitted three whole pairs of socks, and I am well started on the fourth."

"Wonderful," Molly murmured.

"I've knitted ninety-three pair. Two a week since I started."

"That's wonderful. It's—it's really . . . wonderful." Molly cast about desperately. "Amazing," she added.

Molly's contribution to the exchange was feeble, she knew, but it wouldn't have made any difference if it hadn't been, for with her usual deflating habit of abruptly terminating things, Clytie suddenly dismissed her.

"It's little enough that we can do," she said crushingly.

You'd think from her tone, thought Molly indignantly, that I'd said it was silly. She was darned if she'd be brushed-off like that!

"British War Relief?" she asked.

"Of course."

This time the dismissal was final.

"I think I'll have Sherman drive me to the village." Clytie fixed her look firmly on Sherry, sprawled longleggedly in front of the fire, quite as if she expected to see him drawn to his feet by the mere power of her gaze, and tucked the parcel under her arm. "I want to get these socks to Mrs. Layton-Hoyt."

"But Clytie," Helen objected in her soft, helpless way, "won't tomorrow do as well? It's practically dark already outside and it's awfully cold—"

"The fresh air will do me good. Are you coming, Sherman?"

Sherry stretched, gathered in his long legs, and stood up resignedly.

"All right, if you insist." He started lazily in the direction of the door. "Anything that I can bring you from the village, Molly?"

"Darling boy," Helen's indulgent chuckle took possession of him, "aren't you forgetting that it's Sunday? Everything will be shut."

"Thank you, Sherry," Molly fought down the sudden anger in her voice. "It doesn't matter, I don't need anything."

The sharp little pang of jealousy had stabbed inside her again, just as it had last night when Helen had laughed that way. And must she say things like "darling boy"! Of course, it was Clytie whom she really disliked, Helen had been sweet, it was only that—

Molly got up. It was a good time to go upstairs again, and perhaps she could catch Sherry in the hall.

"Will you—" she began. She didn't know quite how to go on. It reminded her of her kindergarten days when you raised your hand and said you needed, "Absence, please." There was a classroom atmosphere about it all, you couldn't simply walk out of the room. Probably she couldn't do better than the old frank one: "Will you excuse me for a moment?" She took a breath for it, and her lips parted—

"Let me tell you about Mrs. Layton-Hoyt," Helen said cozily; "she's such a fine woman and it's awfully sad. She's English, you see, and—"

Molly sat down again. She was trapped: Helen had embarked on her story. What was more, she appeared completely unaware of Molly's abortive effort at escape. But was she? Looking at her, Molly wasn't sure. The smile Helen sent her was almost too bland and innocent. And it was odd, too, that Mrs. Layton-Hoyt should last out exactly the sounds of departure: the voices in the hall, the closing of the front door, the driving away of the car. . . .

And yet wasn't her suspicion rather far-fetched? All that day and last night it had always been Clytie who had cleverly managed to keep her away from Sherry (you could hardly count the unforeseen occasion on the lawn), skillfully maneuvered things so that—without open rebellion—they had had no chance to be alone together. It wasn't Helen. No, she must be mistaken.

As to the 'open rebellion,' Molly couldn't do that without Sherry, and Sherry, she felt, was biding his time. And that had something to do with last night—with this mysterious, "Victorian" thing she was supposed to have done. . . .

She had to see him. She would give him the rest of the day and then if nothing had happened, she must be ready to take matters into her own hands. The situation was both ridiculous and intolerable, and it couldn't be allowed to go on. No matter how much she funked it, she'd have to carry through with the plan that had already formed in her mind. . . .

"—so brave, her house bombed and everything gone, and practically no money coming out of England. She's a remarkable woman." Helen's story came to an end.

"I know, it must be awfully hard for them," Molly said.

The sound of the car was quite gone now. She smiled and stood up.

"Will you excuse me for a moment, Helen? I'll be right back."

"Of course, my dear." Helen made an inviting little gesture with her fingers against the skirt of her dress, and the big black cat, who had been lying before the fire, yawned with a very pink mouth and jumped into her lap. "Do come down again, and we'll have some Russian Bank."

She nodded at Molly as her white fingers began to slide, slowly stroking, over the cat's black fur.

CHAPTER EIGHT

Molly looked at herself in the bathroom mirror. It was a disinterested look, for her mind wasn't on her face, and she was only doing it because it was one more thing she could legitimately use to waste time. She knew she had to go downstairs to Helen, and she didn't want to. Staring at herself, she began to play one of her mental games. . . .

Bathrooms were like a modern form of sanctuary. In the Age of Faith when you were hunted or pursued you ran into a church and then they couldn't come after you, and you were safe. It wasn't the same, of course, really. . . . . And as to that, she supposed you could still run into a church, only she couldn't imagine anyone doing it. Probably the reason for that was that in the Age of Faith all sorts of 'right' people were always being pursued and now only 'wrong' ones were. It showed how things had dwindled, somehow. Here in the modern world, this Age of Science, you fled to chromium and glass rods and faucets, and to porcelain that flushed.

She remembered the beautiful matinee idol of stage and screen—he had an exigent wife plus agents and secretaries and a mistress or two—who had said to her once, his gently bloodshot eyes caressing her thrillingly out of mere habit, "My dear child, you are kind—but *simpatico!* and I am saying to you what I could not say to another soul. Believe me, *jamais de la vie*, never. I am a driven and desperate man. In all the rich, wide world there is left only one place where I can be alone: the toilet. My last, ignoble refuge—thank God for it! Even my wife hasn't come in there after

263

me . . . yet." And wasn't it George Moore who had said to a slightly astonished vis-à-vis: "Dear lady, haven't you found that your most beautiful thoughts come to you in the lavatory?" Although in George Moore's case privacy, perhaps, wasn't the reason. . . . But this, none of this, was getting her down to Helen.

She had to go.

Conscientiously, she whistled her thoughts back to heel; her eyes became aware once more of her face. Molly leaned closer across the bathroom basin to the mirror of the medicine closet and gave her reflection a moment's scrupulous care. Everything was in place—nothing needed to be done. She opened the medicine closet, took out her bottle of Anacin, shook a tablet into her hand, and (a feat she was childishly proud of) tossed it into her mouth and swallowed it dry. She sighed, said "'Here we go again, boys,'" and opened the bathroom door.

At the head of the stairs she paused. There was something she wanted to do. She should have done it that morning while they were all at church, but she hadn't known then that the Ignoring was to go on and that it would be made necessary. It wasn't something she *liked* to do, for it was—her mind stopped to add quotes— it was "ill-bred," and, even worse, smacked most unpleasantly of spying. Nevertheless, if her decision was to be carried out—and she was bravely determined that it should be—she had to do it; and this was her best, possibly her only opportunity. Her diffidence caused her to continue to shy away from the rest of her plan: the implied probabilities were a hurdle her reticence, and her—more quotes were needed—her "maidenly modesty," would have to take later. But one thing was unescapable: she had to find out which of the bedrooms was Sherry's. And the time for that hurdle was now.

There were many doors, all of them closed. Down at the very end of the long upstairs hall, at the front of the house, a door stood ajar. Molly crossed her fingers and prayed fervently that it might be Sherry's. It would be utterly loathsome to have to open those discreet closed doors—prying on privacy; she didn't think that she could do it. Holding her fingers before her, Molly began her stealthy, tiptoed approach.

In the dim long hall, her body rigid, her hands with their crossed fingers raised as though in a gesture of awed invocation, she looked like one engaged in some strange and primitive ritual— a priestess of some lost, forbidden rite. . . .

"That's another Stop, I'm afraid," said Helen. "If you put the three over on the other four, and this four in the space, and the five of diamonds onto me, you can get at the six."

"Of course!" Molly picked up the card she had played and put it back on her pack. "How stupid of me—I'd entirely forgotten that we wanted the wretched thing."

She sat inertly, blinking down at the cards, telling herself that she simply must pull herself together and concentrate— Black on red, red on black, the cards blurred in a patternless jumble; they had no meaning for her brain: it was as though she had never seen them before; she was helplessly sleepy.

Helen played briskly.

"What a delightful run I'm having. . . . You know, my dear, it's odd to think that I have often seen pictures of you when you were little. Sherry tells us that you are the daughter of Stanley Nash."

"Yes," Molly murmured, waiting wearily for the rest that would come.

"Such a truly great actor. . . ." Helen put the finished suit of clubs to one side and began building on the hearts. "I saw him many, many times. . . . And your lovely mother—she was very beautiful. . . . But that was a good many years ago; you could have been only a little child when she died."

"I was three."

"Ah, how sad. . . . And then, still no more than a young girl, to lose your father, too! . . . Looking back I realize that it must be ten years or more since we went to see your father last—yes, it must be at least ten years. He came to Boston, in *Othello* I know it was. . . ." Helen's gentle voice went on, unheeded, reminiscing; while her deft white fingers placed black on red, red on black, and the little pile of hearts grew toward the king.

(Twelve years, corrected Molly's mind, remembering, too. Twelve years— She was thirteen. *Othello*—the last tour on the 'big circuit'; the final, magnificent gamble; the last, defiant challenge to obscurity: so disastrously lost, with all that remained of Stan Nash's fortune, all that remained of fame— Oh yes! she, too, remembered *Othello*.)

"Father died only last year," Molly said brutally.

Helen flushed.

"My dear, I am sorry. . . . I thought— Because I hadn't heard anything about him, I presumed— It was foolish of me, we go to the theater very seldom. Old fogies like ourselves, stuck away out here, we don't keep up with things, so really you can see how ridiculous it was that I should have thought, merely because we hadn't happened to hear of him, that he had—that he was—"

"Dead," Molly finished for her quietly, ashamed now before the distressed pink in Helen's cheeks, the tumbling haste in the soft voice, anxious to cover it up. "No, it wasn't ridiculous, Helen. You were right. The Stanley Nash you remember *was* dead. He died, just as you thought, with *Othello*. Only . . . my father did not die. He went on living . . . on and on hoping, and believing, and loving the theater, to the very end."

Unconsciously, Molly's head came up in a small, proud gesture of implacable tenderness.

"He was—he was an idealist. A damn fool, cockeyed . . . darling idealist."

Helen had stopped playing. She looked at Molly now with eyes that were all at once young—and very bright.

"What a wonderful heritage! And you? . . . You must love the theater, too."

"Love?" Molly echoed with a sort of driven despair. "Love?" . . . She flung out her hands, warding it off, threatening it away. "Oh no, no, I hate it! It's tawdry and sordid and cruel. I never want to go back again . . . never. It's lonely and—" Molly dropped her hands once more to her lap; against the dark of her skirt her wedding ring winked derisively up at her. "I'm sorry, Helen," she said gently.

"I didn't know." Helen was like a puzzled child. "I don't think I understand. You see— All my life I've always wanted to be an actress. Malcolm and I, we used to put on little shows, magic and things like that, and I always thought that I— But perhaps I was wrong—maybe it wouldn't have been the way that I imagined it, after all."

"No . . . it is just hard; and then there is nothing left. You have nothing, no Everyday that you can count on. Helen," said Molly suddenly, "why don't you and Clytie want me to be married to Sherry?"

Helen's head jerked up: and for an instant Molly saw the deft fingers splayed uncertainly over the pattern of red and black: two cards slid over the edge of the table and fell to the floor. They fell with a curious, hushed slowness. Everything that was happening seemed to take a very long time.

"What!"

"I know," Molly began to talk in a rush of nervous candor. "I know I've startled you, it was unpardonable of me to burst out with it like that. But don't you see I didn't mean to? You can't be half as surprised at me as I am at myself—and you can't be nearly so . . . so frightened."

"Frightened . . . ?"

"Yes. Yes, of course, I'm frightened. It was an impossible thing to say against—against the Ignoring. It's been awful—like being made to play some horrible game. And now I've lost my head and cheated, broken the rules. I didn't know I was going to say it. I didn't believe that I could— But now that I have—" Molly raised her eyes and met Helen's unflinchingly— "I want you to tell me, Helen. I want to know what is wrong."

Helen looked old again now. Pink and white and guileless—still, once more, an old lady. Old and . . . wary. Wary? Molly's mind touched the word with amazement: guileless and wary, both? Yet it was there. It lay over Helen's innocence like a dirty cloak: a penance for trustfulness Clytie had flung at her, and that she wore because she must—awkwardly, like a foreign garment, ashamed of

its incongruity. . . . "Helen—" Molly murmured. She felt hatred for
Clytie twist inside her, indistinguishable from pity. "Helen, dear—"

Helen played a card with elaborate care.

"This," she said softly, "is all most bewildering. I do not know
what to say, because I do not know what we have done, dear child,
that you should feel as you do—in what way we have been remiss.
We have welcomed you into our house, tried our best to make you
feel at home; and, although you may, perhaps, find us stiff and
old-fashioned, I should be grieved to think that we had wholly
failed. Our New England hospitality is something that we treasure
very highly, and that you should find us wanting in it distresses me."

Hospitality! Oh God, thought Molly, what a dirty trick. She met
Helen's eyes again: helpless, accusing, and hurt. Oh Lord, thought
Molly with shamed wonder, that's worse—she's perfectly sincere.

"But Helen—please! It's not that. You've been kind and polite
and awfully nice to me—of course you have. It's only that I—" Molly
dived under the table and came up again with the two cards. "That
I felt—" she hesitated miserably. "Oh, this is most unfair! I should
have spoken to Clytie, not to you."

Helen took the cards from Molly's fingers.

"They belong here, I believe," she said. Both her tone and her
gesture held a sort of quiet reproof. "Clytie . . . .?" She put the
cards in their place and bent over them, straightening them with
fastidious exactitude; she gave the impression of having, out of
sheer lack of interest, forgotten what she was about to say. "Clytie?"
she repeated. "Don't you think, my dear, you may have misjudged
her? Her manner is somewhat forbidding, I know, but—" Helen
smiled—"she is really quite harmless, I assure you. . . . Let's see,"
Helen looked down again at the board, "where was I?"

"You were going to play the queen of hearts, I think," Molly
answered, feeling surprise that she could remember so unimportant a thing from such a long way off.

"Oh, yes— No, my dear, forgive me, but much as it distresses
me to have you feel as you do, I still fail to see what we can have
done, so—" Helen picked up the queen of hearts—"don't you think
it would be best if we were to forget all about it?"

"Yes—I'm sorry, Helen," Molly mumbled and watched, with a sort of hynotized despair, Helen's ruthless excavation of the buried king.

Now, indeed, she was defeated. With foolhardy valor she had tilted against the windmill of their Ignoring, and lost. For there were things, she told herself, that no one could say; and these, the unsayables, were all that were left. They were safe again now behind their proprieties—twin maiden ladies, impeccable and secure. All the warm and human truths denied in single beds and lonely rooms; all the dark, bright awe of love and need and bodies' wonder—these could not be said . . . . claimed or affirmed. No, even had they not been denied thus by action, they must have remained unsayable still—assumed but always hidden.

Her eyes on Helen's moving fingers, she saw her love and Sherry's, gay and cleanly free, change in this house to a furtive thing: saw desire turn, wearing the face of borrowed shame— Oh, why, why, why, had Sherry brought her here! Molly cried to herself again. Even if it had been different, even if Clytie and Helen hadn't— Even then, how could one come intimate from love and happiness and fulfillment—all warmth!—to cold breakfast tables and porridgy-hypocrisies and maiden aunts! She wished—

"Well, that's the end of my nice run. Now, my dear, let's see what you've had waiting for you all this time," Helen said.

Molly turned over her card, and a little smile twisted her lips as she laid it carefully in the center of the table.

"Poor Molly! and just what I wanted, too. The game's mine," Helen said.

It was the ace of spades.

CHAPTER NINE

It was quarter past eleven. Molly stood in the middle of the big lonely bedroom in an agony of indecision.

Once more she had been outmaneuvered. She had clung on manfully at the finish of the last rubber only in the end, lacking again the courage of positive rudeness, to find herself shepherded up the stairs between Clytie and Helen. She could still feel the warmth of Helen's arm slipped amicably through hers, still sense against her other side the ramrod chill of Clytie's stiff ascent.

And Sherry—? Sherry was winding clocks! The grandfather clock, and the ormolu clock, and God knows what other clocks. For it was Sunday, and on Sunday night at Prescott Point the clocks were wound. So Sherry had (oh, quite as a matter of course!) stayed behind to wind clocks.

The question was, what was she going to do? Should she go now to Sherry's room or wait until she had undressed? The difficulty was she didn't know how long the clocks would take. . . . She wished that she could hear him coming up the stairs; but the stairs were too far away, the walls and door too thick. . . . And while she'd feel less—less importunately brazen, should she say? if she could go now fully dressed, nevertheless it would never do to show that she was self-conscious about it, and so if she waited and had had time to undress, well—she'd have to *be* undressed, wouldn't she? The point was, to appear as natural, under the circumstances, as she possibly could. Positively casual, my dear—

"Golly, this is grim," Molly said.

She was suffering the most acute attack of jitters. Stage fright, shyness, reticence, the much scoffed-at "maidenly modesty," all piled up together to make what she had to do well nigh undoable. But she knew that she would do it. Ashamed in one pride, she had a pride that was greater still: the pride of her love. And she knew there was one way to save it, only one way to fight this strange, hidden battle—and that was, together. Man and wife, flesh of one flesh, Molly and Sherry, together. Married, consummated, and sure. . . .

Molly closed her eyes; and in the cold, empty room her arms moved in a gesture, tenderly encircling.

"They could never harm you there, my darling," she whispered.

She turned and went swiftly out of the room.

The decision had been made. Inwardly timorous, but as ruthlessly determined, she shouldered the weight of her diffidence and her inadequacy as a soldier shrugs onto his back his heavy pack; and with the shutting behind her of her bedroom door, carried the fight into the open at last—her 'naked steel' the brassy gold of a too-new wedding ring.

The long hallway stretched before her empty. Disdaining secrecy now, she went quietly, but with no suggestion of stealth, past the discreet closed doors, the well of the staircase, down the full length of the long narrow hallway to Sherry's room.

His door was again slightly ajar and the room beyond was lighted. She rapped, and when there was no answer, pushed the door more fully open. The room was, as she had seen in her brief glance that afternoon, half study and half boy's 'den'; and, thinking that Sherry might be in the bedroom which she supposed must adjoin it, she stepped rather hesitantly inside.

"Sherry—?" she called, but at the same moment, she knew that he wasn't there. She could see the bedroom door now; it hung open upon dark emptiness.

Conscious of an absurd feeling of guilt, she stood motionless just inside the room where her first steps had taken her. She could not rid herself of the feeling that she had no right to be there, that she was obtruding herself upon a privacy and a past toward which she had no claim inasmuch as it was as yet unshared with her. She felt that, although the room in which she stood was so typical as to be curiously impersonal—wholly noncommittal of Sherry himself. All that marked it was its masculinity: it could have been any boy's room—any room in which any boy had grown into a man.

And seeing this, Molly felt again her old unease. In its very impersonality there was secrecy. The room showed its wares: the scuffed baseball glove, the faded pennant, the rack for pipes, and the battered typewriter; but it was as though they had been treacherously assembled from some dog-eared property list held by grubby fingers—as though some stage manager of life had arranged them there to give the semblance of truth. . . .

What, she asked herself again, did she know of Sherry?

And that the old questioning should have come back upon her now, at this moment when she felt herself so irrevocably committed, seemed to her monstrous. Now, when she must lay exposed to the unknown in him all that she held fastidiously guarded; render up in an act of homage-intimacy all that the years had watched—thoughts, dreams, growth, and maturity: the sum total of herself. . . . Standing there, uncertainty heavy within her, she was aghast to know herself capable of such stupendous trust: as if in wanton assurance that it could not be lost, she buried in the sands of an unknown shore a tiny priceless jewel. . . .

She shook her head impatiently. It was the only way—the right way. What place had self-preservation—even of so inmost a kind—with love, composed, as it was, of instinct and blind faith, elements too rare for caution to take breath in? And if the old doubt must be added again to all the rest, then she must carry that, too. Had she not her invocation against defeat?

"I love you, Sherry," she said.

"Molly . . . ." came Sherry's voice in answer to her.

And although it was odd in timbre and strangely disembodied, Sherry's voice belonged so naturally with her thoughts just then, that Molly did a mental 'double-take'—for an instant she simply accepted it. Then, with the realization that she had in fact heard it and that that was impossible, she gasped, painfully startled; and for the next split second or two atavistic terror and a sudden belief in black magic were most unpalatably blended: fear was in her mouth with the taste of copper.

Molly wet her lips. . . .

The voice came again, and with it, terror and black magic were gone. As she recognized its source, Molly leaned back against the wall overcome by a helpless attack of giggles she strove desperately to silence.

In the reaction to her fear of a moment before, she found it quite irresistibly funny that she, of all people, should have ascribed to the supernatural a phenomenon that was all too common to brownstone boardinghouses and cheap, old-fashioned hotels. Had she not lived for years an unwilling auditor, while through the rusty vocal pipes and fretted iron mouth of countless walls in countless rooms had come that hollow fragmentary speech: the poker party in 62, the night love-approach and the morning quarrel of the couple in 117? The acoustical indelicacy of the old system of hot-air heating was well known to Molly. She was astonished that she had not recognized at once its peculiar muffled resonance.

What had happened was plain. Prescott Point had been built at the time of that old type of hot-air furnace, and although it had long been superseded by a more modern form, neither the pipes running through the walls nor the flat iron registers set knee-high in the walls of the rooms had been removed. She was standing by one now, and somewhere in some other room Sherry stood by another. . . .

His voice came through to her again, sentences fragmentary and broken up as he moved away and near once more: he was apparently walking up and down. The person or persons to whom he was talking (Helen or Clytie or both?) were too far within the room to be audible except now and then as a faint and wholly indistinguishable murmur.

Molly had started to move away, she had no wish to eavesdrop, when she was arrested by a curious quality in Sherry's voice. The element that was strange and unusual to it came through in spite of the distorting medium of hollow pipes and caused her to stand dead still, her heart thudding on an indrawn breath of sharp distress.

What was it in his voice? Fear? Not exactly. More the agitation of a realized dread. The emotion of recognition, that was it, quick and emphatic as it is to joy, but here going out to greet malevolence: as though one said 'hello' to horror. And yet in the words themselves. . . .

Motionless, stilled in apprehension, Molly stood listening, hunting behind the words, the broken phrases, the face and form of evil. But they came at her empty of significance, like the blank faces of passers-by among which she sought in vain to identify the features of a mortal enemy. They told her nothing. . . .

"One gets used to things. I hardly noticed."

A pause; he had moved away.

"—over and done with, don't you see? Otherwise it would have been unthinkable."

The faint murmur of an answer; then, very clearly:

"I had to come back, I had to know."

Those same words—where had she?—last night, in the taxi. . . . His voice again now, suddenly harsh:

"No, I won't take it, I'm going to stick it out this way. I'm convinced—No! I say."

Another pause, and in it the sound of a deep, slow bell. . . . Where was it? Did it come from outside, or from that room? And with his words, the answer:

"The bell buoy, there it is again. I can hear it tolling . . . . tolling. God, how I wish it would stop!— Don't shake your head, I know damn well you can't, but you've made too much of it always. That's what I'm telling you. I'm through with being afraid. Molly—"

Molly—her name leaped at her out of the rest, a pointed finger, accusing her. Molly clapped her hands to her ears, pressing them close against her hot cheeks. She was trembling. What was she doing, listening like this? What had she become, a spy and a sneak?

She wanted to know what was wrong—of course, most desperately she wanted to know!—because if she knew, she could fight;

not blindly like this in the dark, but surely with knowledge and strength. But this wasn't the way, this ignoble ambushing of truth. Sherry must tell her himself; when he was ready—when it was right for her to hear.

She must go, at once. Go, and come back to Sherry later. . . .

In shamed haste, Molly was all at once out of the room and running swiftly and silently down the long hallway. And, as she ran, she thought that she heard again, very faint and far away, the slow tolling of the bell, portentous and mournful: Dan-ger. . . . Dan-ger. . . .

She reached her room and plunged in.

For a moment she stood, her shoulders and palms pressed back hard against the closed door, her breath coming and going in little gasps as though she had been running a very long way. She felt spent, as if she had missed by seconds some appalling disaster; as if, even now, she held the door against an illimitable peril, silent and unseen.

She pushed herself free and, going over to the window, flung it open and leaned out, drawing in great breaths of the frosty night air. Slowly her breathing steadied, her foolish panic subsided, but she lingered, letting the last dregs of the hot turmoil within her drain away into the immensity of the winter night, the cold, astringent glitter of the stars.

Three quarters of an hour later, Molly, charmingly flushed from her bath, powdered and serene, emerged from her "modern sanctuary," and, naked except for a pair of bedroom slippers and a little swirl of steam which followed her out, walked with purposeful directness over to the chest of drawers and, lifting out her nightgown, slipped it over her head. She caught up her bathrobe from a chair, put it on, and tied it around her with determined tightness. For an instant she hesitated, drawing the silk fringe of the belt slowly through her fingers, then with an abrupt gesture she spread her hands in a shrug of resignation, turned on her heel, and said aloud: "Here goes."

She was ready.

Her chin held just a suspicion of a shade too high, she walked across to the hall door and dropped her hand over the knob. She turned it firmly and pulled the door toward her. Nothing happened. The door remained closed. Brought up short in what had all the makings of a magnificent exit, Molly was justifiably annoyed. She gave the knob an impatient twist. Things remained obdurately as before. She rattled it angrily, tugging backward at it with all her strength, while slowly inside her, with chill certainty, the knowledge grew:

The door was locked.

Molly swore. . . .

She was angry. Immensely and completely angry. She lifted her clenched fists to the door and opened her mouth in what was to be a bellow of incensed outrage—she was on the point of battering the damn place down. She wouldn't, no, no, no, by God, she wouldn't be locked in her room! She'd yell and she'd scream and she'd pound—

(Wait a minute, said Molly's wayward memory. Wait a minute, that's like something. So you'll "Huff and you'll puff, and you'll blow the house in," will you?)

—she'd pound until . . . .

Molly dropped her hands and took a deep breath.

She couldn't do it. Of course she couldn't do it. It was late, awfully late, and they were all in bed. She couldn't make a scene like that, it would be too humiliating and dreadful. They'd beaten her again, and there was nothing at all that she could do about it.

With commendable stoicism, Molly went back to the chest of drawers, took off her nightgown, got into her pink rayon slip, and sat down on the edge of the bed to review the situation.

Someone—Clytie without a doubt—had locked her door while she was in the bathroom taking a bath. That was why she hadn't heard her— Then, last night? While she was asleep in the chair! Yes, that would be it. And Sherry had come and found her door locked. The "Victorian" thing she'd done— Oh, poor darling silly idiot, he'd thought that she had locked him out! No wonder he'd been angry and hurt— But it would be all right now, she'd tell him all about it in the morning.

They were fools, after all, Clytie and Helen; they'd overreached themselves badly this time, and the next battle was hers. Tomorrow—

Tomorrow? Molly slipped off the bed and went back to stand for a moment before the closed, locked door. It came to her with insistent force that tomorrow was too late. She had a compelling urge to beat on the door and call until Sherry came to her—now, this moment, tonight. . . .

Very, very slowly she turned away and crossed again to the window to open it for the night. Once more, for a brief minute, the black cold darkness flowed around her; she heard the pounding whisper of the surf; and this time it occurred to her to wonder, as at something curious but unimportant, that in all that ocean speech, the bell was silent.

CHAPTER TEN

And it was of the bell that Sherry was thinking as early the next morning he eased the front door quietly shut behind him, vaulted the low railing of the veranda, and, avoiding the gravel driveway, made his way quickly in the direction of the garage. It was still dark—the grandfather clock had been striking six as he left the house—and it was bitterly cold. The headlights of his aged Ford showed a thick white mist, practically impenetrable. It would be slow going until he had struck inland far enough to be out of the reach of this damn sea fog. He calculated that it would be light by then—that meant two hours of tiresome crawling driving. But he was in luck on one score, the car had started up without trouble; and he had plenty of gas, the gauge showed over a quarter full— fifty miles, two hours, and he'd hit the Post Road. The filling stations would be open and he could pick up some breakfast, too.

He felt groggy with lack of sleep and cold. The left-over coffee he'd found in the kitchen and heated in a saucepan hadn't helped. It was pretty foul, he wished he hadn't drunk it. He missed old Lizzie—he'd have wakened her up and she would have gotten his breakfast; waddled down in that old woolen wrapper of hers, her hair twisted in knobs of kid curlers, wheezing her oath of secrecy. "Sure the Devil himself would be after ripping the tongue from me mouth and me uttering the sound of a word of it!"—she'd been covering up for him and helping him out of holes ever since he could remember. It was like the twins not to tell him that she had died, to let him go bursting into the kitchen shouting, "Liz, guess what!

I'm married," and find a strange female there. He'd felt an awful fool. Helen was firing the poor woman today, God knows why, she seemed all right as cooks went. . . .

Sherry shut the garage doors and got back in the car. He tossed his attaché case on the ledge behind his head out of the way and dug around in the dashboard compartment until he had found an old pair of fur-lined driving gloves; already the steering wheel was like ice under his fingers.

It was going to be a hell of a business until daylight; well as he knew them, cutting across on these small back roads was a tricky job.

The glare of the headlights reflected against the white mist blinded him; Sherry switched onto dim and then again over to the parking lights. Guided more by memory than by sight, he nosed the car cautiously round the curve at the corner of the house and started down the long straight driveway. Gradually his eyes became accustomed to the darkness, the confusion of the mist had gone with the turning down of the lights, and slowly the road began to define itself, a pale glimmer stretching ahead. By the time he reached the gates a mile from the house, Sherry was managing a satisfactory and fairly steady twenty-five.

He was glad of the need for concentration, relieved to find in this mechanical demand upon his attention some measure of release from his thoughts. He had not slept, and at five, stubbing out the last cigarette from the three emptied packs by his bed, he had crumpled the packs one after another into a ball, hurled them across the room, and given it up. Further inaction was impossible. There was one person who might be able to help him, and he was going to see him.

He got up, shaved, and dressed.

Search of the sitting room produced a half-full package of cigarettes, his overcoat pocket, another. Stuffing the few things he would need into his shabby attaché case, Sherry had been ready to go when he remembered the letter. He needed it for the address, and when he had time he wanted to reread it. He undid his overcoat and got out his wallet. The letter was there as he had expected, but he had very little money—less, even, than he had thought. He recalled with disgust his petulant gesture of two nights ago: throwing away good money because he'd let Fred make him angry—he deserved to be kicked! Still, with care he could make it; and once he was there he could borrow from the old boy to get back home again.

Sherry removed a five-dollar bill from his wallet, folded it lengthwise and tucked it down behind the inside leather band of his hat. Theoretically, that money was now forgotten, to be remembered only in a last necessity when something unforeseen went wrong. Circumstances and the years had varied the amount but never the hiding place nor the act—from the very first time that he had run away, Sherry had always put aside, and reckoned without, his emergency money.

He had gone then along the hall to Molly's room. The door had been locked. . . .

Sherry let the car slow to a crawl, slipped off his glove, and fished in his pocket for a cigarette. He lighted it, took a drag or two, and experimentally switched on the heads. The mist had thinned. He gave a grunt of satisfaction and pressed his foot down on the accelerator.

He had hated to leave without seeing Molly, but there was nothing that he could do about it. Clytie was a light sleeper and her room was right across the hall. If he had knocked on the door it would have awakened her, and then there'd have been protests and explanations and a general to-do. He had to go; there was no point in having a scene about it.

That was how he'd felt; and it was too late to regret it now. Although, damn it! he did. The twins' hullabaloo would have been small change against seeing Molly. The truth was that at the time he'd been too angry and hurt to care. He'd written a hasty note, shoved it under her door, and let it go at that.

The thought of the locked door still irked him. He found it out of character and inexplicable. The first time he had put down to an impulse of pride, a desire to wound him, which he to some extent merited, and which he could at least understand, much as it seemed petty and unlike Molly. The original failure of trust had been his, he had deceived her about the twins; and even now he could not say what compulsion had made him do so. He could find only the word, "test," in his mind, and that presumed an arrogance that was wholly false. The word was strange— This "test," was it of her or of himself? He did not know. And if, probing like this, his motives remained obscure, how could Molly reach a truth which even he could not uncover? Without it, what he had done must have seemed a wanton breach of faith.

Poor little devil, what he had made her go through! She'd put up a great fight, taken it on the chin and never blinked. The way she'd walked into that room and never showed by a flicker of an eyelash that she hadn't known they'd be there—it was swell. She'd said, "Here I am, Sherry," and drunk her cocktail— Yes, by God! he had deserved that first locked door— But the second—

After their quarrel that morning, inconclusive and curiously lacking grip as it had been, he had thought that he had made one thing clear: that she had no need to "protect" herself against him. That until she had forgiven him and wanted him, he had no intention of forcing himself upon her. The whole thing was incredible. It didn't make sense, and it wasn't like her. Jumping Jehoshaphat, what did she think he was! The kind of guy who'd insist on his "marital rights"? It made him boil. Taking it by and large, he'd never been more thoroughly insulted.

Yet it was odd how, in spite of all reasons and of all appearances of lack of faith in one another, when they were together they felt close and warm as though it didn't matter—as though they went on quarreling with their words and their bodies only. Actually, for a while there that morning, he'd thought they were going to chuck it, stop pretending and break down and laugh. But they hadn't—they'd hauled back their pride and gone on. What was the matter with them!—they loved each other. God only knew how much he loved her. . . .

That was a bad moment he'd had, seeing her standing there by the edge of the cliff in her white—that was wrong, it wasn't really white at all, only light-colored—in her camel's-hair coat. So terribly

near to the edge— He'd had that pitching forward sensation, as
though he, too, were plunging into space over the cliff with her.
And he hadn't been able to move, to run forward and stop her from
falling—catch her and hold her and pull her back into safety. He'd
had to wait still, feeling that strange draining-away powerlessness,
as if he were weak and very small— And all the old horrors had
begun again, marching round and round in his head. Terrors, fears,
tramping round and round like gray convicts in a prison yard. Pris-
oners who held their faces averted from him, so that he could never
see their features, recognize them, or call them by name. They
circled there, anonymous and unknown, and yet he felt that he
knew them, every one, would they but turn their heads and let him
see them. They never did—just tramped and tramped, until his head
was splitting with the shuffling pound of their feet. Seeing Molly
there . . . . feeling all this suddenly again, because he'd come round
the house and she'd been standing there at the edge in the darkness with her long, white—no, wrong . . . . he was confused. Dreaming . . . . half asleep.

Sherry braked the car, braced his elbows on the steering wheel,
and pressed his fingers hard against his eyes. His head had begun
to throb. He was dead tired, that was all. He would be all right.
Naturally, it had shaken him—happening again after all this time.
The thing was not to be afraid. What if it had come back? He'd
been all right for a long while now. Ten years, maybe more— He'd
been over it; but he hadn't been over being afraid. That was the
trouble. Stop being frightened of it and what did it amount to?
Nothing. Nothing that couldn't be tackled sanely and with action
as he was tackling it now, and from here in. God! was he a man, or
only a sniveling child, terrified of a bell that rang? He'd never
fought it; he'd been a coward; he'd made it bad by fear. Even when
it had gone, he'd hidden it away and tried to forget that it had ever
been. That wasn't the way. . . .

He should have told Molly, *she* wasn't afraid. She wouldn't have
believed it either, no matter what they would have told her. She
knew him, she loved him. She'd have known, just as he knew,
now at last, that they were wrong. They'd almost made it true by

doubting, and by letting him doubt— That was why he'd had to come back, to make sure. And he was. The future was in his hands, and fear alone could rob him of it. For the first time in his life, and in spite of what had happened last night in Helen's room, he knew with a great lifting of the spirit that he had found in the darkness the way out. Bright and straight, it lay with courage and with him.

Dear Molly. . . . He longed to get back to her, to rush up to her and carry her off and put an end to all this tortuous uncertainty. He could tell her everything now, pour it all out and have an end to it for ever. Lord, he loved her! But blast her stubborn little heart for locking the door. He'd intended to tell her last night. Actually, he'd thought that she would come to him. What a smug fool he'd been—he should have known females better— Probably she'd been expecting, or at least secretly hoping, that he'd break the damn door down. By God! when he got back, he would. Then let her look to herself. "Husband," indeed! He'd fix that for her, the little sweet— Sherry yawned and lifted his throbbing head from his hands.

The headlights showed paler now in the grayness; it was growing light.

He'd come through on the confusing back roads without a hitch. Ten miles more and he'd be on the highway. He was cold down to his bones, and his stomach felt hot with emptiness and fatigue. All sensation focused at last on one simple desire. He wanted a cup of coffee more than anything else in the world.

The man behind the counter scooped up Sherry's plate and glanced at the face of the big electric clock. Seven minutes, and the day shift would be coming on. From a shelf behind his head a radio blared the inanities of early morning.

"Anything else?" the man asked. "Fill her up again for you?"

"No thanks," Sherry answered, "I'm fine." He put fifty cents down on his check and shoved it across the counter. "Let me have a package of Luckies."

The man rang up forty-six cents on the cash register and slapped four pennies and the cigarettes down in front of Sherry.

He began to swab at the counter with a damp rag, his wet hand and white, hairy arm moving in weary, practiced semicircles.

"Going far, Bud?"

"Bangor."

"Maine? . . . Jeese!" The man threw the rag with accuracy into the sink at one end of the counter and rolled down his shirt sleeves; automatically, Sherry reached for his coffee.

The counter man saw the gesture and grinned. "Take your time, pal, we don't close. I'm off now. Harry'll draw you another cup of mud if you change your mind."

He started toward the greasy-finger-marked door at the rear, then turned again.

"Heard the morning weather report, Bud?" he questioned, solicitude in his tired voice. "Seems we're in for a blizzard. It's bad already some places up north."

"That so?" said Sherry. "Well, it can't be helped."

"Yeah, if you gotta go, you gotta go. So long, pal."

The man went through the dirty swinging door, and Sherry was left alone in the warmth and steamy odorousness of the little wooden hash-house. Across a misted window, white porcelain letters seen backward proclaimed with an oddly Russian emphasis that this was: ꓘƆAHƧ Ƨ'ᴙƎM⅃Ǝ . . . . Presently another man came through the door and without a word took Sherry's cup and filled it with fresh coffee. The radio began to play: "There I Go." . . . .

Sherry took a swallow of the hot coffee and lit a cigarette. He was feeling better, his head had almost stopped aching. He'd been worried when it started, that hard pounding, that he might be in for one of his old bouts. He was relieved to have escaped it; the pain got pretty bad, and he didn't want to be driven into taking any more of the strong stuff they used to give him. He hadn't needed it for a long while now, and he didn't want to begin on it again—he'd told Helen so last night. It was no good to him. . . . He ought to get going; he couldn't make Bangor before five or six, if he ran into snow it would be later. It didn't matter, he might as well finish his cigarette in peace; there was no use pushing himself like hell, anxious as he was to get back. He'd be too late, in any case, to catch the old boy at his office.

He would have to go out to the house. That meant staying the night, but that was all right, too. He could do with some sleep.

The door to the street opened, and a prowl-car cop came in and sat down on a stool near to Sherry. He grunted a general good morning, leaned his elbows on the counter, and pushed his cap back on his head.

"Hi-yah, Harry," he said. "Give me a coke and a single stack."

Sherry winced, feeling his stomach contract: people put the damnedest things together!

"That your car outside, Bud?" the cop asked him.

Sherry nodded.

"Connecticut plates. . . . Going through?"

"Maine—Bangor."

"Jeese, you salesmen have it tough. . . . It's as cold as your girl the morning after outside. Weather report says there's a blizzard coming up."

"So I've heard," said Sherry shortly.

The cop lost interest. "Better you than me, brother," he muttered. A crumpled newspaper had been flung down at the end of the counter, he stretched out a thick khaki arm, pulled it toward him, and began to read.

Sherry swallowed the last of his third cup of coffee, and with his thumb against the coarse edge of the saucer pushed the cup and saucer to one side. He took his uncle's letter out of his wallet and laid it open on the counter before him. This was as good a time as any to have a second stab at trying to figure it out. His cigarette had been finished some minutes ago. He picked up the package of Luckies, flicked his finger expertly against the bottom, and a cigarette rose out of the pack. He caught it between his lips. For a moment or two he remained scowling abstractedly down at the letter. Then he shook his head, struck a match, and began to smoke.

The letter had been written by hand. And, looking at the cramped, precise writing, it struck Sherry how significant it was of their whole relationship that this should be the first time that he had ever seen it. Brief businesslike notes had come, accompanying the quarterly checks paid to him by his mother's estate; and at birthdays and Christmas other checks and other notes—less businesslike perhaps as befitting the occasion, but just as brief, and always from the office and typed by a secretary. It wasn't, as a matter of fact, until he had received this letter that Sherry had known his uncle's home address. Reading the address now, 52 Maple Tree Avenue, he realized that, apart from the office, he had never thought of his uncle as having one. He had been a man without a home, a dehumanized entity, severe and aloof; existing solely as a name in a letterhead: "BABCOCK, AVERY AND BABCOCK. Attorneys-at-Law." The central link between two Babcocks, but scarcely less dim than they; for had they not, also, arrived, and doubly! through all his life, with every letter but this?

Sherry had written from Chicago telling his uncle of his impending marriage, and this letter, which had been waiting for him at Prescott Point, was in answer to his:

> "52 Maple Tree Avenue
> Bangor, Maine
> Tuesday, February 12th, 1941
>
> "My dear Nephew:
> "May I be permitted to express my warm congratulations upon your approaching marriage? The intimation did indeed come as a surprise, but it was none the less welcome for all that. It gave me, in fact, great pleasure and I am sure that you, and the charming girl you are about to marry, will be very happy . . ."

There was some more of this, and then quite suddenly came a change of tone. Under the stress of some emotion, personal and difficult of expression, the stiff formality faltered, became unsure:

> ". . . I have occasion to reproach myself to-day for many things, Sherman, but for none more than my

neglect of you. You are my nearest relative; the son of a sister who was most dear to me while she lived and to the memory of whose loss over twenty years have served to bring no measure of reconcilement.

"You, who are a part of her, were left; how is it then that I have been content not to seek a closer bond with you than this meager one of virtual strangers? Indifference is not the answer; and could self-reproach push back the clock, I might rectify much that lies heavy upon my conscience concerning you— And Janet, too! if it be that the dead are troubled in their peace by a care for the living.

"There are answers to both these things. They are not such, however, as may go with any degree of prudence or fitness into the scope of. . . ."

Sherry frowned and raised his eyes from the letter. This was the place where he'd been bogged down before. What things? The old boy's style was heavy and sticky at best, and here even the subject appeared to have gotten itself mired. Certainly it was far from clear. All right— There were two things that had "answers." He knew what the first one was (obviously, his uncle's 'neglect' of him) and he wasn't at all sure that he didn't know the answer to it as well. But what was the second? There seemed nothing in the context to indicate that it so much as existed— Wait a minute!

Sherry's eyes went back to the letter.

". . . . to the memory of whose loss over twenty years. . . ." Was that it? Was that phrase more than a trite expression of grief? Was it, instead, the literal statement of a fact? And did it, too, have its answer? Was there—could there be—a reason why, even after all these years, his uncle could not reconcile himself to his sister's having died? That was strange— Was there, then, something about his mother's death—?

Unconsciously, Sherry's hand tightened about the letter. His thoughts halted before a dark and ancient barrier. From far beyond, over the soundless marshes of his mind, blew, thin and sweet, the bugle call of courage. He did not hear it. This was forbidden territory. He could not go on.

He began once more to read, hurriedly now and a little absently, as if merely to complete an unfinished duty.

> ". . . into the scope of a letter. One is personal to myself; the other may exist merely as the hateful figment of my imagination.
>
> "The first can interest you solely as an explanation which, however, is your due and in which my reticence gives way before the necessity of providing myself with an excuse for my bad conscience!
>
> "The second I must tell you, although I shrink from it. If my conclusions have been false—as unfounded as they are unverified—then my misgivings become, too, of little moment. And I shall have done a great wrong in speaking to you of them. But should they be unhappily correct, too much is jeopardized by silence. Your recent news leaves me no choice: weighing the balance, I know that I must speak. And so, my dear boy, will you come to see me?
>
> "Now in regard to matters of a more practical nature. As you know, the money which you inherited from your mother remained, under the terms of your mother's will, in trust until your marriage. It now comes to you outright. Should you, however, wish me to continue to aid you in the conduct of your affairs, I shall be only too glad to do so.
>
> "I have also a letter written by your mother which she desired me to give to you at this time. It contains a certain request—advice is perhaps the more exact word—which bears more or less directly upon what I have to tell you. It constitutes, in fact, my strongest claim to credence.

"Glancing over what I have written, it occurs to me that you may find it somewhat importunate. Let me hasten to assure you that there is no immediate urgency. But when the honeymoon is over, may I look forward to a visit from you? Apart from all this, it will afford me great happiness—it must be over fifteen years since I saw you last, the occasion was your tenth birthday, I remember! It is hard to realize that you have become a grown married man before we meet again; and I confess to the hope that through this reunion we may find a friendship in the future that we have missed in the past. Should you doubt the possibility of this, believe me when I tell you that I am not quite the old fogy that this letter might indicate. Its unfortunate manner arises from the fact that I am now a helpless slave to the habit of dictation—I can no longer express myself with pen and ink.

"With all best wishes for your happiness and with kindest regards to your wife (please bring her with you when you come, I am most anxious to meet her!)

"I remain,

"Your affectionate uncle,

"Derwent Avery.

"P. S. Have you an address where I can reach you during your honeymoon? I was very lucky in a little flutter I took recently, and I want to send you the results as a wedding present. Do, I beg of you, go off somewhere gay—even if you must go first to Prescott Point, don't let the aunts keep you for long tucked away in that gloomy, forbidding house. In my candid opinion it is an architectural monstrosity and for the aesthetic good of the Nation should be burned to the ground."

Sherry smiled and folded the last sheet of the letter in with the others. The old boy had snapped out of it at the end; disentangled himself from what he would probably call his "epistolary style," and become almost human. Perhaps it wasn't going to be too bad trying to talk to him, after all. His recollection of him was very dim, but he remembered that he had seemed rather jolly and that he had laughed a great deal. The letter was certainly a most amazing mixture, and rereading it hadn't gotten him much further—but it didn't matter, he'd know all about it very soon now. . . . That last bit about the check was great—it meant they could have a real honeymoon. He wondered if Molly would like Bermuda.

Sherry stubbed out his cigarette, put his wallet back in his pocket, and slid off the stool. The cop glanced up from his plate of wheat cakes.

"That was some letter you had there, Bud. Wish I had a girl to write to me like that. What's she do?"

"She's a professional swimmer," answered Sherry idiotically— Molly could swim like a fish, and it would do the cop good; he had more curiosity than ten cats.

"Yeah?" the cop gave him a look of dark suspicion and wiped syrup from the corner of his mouth with a wadded paper napkin. "Leaving us so soon?"

Sherry buttoned his overcoat and picked up his driving gloves. "I've a hell of a way to go."

"You have that," the cop agreed. "Well, good luck to you."

"Thanks," said Sherry, and went out of the warm and comforting fug into the bitter gray cold of early morning. The sky looked close and swollen—they were right, it was going to snow.

Sherry got into the car.

For hours then he was conscious of very little but the cold and the weary strain of driving; and the monotonous miles slipped behind him with their towns and cities blurred, indistinguishable one from another, across his tired eyes and brain.

Once, his thought returned to the letter and to the answer he believed he knew—to the reason why his uncle had remained for so long a stranger to him. The explanation was to be found, he was sure, in something that Nona had told him one summer afternoon many years before. He had remembered it because it had seemed so unbelievable to him—so impossible to imagine as ever having been true.

Long ago, she had told him, Clytie and his uncle had been in love. They had loved each other for a long time and were at last going to be married. But something had happened; they had quarreled bitterly and they had never seen one another again. It had all occurred many years ago, about the time of his mother's death, when Sherry was very little, only five years old. But hearing it as a boy of eleven or twelve, he could not imagine that, even then, in that far-off time seven years before, Clytie could have been in love. He found it incredible then, and he found it incredible still. Not Clytie. . . .

Helen—oh yes, that was very different. Helen was gay and sweet and feminine. Why, even now at sixty, she made you aware of herself as a woman. It was as hard to think of Helen as being an old maid, as it was to think of the possibility of Clytie's ever having been anything else. And yet, according to Nona, it had been Helen who had never wanted to leave home, who had turned all suitors away; devoting herself first to her father, then to her brother, and then, at last, to her brother's son—to Sherry himself.

Surprisingly enough, he remembered, Nona had appeared not to approve. "Christian devotion, they may call it if they like," she had said, "but I call it downright unnatural." Funny Nona . . . she had never liked Helen. Perhaps she had always been a little jealous of her; she was fanatically devoted to Clytie. . . . They were alike, those two pinched, tall, gray women. They had the same erased, still look upon their faces, as if they had come under the same fire; faced life over the battered, shell-marked top of the same trench; stood shoulder to shoulder, comrades-in-arms, against the advancing thunder of days and hours, the long campaign of frustrated, empty years— Yes, he could understand why, in that group of three, Nona's loyalty should be for Clytie. Bitter and tragically unlikable, Clytie, not Helen, had need of it. . . .

Once more, Sherry's thoughts emptied. He was conscious only of the road before him.

Around two o'clock Sherry stopped for a hot dog and a cup of coffee at another roadstand; filled the car with gas and shoved on. Counting his money at the filling station, Sherry figured that if he went light on dinner he could arrive in Bangor with two dollars and a half aside from the five-dollar bill put away in his hat. Then, if for any reason his uncle couldn't put him up for the night, he had just enough for a hotel room. He had to get some sleep; and he didn't want to touch the old boy for money the minute he walked in on him.

He told himself that he was being ridiculously overcautious: of course his uncle would be there, and there wouldn't be any question of his having to go to a hotel. But it would take all of the five dollars in his hat to buy gas for the trip home, and he'd better play safe, just in case. If anything did go wrong, he thought ruefully, if, for instance, through some improbable chance his uncle should be away, he'd have a very thin time of it on the way back. It would be a choice then between sleeping and eating—obviously, he couldn't do both. Sherry yawned, and decided in the event of that very grim improbability, he should most emphatically choose sleep. . . .

The weary miles went on. And at four o'clock, with over a hundred miles still to go, it began to snow.

Somewhere off the coast of Florida, under a gaily striped awning, Mr. Derwent Avery crossed one white-flanneled leg over the other and raised a cocktail glass to his lips. Warmed by a very gold sun and lulled by the gentle motion of a very blue sea, he thought how pleasant and how unexpected had been the chance that had brought him there.

He thought of his nephew not at all.

CHAPTER ELEVEN

Life at Prescott Point, Molly decided dolefully, seemed mainly to consist of frustrated goings-to-sleep and bitter wakings-up-again. She had awakened early Monday morning, bolt upright, aware of an enormous urgency. The vast room with its heavy furniture had the black-and-gray appearance of a negative—it was not yet fully light. Dream-haunted still, Molly sighed with relief and lay down again: there was plenty of time.

She had been dreaming that she had to catch a boat. But she wasn't ready, she hadn't even packed, and all of a sudden it was terribly late. With the guilt-injustice of dreams, she knew that she had known all along that she was to sail, so that for her not to be ready was inexcusable—a grave and incredible slackness. And yet, although she was most dreadfully culpable, at the same time she was not to blame. Through no fault of her own, there had been a strange slip-up: and what had been Then had jumped into what was Now without any warning at all. And here she was with every-thing left to do and no time left to do it in, caught helpless in a panic-sense of awful urgency: Sherry and her father were on that boat, they needed her and she must sail with them. She had a mes-sage for them that was terribly important. If she didn't get to them with it something horrible would happen—and they would never forgive her. She would be guilty. She would have failed them both.

The trouble was, she didn't know the time. Time was the key to it all. She ran down the stairs to look at the ormolu clock. It was there, ticking on the mantelpiece, but for some reason she could not read its face. That was Clytie's doing, because Clytie wouldn't let her. Clytie knew the time, Clytie knew everything. Molly began to plead with her, standing in the middle of the living room, sobbing and begging: "Please, please Clytie, be kind and help me. Oh, it's awfully late! *Please* Miss Prescott, like me a little, and tell me the time." But Clytie wouldn't even look at her, just went on putting purple tulips into a bowl, throwing the yellow and pink ones over her shoulder onto the floor, whispering angrily, "Clash—clash—clash." . . .

And Helen was no good to Molly, because Helen didn't know when the boat was sailing or what time it was, any more than Molly did. But she kept opening her big black lace fan like a *Señorita* and smiling slyly behind it at Molly.

Then Nona was there, too, with the breakfast tray, picking up the yellow and pink tulips and putting them on it. She turned her blank, glittering spectacles on Molly, saying severely: "Waste not, want not," and Molly knew that the tulips were being saved for a funeral, and that the funeral was to be her own. . . .

And all the while it was getting later and later, so she tried once again to make Clytie listen to her, but this time Helen got in her way. Helen was playing with the black cat now. She had something in her fingers, and she was teasing him with it and making him jump into the air up against her skirt trying to get at it. It was something small and white, and suddenly Molly knew that it was the little perfumed hunk of cotton from the folds of her wedding nightgown. But, just as she went to take it from her, the bell buoy began to ring and it was her father on the telephone and he was saying to her reproachfully, over and over, "The boat sails at noon, daughter. Hurry, hurry, hurry." . . . And then Molly was bolt upright in the almost dark room, knowing that it was still very early in the morning, and that there was, mercifully, after all, plenty of time. . . .

For a moment or two the driven anxiety of the dream remained with Molly, and she sighed as though at a reprieve as she lay down again and pulled reality snugly around her. It was Monday morning, and in a few hours she would be seeing Sherry and getting everything straightened out. She turned over on her side to go back to sleep. Her eyes began to close; suddenly she opened them wide and raised herself on one elbow. Out of the corner of her eye she had caught the glimmer of something white.

It lay on the floor by the door and it was flat and square. It looked curiously like a letter, but what would a letter be doing—

Molly snapped on the light and in one bound was out of bed and had Sherry's note in her hand. The dreadful sense of urgency was upon her again, and with it came the certainty that this time she was too late. What she had felt last night, and what she had felt in the dream—both were true. Sherry was gone.

She crawled disconsolately back into bed and opened the envelope:

"5:45 Monday morning.
"Darling, I wanted to see you before I left but you had locked the door. I have to go away for a few days and I would have told you why if I could have gotten in to you without waking Clytie. They don't know I'm going and please say nothing to them about this. I'm off now. When I come back I'll explain everything. Only for God's sake, darling, will you stop locking your damn door! Remember what you promised me? Take care of yourself. I love you,
    "Sherry."

Molly read the letter through a second time, then she put it in the envelope and pushed it out of sight under her pillow. She picked up her watch from the bedside table. It was after seven o'clock: Sherry had been gone for over an hour. She felt quiet and still inside herself now, as if she had come to a clearing in the midst of a thick wood: an empty, silent place where everything waited motionless. There was nothing more that she had to feel. It was too late; she could rest, suspended, until Sherry returned.

Nothing more that she had to feel—only simple things that she had to do. Molly got up and padded across to the door. It was still locked. That was that. Molly went back to bed, turned off the light, and lay down. Someone would be coming soon to unlock it. All she had to do was to stay awake and wait for them. . . . Of course there was no reason why she shouldn't just close her eyes for a minute or two, she wouldn't go to sleep. . . . What was Clytie going to say when she caught her red-handed unlocking the door? That was going to be a wonderful moment. But 'red-handed' belonged only with a murder; she ought to think of a better word. . . . Pink and yellow tulips for a funeral; that was silly, too. . . . Nothing to worry about. There was lots and lots of time. . . .

Promptly at seven-thirty the key turned softly in the lock. It was a very quiet little sound, and Molly did not hear it. For at seven-thirty Molly was fast asleep.

And thus it was that Monday morning had two bitter wakings-up instead of the usual one.

Nona's knock came at a quarter-past eight, and it is merely honest to admit that, fully awake, Molly's language woke up, too. She was absolutely furious with herself, and while she dressed she told herself about it in a full-bodied bouquet that only years of being 'aged' in the theater could have perfected. Brushing her teeth, she took her toothbrush, every now and then, out of her mouth to add another word of vintage flavor. Until, at last, a little drunk with self-reproach, slightly giddy with recrimination, she began to feel distinctly better.

Perhaps, she consoled herself, it hadn't been such a good idea, after all. Just one of those things that seem extremely brilliant late at night, or early in the morning. Bouncing out at Clytie could hardly be called very polite; and incidentally, what would she, herself, have said: "Aha! I've caught you"? It would certainly have created a situation. On the whole, thinking it over, it was undoubtedly just as well that she had gone back to sleep.

So, having reached this soothing conclusion, Molly powdered her nose and, looking as if butter wouldn't melt in her mouth and as beautiful as only Molly could look at eight-thirty in the morning, descended to breakfast.

Clytie and Helen were talking together in low tones when Molly reached the dining room. They stopped suddenly as she came in, looked up and said in unison with her, "Good morning." Molly sat down and did her best to repress a shudder. In a dish in front of Clytie, her worst suspicions were confirmed. There was, she noted with horror, actually porridge.

She would have to eat it; Clytie's voice closed all hope of escape: "Sugar and cream?" asked Clytie firmly.

"Yes please, thank you," Molly answered; and accepted her fate.

Helen had been watching them, turning her head quickly from one to the other. She had, Molly thought, the brightly inquiring air of a sleek and eager little robin. Now she spoke:

"We would have sent your breakfast up to you., dear, I'm sure you would have preferred to have it that way, only we're a bit disorganized this morning. And until—"

"I still say, Helen," Clytie interrupted with acerbity, "that you're making a mistake. You'll find you can go far and fare worse."

Helen went on as though she hadn't heard her. "And until Nona gets used to being single-handed, we thought it was better to have you come down."

"Until Nona recovers her temper, you mean," snapped Clytie, evincing not the slightest intention of being ignored. "There was nothing in the world the matter with that raspberry fool." She turned suddenly on Molly. "What did you think of it?"

"W-ho me?" Molly stammered. "Why I thought— It—it was delicious."

"You see," said Clytie.

The swinging door to the pantry opened sharply, and Nona came into the room.

"What I can't understand, Helen," Clytie continued to drive home her advantage, "is why you should change your mind all of a sudden. Up until Saturday night you did nothing but say what an excellent cook she was. Far superior, you said, to poor Lizzie."

"Clytie dear," Helen murmured deprecatingly, "I should much prefer not to discuss this further."

Nona decided to enter the fray. She swooped down upon Molly's plate of oatmeal and whisked it away.

"If you ask me," she said to Clytie, speaking of Helen in the third person exactly as if she weren't there, "she's got taken by one of her notions, that's all. Can't abide strangers about, things being as they are. Don't matter to her how much extra work—"

They were certainly ganging up on her; Molly began to feel rather sorry for Helen. She needn't have worried; Helen was fully able to take care of herself.

"That will do, Nona," Helen said, and there was surprising authority in her gentle voice.

Clytie declined to be silenced.

"Nevertheless—"

"Clytie!" Still Helen did not raise her voice, although now Molly sensed that she was very angry. "Please don't go on with this. Can't you see that you are making Molly most uncomfortable?"

Thrust suddenly like this into the limelight, Molly went completely to pieces. She nearly burbled brightly, "Oh, don't mind me." Fortunately, Clytie saved her.

What happened then partook of the sheerly impossible.

"I am very sorry," Clytie said. And before Molly's wondering stare, a slow red flush crept up her neck, over her cheeks, to the roots of her iron-gray hair. She dropped her eyes to her plate.

Nona slammed out of the room.

There was a highly charged silence.

My brain feels, Molly thought, as if somebody had pied the type. Helen had defied Clytie and Clytie had blushed, and all Molly's neatly arranged theories lay jumbled together on the floor of her mind. She would have to set them up all over again. Nona and Clytie banded together against Helen. The curious amount of high-voltage temper generated by the dismissal of a cook. It was all very odd.

And when in it all, Molly wondered, would somebody say something about Sherry? His place was not set at the table; they must have discovered he had gone— She'd have to say something soon if they didn't, otherwise it would begin to look fishy that she hadn't asked where he was. What's more, it was going to take quite a nice little piece of acting if she was to make it convincing. Rapidly, Molly began to review her lines.

She never had to use them.

Clytie cleared her throat. She looked impenetrable, granite-skinned and severe—quite her old self again.

"Sherman has gone," she announced flatly.

Obviously, at this point, Molly's script read, surprise, incredulity, dismay: What! What? Wh-at. . . . She got them ready, and produced the first:

"What!" Molly exclaimed.

"My dear child," Helen cut in, "forgive me. I haven't given you any coffee. You should have asked me for it. Sugar?"

"Wh-at?" quavered Molly, dropped with such a bump that a wobbly combination of the second and third "what" got out before she could stop it. "Er— thank you. . . . Two please."

Helen was brightly soothing. She poured coffee.

"It's just for a few days, dear." (The insufferable trained-nurse touch: pat, pat.) "You mustn't look so disturbed. . . . You see, it wasn't discovered until late last night that Sherry had to go. A little business matter— Still it won't take long, he should be right back."

"Oh. . . ." Molly contented herself with that, but she felt like a great deal more. She would have liked to say as Sherry had, "Now, Nell, don't be naughty." For although Helen had, very cleverly indeed, avoided telling a direct lie; and although she was, of course, only doing it at all in order to be kind; nevertheless, the whole thing stacked up to an enormous whopper.

Clytie took over again. She fixed Molly with a let's-get-to-the-bottom-of-this eye, and spoke with her usual, disconcerting abruptness.

"Did you know Sherman was going?"

Helen put down Molly's cup and saucer with a sharp little clatter, picked it up again and handed it to Molly.

"Don't be ridiculous, Clytie! How could Molly have known?"

(How, indeed, thought Molly, locked in a room!)

"Did you?" persisted Clytie.

"No, of course, I didn't," answered Molly, firm in relieved truthfulness; and determining in that instant upon an attack of her own added casually, "By the way—" (the thought-connection back of this was going to be most gloriously obvious)—"while I think of it, Clytie, I wonder if you could let me have a key for my room?"

She was completely successful; Clytie looked immensely startled.

"A *key?*"

"Yes, so that I can lock my door."

"But my dear child," (that came from Helen) "what an extraordinary request!"

"It's a habit—hotel rooms and all," Molly mumbled, refusing to become deflected and keeping her eyes glued to Clytie's face. "Can't seem to get out of it," she ended with inspired double meaning.

Clytie gave her sister a long strange look, oddly beseeching and yet somehow speculative. Then she turned and looked at Molly. There was nothing mixed about this—even softened, it could only be described as withering.

"If she wants it, naturally she must have it," Clytie said.

"Why, of course—" Helen's murmur showed more desire to be helpful than a happy choice of words. "We only want her to feel at home. . . ."

There was no doubt about it, Molly thought, sometimes she did succeed in getting them down. Illogically, she felt a little ashamed.

"Are you sure," Clytie asked grabbing hold of their end and lifting it up by as pretty a piece of puzzled innocence as Molly had ever seen, "are you positive the key's not in your room? It should be right there in the door. Perhaps," this last had an air of sudden inspiration, "it's been knocked out onto the floor."

"I don't think so," Molly said.

Nona came in with a plate of bacon and eggs and put it down in front of Molly. She creaked and straightened.

"Cook's leaving by the 10:10, Obadiah wants to know if he's to drive her."

"Tell him, no." Clytie folded her napkin. "I shall want him this morning."

Nona went out again through the swing door, something about her back suggesting an intense and secret satisfaction— She loves saying no to poor Obadiah, Molly decided. And as for the cook, the poor thing hadn't even got a name!

The cook . . . it was odd to think of her there, still in the house— a stranger, like Molly herself, in this house that didn't want strangers—and realize, with unwantedness making so much queerly in common, that she'd never know Molly's name, nor Molly hers. Molly had been just another dinner to her, and now she had ceased to be even that. In less than an hour, and without their so much as laying eyes on each other, the nameless cook would be gone. . . .

Suddenly, and as if it could be terribly important, Molly wanted to see her just once; to watch her stepping into the car to go away from this place, back to— Like a long-term prisoner who hears of another's unexpected release, like an exile who sees a boat sail for home, like any other cliché of the sort—quite overwhelmingly Molly envied that cook. She bit viciously into a piece of toast.

Clytie rose. "If you will excuse me," she said. "I'll go now and telephone Fred Kirkwood. I must catch him at once if Mrs. Wilkins is to leave by the ten o'clock train."

So she had a name after all! Irrationally, Molly felt cheated, as if Clytie had been looking inside her mind, letting her build things all up around an unknownness just in order that she might spoil it for her now by giving it away at the very last minute. Wilkins! Oh God. . . .

Helen watched her sister leave the room. A little preoccupied frown lay for an instant over her customary expression of child-like serenity. She usually gave the impression, Molly thought, of a well-behaved and happy little girl about to go to a party: life an unopened present she held between her hands. Now she looked perplexed and vaguely troubled: someone had inexplicably taken the present away. It was only for a moment. She turned her head back to Molly and smiled.

"You know, dear," she said with that shyly confiding friendliness which Molly found so difficult to resist, "I am not altogether sorry that Sherry had to go, it will give us a chance to get better acquainted. There's so much, isn't there, that we have to tell each other? We must have a nice long hash together, just you and I."

"I should like that," Molly said, not altogether sure that she would. It rather depended, she thought, upon who did the hashing: events had bred in her a small and unaccustomed wariness.

Helen pushed back her chair. "I'll run along now and let you finish your breakfast in peace. Things have been awfully confused this morning, haven't they?"

Helen giggled, suddenly looking mischievous. Mood shifts without transitions, thought Molly, seemed to be the twins' own specialty. Apparently, she had been wrong: Helen had enjoyed it all immensely. . . .

"If there is anything I can do—?"

"My dear child, of course not! Everything will be—what's the word?—everything will be jake in no time. To tell the truth, Nona's a little spoiled."

Helen got up. The cat, which must have been lying out of sight by the other side of Helen's chair, appeared all at once and, just as he had in Molly's dream, sprang into the air and flung himself violently against Helen's skirt. So violently, indeed, that the impact knocked Helen for an instant off balance.

"Gracious goodness!" Helen exclaimed. "He will do that," she said to Molly. Her tone was disparaging, yet fond. "It's very naughty of him, some day he's going to have me right over." She addressed the cat, who was now purring and rubbing up against her legs. "Did I forget his cream? Well he shall have it this very minute as ever is . . . so he shall."

A mental groan escaped Molly. If anybody was spoiled in that house, it was Helen's cat. She was inclined to agree with Sherry—the creature was a black monstrosity. And like the cook, he was apparently nameless. With a childish feeling of spiking Clytie's guns in advance this time, she said, "What's his name?"

Helen put the saucer of cream down carefully on the carpet, "Matilda."

"But I thought—" began Molly, completely bewildered.

"Oh yes, he is," agreed Helen cheerfully. "You see, he was named before we knew. We were, as it turned out, under a definite misapprehension. Now it seems rather absurd and hardly fair to him; so most of the time we just don't call him anything."

"Oh. . . ." said Molly. Somehow, the explanation hadn't helped very much. Helen seemed unaware of any possible lack, however. She smiled again brightly and bustled from the room.

"Really!" said Molly to herself.

She got up and poured herself another cup of coffee, sat down again with it, and lit a cigarette. She felt that she wanted to pull herself together. As an early-morning exercise, she found the twins far too strenuous. She did her best to ignore the suspicion, lurking uncomfortably at the back of her mind, that they might prove to be too much for her at the very best of times. She had had, after all, a certain measure of success. Offense was, obviously, the best defense. Molly decided upon a firm policy of frontal attack. From then on, she was going to bang right out with things. . . . When, for a second, doubt as to the wisdom of this poked its head out, Molly told it firmly to go back with that other suspicion and lie down. She finished her coffee with an air of belligerent confidence.

But she almost ran to her room. . . .

She had forgotten the letter. It had been left under her pillow, and suddenly she was seized with panic lest it should be found by someone going in to make up her bed. Even as she hurried up the stairs she told herself that: she was being extremely silly—Nona was undoubtedly still in the kitchen; and although she had all that extra work to do, it wasn't likely that either Helen or Clytie were going to help her out by making beds. All the same. . . .

She flung open the door of her room and took a deep breath of relief. Everything was just as she had left it. She went over to the bed and took Sherry's letter out from under the pillow. She turned holding it in her hand and froze suddenly in incredulous amazement. There, shining a little against the dark wood of the floor, lying in a corner near the door, was a key.

"Well I'll be gumswizzled!" said Molly chastely.

She was too astonished for anything else, and for a moment she found herself wondering if it had not been there all along; actually caught herself arguing wildly that, even if it had been, it could hardly leap from the floor, lock the door, and jump down again by itself. At last, still feeling rather like the victim of a conjuror's trick, Molly walked over to it and picked it up.

It didn't change into a rabbit or a box of chocolates or even a bunch of paper flowers. It stayed a perfectly ordinary key. Skeptically, Molly inserted it in the keyhole and gave it a twist. The lock turned sweetly and with scarcely a sound. She had the last astonishment of all:

It was the right key.

CHAPTER TWELVE

Immediately, Molly was filled with immense uneasiness. She thought: "This is wrong. It concedes too much. It has been too easy." There was slyness, treachery, in this small victory. She felt herself enclosed in hostility, thick, opaque like a fog; imprisoned again in a law of evil where even inanimate things, obedient, bore their own malignity: a rusty sign that creaked in the wind, a bell that rang, a key. . . . Standing there, with the early-morning sun slanting across the rumpled bed, surrounded by the rectitude of prosaic objects—the sedate Victorian furniture, the air of humdrum righteous comfort—she felt the steamy alive-dark of the jungle, the breathing crouched malevolence, secret and waiting— She wrenched the key from the lock.

For the first time in her life, Molly could not afford her imagination, it ran too close to a sensed truth—lighting up her dimmed apprehension with the garish symbols of terror like a child making frightening faces in a glass. Only her reason was any good to her: the 'why' of things. Understanding took the secrecy and hiddenness out of fear and left it open and clean, something to be dealt with. It was because this whole business of the key was inexplicable that she found it so unnerving.

They had locked her in her room—why? To prevent the consummation of the marriage, to keep her away from Sherry. Yes, but she would discover it very soon, as she had, and then she would tell him. (Or he would tell her—except for a silly quarrel, that would have happened yesterday.) It was like the Ignoring, good for only

305

a little time. But suppose that was what they had hoped for? Suppose they wanted to gain time until— Until *what?* that was the question Through it all, behind their ruse of delay, she had sensed a waiting expectancy; from the first that had lain in her nerves a subtle message of danger, awakened in her the instinct of desperate urgency. But social habit, the taboo against making a scene, these had been stronger than instinct—she had not obeyed.

Now they had given her back the key. Was that because Sherry had gone? Because it was useless now that she knew? Or because— this, the treachery behind her 'victory'—its purpose was already accomplished? . . . . But how could that be? How could they believe they had won? Nothing had changed; Sherry was coming back.

What did they hope for? *What* did they wait for? Until—they had persuaded her away, annulled the marriage? Once, was it only yesterday morning? she had almost gone; but she would never go now. Until they made her desert? She thought of it with shame. No matter what happened, no matter what they tried, she was seeing this through. She was loyal. She would stick.

They forgot the most important thing of all: her love for Sherry and his for her. That was their greatest weakness. They were old, they did not remember—perhaps they had never known— Staring down at the key lying in her palm, Molly felt obscurely sorry for them. She had everything on her side—the strongest force of all. She thought: "Hatred and malice? Even death cannot stop love." When you came up against love, you came up against defeat.

With a little grimace of defiance, Molly put the key back in the door, turned away, and began to make the bed.

Secure in her faith, confident and very young, she did not know that because she was as incorruptible as a child in her belief that life was good, stubbornly uncompromising and with the appalling tenacity of a saint, she was carrying within her her own danger. She could not be intimidated by doubt; she could be taught nothing contrary to what she instinctively felt to be true. Against her invincible simplicity ordinary measures were useless; inevitably, to attack her at all, was to be forced to extremes. It took drastic weapons to pierce Molly's crusading armor. . . .

Sherry had said: "Happiness through you, Molly, some time, some day—" That, then, was how it was to be . . . . Molly executed a beautiful square corner, tucked in the blankets, and went over to fetch the spread. She was very precise about it all, and when she had finished she stood back and looked at the bed with grim satisfaction. She had achieved its pristine look of conventlike rigidity. It looked as it should: as though it had never been slept in.

The day loomed ahead of her, long and lonely and impossible to fill. She fought down a rising sense of utter desolation. Emotion was forbidden, too, along with her imagination. It struck her that it was going to be awfully chilly and very dull with only reason to keep her company. She was going to miss her two habitual playmates, although there was no doubt about it, they were bad for her just now. Reason was so very formidable, like a carping and censorious grownup. Molly gave her pince-nez and a stiff upholstered bosom—it did not occur to her that in this dressing-up, playmate number two had surreptitiously sneaked back. . . . She tidied the room and the bathroom and at last wandered over to the window. The sun had gone in, and it looked as though later it might be going to snow. She wondered where Sherry had gone and wished that he had told her. If only the door hadn't been locked she might have known everything now, there might have been no mysteries, no "whats?" or "whys?" to worry her any more.

His note was so terribly unsatisfactory— She turned and looked over at where it lay on the top of the chest of drawers. What should she do with it and with the key? Unsatisfactory as the note was, she didn't want to destroy it; it was something of Sherry, a confidence—something to touch and have near her until he came back. She couldn't leave it in her room; she couldn't carry a handbag around with her all the time—an insulting hotel-like touch— Let the key stay in the door? They'd hardly— On the whole, she'd feel better if she had them both with her. The difficulty was, *where?*

In the end she solved her problem in a way that was practical if distinctly uncomfortable, and smacking, moreover, of secret agents and desperate missions. She put the key in the letter and the letter inside her elastic girdle. After considerable experiment in walking and sitting she found the least painful and conspicuous position to be at a point slightly off center and to the left. Although it was inclined to bite her with disconcerting suddenness and sharpness at moments, she told herself firmly that if the Spartan boy could take the fox, she could certainly take this! After all, she supposed she'd get used to it in time, and there was one good thing: her suffering, like his, was silent—the letter was too tightly cemented onto her flesh to do any crackling— That was settled . . . but what now?

Molly moved restlessly about the room. Underneath everything she thought, everything she did—all attempts at distraction—she was increasingly aware of the taut suspense which drove at her nerves giving her that sense of desperate urgency, impelling her to action: do something, do something! But what *could* she do? It was all so intangible. With every instinct crying for haste—against what or before what, she did not know—she was compelled to wait, bound helpless in inaction. It was as though she saw happiness to be gained, like a last train for home slowly leaving the station, and could only mark time, lifting her feet in a dreadful parody of running.

The feeling of her dream haunted her. Over and over she told herself that there was nothing she needed to do: when Sherry came back and they talked together wouldn't everything be made clear? Yet the sense of having-to-be-ready persisted: she, herself, must uncover the secret. The unsolved mystery was like the unpacked trunk in her dream—she must have the solution ready, or in some obscure way she would have failed Sherry. She was responsible and trusted; he had needed her help, and it had been necessary to him to know that she could sense this: a test of her love made vital by not being expressed. An ordeal by silence.

And perhaps it was not only that, perhaps, even now, there were things he could not reach, hidden places he could not find unaided, needing her to discover the way. He was the native, bewildered and lost in familiar terrain, she the explorer with maps and charts. . . .

But, if she was to do it, she must stop vacillating; stop seesawing between smug confidence and vague fear, neither exaggerating the one nor deluding herself with the other. She must put her feet on the ground. Get down to it, and work it out— Above all, at the moment, she must cope with her damnable restlessness. Prowling between the bed and the window wasn't doing her any good— she'd better go for a "nice brisk walk." Here was her schedule: Exercise the nervousness out of her body. Quell all signs of Imagination. Quash all Emotion. Rely solely on Reason (sic!). . . . Attractive regimen, wasn't it? A little on the stark side, perhaps?

Molly went to the closet and got out her camel's-hair coat. She pulled the belt tight around her waist (repressing a start as she ran foul of the key) and turned the collar up about her ears. Everything was happening all over again, yesterday morning repeating itself: the same gesture, the same act. Monotony without peace.

"I give it to you," Molly said aloud, "as a recipe for hell"—and suddenly with alarming treachery tears stung her eyes. "Bloody ass," Molly added. "Come on Reason, make it snappy!"

Pince-nez and bosom appeared. Safely escorted by the dowager, Molly left the room.

Again the upstairs hall was empty, the doors all closed. Again the house produced its malevolent impression of vacancy, of tenantless desertion. Again, almost furtively, Molly slid through the front door, conscious of a palpable feeling of escape. She took an incautiously deep breath of release and choked as the biting air reached her lungs. It was as piercingly cold as an anaesthetic. She decided first on an exploration of the cliff.

Rounding the corner of the house, Molly paused to look up at the windows. After spending two nights and a day at Prescott Point she still did not know which rooms were Clytie's and Helen's. From Sherry's note, however, she gathered that Clytie's door must be near her own—obviously, in that case, the one diagonally across the hall from hers. Clytie's bedroom, then, was at the back facing the sea. . . . Looking along the house Molly could identify her own windows now. They would be the last two on this side, for if she leaned out of the farthest one she could just catch an angle of the cliff and a bit of sea between the windbreak of pines and the corner of the house. Helen's must be here farther toward the front on this, the sunny side of the house. Undoubtedly the two windows directly above her head as she was standing now.

Staring up at them, Molly had confirmation. Behind one of the panes there was a flash of movement and the big black cat appeared. He glanced in royal indifference at Molly below and began to sink down upon his paws with a smooth, melting-into-himself slowness, rather as if his legs were being dissolved into his body instead of being bent. Crouching on the window sill he basked in a momentary gleam of thin winter sunshine. Helen's cat and Helen's room— that minor problem was solved.

Behind her a voice spoke. "Ain't manners to stare," it said. "Can't see nothing nohow," it added practically.

Molly turned round. Obadiah was standing across the gravel drive. He gestured toward the garden. "Said she wanted me," he complained with a sort of outraged dignity. "Wouldn't let me drive the car." He had the air of one who suffers a monstrous injustice.

"I'm sorry. . . ." Molly moved closer and raised her voice. "That's too bad," she shouted.

Obadiah held up a calloused palm, cutting off waste effort. "'Tain't no good answering, I'm hard of hearing." He gestured again at the garden, this time more angrily. "Don't get to go to the depot 'cause she said she wanted me. And *then* what happens?"

"I don't know," murmured Molly automatically; "what did?"

"She goes off, that's what she does. Don't pay no heed to me. I tell her it's there, but she's got to go and see for herself. And then she don't come back. Piddling nonsense, that's what it is! Getting herself all worked up for nothing— Sherry hain't got took by the notion for a good spell now—no call for her to be feared he would. I tell her the boat's there, but she—"

"Obadiah," desperately Molly grabbed his arm, "what are you talking about?" She put her mouth close to his ear. "I don't understand!"

Miraculously, he appeared to have heard her. "'Course you do," he corrected reprovingly. "Hain't you never done things just 'cause you're feared to? That's natural, that is. Leastways for menfolks—

Why ever since he's a little shaver Sherry's been scared pink of the water. Sick scared."

(Of course! Molly remembered now . . . that was the other thing that Sherry would never speak of— the other thing that had a sentry.)

"When the spell came on him extra bad seems like it made him plumb angry. Kinda couldn't stand to let it get the best of him. Usta take out that there catboat in all sorts of dirty weather, risked his fool life time and time again. . . . Didn't do no good, he never quit being scared. Lately though he hain't been doing it, 'pears like he's outgrown the need . . . sorta accepted it, I reckon. . . . That's why I knew she was getting all stewed up over nothing. I tell her so, but she pays no heed." The strange monologue had worked itself round to the beginning again. "Off she traipses to the boathouse to see for herself. . . . Could have been to the depot and back long ago. Won't let me drive the car. Says she *needs* me."

Obadiah took a step nearer Molly. He drew himself up—a man standing for his rights against unreasonable tyranny. "Women!" he pronounced with weary scorn. "If you was to see her, mind you tell her from me I'm awaiting on her and I'm getting mighty tired of doing it. Just say, 'Obadiah's mighty riled.' That'll fetch her like as not." Obadiah turned away. "Good day to you," he said.

The monologue was over.

For a moment Molly stood still, watching his retreating back as he shuffled off in the direction of the garage. She felt a little stunned. But yet it was curious that in a conversation in which she had had no share, been able to take no part, she should have learned more than in all the others: been given, through it, one number of the intricate combination—because, somehow, she knew that she had. Her instincts like sensitive finger tips had felt the fall of the tumbler; soon others near it would fall into place, and when she had them all in the right order she could unlock the secret.

She knew now what had been the emotion in Sherry's voice when he spoke to her by the cliff—it was fear. And as a symptom may reveal the malady behind it, so that fear was important: in knowing the effect she might be led back to a knowledge of its cause. . . . Sherry's fear of the water was an obsession strong enough to compel him to risk his life in an attempt to conquer it. And yet, when once she'd happened to tell him about her father's curious insistence on swimming as part of her training for the stage—that quaint theory regarding bodily co-ordination that had meant hours of practice in pools from Maine to California until she bulged with unwanted muscles—Sherry had only laughed and teased her: his reaction had been completely natural. "You'll see how good I am," she'd said, "when summer comes." He'd shown nothing. . . . But when he'd seen her standing on the cliff leaning out over the sea, he'd been afraid for her—unreasoningly afraid, for she was in no danger. Was there a significant discrepancy in those two reactions? Or was she torturing her one poor clue trying to wring truth from it? She'd better not moil over it any more, simply let it wait in her mind—often when you put things away naked you came back to find them fully clothed. . . .

Molly went round the windbreak of pines, and again, prepared as she was for it, the nearness and suddenness of the sea was like a physical impact. Its vastness was as gray and sullenly still as it had been yesterday, but today from the point of the cliff a long line of breakers stretched like a white road out into the grayness. A spine of submerged rock apparently ran out from the cliff into the water and at the change of the tide contrary currents meeting above it formed a race which extended, Molly judged, nearly a quarter of a mile out to sea. No wonder Sherry risked his life sailing a catboat in bad weather! Even in good, the currents must be extremely treacherous.

Where was the boathouse? In all probability it was below the cliff on the far side of the house. . . . Looking diagonally across the lawn, Molly saw what she had failed to notice the morning before, a second break in the line of the white posts: undoubtedly steps led down from there to the boathouse she could not see.

She started walking in a direct line toward it. This took her straight past the post that guarded the fissure in the cliff and she stopped to look down. The sides were as smooth and as sheer as those of a well; it was as if a precise and clean incision had been cut deep into the stone flesh of the earth. Held securely by the stretched white chain, she leaned out farther: far below was the gleam of water, and at the narrow mouth of the wound waves broke and curled. With an involuntary little shudder she straightened, gave the guardian post a commendatory pat, and went on.

She was right about the steps. Although completely invisible until one stood directly above them, they were there as she had supposed. Supported by a stout wooden scaffolding against the side of the cliff they led steeply down to a tiny rocky cove lying below. Farther back, approximately on a line with the corner of the house above, and sheltered in the lee of the cliff, was the boathouse. From its wide door a launchway of wooden rollers crossed the narrow shingle to the water's edge, and beyond, a sturdy little pier with a landing stage extended past the breakers into the sea.

It was all tidy and complete, even to the miniature searchlight at the top of the steps by her hand. Experimentally, Molly switched it on. Pallid and pink in the daylight, by night it would illumine the whole cove like a welcoming beacon. Molly had a feeling of delighted discovery. Yesterday, standing at the point of the cliff, it had all seemed so stark and forbidding, just the lonely ugly house and the vast empty sea—always drab, always winter. But now, looking down at the white boathouse with its gay green roof, summer came true in anticipation: blue sea and bright hot sun, they would have such fun together, Sherry and she, swimming and sailing. In only a few months now, if—

Molly frowned impatiently. There was that 'if' again, incessantly intruding itself, perpetually turning up to spoil every dream! There was no 'if'—everything was going to be all right. She was going to get to the bottom of what was wrong and make it right. Long before summer came, this dark haunting mystery would be over forever. Sherry would be happy and free and not afraid any more. . . . Molly clicked off the switch of the searchlight and ran down the steps; she wanted to take a look at the boat.

The deep pebbles of the beach slipped and slithered out under her feet, Molly looked down at her best shoes with concern. But it was warmer here out of the wind and small and sheltered—like being in an altogether different world. The big, sprawling menace

of the house was gone and the vast expanse of the sea. The tall cliff
at her side and the lower one beyond narrowed everything into
cozy, friendlier proportions. They were like great stone blinkers,
Molly thought, shutting off what was too much to see. Even the
sky seemed smaller for the pines growing along the top of the steep
bluff behind the boathouse; except for the steps up the side of the
cliff, the tiny cove was completely cut off.

The wide double doors of the boathouse were padlocked. Molly
went around to the side. There was a window there but it was too
high for her to be able to look in. She stood on tiptoe but her head
barely reached the sill and she half-turned to go back. She was
worrying about her shoes. The trunk would come today, and when
it did she could unpack her old pair of brogues and explore to her
heart's content. In the meantime she ought to confine herself to
less disastrous going. . . .

Molly chuckled. She had remembered a funny French sign
which she had seen once in a window in Paris. It was propped up
against a pair of stout English walking shoes, and it said: "*Pour le
footings.*" Well, it was typical of her luck to find herself stranded
without proper "footings"—shoes she shouldn't wear and a nightgown she wouldn't wear; it made both day and night quite a problem. . . .

Just the same, she thought, it's hardly any farther to go on.
Curiosity won over caution. There must be another door at the back,
and, although it was undoubtedly locked too, she might as well
circle the boathouse and see.

There was a door, and to Molly's delight and surprise it was
not locked. She pushed it open and went in.

It was very dim inside the boathouse, dank and sea-weedy
smelling, and the sound of the waves beat in it with a hollow echo,
suddenly loud. There was another sound too, somewhere inside
there, softer and more broken. . . . Molly could make out the dark
bulk of the boat crouching like a great sleeping beast in the semi-
darkness of its cave. And over there, half-hidden by the curve of
its flank, was a smaller huddled shape that moved ever so little. . . .
Molly stood stock-still. The soft sound came again—someone was

sobbing. Again something moved, and all at once the huddled shape, half-seen, took form: the bent shoulders of a woman and across them the protecting arm of another, a pale hand that moved in the dimness, stroking, consoling.

"Don't . . . don't take on so, Miss Clytie." Nona's voice—but so changed that Molly hardly knew it. There was a sort of angry tenderness, a compassionate impatience in its flat tone. "Come now . . . come. You mustn't, dear—you mustn't. . . ."

But the low terrible sobbing went on shaking through the stillness, seeming now for all its muffled softness the only sound—closing her senses to itself alone, making unheard the empty hollow drumming of the waves. . . . . Molly turned her head back to the bright rectangle of the open door—if only she could reach it undiscovered.

Her position was a miserable one. If Clytie and Nona should realize she was there; if they ever knew that she had heard Clytie crying—that she had witnessed this moment of closest privacy—it would be intolerable, and they could never forgive her. Embarrassed shame would cause Clytie to loathe her, to see her always as a crass intruding sneak. They had been too absorbed to notice her; she must try to slip out unseen.

Molly took a cautious step toward the door. . . .

Clytie's voice now, broken and desperate:

"I can't bear it . . . I can't!" The words came through the dimness with a sort of driven despair. "Such hate . . . and I can't stop it. I can't fight it. I'm weak . . . guilty. I can't help it. I'm too weak, I tell you. No good . . . no good. Oh, must it happen all over again! I can't bear it, I can't!"

"No, no, dear. It's not going to. Listen to me—"

"Listen? What's the use! Poor Nona. . . . Don't lie to me, Nona, it's no use." In Clytie's voice the quick despair had grown weary, dull with bitter acceptance. "You feel it and you know. Now it will happen again because it must. It is the same, and it must. Horrible . . . all over again. Merciful God, why am I—"

"Hush, Miss Clytie. It doesn't have to, you can stop it. I know you can. This time—"

Molly was through the door, slipping and stumbling in her haste, the noise of the slithering pebbles loud in her ears. Reckless now of her shoes, she plunged across the beach, up the steep steps, running blindly across the lawn, swerving just in time round the white post, until gasping and painfully out of breath, she reached the corner of the house. She stopped there, steadying herself for a moment, waiting for the hard thudding of her heart to subside, the salty taste of blood to leave her mouth. Then she started walking as fast as her legs would carry her, past the windbreak of pines, the garage, the garden, down the long gravel driveway in the direction of the village.

CHAPTER THIRTEEN

She walked without thought, conscious of nothing except the compelling instinct to get away—to put as much distance as she possibly could between herself and the hateful, brooding house. Nothing that had happened had shaken her so as the low, tearing sound of Clytie's sobs. Nothing had seemed half so frightening, so terrible a part of evil, as the hopelessness awake in that small rasping noise of utter despair. Remorse? . . . A haunting dread . . . a memory? She could not probe in it for meaning; she could not lay cool curious hands upon it. Not now . . . not yet. It existed in her as something felt, too immediate for reason. Looming too close and large for thought, it needed the dwarfing perspective of time for her to see it clearly.

She walked hard and fast. Cars zoomed by her on the road, the sucking swoosh of their passing whipping her coat against her legs. She did not look up or turn her head, but with her eyes on the road ahead of her trudged steadily on. About three miles from the village Fred Kirkwood passed in an open truck as dilapidated as his taxi. In the back along with some chicken crates and a bicycle was Molly's trunk. As he rattled by he gave Molly a long stare. He wasn't sure that he recognized her, for he had only seen her once and in the dark. The set expression on her face caused him to purse his lips in a soundless whistle. "If it's her," he thought, "she's not lasted long. She's skedaddling mighty quick." He had an obscure feeling of disappointment: he'd taken her for a sticker. "Ain't got no guts, be gosh," he said to himself. Those twin she-devils! Two in one morning, first the new help and now Sherry's girl. Like as not, he'd have to cart that trunk right back to the depot again. . . . Still, maybe it wasn't her, after all.

But when, a quarter of a mile farther on, he saw the Prescott sedan coming toward him with Obadiah driving, he knew that it was. Fred waved as the cars passed each other and gestured with his thumb back down the road. Yet, although he had seen him, Obadiah did not respond to Fred's signal. His rigid concentration could not be broken by even a nod, let alone a hand raised from the steering wheel. He went by bolt upright, eyes fixed sternly ahead, clutching the wheel stiffly with both hands, on his face a compound expression of reckless glee and awe-inspired anxiety. Fred chuckled and then suddenly put his foot on the brake. The truck rattled to a stop.

Leaning out watching the slowly retreating rear of the Prescott car, Fred shifted his plug of tobacco to the other cheek and spat meditatively into the road. His mind had made a sympathetic right-about turn, and in his breast stirred the immortal fervor of Galahad: he wanted to swing round and ride gallantly back to the rescue. There she was trying to escape, poor critter, and those she-devils had sent Obadiah to stop her. Why shouldn't she beat it if she wanted to? Sure as shooting, she'd never known what she was getting into with that pair of cantankerous old maids. . . .

Where was Sherry? He wasn't doing any stopping, not so's you'd notice it. . . . Abby was right. When he'd told her, she'd said it wouldn't work. Young pretty wives never lasted long in that house. Hadn't they done for Mrs. Malcolm in the end? "Accident"? Fiddlesticks! Fred spat again. Didn't the whole village know they'd plumb worn her down—driven her to her death? Prescott Point didn't forget, not if it was twenty years ago. But Abby wore the pants in his house, and she was a great one for keeping things to themselves. She'd made him swear he'd not tell a soul that Sherry'd come back bringing a wife. . . .

Pesky nuisance Abby was so close-mouthed—Prescott blood, he reckoned, though it made her mad as a hornet if you told her so, seeing as how Carrie Warner's "disgrace" didn't get alluded to.

Fred sniggered. Old Jeremiah Prescott sure must've been a wild one by all accounts. No call for the Warners to stay all het up about it for seventy years though; 'twasn't like they was the only ones, three or four families round about could've owned to Prescott blood if they'd a mind to. His own great-aunt Sarah now— Grandpa Curtis always said the Kirkwoods had acted mighty strange, and there'd been some funny goings-on when that second boy of hers was born. . . .

Fred spat a final time and shook his thoughts back to the present. The Prescott car was just disappearing out of sight around the far curve. He'd better leave things be and not go after it. Abby'd give him the deuce if he butted in. He could hear her doing it: "Land sake, Fred Kirkwood," she'd say, "when are you going to learn to mind your own business? I never did! And after promising me, too. If you aren't the most aggravating man, forever sticking your nose into what don't concern you. I declare, it's enough to try the patience of a saint!" . . . Yup, he'd catch it all right. Chivalry shriveled in Fred's breast—it wasn't worth it. Fred sighed unhappily: for now that he had seen her clearly, he belonged to the ones who thought Molly lovely.

Reluctantly, he coaxed the aged truck into motion again and drove on. It was a goldarned shame, she was a sweetly pretty girl. When in tarnation was Sherry going to kick over the traces? Abby be blowed, if he wouldn't give him a piece of his mind the next time he saw him! "The House of Gemini" . . . parcel of ornery fools, the whole kit-and-boodle of them. For the second time that morning Fred swung in through the gates and rattled up the drive.

Molly, trudging ahead, did not slacken her pace when she heard the car tooting behind her; she merely moved a step or two nearer the grass verge of the road and marched on. She had come about four miles, and the village could not be more than another mile away. The impulse to escape, if only for a few hours, which had started her off (best high-heeled shoes, notwithstanding), had turned now, as such things will, into a simple determination to reach the village at no matter what cost to shoes or weariness. It was pointless and unreasonable, and the thought of the long walk back appalled her; her feet hurt, and she might easily be late to lunch: but she had started out for the village, and to the village she was going to go. There were times when Molly's steadfastness became plain stubbornness, and this was one of them. . . .

The car tooted again, impatiently. Still Molly paid no attention: what more did he want? He had the whole road to pass in: some fresh yokel, probably, trying to pick her up. Molly's head went higher and she quickened her step. There was a last despairing blare of the horn right on her heels and the car drew level with her; she would have to deal with this.

"Hi!" said a voice.

Molly stopped. With an uncertain little shudder the car stopped, too. "Hi—you!" said the voice again. To Molly's surprise, it sounded more angry than coy, and strangely familiar. She looked up.

"Obadiah!"

"It's high time. What do you think you're playing at?" Obadiah demanded crossly. "Have you gone deaf the same as me? Making me chase you all over creation—why didn't you stop?"

"I'm sorry," said Molly. "How was I to know it was you?"

"Don't answer back. Told you once, 'tarn't no good." Obadiah was obviously nettled. "Git in and quit making trouble."

Molly shook her head.

"Git in, consarn you, I've been sent to fetch you home."

"No!" said Molly loudly—she was damned if she'd be bullied like this. She pointed down the road. "I—am—going—to the—village."

"No you ain't!" bawled Obadiah. It was rapidly becoming a fracas. "Not if I have to drag you in and hog-tie you, you ain't."

"Yes, yes I am!" Molly screamed.

The whole thing was ridiculous. . . . There was a deadlocked pause.

Suddenly Molly giggled.

Obadiah groaned. "Well, I never did!" He cast his eyes to heaven, in this case the top of the car, and sighed in pious resignation. "If females ain't the beatenest critters, screaming one minute and laughing the next." He peered at her suspiciously: "You ain't fixing up to cry some, are ya?"

"No—" Molly reassured him, shaking her head again. What was the use? She opened the car door and smiled sweetly. "No, I've decided to come quietly, you hilarious hayseed Hitler— You—you bucolic baby-Benito—" This was rather fun, she'd often wanted to do it to managers— Unhappily, they'd never been deaf. Obadiah grinned broadly.

"For the land's sake, get in, I hain't got all day. And don't pride yourself," Obadiah added as she sat down beside him, "that just 'cause I can't hear 'em, I don't know what you're up to, calling me names. Taking advantage of a person's infirmity ain't nice, now is it?"

Molly turned uncomfortably pink. "No, it certainly isn't," she said humbly. Hesitantly she put her hand on his sleeve and leaned over until her lips almost touched his ear. "They weren't such very bad ones," she said. He was a nice old man—she liked him, really.

Obadiah gave her hand a little pat: apparently he was quite ready to forgive. "'Tany rate," he said, "I did get to drive the car." Together on that they both burst out laughing.

And with their laughter, the awful sense of aloneness lifted from Molly. Crabbed and old and stone-deaf as he might be, and a gosh-awful driver as he definitely was—she had a friend now at Prescott Point. All the way back, she chatted ninety to the dozen at him; and although Obadiah heard not one word, companionship was warm and happy between them. Never, Molly felt, had she had a more sympathetic listener. . . . As they neared the gates a truck careened out.

"You'd oblige me if you was to wave to Fred Kirkwood there," suggested Obadiah. "I dursn't leave go of the wheel."

Gladly, Molly complied. She waved, but she wholly failed to see the look of slavish adoration which her gesture brought her: bent on making a conquest, she had eyes only for Obadiah. . . .

CHAPTER FOURTEEN

"It's nice of you to come with me while I take my little constitutional," Helen said. "I hope you weren't really too tired."

Molly glanced down with affection at her comfortable old shoes. "No, not at all," she murmured politely.

It was half-past two in the afternoon, and Molly and Helen accompanied by the black cat were strolling along the top of the cliff. It had been obvious when, immediately after lunch, Helen had buttonholed Molly and asked her to come, that the dreaded heart-to-heart talk was upon her. But although they had been walking for more than a quarter of an hour, nothing of importance had so far been said. Bareheaded like Molly and looking absurdly young, her cheeks whipped pink by cold and her white curls bobbing as she walked, Helen had chatted inconsequentially of this and that, while the black cat made darting little scurries past them and from the overturned pewter bowl of the sky a few desultory snowflakes fell.

"Does he always come for walks, like this?" Molly asked. The black cat, ahead of them now, pounced upon some small imaginary prey and then crouched down by the side of the path waiting their approach.

"Oh yes, he loves coming. He's very independent though, he goes home as soon as he's bored. Watch out!" Helen exclaimed, "I'm afraid he's going to jump."

At her words, with devilish precision, the black cat hurled himself against Molly's knees. Molly staggered and knocked into Helen. "Oh dear," said Molly chagrined, "did I step on your foot?"

322

"No—it's quite all right, it didn't hurt. Look—what did I tell you! There he goes scuttling for home. He's had his fun."

"Rather a practical joker of a cat, isn't he?" Molly hoped that she didn't sound as annoyed as she felt: the cat was exactly like a spoiled child, and Helen a doting mother. "I tried to be ready, but I had no idea how strong he was."

"He's terrific." Helen made no attempt to hide the pride in her voice. "But it's even more the clever way he does it. He knows just how to throw one off balance. Clytie says he's a positive menace to life and limb, so I've done my utmost to break him of it, but it's no use. You see, when he was a kitten I taught him to jump up like that; I never stopped to think how disconcerting it might be after he grew up."

Helen chuckled reminiscently.

"One day he caught Nona off guard right at the top of the stairs. She was carrying a tray and on it was Grandmother's gold luster tea set. Well I'll have you know, she fell all the way to the bottom and kept the tray upright the whole way down! Poor Nona, I think she'd rather have broken her own neck than one of Grandmother's best cups— Luckily she wasn't badly hurt but she was awfully mad. Matilda was certainly in disgrace and quite subdued for a day or two, not at all like his usual self. He's never jumped on Nona again, and I have a shrewd notion that behind my back Nona gave him a whipping. She has a temper, you know, although you might not think it. . . ."

Helen slipped her arm companionably through Molly's. "I suppose I'm too lenient and that I spoil anybody I love, even a cat. Clytie says that too much gentleness can be a vice, but I can't help it. I simply can't abide violence of any kind."

They walked on a few more steps in silence.

"I was terribly distressed," Helen said then, "by the way Clytie spoke to you at lunch. I hope you can forgive her. The villagers are an extremely nosy and curious lot, always trying to pry into one's affairs, and we keep very much to ourselves—so you can see why we'd prefer that you wouldn't go to the village. It would give them something to gossip about and that's very distasteful. We have reason to know how they can distort the most innocent things. . . . For twenty years now we have kept from them, as much as we possibly could, everything that concerns us. Still, unless Sherry had warned you, you weren't to know that, and there was no occasion for Clytie to speak so sharply. I do hope you'll forgive her."

"Of course," Mumbled Molly. She found Helen's habit of apologizing for Clytie very embarrassing. "There's nothing to forgive, really. I'm only sorry I caused so much trouble."

"Trouble, dear child? Obadiah's tickled pink if he can drive the car. . . . No, you must understand that Clytie's hardly herself today. She's terribly upset because Sherry has run away again."

"Run away?" exclaimed Molly. "But I thought you said—"

Helen gave Molly's arm a little squeeze. "—that he'd gone on business," Helen laughed a little. "Yes, I know I did. But to tell you the truth, dear, that was a sort of white lie. I didn't want you to—to have to be unhappy."

Molly took her arm away from Helen. She stood still. "Unhappy?" she repeated after her. "Please tell me what you mean. Why do you say, *again?*— 'Run away again,' as if—"

"As if he often did it?" Helen finished gently. "Because I'm afraid that he does."

"But *why*," Molly cried. "*Why? . . .* I don't understand!"

Helen put her hand coaxingly on Molly's unresponsive arm.

"Come on, Molly dear, let's walk on— There's a lot," said Helen softly, "that you don't understand. Such a lot that we must talk over quietly together. . . . . You don't know Sherry very well, do you? I mean," Helen amended as she felt Molly stiffen, "that you don't know much *about* him. You can't, for you have known each other only a very short time." Helen drew Molly into step again beside her. "Just how long is it exactly?"

"Three weeks tomorrow," answered Molly. "But time," she protested vehemently after a second, "time has nothing to do with knowing a person!"

"Ah, my dear . . . don't you mean, nothing to do with *loving* a person, perhaps?"

Molly stopped again to stare at her with incredulous astonishment. "Loving *is* knowing," Molly said, and with such valiant finality that Helen gave in and made no reply.

They moved on once more in another silence. "Strange, isn't it," Helen murmured at last, "how the snow continues to hold off? Every moment it looks as though it were going to start in really hard and then it doesn't. . . ."

"You see," Molly said, "we never seemed to have time to tell each other the unimportant things. They didn't matter and there was to be all the rest of our lives for them— There will be all the rest of our lives. But since I've come here I've realized that there is something terribly wrong, something that's troubling and strange. I've felt it from you and from Clytie—oh, don't you know that I have? I said so to you last night. I thought that perhaps it was just that you didn't want me—that I wasn't the kind of girl you wanted Sherry to marry. But now I know that there's more, that it isn't just because I'm me. Oh, Helen what is it? I've got to know for I want to help Sherry. I love him— Helen, please. . . . understand that! I love him most awfully. . . ."

This time it was Helen who stopped walking. She turned in the path to face Molly, laying her hands with forceful gentleness one on either side of Molly's arms.

It was as if she sought to convey through the sense of touch the urgency of her appeal.

"I know that, Molly. I know that you love Sherry. But won't you believe me, dear child, when I tell you that it would be far better for all of us—for yourself and for Sherry—if you were to go away? No, hear me out," Helen begged as Molly started to speak. "Listen to me quietly for just one minute. . . .

"There is a reason, a very good reason why you should go. You are young with all your life still before you—you will forget. I know you love Sherry . . . . but in three weeks, in such a little time, love cannot go very deep. It isn't even as though you were in fact truly husband and wife. That hasn't happened yet— Leave before it does, I beg you, Molly! Keep it as it is best that it should be—a romance,

impermanent, sweet to remember perhaps, but possible to forget.
. . . I know it will be hard at first, but we will do everything, dear,
to make it easier. Things can be arranged . . . an annulment. Anything you want that is in our power to give you."

Helen tightened her hands on Molly's sleeves.

"Trust me, Molly. For your own sake—trust me. . . . . Oh, my
dear, I wish with all my heart that it didn't have to be this way!
Clytie has always despaired, but I've gone on. And lately I'd begun
to believe that she was wrong. I hoped— But last night something
happened again which frightened me. And when, this morning, I
found that Sherry had run away—then, I *knew*.

"That's why I lied to you at breakfast. I couldn't bear to tell
you. Because it meant, don't you see, that Sherry knew, too. And
he was running away from it as he always has. Running away from
his responsibility, the consequences of his own action, from
everything he could not face. . . . I did not want you to know that.
I did not want you to know that this time, Molly, Sherry was running away from *you*."

Helen stopped, arrested by the curious expression on Molly's
face. It was a look almost of exaltation. As if in search of something, Molly's hand went in an abrupt little gesture to her belt and
rested there for a moment.

"Never," whispered Molly fervently. "Never!" In Helen's ears
it had the sound of triumph and for a second Helen turned her
head away, filled with a sick pity. Was there nothing left? Nothing
else that she could do?

"Sherry loves me," Molly said. Through her heavy coat, she felt
beneath her fingers the contour of the key, the sharp edge of
Sherry's letter. "It wasn't like that. I know. *This* time Sherry didn't
run away, not from me or from anything. He went for some good
reason, and he'll be coming back— I've said, loving is knowing,
and I know this: Sherry wants me and needs me, and he can no
more go from me than I can go from him. He'll be coming back.
Very soon. And when he does—"

"My dear . . . my dear," Helen's words came wearily. "Don't
you realize what I have been trying to tell you? You are loyal and

brave and very much in love—but you are marching on tragedy. . . . Sometimes these are not enough. For although love may work miracles, there are things it cannot mend. I, too, love Sherry. He's my child . . . . for twenty years I have been father and mother, everything to him. Can you question that my love for him, though different from yours, goes less deep? He is all that I have of a brother who was life itself to me—Malcolm, whom I adored above any living creature, and always shall. . . . Is it not then, perhaps, a little presumptuous, Molly, to think that you can succeed where I have failed? You have asked me for the truth—will you listen quietly to me for just a little longer?"

"Yes, Helen—please," Molly said. "I want to know."

Once more Helen linked her arm in Molly's. And once more they walked slowly on through the cold gray stillness, heavy with the threat of snow; while to Molly, listening, the hushed waiting afternoon took Helen's gentle voice, like the murmur of the waves, as its own. . . .

A lonely house and three children who made a world to themselves. A beloved younger brother—throughout Helen's story were woven the threads of that passionate attachment. They grew older, and Clytie sought other interests, but to Helen, Malcolm remained enough—all that she ever wanted.

Brilliant, absorbed in his career, at thirty Malcolm had unexpectedly married. It was a grave mistake—flirtatious and gay and "emptyheaded," pretty eighteen-year-old Janet Avery was not the wife for him, Helen said. She had had serious misgivings from the first; however, for two years or more she saw little of them: Malcolm's work took them constantly here and there, often to quite distant places.

During that time Sherry was born and then, just before the child's fourth birthday, Malcolm had come home bringing his wife and son. Janet had not been very strong ever since Sherry's birth; and where he was going now, was not, Malcolm felt, the place to take a delicate wife and a small child. So might they stay at Prescott Point where he knew they'd be safe and well looked after? . . . He had been gone for nearly a year. . . .

The twins had welcomed Janet and the little boy and they had done everything, Helen said, to make Janet happy. Yet little by little they had come to realize that there was something dreadfully wrong. Janet's spells of depression, which at first they had put down to a natural nostalgia at being separated from her husband, grew, as time went on, more and more violent and pronounced. Morbid fears and obsessions of persecution—directed mostly at Helen, herself—had made Janet's life a misery and theirs as well.

Clytie was at this time engaged to Derwent Avery, Janet's brother and senior by fourteen years. Helen had wanted to go to him for help, but Clytie would not hear of it—maintaining with characteristic stubbornness that there was nothing wrong with Janet the return of Malcolm would not cure. . . .

Things were at a sorry pass (Helen grew vague here, but Molly gathered an impression of either drugs or drinks: which, was not clear) when, at last, Malcolm had come back.

His return, Helen said, acted like a miracle upon Janet. It looked, then, as though Clytie had been right. Janet was gay and happy and her laughter filled the house; those terrible moods of black despair seemed a nightmare of the past, gone now forever.

Malcolm, too, appeared happy and, as he always did, devoted to his young wife. Helen alone sensed, she said, that he had long ago realized the mistake his marriage had been: ("Separated from his wife both by years and by temperament, what could it bring to him?") However, neither by word nor by action did he admit to any of this and, shallow and insensitive—flibbertigibbet was the word Helen used—Janet remained, of course, wholly unaware of what only Helen guessed. ("Malcolm was very angry," Helen said in telling about this, "and shouted at me that I had 'everything all wrong.' Naturally then, I knew that I was right.") Malcolm had not listened, either, to the warning which Helen tried to give him. "Janet's okay, you simply don't, understand her," is all that he had said— And so what was to happen came to him as a severe shock.

They were going away again: a dam or a bridge to be built in Peru: and this time Malcolm had decided to take Janet and Sherry with him. Their trunks were packed, they were to leave at the end of the week.

The day of the tragedy dawned bright and clear, a perfect summer's day. Malcolm had got up early to go deep sea fishing with a party of friends—the men had put off in the boat a little after four that morning. At breakfast Helen noticed that Janet was not looking very well; she seemed despondent and tired. As the day wore on she became increasingly restless and distraught—she appeared unbearably nervous. It had turned very hot. The heat grew more and more oppressive, and around six o'clock that evening, with sudden fury, the storm broke.

For five hours it raged: thunder and lightning and a deluge of rain, the sea lashed into a churning lather. Hailstones the size of a man's fist rattled down breaking windows: the noise was deafening. Through the rolling crash of the thunder, the howling of the wind, could be heard the frenzied tolling of the bell buoy. Houses and trees were struck; during the space of more than an hour the electricity failed, and for miles around the telephone wires were down.

"It was the worst thunderstorm in all my memory, Molly," Helen said. "We were all worried for Malcolm's safety, but Janet was frantic. We could do nothing to soothe her. . . .

"Then, about ten o'clock, she became strangely quiet. She—she had taken something, I think. She had undressed—we had all gone upstairs—and I persuaded her to come into my room for a while with me. Sherry hadn't been able to sleep, of course, and she came in bringing the little boy. He was five at the time.

"Janet was very pale and still: in her nightgown and long white robe she looked like a ghost—insubstantial, somehow unreal. She sat almost motionless, Sherry standing, leaning against her knees. I can see them now. . . . Sherry was very quiet, too, his eyes enormous in his small face and his hair like a tousled gold halo in the lamplight. He was awed by the storm, but not afraid, I think. . . .

"I talked to Janet and tried to comfort her. I reminded her that the men were all excellent sailors and that they must have realized that the storm was brewing. Long before it broke, I assured her, they would have made for port and put in to safety somewhere along the coast. We had had no news because Malcolm had been unable to reach us, that was all. While our own line was still working, the wires were down in many places, and he was having difficulty trying to get through to us, I said. I did not let her see my own anxiety. 'Malcolm is safe,' I told her. 'I know that nothing has happened to Malcolm.' I repeated those words over and over. . . .

"At last I began to feel that I had succeeded in calming her fears. She seemed better to me, less tense and unnaturally still. Her face lost its carved white stiffness, its dreadful look of a death mask— The storm was abating: she said something about Sherry being able to sleep now, took the child's hand in hers, and left the room.

"A moment afterward I heard running footsteps on the stairs. Janet's voice cried, 'Malcolm!' and I heard the front door slam. I waited only long enough to snatch up a coat and then I ran down the stairs, out of the house, after her. I was filled with foreboding. I feared that the long hours of terror and suspense, the heart-racking uncertainty, had snapped her last frail hold upon reason. . . . That in her poor crazed mind was only one thought, one obsession—Malcolm was dead.

"I called to her, I think: 'Janet—Janet—' And somehow I must have known which way to go, for I did not hesitate. I raced round the corner of the house, running, calling— But I was too late.

"She was poised there, at the very edge of the cliff—a long white figure that glimmered in the darkness. For an instant I saw her, and then— It was as if she were going to take flight— She flung up her arms, plunged over the cliff, and was gone. . . ."

Through the merest breath of pause, Helen stopped speaking; then her gentle even voice took up her tale again.

"I ran to Sherry. He was lying on the ground halfway between the house and the cliff. He had fallen and cut his head, for when I reached the light I saw that his face was covered with blood. I picked him up and carried him into the house. He was drenched through with rain and trembling; but, although he was hurt, he did not whimper. I remember how good and exceptionally quiet he was— I do not believe that he said one word. . . .

"When I came through the front door with Sherry in my arms, the telephone was ringing. . . . It was Malcolm to tell us not to worry . . . . that he was safe."

For a minute again Helen was silent. Then she said—and it was as though for her this was the end, not only of the story, but of all there could ever be—"Malcolm went away . . . to Peru. He caught some kind of fever there. He . . . he never came back."

All at once, now at the very last, Helen's voice lost its even gentleness. She added almost shrilly:

"I did not expect him to go. I never dreamed that he would. After what had happened, it was wrong of him to go—wrong, wrong!" Her voice dropped again to softness. "It was all such a waste," she whispered. "Such a terrible, tragic . . . waste."

Helen had spoken as if to herself alone; those final whispered words had made Molly an intruder: she had not found anything then that she could say. For a long time they had walked on without speaking. A gulf lay between them which Molly's vague murmur of sympathy, when at last it came, could do nothing to bridge. What Molly had taken from the story was not what Helen had sought to give her, and the failure lay, palpable, between them. They saw it, as they must, through different eyes. To Helen, it was Malcolm's story, to Molly, Sherry's. . . .

No, Sherry had remembered nothing, Helen said. He was so very young—only five. A few brief hours, perhaps, the memory may have remained, and then it was gone like a dim, bad dream. He had forgotten, as children will. He had never asked for his mother— he accepted her absence, as he did his father's, without question. Like his father, she had simply gone away. ("We have never told him what happened, Molly," Helen warned, "and you never must.")

So at first, although necessarily lonely, Sherry had appeared a happy and perfectly normal child. It was only later that they began to notice in him disquieting signs of his mother's malaise.

He had spells of extreme and irrational moodiness: "black days" when he would say hardly a word; when he brooded, all to himself, over some hidden misery, some imagined woe that they could not guess. If they questioned him or tried in any way to reach him, he would go away and hide. Sometimes it would be hours before they found him—he had pathetic ingenuity.

That was, Helen supposed, the beginning of his running away. . . . He had been barely seven when he went the first time and they had been nearly mad with anxiety. But as the years passed, they had grown almost inured to this. After Sherry was sixteen they had ceased, in fact, even to try to find him—he always came back in the end. And never once in all that time had he given them an explanation of why he had gone: he went and he returned, and that was all. . . .

This unnatural secretiveness of Sherry's, Helen said, was like a barrier erected before the dark unhappy recesses of his mind. By it, he shut off from himself in his trouble even those whom he loved best. Close as Helen had always been to him, he did not confide even in her; and she had found out about the terrible headaches and the stranger, and so much more frightening, aural hallucination, quite by accident.

She had discovered him, a small boy of six, one winter afternoon, holding his head under the cold water faucet of his bathroom. The icy water was running down over his head and he was being pitifully sick in the basin. Very reluctantly he had told her at last that this was "just a day when his head hurt him." The cold water, he explained, "sometimes made it feel better." When summoned, the doctor's tactful questions had revealed that the headaches had been both protracted and frequent; the pain, as was obvious, severe. However, the extensive examinations, which were then made, only served to confirm the first doctor's original opinion: there was nothing physically wrong with the child. The trouble was 'psychic': an hysterical manifestation of a psychic disorder, a psychosis— He had used some such words, Helen said. It didn't matter—what he was telling them was plain enough. . . .

As to the other—the strange aural hallucination—it had been her own stupidity which had kept her so long in ignorance of that. One paid so little attention to what children said they had seen or heard—one did not expect them to make much distinction between the vividly imagined and the real. But in the end it had been brought home to her in a way that left no doubt: Sherry actually heard the sound of something that was not there.

This last, to her the most significant and disquieting sign of all, she had kept to herself: until this moment, revealing it to Molly, she had told no one. Sherry, of course, knew. It had been impossible to keep it from him. . . .

Helen ceased speaking and in the pause her last sentence, so casually spoken, grew monstrous with implication in Molly's mind.

"Do you mean," Molly said slowly, "that you have let Sherry grow up all these years believing that he is— That he is— Oh I can't even say it! Helen, that was horrible . . . horrible. How could you!"

They had stopped again now and faced each other across the narrow path at the cliff's edge. The short winter's day was closing around them and already it was growing dark. They stood there—unconscious of the cold and the deepening twilight, absorbed in a conflict no longer hidden between them. Helen raised her hands and let them fall again to her sides, but she said nothing.

"Because he isn't," Molly cried. "He isn't! He is as sane, every bit, as you or I! Do you think, loving him, that I wouldn't know? All of us—every one of us, almost, that's ever lived!—have hurt, dark places in our minds that need bringing to the light for healing. Does that make us mad? But to be allowed to believe— To doubt— Oh, that poor little boy!— My own poor, darling Sherry. . . ."

"Do you judge me, Molly?" Helen's gentle voice was sad. "Remember, there was Janet."

In the dimness, Molly shook her head. "I don't know about his mother—only that what happened was pitifully dreadful and tragic. I *do* know about Sherry. I know with my faith and with every instinct that's in me— Sherry will be all right. Understanding and love and . . . happiness. He said that to me, Helen. He said,

"Happiness through you, Molly, some time, some day." . . . That is coming true, Helen. I am going to stay and make it true."

"You are going to stay?—then there is no more that I can say. I have told you because it was right that you should know." Helen's tone was all at once queerly impersonal, she spoke almost coldly. "You have chosen. It is your own decision."

She stopped, and there was a brief silence. Then she put out her hand and touched Molly's; her voice changed.

"Do you think, my dear," she asked softly, "that I do not wish with all my heart that it could come true? That I would not pray that your faith might be enough? . . . Never forget, Molly, in the arrogance of your different love, that I too love Sherry. He is all I have. As he is, as he may become— This way, or any way— I love him. . . . And Sherry loves me."

"Yes, I know that," Molly answered, "I've seen it. And if because I love, I am arrogant . . . and if because I believe, I am presumptuous (for you said that, too, Helen) . . . I am sorry and ashamed. I realize what you mean to Sherry, and I hope that I shall never have to do anything which would make me come between you."

"Between us? Between Malcolm's son and me? *My* son in my love. . . ." The words hung there a moment in the stillness and then, almost gaily, Helen laughed. "No, Molly, you will never do that.— Why look, child, you're shivering!" Her eyes found Molly's.

"Am I?"

For an instant neither moved; then Helen turned abruptly.

"It is nearly dark," she said; "we must be getting back."

They walked rapidly now, and they spoke very little. But this time their silence was the silence of completion. It was as if everything had been said and there was no longer any need for speech. They were absorbed in words that were past—each hunting among them those she would lay aside for remembrance.

A rough and vivid phrase in a tale worn smooth by telling. . . . This, Molly's memory touched and selected. An anecdote false for 'gentleness' to delight in. . . . An intimacy known, which betrayed in the knowing. . . . Significance to be glimpsed through the opening shutter of the insignificant: a pause, a tone of voice, the surprise of laughter. . . .

It was very quiet—only the languorous murmur of the waves and the sound of their hurrying footsteps.

Something was nagging at the back of Molly's mind, asking for recognition, but she could not reach it—

"How still it is . . ." Molly said, ". . . so hushed and dead . . . curious that one cannot hear the bell."

"The . . . bell?" Helen turned her head toward Molly; in the gray half-light her face seemed drained of color, expressionless.

"The bell buoy. Last night it was so clear, and yet all day today. . . ." Molly faltered; there had been something oddly disturbing in the wiped-blankness of Helen's look, and for a second she lost what she was going to say. "I—I suppose," she finished, "the wind has to be in the right direction."

Helen made no answer. Out of the dusk, the grotesque bulk of the house loomed before them, one bright window like a solitary orange eye, lidless and watchful.

"I wish," came Helen's gentle voice at last, "that Nona would remember to pull the kitchen curtains. . . ." Once more her arm slipped cozily through Molly's. "Won't tea taste wonderful?" she said.

And at her homely words, the nightmare sense of unreality again closed tight, cold fingers around Molly; and there was an instant when she felt as if she could not breathe.

CHAPTER FIFTEEN

Two elderly women, one on either side of a fire . . . . gray knitting and black cat . . . . firelight winking in the soft brightness of silver and china on a tea table . . . . lamplight warm over the shabby comfort of a cluttered old-fashioned room. . . . The curtain rises, Molly thought, upon a tranquil, domestic scene. The girl seated on a low stool between the two women, her hands clasped around her knees, has been talking—telling of a past far removed from any of this—but now, feeling her words to be empty of meaning, she falls silent. . . .

There was the setting—familiar to a hundred plays, cherished in a thousand dreams. Life going on behind the walls of houses— the lovely life of homes, imagined and achingly longed for through all the wandering nomad years of stations and theaters and hotel lobbies.

There it was, just as she had imagined it. There it was— And there was she, Molly, inside it: belonging to it, part of it—part of a *home* at last. And never—oh never, never!—had she felt so homeless and so forsaken. The firelight was warm on her cheek, she sat wrapped in the outward semblance of her heart's desire—could any torture be devised more keen than this mockery of a dream come true! Against it, she wanted to show herself as impervious—to claim for her own shifting background something of permanence: in the lengthening silence she heard herself saying:

"It's warm and cozy here and I hate to go . . . but there are letters . . . friends to whom I must write. . . ."

And back in the vast forbidding bedroom, sitting in the big chair, she put her head in her hands, fighting depths of total desolation. There were no letters and no friends. . . .

In her changing world, friendships were made and lost and regained anew if chance threw them back together once more. But contacts were never kept, nothing was continuous. There were hundreds of people to whom she was "Molly *darling*"; she could not have walked six Broadway blocks without being gushingly hailed by someone; but of those ebullient hundreds not one knew where she was—nor cared. Uncle Ned?—a nostalgic longing seized her: he was the nearest thing she had to any "family." Where he was now she had no idea; a letter to the Player's Club would some day reach him—in a week, in a month, sometime.

The old panic-sense of desertion gripped her as it had before in the bright chatter of the restaurant in Chicago, on the cold dark platform of Prescott Point, where a rusty sign creaked in the wind and the red light of a train went away into the blackness: Sherry was gone and she was alone. . . .

She had said she must learn to trust happiness, learn security as a child learns a lesson by its being repeated over and over. But what opportunity had she had? The pages of the book were blank: she had found no happiness and no security. Only, ever since the door of this house first closed behind her, a growing knowledge of malevolence, a still certainty of fear, and utter loneliness.

Down underneath all her brave parade of confidence there was doubt; and down underneath all her valiant defiance she knew herself to be mortally afraid.

And yet she had the answer to the mystery now; almost every number of the combination was in place. Helen had given them to her—more, indeed, than she knew. For Helen was wrong: Sherry had not "forgotten." . . .

The jargon of psychoanalysis came readily to Molly's mind, but she had little need of it—the story was plain for anyone to read. A sensitive and impressionable child and a lost and hidden memory— The terror of the mother communicated to the little boy . . . and then a white figure glimmering at the cliff's edge, upflung arms, and the plunge over and away into the blackness— Small hands that had clutched, perhaps, at her skirts trying in vain to hold her back. . . . The stumbling fall, the cut head, and the sharp stab of pain. . . . Pain that alone was left—the heritage of horror too searing for remembrance—to return again in the form of racking, blinding headaches.

Oh yes, much was plain. . . . Sherry's fear when he had seen her, Molly, standing at the edge of the cliff—his dread of the water. She recalled how he had stood still in the middle of the lawn as though he could not come any farther, and the look on his face had been the same as she had seen over and over upon her father's. The look of a man haunted. . . . She had been near the truth that first night when she knew that they were alike: love had dredged it up for her, shown her their tragic kinship. Were they, she had asked herself then, the same all the way through? Even to a sense of guilt?

She thought now that this was so. Her father had gone to his death blaming himself, the words *if only* a lash across his heart. Did those self-same words cut deep into Sherry, too? Did that small child of five blame himself: did he say if only he had been stronger and bigger he would have saved the mother he loved? If only he had not been so weak and little, so shamefully useless. . . . Had he grown up through the years believing in that forgotten core of himself that he had failed?

Perhaps. . . . Her reconstruction was neat and finished, it rang true. And, if that were all, it needed, as she had said to Helen, only bringing to the light for healing. She had only, warily tender, to lead Sherry back to that lost memory so that, looking again with adult comprehension, he might see it clearly at last. . . . . If that were all— It should be, and yet—

Molly's doubt stood there before her.

Why? . . . .

Why had Sherry not truly forgotten? Why in his child's brain had it not all gone away like a bad dream? What had made it stay? Why had the scar of that night never healed? In a healthy mind would it have become a festering wound that poisoned with fear? In a *healthy* mind. . . .

Molly had reached the low ebb of her faith. Helen had called her arrogant and presumptuous and perhaps she was. . . . She had trusted in the instinct of her love to find truth, and now, questioning its validity, she was lost. Without it, alone and frightened, there was nothing to sustain her. Doubt had come. . . . For a bad moment; Molly abandoned Sherry.

"No," whispered Molly fiercely. "No!"

She got up from the chair and began to pace back and forth, back and forth, as though her body kept sentry-go before the intolerable question in her mind.

It couldn't be true—it couldn't! There must be some reason, some explanation other than that. A last twist to the mystery that she didn't know—a key number of the combination that still was missing. Something that was right there before her, perhaps, and she was too blind or stupid to see it. Indeed, the strange thing was that, as she hunted for it, she felt that she had had it—that she'd known it but had somehow mislaid it in her mind. . . .

If only, at this moment, Sherry didn't seem so dim and so unreal. If only she could bring him back and make him no longer like a problem to be solved, but emotionally vivid and alive in her senses once more.

She stopped and got out his letter. And somehow, the very incongruity of what she had to do to get it helped her. The absurd disparity between her tortured thoughts and the necessity of coping with skirt and slip and girdle, made both thought and action equally fantastic; and the letter, which before she had found so unsatisfactory, now seemed reassuringly casual—soothingly wholesome in the way it took everything blandly for granted.

"Remember what you promised me? I love you—Sherry." Just like that! . . . Molly sighed, a mixture of exasperation and relief.

She had succeeded: Sherry was real again.

She folded the letter and stood for a second holding it and the key in her hand. Carrying them around in her girdle had been childishly melodramatic and extremely uncomfortable—she had no intention of continuing the practice.

Her battered wardrobe trunk stood open in one corner of the room. Molly went over to it and hid Sherry's note under the odds and ends in its top drawer. The note could stay safely there until she unpacked; and that she wasn't going to do before Sherry came back. . . . For to unpack would be, she had decided, an unequivocal concession to a situation that was plainly impossible.

Everything waited upon Sherry's return. Probably they would be leaving then—devoutly Molly hoped so—and even if they were to remain, it would not be on the twins' terms. And speaking of that—

Molly's lips curled and she closed her fingers over the key in her hand. Helen had given herself dead away this afternoon. What had she said? "It's not as though you were, in fact, truly husband and wife. *That hasn't happened yet.*"

Yes, those were her words. And how could she have known about that, unless— Molly tossed the key with vicious scorn down on the chest of drawers—unless she knew about *that*, too!

"Breakfast innocence," muttered Molly bitterly. "It won't wash!"

At this point, there was a knock on the door.

Good God! Molly thought. What now? She felt that she lad had enough of everything just then, especially Helen. Rebelliously, she marched across the room and jerked open the door:

"Oh!" exclaimed Molly in consternation.

It was Clytie, not Helen.

"May I come in?" Clytie recovered the startled step backward which she had taken upon the violent opening of Molly's door and walked past Molly into the bedroom.

"I am sorry to disturb you," she said. Her austere gaze swept the room and lighted pointedly upon the writing table conspicuously virgin of use. "But you've finished your letters, I see."

"No," said Molly, coming away from the door, "I haven't written them."

A heady and liberating defiance surged through her—she wasn't going to be baited by Clytie any more. Or frightened . . . or overawed. She'd hold on to that, no matter what came of it. "Won't you sit down?" invited Molly.

"Thank you, I prefer to stand. I am staying only a moment."

Clytie's inspection reached the chest of drawers.

"So you found the key," she said. Her tone was filled with smug satisfaction, but there was something about it which curiously suggested relief. "I presume that it was here, as I thought, all the time."

"On the contrary—"

Molly walked over to Clytie and stood, determined and straight, in front of her.

"Look here," Molly said, "let's give this up. I'm sick of pretending, and I should think you would be, too. There's no point to it any longer. So what do you say, we agree right now to call it off?"

"Call it off. . . .?" Clytie echoed the words with frigid distaste. "I have no idea what you mean."

"Oh, very well!" Molly shrugged. "Go on with it if you want to, only I'm through." She was behaving outrageously, but she dared not stop; if she let go of defiance for a moment she would lie down and grovel before the chill authority in Clytie's eyes. "The key wasn't here because one of you had it. I don't know which one, although I think it was probably you. Anyway, it doesn't matter since Helen was in on it, too. She gave that away this afternoon. But when I asked for the key this morning, you both pretended innocence. You even said, Clytie, that it 'must have fallen out of the door.'" In her impatience Molly invested the phrase with scathing mimicry. "Then while I was finishing breakfast you came in here and dropped it there on the floor," Molly pointed, "so I should find it just where you'd said it might be. What was the use? Do you think I'm a child to be fooled by such tricks? Why won't you come out into the open and fight fair? For two nights I've been locked in this room, and *I don't like it!*"

Molly gulped and came to a full stop, shocked by a stricken realization of the expression upon Clytie's face.

Throughout Molly's angry tirade she had made not a sound, but her face had gone paler and paler until now she was white to the lips. She moved her hands in a queer incompleted gesture as though she had been about to cover her face, in shame or in some sort of horror, from Molly's sight. Yet when she spoke, what she said was oddly inadequate, and her voice was as flat and as devoid of emotion as usual.

"Aren't you being a little rude?" Clytie amazingly asked.

"*Rude?* Oh heavens above!—yes, terribly. I'm sorry. But really, Clytie, there are other things more important than that. I have to be careful with Helen, she seems so gentle and helpless, so easy to hurt—but you— Why can't we be open with each other? Honest enemies, at least? We might get somewhere that way. You've never hidden your dislike of me; why do you want to go on hiding the rest? This morning and now? Pretending. . . ."

Still Clytie said nothing, only stared back at Molly, her cold gray eyes immovable in her ashen face. Before something she saw there, Molly's defiance ebbed away; and what came in its stead felt to Molly strangely like pity.

"Please, won't you answer me, Clytie? I'm so terribly sorry. . . . I shouldn't have spoken to you that way. But it's been so awful, feeling how you hated me, and not knowing why. I've felt so alone. I thought—I suppose I must have thought—that if we could make an agreement together, it wouldn't be so lonely. Even to be ene-mies. . . . There'd be a kind of bond in that. It would *include* me, don't you see? Clytie, please. . . . I know why you're here. You've come to ask me to go away, just as Helen did this afternoon."

Now at last Clytie spoke. She said, very slowly: "What did Helen say?"

"She said I was wrong to think I could help Sherry, and that she wanted me to go away and not be married to him any more."

"And you?"

"I told her I was staying."

"No," Clytie brought her hands together. "No! You must go." Her flat voice issued a command, but her gesture was that of an appeal. "Simply believe me—for your own sake, you must go."

"That's what Helen said," Molly murmured. "You've used al-most her words—"

"Go, and I'll send Sherry to you. I promise."

Molly shook her head.

"But I can't go, Clytie," she protested softly. "Don't you under-stand? It would be like desertion."

For a long time this waited in the silence. At last:

"Yes," Clytie answered. "Yes, I think I do understand. . . ." And her flat voice seemed no longer cold, but surprisingly tender. "It's not good to desert, no matter what it may cost. . . ."

She turned abruptly away and went quickly toward the door. With her hand on the knob she looked back.

A curious little smile, half sad and half bitter, touched her lips.

"Poor child. . . ." she whispered.

Then the door closed behind her and Clytie was gone.

"Poor child." . . . . The first night of all, running up the stairs—it seemed such a long time ago. . . . Those words and that voice came back to Molly. . . . "Poor child."

Molly sat down on the bed. Suddenly, and for no good reason at all, her knees were shaking.

CHAPTER SIXTEEN

Sherry pulled the wheel of the car hard over and turned in through the gates. Forty-one hours had gone by since he had driven through them bound on his futile errand. He had been tired and sleepy then, but now he was utterly all in. It was eleven o'clock Tuesday night, and from early that morning he had been driving without rest, in bitter cold and over roads made almost impassable by heavy snow. The last fifty miles had brought a respite—no snow had fallen here— but it had come too late: behind him lay nearly four hundred miles of grueling going.

To add to that, he was without food or sleep. When, in the midst of a blizzard, he had at last reached Bangor to find his uncle gone, he had been too weary and disheartened to go on. Body and nerves cried out for sleep and he had squandered the last of his money on a hotel room; only, once he was in bed, to toss and turn, leadenly wakeful, the whole night long.

All night and all day he had been haunted by old terrors. Through his exhausted brain had echoed the dread memory of a sound: the low note of the bell buoy, which, in Helen's room, had struck once more, insistent and slow, upon his ears—a ghost bell's tolling, he had thought never to hear again— He felt next to horror, as though now, at last, he was to touch it and to see its face. As though, fearful and yet exhilarated, he waited upon the brink of some tremendous event: a revelation that would mar or mend. The sense of its approach pressed close about him; came now so near, that with awed surprise, he knew it not as something strange, but timelessly familiar—forgotten, yet always known. He stayed stilled in apprehension, for it seemed to him that nothing more was needed than the merest movement of consent, to draw it to him— only that he should will, as he had never done, to remember. . . .

Sherry's hand jerked on the wheel. Before his tired eyes the driveway blurred and came clear again. Concentratedly bright, the headlights swept the corner of the house and reached out, thinned and far, to the cliff's edge.

And then, suddenly it was there.

—Caught for an instant in wheeling light. . . . The greatest of the forgotten fears. The terrible one. The lost shape of terror.

For a second's stab of time, it glimmered there, tall and white with upflung arms, at the cliff's edge. The lights swung by and it was gone—plunged away into the blackness. . . .

At once, out of the dark caverns of the past, memory, released, sprang full upon him. Again, inside him, a voice cried, a child's voice—his: "Mother . . . stop! Don't go. . . . Oh, mother, mother. . . ." Again, through small fingers wet with rain, he felt the slippery escape of silk— Knew again the impotency of loss, the hot shame of failure. . . . The stumbling weak pursuit and the sharp reality of pain.

Pain. . . . And as at a signal, even as memory relived it, it was real. For now, on that instant, came the old agony. . . . whirling away into nothingness the consciousness of all else. Demanding, imperious, destroying thought Hammering through his temples, licking against his eyeballs with jagged tongues of red fire. Beat-ing, pounding . . . accelerating faster and faster in throbbing rhythm, until everything went—knowledge and hope, the past and the future—and there was nothing left but its savage ecstasy.

The headlights glared back from closed garage doors.

Fumblingly, like a drunken man, Sherry stopped the car and switched off the lights. For a long moment he remained slumped over the wheel, helpless in the grip of an anguish which, never to come again throughout the rest of his life, seemed to have gathered all its strength into this final assault. Then, bent half-double, holding his head between his hands, he staggered toward the house.

In the blinding agony, only one thought lived. He must get to Helen. . . .

For in Helen's keeping, in a small round box, was oblivion.

CHAPTER SEVENTEEN

To Molly, Tuesday had seemed endless. The long day had dragged itself by, filled with the suspense of waiting and the strain of things left unsaid. In spite of her determined eviction, a small troubling doubt still hung about on the edges of Molly's mind—a shoddy and disreputable trespasser, which only the actual presence of Sherry, himself, could finally expel. She knew that when she could see him again standing there before her, tall and strong as he would be, and very real—the look on his face she loved best, one eyebrow quizzically cocked above eyes that were steady and grave—the last lingering doubt would go, and everything would be all right.

How petty and unimportant all the other things seemed to her now! Her disappointment at finding the twins at Prescott Point; her hurt anger because Sherry had not told her they would be there; the foolish quarrel over a locked door that a single word could have dispelled—all the barriers of bewilderment and pride which she had allowed to come between them.

It must never happen again. All that long weary day she had held close to her heart a sweet knowledge of the infallible remedy: Once they had been together, loved completely and fully, separateness would go and they would be no longer unsure. There was a sort of sensitive distrust which attraction without intimacy bred. That would have vanished, for they would not be strangers to each other any more. The Bible said it for her, truly and well: "Adam *knew* Eve his wife." . . .

Over and over the worn track of her desires and faith her mind traveled; while the slow hours of morning and evening, of lunch and tea and dinner, ticked themselves away on the ormolu clock and she longed for the sanctuary of her cold forbidding bedroom, where at least she need not pretend or find words far away from her thoughts. She was tired and miserable and, in spite of the tension, very bored . . . it would be wonderful when it was time to go to bed.

But when at last good nights had been said and she stood, as she had for four successive nights, alone in the vast ugly bedroom, she realized that she was too nervous and keyed-up for sleep. Last night had been the same; and finally in desperation she had slipped down the kitchen stairs and gone for a walk along the cliff. It had helped. The sense of escape had soothed her restlessness, and, re-turning, she had been able to sleep. Perhaps, she told herself, that would work for her again tonight. Besides . . . it was not yet eleven, Sherry might still come. His note had said a "few" days, and hadn't two long days already passed?

Although down in her heart Molly knew it was really too soon to expect him, she couldn't resist playing with the hope, so that by the time she wandered abstractedly over to the closet to get her coat her imagination was already busy, building up a happy drama-tization.

As she tilted the hanger, Molly was smiling. (Sherry had driven up, leapt from the car, and was just running eagerly toward her across the lawn); but, when she reached this point and the coat slid into her hands, Molly frowned. She had run into a snag. Her setting was wrong: she had forgotten that it was dark. How, then, had Sherry been able to see her?

A meticulous and realistic daydreamer, Molly always played fair. She sighed, threw over plot one, and began again. . . .

Completely immersed in the intricacies of plot two—her diffi-culty being to maintain exactness with glamour—Molly put on her camel's-hair coat and started for the door. She had forgotten that she had taken off her dinner dress, and now, halfway across the room, she caught sight of her long white figure in the glass and stopped in dismayed recollection.

Out from under her sports coat trailed the intimate folds of her long white woolly bathrobe.

For a moment she hesitated, contemplating herself. Then she shrugged, turned away, and switched off the light. The combination was almost indecent. It smacked of clandestine discoveries and hasty retreats. . . . But it wasn't worth while to dress. Her legs would be warm, and there was no one to see her. . . .

In the darkness her hand found the knob of the door, and, smiling a little—for, still absorbed in her daydream, she had suddenly found that by using the headlights she could overcome the snag in her plot—smiling a little, and mentally far off in a happy reunion with Sherry, very carefully Molly pulled open the bedroom door.

And . . . as she slipped through it out into the hall, the white skirts of her bathrobe swirled, glimmering in the dimness, just as the long silken folds of another's had, long ago. . . .

Pale coat, white in the dark. . . . Long white skirt. . . . Unknown to her, forgetfulness had dressed her for the part she was to play. Out of a drama of the past, chance had rewritten the script. In a few minutes now, the curtain would be going up—

Thus, through the abstraction of a daydream, was created an illusion by which memory returned; and at a cliff's edge, a tall white figure on a winter's night reached across the span of twenty years to bring back a summer's night of storm and terror.

The door to the kitchen stairs was only a few steps away at the end of the hall next to Clytie's bedroom. Silently, Molly tiptoed over to it, eased it open without a sound, and crept down the kitchen stairs. She made her way across the dark kitchen, slipped back the catch of the Yale lock so that she could get in again, and the next moment, closing the back door cautiously behind her, Molly was outside in the sudden immensity of the night.

It was windless and still as it had been last night but not as cold. Nor was the darkness so profound. Tonight there was a kind of luminosity; turning her head, Molly could see the smudged black contour of the windbreak of pines by the corner of the house and, across the lawn, the faint glimmer of the line of white posts marking the cliff's edge. From the kitchen door the point of the cliff lay straight across the lawn ahead of her; and as she walked toward it, the solitary post guarding the gouge on her left slowly defined itself, showing clearer and larger than its fellows.

At the point of the cliff she hesitated. Should she turn to her left, around the gouge, down the steps to the cove? Or— The tiny hope of Sherry's return decided her, and she turned her footsteps to the right, along the edge of the cliff in the direction of the garage.

In the stillness, the sound of the surf breaking below her was urgently loud so that she did not, a minute later, hear the car. But as though by a planned precision, she had just reached the stretch of cliff visible through the opening between the windbreak of pines and the end of the house when the car's headlights swept round the front of the house and fell full upon her.

Caught for an instant in dazzling light, she had only time to wheel, flinging up her arms in greeting, before the lights swung by and she was plunged once again into darkness. For a second more she could see them flickering behind the thick screen of the trees. Then suddenly they went out. And, straining her ears above the noise of the waves, she thought she heard the sharp slam of the car door.

With that quick little sound went all Molly's doubt and loneliness—Sherry was back.

He *had* come, and now everything was perfect and happy and all right. . . . In a minute he'd be hurrying across the lawn toward her, just as she had imagined it.

Rather slowly, because that moment had all of anticipation's enchantment and she wanted to prolong it, Molly went forward to meet him. . . .

The distant noise of the waves had fallen to a soft murmur now, but still in the quiet she could hear no sound of footsteps but her own. At the windbreak of pines she stopped. The grayish bulk of the garage was there before her and in the dim space between them nothing moved.

Sherry wasn't there. . . . He had gone on into the house, for he hadn't seen her. . . .

A brief instant of disappointment touched Molly's happiness: chance seemed unnecessarily perverse. Just for once it would be nice if things turned out as she'd planned. . . . 'I always knew plot one wouldn't work,' thought Molly sadly.

But what did it matter! Sherry was back, and here she stood, moping over a frustrated daydream, while inside the house, at this very minute, Sherry might already be hunting for her. . . .

Molly turned and sped along the back of the house to the kitchen door.

There was a crack of light now under the door at the top of the kitchen stairs. The lights had been turned on in the upstairs hall. Molly opened the door a cautious crack and peeked out: the hall was empty. With one bound, sacrificing silence to speed, Molly had made her room and plunged in.

No one had seen her. Nor, apparently, had she been missed. The bedroom was in darkness just as she had left it. Molly was relieved. She felt rather guilty about her excursions down the back stairs, and she was worried that the light in the hall might mean that Helen, with her room overlooking the garage, had heard Sherry drive in.

Molly switched on her light and stood listening—there wasn't a sound.

That last thought of hers about Helen had been a disturbing one. More disturbing, she realized now, than the mere danger she had run of being caught. If Helen was really awake, what would happen in that case? Would Sherry still be coming along to her here any moment? Or—a distinct possibility—had Helen already waylaid him in order to prevent him? Molly could easily imagine how awkward she could manage to make it.

"Darling boy," Helen would say, "surely the morning will do? You can't be so inconsiderate as to wake Molly up!"

Well, if that had actually happened (and Molly wished that she hadn't become so forebodingly suspicious), there was nothing that Sherry could decently do. He'd either have to give up or wait until Helen, herself, had gone back to sleep. And that might be one hour—it might be two. . . .

But whatever happened, whatever Helen did, Molly resolved, she was going to be with Sherry tonight. If he didn't come soon, she would go to him. Yes, even if this house turned beauty into ugliness . . . even if it must be furtive and difficult and not at all as she had dreamed. She had learned now that all that was unimportant beside the certainty and wonder of the accomplished act. "Made man and wife": sweet and infallible remedy. . . . Against that nothing could prevail.

Molly knelt down by her chest of drawers and reverently lifted out her wedding nightgown. Then, very efficiently and quietly, she began to undress.

Three quarters of an hour later Molly stood at the crack of her bedroom door. Softly, and as though from very far away, the grandfather clock at the foot of the stairs struck midnight. In the long upstairs hall the lights still burned, but it was deserted; and with the last dying sound of the chime below, there was absolute silence over all the house.

The lights burned on in the sleeping quiet as though forgotten, glinting upon the varnished panels of closed doors shut tight against the hall's bright emptiness. Stretching before her, hushed and stark, the hall wore for Molly the reproachful menace of hotel corridors in the small hours of the morning. It seemed to lengthen, to grow endless, until now Sherry's door became an immeasurable distance from her own. . . .

Molly took a breath and stepped out over the threshold. Her heart was pounding: she was afraid. Of what? Of an empty upstairs hall, a sleeping house? That was absurd. . . . She ought to be glad they had forgotten to turn out the lights. . . . And she wouldn't run. "'Walk do not run to the nearest exit,'" she said sternly to herself through clenched teeth and, cutting off her retreat, heard the latch of her bedroom door click softly home behind her.

Stiffly, resisting with every forward inch the impulse to bolt headlong for Sherry's room, Molly crept silently down the hall. Away from Clytie's door back there near her own . . . past the head of the stairs, the two guest-room doors on her right . . . and at last, stealthily with infinite caution, past that single door on her left—the door to Helen's room.

Now her hand was on the knob of Sherry's door and her heart was thumping so hard that it was suffocating her and she could see the folds of her bathrobe, where they crossed over her breast, jumping up and down with the fierce thudding.

Again Molly caught her breath—a long, shivering, indrawn sigh, that seemed to rasp in the quiet with the loudness of a sob. Slowly, very slowly, she turned the knob and pushed open Sherry's door.

The lights were on in here, too. . . .

The little sitting room smelled faintly of cigarette smoke, but it was empty and very still. Sherry's hat and a shabby leather attaché case lay on top of the desk. His overcoat, flung across a chair, had one arm dangling limply toward the floor. It worried Molly—the vacant sleeve looked helpless and somehow uncomfortable.

Barely conscious of what she did, Molly went over and picked it up. The familiar touch of the tweed's harsh softness steadied her. Known and memorized, under her fingers it was like a reassurance . . . almost as if she had touched Sherry himself.

"Sherry—" she called softly, and heard from behind the half-closed bedroom door the low murmur of his voice.

Then she was in the doorway and Sherry was there, propped up in bed, looking at her.

"Darling," she cried, "it's good to have you back! It's been awful— Listen, darling. *They* locked the door, not I. They took the key, I didn't even know. I kept waiting for you and—" Molly faltered. There was something wrong, something she did not understand. . . .

Sherry was looking at her, but he did not speak.

"And then you went away before I could—"

She stopped. Fear, like a cold smooth snake, moved coiling inside her.

"Sherry," she whispered. "What's the matter? . . . Why don't you . . . answer?"

He was looking at her and . . . *he didn't see her.*

She stirred, and the bright glazed eyes followed her, indifferently, automatically, without recognition. . . . While now the low murmur of his voice began again, talking out from a strange, closed, far-off place where Sherry was.

"The boat . . ." he said. "I . . . must . . . remember . . . the boat."

The words came clear, separate, uncannily devoid of emphasis, as if they were being sent out through unimaginable space to reach the near-by silence where she stood.

"Ringing. . . . Ringing. . . ."

Timed and precise like some repeated and portentous message, the broken phrases followed one another without pause and without connection.

"And then I'd say, 'I hear it,' and she would—do you think that's funny? . . . It's horrible . . . horrible. Not afraid any more, now I know. . . . The boat's the proof . . . mustn't forget the boat. . . . Tonight, tall and white there by the cliff. I saw it. . . . It flung up its arms just as it did—"

"That was me," Molly whispered. "Sherry!" Her voice, shrill in desperation, cut suddenly across the low monotony of his. "Sherry, look at me!"

She ran to the bed, throwing herself on her knees beside it.

"Look at me, Sherry. I'm here—Molly. Oh God—, please, darling, look at me." Her words tumbled out, incoherent, pleading. "I was there on the cliff. I waved to you— Can't you hear me, darling! I put up my arms and waved to you because I was glad you were home. . . . You saw *me*, darling, only me don't you understand? It's all right. . . . Oh, why won't you answer? Darling . . . darling. I can't bear it, I—"

Someone was behind her. Strong hands were under her elbows, pulling her suddenly to her feet.

"You rash, intruding little fool!" Clytie's voice, angry, incisive, cruel. She spun her around to face her. "What are you doing here?"

"Sherry—" Molly pointed like a child and tried to stop the shaking of her hand. "He stares and stares at me but he doesn't answer—he doesn't even know I'm here. . . . Oh, Clytie, *do* something! He's—"

The blank questing eyes had left hers now. . . . Slowly, they began to close.

"Look, Clytie!" Thin with anguish, Molly's voice mounted perilously. "Look at him—Oh God, is he going to—"

"Stop it!" Clytie seized her by the shoulders, shaking her. "Be quiet, he's all right. It makes him this way. Have you never seen—" Clytie broke off, she seemed to be listening. Her fingers bit viciously through the soft wool of Molly's bathrobe. "Get out of here. I've no time to explain."

Again she spun Molly around, propelling her toward the door.

"Get out. And stay out. Do you understand? . . . Go to your room—"

They reached the bedroom door.

"—Go quickly. At once. As fast as you can. Do you hear? Go to your room and— You have your key. *Use it.*"

For a split second, suspended in a queer little hiatus, close together they stood gazing at each other. Clytie's face was inscrutable—only her tone, and the harsh compelling pressure of her hands, betrayed her urgency. Against the cruel mauve of a flannel wrapper her skin had a greenish tinge. Over one shoulder, looking dreadfully false, like sample hair in a beauty shop window, hung a heavy pigtail of iron-gray.

Molly closed her eyes. In that moment, all horror seemed to her to be caught and woven into a thick braid of lifeless hair.

"Get out. Hurry. Didn't you hear what I said?" Clytie gave her a sudden shove. "Go to your room and lock the door."

Clytie's shove sent Molly stumbling forward across the threshold into the sitting room. Behind her with quiet and irrevocable finality, she heard the door to Sherry's bedroom shut to.

Dazed with misery and shock, Molly had no thought but to obey. She did not question or wonder, she simply went as she was told. . . . Across the small sitting room, past the chair, where now Sherry's overcoat lay folded neatly, the sleeves crossed one over the other like the arms of the dead. . . . Past the desk and Sherry's familiar hat, its brim still showing its jaunty curve. . . . . Out of the farther door, into the hall.

Helen was coming up the stairs.

Molly saw her without surprise. Helen was fully dressed; and with that curiously detached part of the mind which goes on functioning even in moments like these, Molly knew that she had been outside. Little drops of moisture clung to her white curls—that hair of hers, which was so endearingly young and so alive. . . .

"Helen—" It was a broken cry of pain.

"Molly! I thought you were asleep. What are you doing out here in the—"

"Oh, Helen, Helen . . . I've seen him. I've seen Sherry. It was awful—I went and . . . he didn't know me. He didn't even know that I was there. He just kept talking—all queerly, to himself. About that night. . . . About the bell and a boat and his mother on the cliff. . . . Over and over, it was horrible. And then Clytie came, and she—"

Helen's face had gone as white as the curls above it. She said softly—and the pause before she spoke was the merest wing-tip brush of time—

"My poor child. . . . My poor, dear child. . . ."

Helen's voice was kind. . . . Her arms were held out. Molly went to them as a child goes to the shelter of home. They took her in, folding around her tenderly, closely.

"What am I to do! I loved him so—I can't bear it. . . . Oh, Helen, if you only knew—"

Molly let her head fall against Helen. The fight had gone out of her. She couldn't go on hoping and struggling any longer. She wanted to be comforted—to accept unquestioningly the healing anodyne of Helen's sympathy and ask no more. . . . Helen felt soft and warm. She smelled sweet: a faint, spicy, sunshiny smell. It was enough—

"You shouldn't be holding me—" Sentimental contrition mingled with the sharp agony, blurring it. "I don't deserve you to be kind. I've thought the most dreadful things. . . . I wouldn't listen, I thought that you— And you were only trying to help . . . being so good to me. And I was wrong and you were right, right all the time. . . . Sherry—he's so lovely and strong and gay—I can't stand it. Helen, I can't stand to have Sherry m—"

Helen put her hand gently over Molly's lips.

"Hush, dear. Hush. It's been a dreadful shock. . . . Tomorrow—"

"Tomorrow—?" Molly found the word at the end of the world. "We'll do something, won't we, Helen? Together. . . . Tell me we can. I'm not going to go away."

"No, dear, of course not." Helen's arm pressed soothingly tighter, coaxing Molly imperceptibly forward along the hall. "Try to stop shaking, dear, now, if you can. . . . Poor child— Come. Come on into my room with me. We'll talk, and perhaps things will get a little better. And later there's something I can give you to help you sleep. . . ."

They were outside Helen's door. Helen swung it open, and the big black cat ran purring to her legs.

For a moment then, Molly hung back. A warning memory of something forgotten poised for a second upon the edge of consciousness, and was gone again. She said hesitantly:

"Clytie told me to go straight to my room. And to lock my door. . . . In a way, I promised."

"Molly!" Just for an instant, Helen's tone was edged with sharpness. "You sound about eight years old! Clytie *said*—? My dear, you hardly know what you're doing or saying. You must not have understood. Can't you see that's absurd? . . . Come on, dear child. It's cold out there in the hall."

Helen reached out her hand, drawing Molly into the room. And, in Helen's voice, on the slowly closing door, came again, like a fateful echo, Clytie's words: "Poor child. . . . Poor child." . . .

Once more the hall's bright lights burned down upon stark and empty stillness; once more the grandfather clock below whirred and began its clear inexorable chiming—those notes that children sing this way—

> Dear . . . child . . . of . . . God,
> Be brave. . . . Go on. . . .

CHAPTER EIGHTEEN

Helen had been talking for a long time. How long, Molly didn't
know. Things had become very vague, and the sense of the passage of time had slipped away with all the rest.

She sat very still in her chair, her quick hands passive and upturned in her lap, quiescent and motionless as Janet had sat twenty
years before. Her face was in shadow, and in her long white bathrobe it might have been Janet who sat there—only her pale hair
marred the memory-picture of the woman who watched her. Janet's
hair had been dark, but it had lain curled on her shoulders in just
the same way—color alone, a stroke of the brush and the portrait
would be true.

Helen's voice flowed on . . . a lapping, soothing sound, like cool
water over stones, sun-dappled on a sleepy summer's day. . . .
Sometimes it seemed to Molly that she answered Helen, but she
wasn't sure, nor did it matter. . . . The drug Helen had given her—
how long ago?—must have been very strong. She could hear and
see, and her brain felt clear, it was only that everything appeared
to be standing still, to have lost its motion back and forth in time.
There was no moment ago and no moment to come: everything
waited, separate and self-contained, no impulse of meaning or time
linked them any longer together. It was a magic sort of suspension
where there was no thrust of thought or action, and reality had
laid aside all urgency: an enchanted garden where "birds in middle
air hung a-dream" and nothing stirred.

She was not drowsy, she could mark and focus on the things about her. There on the table lay the round black box out of which Helen had taken the tablet she had given her. By it was a glass of water, and she could reach out and touch it if she so willed— She was thirsty, and the room was very warm— The impulse dropped behind; she could not remember what she had been about to do. It no longer mattered— For a moment more her eyes stayed on the round black box. The box had a message for her if only she could bring it back. Sherry— Gropingly, through bewildering folds of inertia, Molly caught hold of the thought that was already slipping so swiftly and treacherously off over the horizon-edge of her mind—

Sherry—the bad headaches and the pain. . . . On the pasteboard lid of the box a druggist's label, turned away from her and upside down— Beneath the heading, small typewritten words and figures, difficult to see and read. . . . A date five, six years ago. . . . A name—

Of course! What was it Clytie had said?— "*It makes him this way. Have you never seen—?*" . . . One obvious ending, one possible meaning. . . . And yet, because she was afraid, she had misinterpreted—found in Clytie's words only confirmation of what she feared. She could complete that sentence now . . . complete it, correctly. There was nothing wrong except in her own terror.

Sherry . . . drugged, as she was now. . . . Not answering her, yet believing that he did, even as she believed that she was answering Helen. She could understand. . . . It was hard to think . . . to put things together. They were so gray and moving so very fast. . . . And all about them there was this queer deep peace . . . this lovely need not to do anything at all. . . .

But she ought to try, for there was something more . . . a quite important thing that worried her. Helen—it had to do with Helen— Helen, who had the round black box. *Helen must have known*, because she, herself, had given Sherry— Then why hadn't she— Why hadn't she—

The thought dropped away—

"Why didn't you tell me?" Molly said.

But now the thought was gone; and she no longer knew what it had been, nor if she had spoken.

The room was very warm . . . unbearably close. She could hardly breathe. . . . Why didn't somebody open a window?. . .

Helen got up from her chair.

Time telescoped; and Molly, hunting still for her lost words, believed she had found them.

The window. . . . *That must have been what she had said.*

A sensation of relief moved through the torpid, numbing peace. She was glad to know—it was disturbing and strange not to be sure. . . . But that was what it must have been, for Helen was crossing the room, drawing back a long tapestry curtain.

There was a window behind it . . . a narrow, sill-less little window set in an angle of the room where one would have expected to find a cupboard. . . . A third window which she had never seen. Molly experienced a faint surprise—looking up from outside, she had been certain that there were only two. . . .

Briefly, this puzzled Molly. Then it, too, fell away with all the rest, into the dim demandless peace.

The questioning past ceased to trouble her remote and timeless present. The drug had its way—sensation, preternaturally absorbing, became all she knew. Like a person hypnotized, her eyes followed Helen as Helen went back to her chair, and then, blank and questing as Sherry's had been, they returned once more, to rest without wonder or speculation, on the black glittering panes of a window still tightly closed. The dark glitter fascinated Molly, but that was all. She had long since forgotten anything else.

Helen began talking again . . . or perhaps she had never stopped. Her words were sounds, disjoined and valueless when Molly's thought lacked cohesion to link them together. They came as if alone, each one familiar and known, but, like words read swiftly backward, they had no continuity of meaning in Molly's mind.

Names—Sherry's and Malcolm's, wove themselves in and out, mingling with others of a legendary past: Castor and Pollux, Helen and Clytemnestra. The House of Gemini. . . . The Heavenly Twins. . . . Stars and portents. . . . Old legends curiously cherished and made into their own by a lonely boy and girl. From over forty years ago, Helen brought them now to Molly. Her apologia: memories to fashion for her an exoneration and a pardon. . . .

Molly heard without understanding, and, safe from Molly's comprehension, Helen talked on—watching the still white figure, the quiet hands, the eyes fixed unwaveringly on the windowpane, glittering and blank against the dark beyond it.

Soon, Helen thought, very soon, it would be time.

And on her unspoken thought, as if a signal had passed between them, the big black cat uncurled from his sleep and with alert pricked ears sat waiting—his yellow unblinking eyes fastened like Molly's on the windowpane.

A little smile of gratification curved Helen's lips. Her voice fell silent; and for a long moment the tableau held—three motionless figures in a lamplit room: a cat, a girl, and an elderly woman. A sentimental tableau, prettily posed, where was there anything sinister in that? In the golden lamplight nothing moved . . . not a hair quivered on the cat's sleek back, not a ripple swayed the table cover's silken fringe . . . and yet, through the warm closed room, blew like a wind the impalpable chill of evil.

Molly stirred, lifting her hand to her throat, pulling the folds of her bathrobe closer around it. A sudden sense of dis-ease had penetrated her tranced peace. Dimly, she fought against it, trying to banish it; resenting its intrusion as one resents the voice, the touch, which is awakening one from sleep. It would not go. . . . She knew its cause—the beating, insistent tolling of the bell. . . .

She seemed not to have heard it when she first came into Helen's room. It had begun softly, almost imperceptibly, so that she had been hardly aware of when it first began; but it had been ringing now for a very long time, growing louder and louder, more and more insistent, until, at last, all her consciousness was filled with its mournful, throbbing rhythm.

Re . . . mem . . . ber . . . Re . . . mem . . . ber. . . . The low notes tolled it over and over, importuning her, urging her . . . never varying, never stopping, muffled and yet curiously near, as though they were beating back from the very walls of the room itself.

Molly stirred again, restlessly. She was imprisoned in sound, monotonous and inescapable. If only she could awake and go— But the tranced stillness held: her hand dropped again to her lap: her eyes remained fixed on the windowpane: and she was motionless as before, except for the barest movement of her head, which, watching her, Helen saw, had begun to sway ever so little, back and forth, in tempo with the ringing of the bell.

The time had come.

Helen's face tightened; her eyes left Molly, and slowly, almost reluctantly, she, too, looked toward the windowpane.

Seconds grew taut and thin . . . everything waited motionless. Waiting had indeed such stillness that the low ringing of the bell buoy seemed to be more than sound, to have a sort of motion in that hushed air. A minute passed . . . another. . . .

The cat saw it first.

He did nothing. The compact black body did not alter by a muscle or a hair its patient immobility. He never budged, and yet the very instant at which watching became awareness could be sensed in him like a gathered violence.

Molly's eyes widened.

Behind the dark windowpane something moved. . . . A patch of darker darkness, rocking, jerking. . . .

An eerie luminosity defined it suddenly: a little boat, sails set, far out upon the tumbled waters of the Sound. The light came again, a blue flickering flame—clinging and waving from the mast like a single tendril of blue fire.

The cat growled.

Fear reached deep into Molly, tearing away her dulled peace, showing her with quick and awful instancy, terror's culmination. She had waited upon bated horror, but here it was, alive and swift in her caught breath—

"Look," Molly whispered, "*look!*"

Without knowing it, she was on her feet.

"Look, Helen, look!" she whispered again. "Out there on the water. A little boat, tossing and plunging. . . . Can you see it, Helen? Oh, Helen, I'm afraid. Afraid, because. . . ."

Molly's whisper died. Her hands reached up, pushing against a dread that would not go—covering her ears against the words her mind had begun to repeat over and over:

"*Sick scared . . . risking his life time and time again. Sick scared, that's what it is.*" Obadiah's voice, and then, lost and haunted as she'd heard it tonight, Sherry's voice as if in answer: "*Not afraid anymore. . . . . The boat's the proof. . . . Remember the boat.*" . . . .

Dread gathered and broke. Oh, God! was it Sherry out there? . . . It couldn't be. She was all confused. He was drugged . . . asleep. And Clytie was with him. . . .

Minutes seemed to have gone by with her standing there, and yet Molly knew that only seconds could have passed. Helen had not yet even answered. And, exactly at the same point of the windowpane where she had seen it first, the little boat had made no headway. It plunged and heeled, helpless in the savage water. How rough it was . . . when only a short time ago it had been so calm. . . . The eerie blue light ran and flickered over the mast, tossed from its tip a jagged feather of blue fire.

"Beautiful and horrible," Molly whispered. "Do you see it, Helen? There's a queer light—"

Now, at last, Helen spoke. But it was not as if she answered Molly. Her words seemed to seek a listener and a time long gone. . . .

"The corposant," murmured Helen softly. "St. Elmo's fire. . . ." She paused. A look almost of exaltation crossed her face and, text-book-dry, her next words held an odd intensity. "The single flame that ancient mariners called 'Helen.'" Again she paused. She said, even more slowly, "Portent of the evil that is still to come. . . ."

Molly hadn't heard her. She was leaning forward; tense, absorbed, her lips parted.

"Look, Helen! Oh look— The little boat, it's plunging and tossing horribly—heading straight into the race. It's moving so slowly it seems to be standing still—it must be on the very edge. Oh why doesn't it put about while there's still time! When the current catches it, it'll be sucked right in. It'll never—"

Molly started for the window.

Helen seemed to rouse herself: What was she thinking of, dreaming here? Already it was almost too late— Molly was half-way across the room, nearly to the window. If she got any closer . . . put the light behind her . . . even in her drugged state, she was bound to see—

With one swift, surprisingly agile movement, Helen was out of her chair; and, running forward, she cut across Molly blocking her view—practically hurling herself in front of the windowpane. She stood right up against it, covering it with her body, and, cupping her hands round her eyes, thrust her face close to the glass. Her scream, tearing into the hushed air, had a monstrous impropriety.

"Oh God! Molly— It *is!*" Horror, confirmation of her worst fears, rode in her voice: a superb performance. "Molly, *don't you know who's in that boat?* It's Sherry— *Sherry*, who's out there!"

Molly's hands flew to her throat. She gave a little whimper, a small heart-breaking sound—the inept animal speech of grief.

"Oh no, Helen . . . no. . . . It can't be. . . . I don't believe it. He's in his room . . . ill. He couldn't—"

Helen whirled around.

"What do *you* know about it?" she demanded fiercely. "How do you know what he will or will not do? He's done it before. He's deranged, I tell you— When he's like this he'll do anything. *Anything!*" Her voice rose, she seemed goaded by an unbearable impatience—angry. It was as if in some obscure way Molly had deliberately driven her beyond her control. "You didn't choose to believe me, did you? Oh no, you knew best!" It was amazing— At that moment of all moments, Helen stood and scolded Molly. "You knew it all. Well, I thought after what you saw tonight, you would at least—"

Helen broke off. With an effort she appeared to recollect herself. She swung back again to the window, pressing her face once more against the pane.

"What are we going to do?" she cried. "Oh, God! He hasn't a chance—the mad, crazy fool. . . . Not a chance. . . . Unless—"

She whirled about again, running to Molly and catching her by the arm.

"Listen to me, Molly, listen. . . . There isn't a minute to lose. You can save him, Molly, do you hear me? You can save Sherry— He'll come in for you. . . . I know he will. . . . The searchlight by the cove—we must turn it on. He'll see you signaling to him. . . . He'll turn back, it will guide him in. Quick, Molly, quick, before he reaches the race, and it's too late. Run, child, run—you're young and faster than I am. It's our only hope. Get to the light. It's at the top of the steps—"

But Helen's last words were wasted— Molly had already gone. . . .

Helen waited only a moment. She smiled, a pleased smile as at a task well done; and with a deft gesture her hand reached up, pulling the tapestry curtain once more into place over the dark glittering panes of the sill-less window. From the stairs came the diminishing sound of Molly's running footsteps: Twenty years fell away to find again that sound . . . that moment— And, swift and sure as then, moving with supple quickness, Helen followed Molly. . . .

In the quiet room, the bell's low notes still tolled of danger. The cat yawned, curling himself to lay his head along his paws. And, safe from sight behind the tapestry curtain, a little toy boat rocked on upon painted waves.

CHAPTER NINETEEN

For seconds that seemed eternity, the front door wouldn't open. In an agony of delay Molly struggled with the old-fashioned double lock: her desperate haste had made her awkward—it refused to yield.

A sobbing hatred shook her. Like something apart from herself, she saw her hands, white against the polished wood, twisting and turning futilely; and for a slipping moment a primitive rage took hold of her. She wanted to scream, to hurl herself bodily against the blank and obdurate wood, to beat the door down by the sheer fury of the hatred she felt toward it. She caught her lower lip between her teeth and forced herself to calm.

The second's delay had been enough. Helen was right behind her now. Molly could hear her leave the stairs and start across the narrow entrance hall. That ugly boxlike hall, where once so long ago, a girl Molly could hardly remember, had stood and dreamed, planning to paint the woodwork white. . . .

The door came free. Molly wrenched it open.

Her forward lunge carried her away from Helen and, clearing the porch, landed her with such force on the driveway below that the gravel stung her feet through her thin slippers. She stumbled, caught in her long skirts; and then she was up, racing like mad for the corner of the house.

A curious exhilaration possessed her, an instant's surging sense of physical power that was akin to joy. The numbing drug had lifted from her limbs: her body obeyed her perfectly now. She was running fast—very fast. . . . The moment passed, and as in a bad dream she seemed to be standing still—heart and lungs and pounding legs laboring in a nightmare effort that availed her nothing.

She rounded the corner of the house.

Helen's voice came from behind her, urging her on.

"Run, Molly, run— Hurry. . . . Hurry!"

And, born of that cry, a half-formed thought, the emotion of recognition, lived for a moment in Molly's mind. *This was all like something else. . . .* Something remembered or experienced, she wasn't sure. *All too much like something else. . . .*

Above her head, the twin squares of Helen's lighted windows threw down their shape in two thin rugs of light across the flower beds below. *Two*, a part of her mind said to her. *Only . . . two! . . .* She sped on. Past the garden . . . the garage . . . out through the windbreak of pines—

The sea stretched before her, dark and limitless.

Where was the boat? The little boat with St. Elmo's fire in the rigging? Already close to the rocks beneath the cliff, or—its ghostly fire quenched—invisible, far out upon the reaching blackness?

"Hurry, Molly. Hurry!"

Hurry— Swiftly, she veered to the left, cutting across the dark lawn toward the steps at the top of the cove. Ahead of her glimmered the line of white posts—a line that appeared unbroken, for this was the angle of optical illusion where the solitary post guarding the cleft did not show. In a moment she would pass right by it, but until she had drawn much nearer, it would stay one with the others—she would not see it. Her breath came in rasping gasps, staples driven through her lungs. She thought incongruously: I smoke too much. . . . In her mouth was the taste of blood.

Again came Helen's voice.

"Run, Molly, run. Get to the light. . . . Hurry. Hurry."

The line of white posts glimmered still ahead. How slowly she seemed to be running! The single post had not, even now, drawn away from the others. And yet she would have thought herself almost upon it; to have seen it, separate and distinct, standing guard by its black hole. . . . Distance and Time were an agony—a vacuum of pain where nothing altered, nothing moved.

All her senses were gathered up into one compelling purpose: the forward thrust of her speeding body. Hearing alone came now a rebel, demanding her awareness. . . . There was something missing— Something else she should have seen, or—

As if the action had taken place in a silent film to which the sound track had been suddenly restored, Molly became aware of sound. She could hear her panting breath, the beat of the waves, the thud of her running footsteps echoing back from the hard earth, but— *She could not hear the bell. . . .*

"Quicker, Molly, quicker. Hurry. . . . Hurry. . . ."

There was no boat . . . no bell. . . . Only—there on the ground by her running feet a white post . . . *which should have been upright!*

Too late, Molly tried to stop herself. Her forward momentum was too great. With all her strength she threw her body backward. Emptiness sprang at her feet.

For a terrible instant she balanced there. And in that split second, the emotion of recognition clicked home.

This had happened before. . . . *This is what had happened to Janet!*

She, too, with darkness and urgency distorting all sense of distance—she, too, had trusted for safety in a white post that was not there. She, too, had heard that treacherous voice which, always behind her, had urged her on; and, listening to it, had gone not to save the husband she loved, but to die. . . .

For a second of appalled incredulity, Helen's face rose before Molly, gentle and smiling. The gentle face of one who had cradled a child in fear. . . . The sweet pink-and-white mask of malevolence . . . madness . . . evil unutterable. . . . A murderer's face. The murderer of Sherry's mother. . . . *Her* murderer. . . .

Molly screamed. And, as she pitched forward, flung up her arms in a last attempt to save herself. Then, instinctively jerking her body straight, she plunged like a plummet feet foremost into space.

Roaring blackness rushed up at her. Emptiness tore, icy cold, along her bare legs and thighs, billowing the long skirts of her bathrobe about her waist.

And again, in a queerly halted split-second, she had time for so much. Again, with a curious acceleration of perception, came the detailed recording of sensation, the flashing awareness of her thoughts.

She thought—and could even distinguish it as irony—that whereas she now knew Sherry to be physically safe while she, herself, was perhaps about to die—her danger was, nonetheless, his too. For should Helen succeed—if dying as Janet had done was to be the end of her blind little fight for Sherry's happiness—then Sherry was lost indeed. What hope could there be for him when he was told that Molly, like his mother, had committed suicide? What way out from his tragic pattern of guilt could be found for him then? "*She believed you mad so she killed herself.*" That was the monstrous horror Helen would lay at his feet. . . .

She mustn't die!— Sherry would never be free or happy or whole again as long as he lived. And with this realization, even as she fell—through the rush and hubbub of sensation, of plunging, hurtling downward—anger against Helen rode over everything, even physical fear; and, craftier and more effective than mere self-preservation, a fighting determination to live took command of Molly.

Between the top and the bottom of the cliff she had time for one prayer. . . . A prayer that, alone of all her flashing thoughts, was made corporate by words:

"Dear God," Molly prayed, "let the water be deep. Don't let me strike the rock."

The prayer was answered. . . .

Toes pointed, body rigid; like an arrow and with hardly a splash, Molly broke the surface of the water and its icy blackness closed over her head.

Immediately Molly struck upward, and, as she did so, she felt a sharp pain run up her leg. She had struck her foot against the rocky bottom. The water was paralyzingly cold—so cold, that in an instant the pain was numbed and she could no longer feel it. The black water sucked and dragged at her: there was a powerful undertow, and all her strength was needed not to be swept out by it to where the waves broke viciously against the narrow mouth of the cleft.

Without a foothold, the narrow shaftlike walls rose steeply above her—as smooth and perpendicular, she knew, as the sides of a well. No hope lay in them. . . . The heavy sodden skirts of her bathrobe clung about her legs, dragging her down under the sucking water. Before anything else, she must get her bathrobe off.

Resisting the impulse to struggle, Molly let herself go under; and, for a long suffocating moment, there was nothing but sucking blackness and her frantic fingers tugging on the knot of her bathrobe's sash. Then at last it was free, and her bathrobe was gone; and striking upward again, Molly gulped air into her bursting lungs.

There was still her nightgown . . . light as it was, tenaciously wrapping itself about her, impeding her movements. . . . The wet chiffon stuck to her body as though it had been glued onto her flesh, and the effort of pulling it off and up over her head dangerously exhausted Molly's strength.

"It's been a jinx," Molly angrily thought. "A jinx from the very beginning. This is the end of you," she said. "You Off-again-on-again-Finnigan, wedding nightgown. . . ."

She must hurry, for already she was becoming numb with cold—she couldn't hope to last long in this icy water. She had assessed her chances and knew that she had only one. If she stayed there treading water, fighting against the pulsing drag of the powerful undertow, she would very quickly became exhausted. Then, robbed of her last resistance by the paralyzing cold, half-conscious, she would be sucked out into the breaking surf, to be thrown battered and drowning against the cliff—until, the cruel sport ended, the remorseless current claimed her for its own and, sweeping her body into the churning highway of the race, carried it triumphantly out to sea.

Her one chance was this: To gauge the moment of the outward drag; and then, diving deeply under the arching, curling waves at the mouth of the cleft to strike with all her strength diagonally out to sea—swimming as hard as she could, away from the waves and the rocks, away from the pull of the race—in the hope that, before her strength failed her, she might reach the lee of the cliff, and, turning shoreward again, gain the shelter of the cove.

She saw it all clearly in her mind: The opening of the cleft perilously near the center of the cliff; at her right, the cliff's furthermost point, and, beyond it, the race; behind her, and to her left, the cove. As though it had been drawn for her, she saw the line that she must travel: an inverted and slightly tilted Λ. A "V for Victory"?—. . . .

It was a tall order, but it might be done. . . . And now, for the first time in her life—and, thought Molly ruefully, perhaps the last—Molly sent up a message of thankfulness for the long, arduous hours of training that had gone to make her a strong and resourceful swimmer.

"Bless you, Father," Molly said.

She took a deep breath, throwing her head back, filling her lungs. And, doing so, looking up—there, at the very end-moment—she knew the last horror of all.

Silhouetted against the sky, she saw the outline of a head and shoulders—Helen crouching, kneeling on the very edge of the cleft. Helen's arms were raised, outstretched in a gesture that was oddly familiar. And, sick with revulsion, all at once Molly knew what that gesture was. Helen was *praying*—offering up, as though upon a pagan altar, her human sacrifice.

As if the waves, the tearing menace of the sea, were cleanness and release, Molly dived deep and hard into the water's icy blackness.

Up on the top of the cliff, a small squat figure struggled with a heavy post; lifting it back into place, tugging and dragging on its white chains until once more they stretched straight and taut.

Helen was very tired—an old woman again, suffering the slowness of an aging body. Ecstasy had left her drained. Twice in the gray and monotonous journey of her days—her dull, sweet gentleness—had come this ecstatic moment. Twice had she felt striking through her, sharp and vivifying, the ecstasy of ultimate power: the beauty and godlike power of death. Twice she had killed; and for the wonder and glory of those two short moments, she gladly rendered up the rest.

And it was Malcolm who had given them to her. Clever, ingenious Malcolm. . . . But he would never know, because Malcolm, too, was dead. . . . The old pain twisted in Helen. An old bitterness assailed her.

"He should have loved me as I loved him!" Helen cried; and suddenly down her cheeks ran tears of self-pity, spoiling the aftermath of her triumph and her exaltation.

He had given those moments to her, and yet, if he knew that he had, he would not be glad. . . . She had loved him, but she knew him to have been made of ordinary stuff—too weakly pitying to savor ecstasy such as hers. . . . Clever, ingenious Malcolm . . . a child's toy, a magic illusion. . . . In her hands, the potent and perfect instrument of murder. For she, Helen, his sister, was clever and ingenious, too.

And because she was, she had safely for her own forever, all that remained of Malcolm: Sherry—Malcolm's son. Sherry could not escape her now— A cold finger touched Helen's thought for a moment, checking it. A sly fear moved like a shadow across her certainty.

What had happened tonight? Why, without her having induced it, had Sherry had an attack? . . . This was the first time. Would there be others? Had she unwittingly played too long with that most subtle and dangerous thing—the balance of a human mind? . . . Could it be possible—Sherry had always been so strong, so resilient—could it be possible that she had pushed him too far at last? . . . She had been cautious. For several years now, until the other night, she had not used the bell.

The bell. . . . If it hadn't been for that, perhaps she need not have had to kill Molly. Perhaps in the end, she could have succeeded in making her go away. But from the time, when walking along the cliff together, Molly had spoken about the bell, Helen had known that she must kill her.

More, that she must kill her before ever she had the chance to speak alone with Sherry again. That was why, when Sherry came back so unexpectedly, she had had to act before her plans were fully completed. She had gone out and put down the post; but she still had not known what she was to do—what excuse she was to find for awakening Molly. Fate had played into her hands—no plan she might have made, could have been more perfect. . . . Although, just for that first moment when, returning from outside, she had come across Molly in the hall—Helen had been frightened that she was too late.

She had been quick-witted—that tiresomely stubborn girl whom Sherry had married. And sooner or later, in the light of what Helen, herself, had been foolish enough to tell her, she would have worked it out. Even if she hadn't, at the very least, she might, quite naturally, have mentioned hearing the bell buoy to Sherry. Or, for that matter, to Clytie or Nona. And when she did—

It was very puzzling. . . . How had she heard it in the first place? Helen still didn't know. Helen had thought her, at the time, safely disposed of in her room. . . . . No matter, she was dead now. Drowned. . . . Her body, like Janet's, carried by the current out to sea.

Helen turned, looking out at the dim, white roadway of the race. She could just distinguish it, stretching out and out, until it was merged into the darkness of the night.

"Good-bye, dear child. . . ." Helen said softly. And even in her own mind, perhaps it was not wholly clear whether or not she said it in parody.

Molly was gone. . . . But, Helen told herself, she would have to be very careful about that. It might not be safe now to tell Sherry— as she had so looked forward to doing—that Molly had committed suicide. . . . Not, at least, until she had made very certain what had caused that worrying attack. . . . Sometimes it was all too much for her. Sometimes she wondered if it was, after all, worth while. . . . Clytie and Nona. . . . There would be Clytie and Nona to cope with, too.

She was very tired. . . . Ecstasy had left her tired. . . . She must remember that it was ecstasy which had tired her. . . . She must try to remember the ecstasy. . . .

There was much still that she must do. She wanted sleep, only to sleep. But she must go to Sherry. She must make sure that he was quiet and would not wake. . . . In the morning, after she had rested, she would be herself again and able to plan. She was not as young as she had been that other time— She was afraid of forgetting things, unsure of herself.

Forgetting things. . . .

Oh, God! she must hurry. Already she had forgotten. She had not had time to turn it off, Molly had run so fast. . . . In her room the bell was still ringing! What if Clytie had heard it! Careless . . . careless. . . . Always before she had been so careful.

Suddenly, Helen was afraid.

"I am getting old," Helen whispered.

And, pressing her fingers to her eyes, Helen was sorry for herself.

CHAPTER TWENTY

It was twenty minutes later that Clytie stood at the head of the kitchen stairs, her whole body tense and rigid with waiting.

The lights in the hall still burned, and in their stark, uncompromising glare Clytie's face showed tired and drawn. There were set, hard lines about her mouth, and her fingers holding the edge of the door were white at their tips from pressure.

Every now and again, she turned her head to look apprehensively over her shoulder along the empty hall behind her. But for the most part she stood absolutely motionless, peering ahead of her through the half-opened door into the darkness below. Once she whispered: "Why doesn't she hurry!"; and her long iron-gray pigtail jerked agitatedly as, again, she glanced backward down the hall toward the closed door of Sherry's room.

There was a faint sound of movement, and Nona's head and shoulders rose out of the darkness of the stairs into the narrow slit of light thrown through the crack of the half-open door.

"Well . . .?" Clytie questioned.

Nona nodded.

She gained the top of the stairs and came past Clytie into the hall. She was breathing hard as if she had been running. Like Clytie, she was undressed for the night, but over her gray wool wrapper she had on a heavy coat, and in one hand she carried a small flashlight. She thrust it now into her pocket, and, meeting Clytie's eyes, she again nodded slowly, but she still did not speak. Her face had a soft and queerly vulnerable look—she was not wearing her glasses. Clytie had not moved; Nona reached round her and quietly shut the door at the head of the stairs.

"In my room," Clytie whispered.

Safe inside Clytie's bedroom, with the key turned in the lock, they faced each other.

"Well?" Clytie said again.

"Yes." The single word was harsh as though assent must be forced through throat and lips stiff with reluctance.

Clytie said sharply, "Speak up, Nona." After a moment, she added more gently, "Why do you try to spare me?"

"I— I'm sorry, Miss Clytie."

"It's true, then." Clytie accepted it wearily. "It's happened, just as I knew that it would. I told you it would . . . there in the boat-house. I said to you, 'It'll be like the first time . . . all over again.' I was frightened and cowardly and too weak to want to face things. But I was going to do something to stop it, only you— You soothed, and begged, and—"

"Miss Clytie!" Now it was Nona's voice that was sharp. "How can you! How wickedly unfair. . . ."

Clytie put her head in her hands, pressing her fingers against her temples. She murmured almost inaudibly, "Forgive me, Nona. . . . Please forgive me." Her head came up. "Don't you see I haven't any courage about this? Just as I never have about anything. I've known it was to happen. . . . Yes, Nona, *known* it . . . ever since I talked to Molly last night. And I wanted to tell her then, only I didn't. . . . couldn't make myself say the words. I put it off, telling myself that next time, some other time, I would be braver. . . . My own sister I couldn't. . . . Yes, I knew it had to happen, and now that it has, I'm still a coward. I can bear everything else, I think, but one truth about it—that I, and I alone, could have prevented it. Oh why!" cried Clytie with a sort of sad anger, "why, even if I didn't explain, why couldn't Molly do as I told her to? Why didn't she shut herself in her room and lock the door! I thought she was going to. I thought she had."

"Please, Miss Clytie," Nona said. "It isn't right to be blaming yourself like this. You didn't *know*, not for all that you say you did. Not for twenty years, we haven't been sure. Not until . . . to-night."

Clytie shook her head. "Weren't we, Nona? I think we were. . . . Didn't I tell you, just now, that you must stop trying to spare me? . . . Go on, Nona. . . . The post . . . it was like it was that first time?"

"Yes, the ground around it all disturbed. And I could see foot-prints where she'd pressed the earth down again. Only this time it wasn't nearly so tidy, much easier to see. . . . The post isn't in prop-erly straight, really. . . . I can't lie to you, Miss Clytie, I wish I could—there's no doubt about it this time, no doubt at all."

There was a dead pause. It was as though in Nona's homely words, horror had reached its close.

Suddenly, Nona moved. She raised her clenched fists in a ges-ture as old as melodrama, and as true as life—

"I hate her!" Nona screamed. "I hate her, I hate her, I hate her! For over forty years, I've hated her! Sweet and gentle!—selfish and sly and cruel. . . . So greedy in her wicked, unnatural loving, that there's to be no love or no happiness left over for anyone else. She took Janet away from Malcolm. And Mr. Derwent away from you. And now—now she's taken the girl Sherry loves away from him. She hasn't only killed two people—she's killed us all. Why did Mr. Malcolm go away to that awful place that was to be the death of him? Tell me that! And tell me if you call the life we've had, you and I in this house ever since—tell me if you call that living? Won-dering and grieving and dreading—Hasn't that been our death, too? . . . I hate her! If I knew how, I'd kill her, so help me, I would!"

She knew no other way to stop her: Clytie slapped Nona hard across the face. Her fingers left red marks across the gray wrinkles of Nona's cheek. Nona gave a sort of sob and became, all at once, very still.

"Thank you, Miss Clytie," she said.

There was another pause.

"What are we going to do?" Clytie asked slowly.

"What is there to do, Miss Clytie? That poor girl's gone like Miss Janet. We can't save her now, if ever we could. It must have happened almost an hour ago, while you were in with Mr. Sherry.

You don't even know that it was just over when Miss Helen came
in to you there—and you came and got me because you'd seen that
the bedroom was empty. . . . And, whenever it was, the time of it
makes no difference."

"If she could swim—?"

"It's no use, Miss Clytie . . . no use, hoping. It's over . . . that
current doesn't leave anybody a chance. Do you suppose Miss Helen
would do it this way if it wasn't sure? She's gone, poor young thing.
And like Miss Janet, there won't be a trace—her body will never
be found." Nona stopped for a moment. Then she asked, ever so
gently, "Do you want to let it be, Miss Clytie? . . . I can . . . . fix . . .
the post."

"No, Nona . . . no. . . ."

"There's nobody need ever know. . . . It would be quite safe.
Even if folks were to question like they did that time there's nothing now more than there was then that they can prove. . . . Soon as
it's light, I could go out and fix the post."

"No, Nona, no. I can't do it. Not this time. . . . Last time it was
different, we could try to tell ourselves it wasn't true. But this time,
we *know*. Molly has been murdered, Nona. I'm saying the words,
do you hear me? My own sister is mad and a murderess. That was
what I meant when I asked you, what were we to do?"

"I don't know, Miss Clytie. . . . Miss Helen will be counting on
our—"

"On our being cowards again. . . . Oh, God! if only it weren't all
so horrible! My own sister . . . my *twin* sister. . . ."

"You love her," Nona said, her voice filled with a shocked surprise.

"Love, Helen? . . . Yes, I suppose that I do. But I have no right
to think about that. She is dangerous and bad, and she must be
put away where she can no longer harm or make unhappy, innocent people who are unfortunate enough to stand in her path. . . .
And if for no other reason—there's Sherry."

"Poor lad. . . ." Nona agreed. . . . "How are you to tell him, Miss
Clytie? Mightn't it be better, maybe, to leave him believing the kind
lie Miss Helen will have ready for him?"

"*Kind* lie?" Clytie repeated bitterly. "What makes you believe it would be kind? . . . I'll tell you something. . . . For a long while I've dreaded facing the ghastly suspicion that has been growing upon me. . . . Even now, I hope that it, at least, isn't true— But. . . . I have wondered, Nona—it's been like a canker in my mind—whether Helen was not, in some secret way I cannot understand, continually torturing Sherry."

"Miss Clytie! . . . that's horrible. Oh, you must be mistaken! Why, he's simply crazy about her, always has been ever since he was little. . . . He's never had much love for you and me—it all went to her."

"Yes, I know that, and I keep telling myself over and over that I must be wrong. Yet. . . . Don't you see, Nona? It could still be true if— If he didn't realize that she was doing it? If he didn't know that it was . . . well . . . *deliberate*?"

"No, Miss Clytie, no. That's too mixed-up," rejected Nona, practically. "You've got to worrying too much and seeing things that aren't there. What have you got to go on? It isn't good sense."

Clytie turned up her hands in a tired gesture that was half a shrug of despair. As though, suddenly, she realized that she had been standing quite unnecessarily for a long time, she went over and sat down on the edge of her bed.

"Sit down, somewhere, Nona. I don't know what we've been doing, standing. . . . I don't really know what we're doing at all. . . ." Clytie sighed; and for a moment she was silent. Then, as if she had been driven back into speech by the goading anxiety of thoughts which would leave her no peace, she began once more at the point where she had broken off.

"I daresay you're right about it, Nona," she said hesitantly. "God knows, I hope with all my heart that you are. For if I ever find out that it's true— Then— Then, even I, would be ready to kill her. What she has done—yes, even murder!—would seem clean by comparison. . . . And I have nothing to go on, as you say. Only a queer sort of instinct—a look I've seen on Helen's face sometimes when, like to-night, Sherry was having one of his attacks. It's a look almost as if Helen were glad that he was suffering. . . . A look of . . . gratification,

I suppose I might call it. . . . And, you see, Nona, I have never understood *why* Sherry should have those strange headaches. I have never believed for a moment that he isn't mentally sound. I *know* Sherry's not insane, no matter what Helen may say."

Clytie's tone was confident, but her eyes sought Nona's for confirmation. Nona's answer was crisp and firm.

"Of course he's not, Miss Clytie! Mr. Sherry's all right."

Clytie closed her eyes. She looked spent, unutterably weary. A few slow tears forced their way out from under her closed eyelids, and, unnoticed by her, ran leisurely down her cheeks.

"It's been all so awful, Nona. All these years. . . . Living with myself, knowing what a coward I've been. Feeling that I, too, was guilty with her—sharing her guilt, having a part of that sin, because out of cowardice I had condoned. Turning myself even away from Derwent, whom I loved, so that he might never see that his suspicions were mine as well. . . . Oh, I've deserved to be unhappy, Nona!—a bitter old maid. . . ."

"It's not too late," Nona said gently. "You can try to make it right even now, Miss Clytie. Send for Mr. Derwent. Will you do that, Miss Clytie? We need him—he would be able to help us."

Clytie opened her eyes. For the first time there was a look in them that was something other than utter despair.

"Yes," she said, as if she spoke of a miracle, "I can telephone to Derwent. . . . He'll come at once, I know that he will. We can wait for him, can't we, Nona? He'll be able to tell us what we should do."

A little flush stained Clytie's cheeks. She glanced shyly at Nona, ashamed to be glad . . . conscious of the secret happiness quickening within her. . . . After twenty long years . . . Derwent. . . .

But Nona was thinking of something else. She didn't even answer Clytie, for she was absorbed, all at once, in a train of thought of her own.

"You know," she brought out abruptly, "how you said you knew it was going to happen ever since you talked with Miss Molly? Well, I've been thinking, and I guess I've known, too. Long before that—from the time Miss Helen sent Mrs. Wilkins away."

Clytie jerked her own thoughts back.

"The cook? What possible connection is there—"

"Why, don't you see?" argued Nona earnestly. "Miss Helen was getting things ready. Taking her precautions in case it had to be done. She thought she could count on us—that old fool Obadiah, and you and me. . . . But she didn't want any strangers about, if it came time to do it. . . . Whatever you say, Miss Clytie, there was nothing wrong with that raspberry fool."

"Nona!" The absurd inconsequentiality of this snapped Clytie's tight hold on herself. She began to laugh hysterically. She stopped as suddenly as she had begun. She said angrily, "Good God! What's come over you, Nona? How can you possibly concern yourself with a thing like that at a time like this? Don't you realize—"

Nona was unperturbed. Inexorably, her slow mind pursued its speculations.

"Miss Helen isn't what she used to be, Miss Clytie. She's not shrewd and careful as she was once. She's gotten so sure of herself, I guess, that she's lost her sense of proportion. The second time's not as easy as the first. It's more dangerous, just because it's the second time. How could she think she'd get away with it this time, for sure? She'd sent Mrs. Wilkins away, but there were others that knew Miss Molly'd come here— Fred Kirkwood, for instance. . . . He's no friend to this house, as well she knows. And he's a great one to blab. . . . Then there's her friends—Miss Molly's—wouldn't they ask questions if she was to just up and disappear?"

"I don't know, Nona," Clytie replied wearily. "It doesn't matter anyway. I've told you this isn't going to be covered up. If you're still thinking of trying it for my sake, I want you to forget it right now. . . . I forbid you to touch that post, Nona. Do you understand? What's more you're to see that Miss Helen doesn't either. . . . I hope to be able to wait until Mr. Derwent can get here, but if you force me to shall act on my own. I'm through with being a coward," ended Clytie. And for all its weariness, there was a note of sad relief in her voice that made her sound almost happy.

She smiled at Nona and, leaning forward to where Nona sat in the chair beside the bed, she patted the hands lying crossed in Nona's lap.

"You're a faithful friend, Nona, my dear," she said.

"I wasn't thinking about covering it up, Miss Clytie," Nona protested. "You had me wrong there. I know you're right, and it would be sinful of us and bad for us, too, if we should do that again, now we're sure. What I was thinking of was, are we going to be able to do it our way? Nicely and quietly, so's not to hurt Mr. Sherry or any of us—even Miss Helen—too much. Are we going to be let alone? Or will it be taken out of our hands, with the police and newspapermen and everything that will make it more horrible than ever—dirty and sort of prying—besides being as it is, terrible and sad? That was what I was thinking of, Miss Clytie."

"I see, Nona. . . . I hope that we can do it our way. We should call ourselves fortunate, I suppose" (Clytie's tone touched the word with distaste: "fortunate" seemed such a cold-blooded word to use) "that poor Molly had no people—her mother and father are both dead—and that her friends are not the sort that ask questions. From what she told us, she had nobody close—everyone she knew, belonged to the casual, come-and-go, crowd of the theater. Probably few, if any of them, even knew that she had married. Or if they did, knew where she had gone . . . No, Nona, on that score, we have nothing to fear. . . . Poor child. . . ." said Clytie softly. "I liked her, Nona. I liked her very much. . . ."

All at once and without any warning, Nona began to cry. She covered her face with her hands, and under her gray wrapper, her bony shoulders shook with her hard sobbing.

"It's . . . Mr. Sherry I'm . . . sorry for," she gulped brokenly. "What will happen to him . . . when he knows that Molly's . . . dead? It's going to break his heart. . . . Oh, how could Miss Helen do it! How could she be so cruel . . . and so wicked!"

Clytie got off the bed and put her arm tight about Nona's shaking shoulders.

"Please, Nona," she begged, "please don't go back on me now. I can't stand it alone. . . ."

Nona's body tensed. She gave a long shuddering sigh, and her sobs ceased. "I'll be all right . . . in a minute, Miss Clytie. I'm sorry I went . . . to pieces."

She reached blindly behind her, hunting into the pockets of her coat thrown over the back of the stiff bedroom chair. She scrabbled in them desperately, keeping her head down, ashamed for Clytie to see her tears. She did not find what she was hunting for. "Could . . . could you give me the loan of a handkerchief . . . Miss Clytie, please?" she asked humbly.

"Of course." Clytie went over to her chest of drawers and taking out a handkerchief brought it to Nona. She laid it on Nona's lap and sat down once more on the bed.

Nona blew her nose vigorously, mopped her eyes, and, lifting her head, faced Clytie—her own master again.

"We'd better be making some sort of plans, Miss Clytie, hadn't we?" she suggested briskly. She sounded, Clytie thought, just as she did when they were about to discuss the day's ordering. "Miss Helen's in there with Mr. Sherry now, isn't she? Will she be sitting up with him the rest of the night?"

"No," Clytie answered, "she never has. I think she's only staying until she's sure that he's sound asleep. She'd given him some of that drug the doctor let her have for him. I don't know what it is, but it's awfully strong. After Sherry's had it, he always sleeps heavily all night. Although—" Clytie shook her head a little, "I think Helen must have given Sherry more than usual, he was very excitable and strange when I was with him. I was really worried about him, Nona, there for a while. I've never known it to affect him like that before—it frightened me. . . . But he got more quiet; and by the time Helen came in, and I left, he was growing drowsy. Once he's in that deep sleep, Helen will undoubtedly leave him, for she'll know that she has hours before he wakes. And by then— Well, she'll feel ready for all of us." Clytie sighed and shifted her position. Her back was aching. "It's more than likely, Nona, that while we've been talking here, Helen has already gone to her room and gone to bed."

"And . . . to sleep!" Nona exclaimed caustically. "I wouldn't put it past her—she's got no conscience. But what I was thinking, Miss Clytie, is that we shouldn't leave things to chance. We'd better take spells through what there's left of the night, you and I, watching over Mr. Sherry. It's got to be one of us that's with him when he does wake up."

"Yes, Nona. . . . I'd thought of that. Only . . . I wasn't going to ask you. I was going to do it alone."

"No, Miss Clytie, you're not to. I'm twice as strong as you, for all that I'm four years older. . . . Shall I take a peek out into the hall, to see if the lights are still on? If Miss Helen's gone to her room, she'll have turned them out."

"Yes, do, Nona," Clytie murmured. She was all at once conscious of being appallingly tired. "That's a good idea."

Nona got up, unlocked the door, and opened it a cautious crack. She closed it again softly.

"They're still on," she told Clytie as, patiently, she returned to her chair.

"There's nothing to do then," Clytie said, "but wait."

"That's all," Nona agreed, folding her reddened servant's hands, once more over one another in her lap.

There was a very long silence.

Clytie broke it at last.

"The strangest thing happened to me tonight, Nona," Clytie began. She sounded tentative and a little abashed. "I'm afraid when I tell you, you *will* think I'm crazy—that I'm really imagining things. I . . . I heard the bell buoy."

Nona sat up straight. She was extremely startled. "You did *what*, Miss Clytie?"

"I thought that I heard the bell buoy. . . ."

"But you couldn't have—it's been gone for nigh on eighteen years!"

"I know it— But listen, Nona. I heard a bell ringing, I'm sure that I did. Deep and slow . . . a sort of tolling. . . . Just as the bell buoy used to do. . . . It was when I was in with Sherry. I'd left him for a moment and gone out into his sitting room to get something— I've forgotten what now. I was standing there near his desk, and all of a sudden I was aware of a bell ringing . . . tolling. . . . I heard it clearly, Nona. As clearly as I have ever heard anything. I could not have imagined it. And . . . there is only one bell that I have ever heard that sounds that way— Only one. . . ."

Clytie's voice trailed off. Slowly across her face, came an expression compounded of so many things that it became none at all: a completely blank, dead look.

"No other bell that sounds that way. . . ." she repeated in a whisper, "*except*. . . . Except . . . long ago . . . the one that Malcolm—"

Shocking in its suddenness, Clytie's voice came alive.

"Oh God—Nona, Nona . . ." she cried. "I've remembered. . . . And now it's all falling into place. . . . It's there for me to see. The whole monstrous plan. . . . Evil . . . diseased . . . cruel beyond belief. . . . Her *pastime*, Nona, for twenty years! . . . My instinct was right, horrible and right!"

Suddenly Clytie was on her feet, holding to the bedpost, her face chalky white.

"Oh, Nona, help me now," she whispered. "Because . . . *my dread has come true*."

Nona's strong arms closed around her.

"Quiet, Miss Clytie, quiet. . . . Hold on to me. . . . Everything will be all right."

She held her, soothing her, comforting her, as she might a child.

"Nona. . . ."

She bent her head to catch Clytie's whisper.

"Nona . . . I'm afraid," Clytie said then in a very small voice, "I'm awfully afraid, Nona, that I might be going to be sick. . . .

"There, Miss Clytie, there. . . . Over here," Nona urged gently. . . . "Oh poor . . . Miss Clytie. . . ."

CHAPTER TWENTY-ONE

Helen sat alone and very still by the side of Sherry's bed. Perhaps ten minutes had gone by since Clytie had left the room, perhaps more nearly twenty had passed—Helen was not aware of time.

Her white curls, which had been twisted into tighter tendrils by the moisture outside, gleamed softly in the lamplight, framing her rosy, childlike face with a fleecy nimbus like a careless aureole. The little hollows at the base of her throat moved gently in and out with her quiet breathing: she seemed peaceful, confident, and utterly serene— But she was none of these things. . . .

The sudden feeling of uncertainty which had assailed her on the cliff had not lessened its disturbing hold upon her. It had, indeed, sharpened in intensity with the hard, still look which Clytie had given her when, in the doorway, Clytie had glanced back, and for the first time her eyes had met Helen's own. It was an appraising look that Helen had seen in them; and yet it was oddly impersonal, too, as if Clytie had looked at a stranger. There had been no rancor in it, no censure or blame, for it had had in it nothing of emotion—but, seeing it, Helen had thought: I am hated.

A link was snapped. . . . An old source of strength failed and was no more. . . .

Helen did not love. The bonds of twinship, exigent for Clytie throughout their lives, had not fastened her. But, free, giving no love, she yet had need of Clytie's. Without it—knowing it, in that still look of Clytie's, so suddenly and strangely lost— Helen was weakened. Uncertainty grew strong; and slyly, treading at uncertainty's heels, fear entered in upon her. . . .

Sitting there so quietly, watching Sherry, Helen did not admit its presence. Valiantly—or was it cravenly? for perhaps just then they were the same—determinedly, Helen denied her fear. She gave to the cold, tight feeling within her other names—she exorcised it with many reasons. She explained to herself that she was cold and tired and very, very sleepy: that the past three days had been an exhausting strain, and the last three hours an agonizing effort. This feeling, she told herself, this unpleasant sensation of thin clammy fingers slowly closing tight around something way inside her—this feeling could come from nothing more than—Helen found her innocuous phrase—than, "the inevitable reaction." . . . She was being extremely silly, stupidly overanxious. . . . Why didn't she pack up and go to bed?— Sherry was asleep. . . .

Of course he was asleep.

What made her think that he wasn't sleeping?

He was lying there utterly still. . . . His eyes were closed, and he was breathing evenly. . . . Too evenly . . . was that why she thought he might be, after all, awake? It was nonsense . . . completely fantastic. . . . Hadn't she made sure that he wouldn't wake. . . . Taken an awful chance, and doubled the amount of the drug? Of course he was asleep; he must be. . . . She was being very foolish; everything would come out all right, in spite of the upsetting way Clytie had looked at her. . . . There was nothing to worry about— Sherry was asleep. She had plenty of time to plan: Sherry would go on, sleeping like this, dead to the world, for hours. . . .

Sherry spoke without opening his eyes.

"That's you, isn't it, Helen?"

"Sherry!" Helen's startled gasp was loud in the hushed room. "I—I thought you were sound asleep."

Sherry chuckled, but his laughing had no mirth. His voice, slurred and thickened by the drug, was bitter.

"You gave me too much for that. Sleep! . . . I've been through hell."

The words, coming from the motionless figure on the bed, still stretched in an attitude of utter repose . . . the eyes closed, the long arms quiet upon the counterpane . . . had an effect of added violence.

"I'm sorry," Helen faltered. She moved her shoulders, offering up . . . to the still figure, the closed eyelids . . . a little gesture of deprecation. She lied. "It's been so long. . . . You frightened me. . . . I had . . . forgotten . . . how much." She said in a warm rush, "Darling boy, you were in such pain! I only wanted to help. . . ."

She waited then. While inside her, uncertainty grew great with fear, like a woman with child. And but for an imperceptible arching of the eyebrows above the closed eyes, she would not have known that she had been heard. . . . First Clytie and now Sherry. . . . Could it be possible that he no longer believed her? Was she, in this moment of her need, to be utterly bereft? She tried again:

"Dearest, I was alarmed, confused— I can't bear to see you suffer. When I realized what I had done—that I'd made such a dangerous mistake—I was sick with anxiety. Please, dear boy, speak to me. . . . Tell me that I'm forgiven and that you understand . . . ?"

It was going to be all right, after all. . . . She need not have worried. . . . Sherry had opened his eyes and was looking at her.

"Where is Molly?" Sherry said.

"Molly . . . ?" To Helen's own ears, the word sounded shrill. She steadied her voice. "Molly? Why she's in her room, of course, sound a—"

"Get her, please."

"Why Sherry, she's sound asleep!"

"That doesn't matter. I want to see Molly; will you go and get her, please, Helen?"

"No, I won't."

Face to face with the danger she most dreaded, Helen's uncertainty left her. Largely the terror of anticipation, the fear of the unknown about-to-happen—now that it was here, concrete and upon her, Helen's panic subsided. She was calm and confident once more. Briskly, she proceeded to deal with the matter. If, in her heart, she knew that she but held time back, she soothed herself that it was enough. The morning—those daylight hours, only now a short span away—had become for her a magic elixir, remedying everything.

"No, I won't," said Helen flatly. "The idea is perfectly ridiculous. And very inconsiderate and selfish of you, as well. I absolutely refuse to go in and wake poor Molly out of a sound sleep, merely because you say that you wish to see her."

Sherry's eyes had closed again. He said dreamily, as if recalling something from a long way off:

"I saw Molly tonight." He paused for a moment; and then, drawing it in, the haunting image in his mind: "She was there . . . on the edge of the cliff. . . . Tall and white and glimmering. . . . She flung up her arms, just as—"

Helen was too quick. Fear betrayed her. Caught off guard, she said before she could stop:

"You couldn't have! You were here—in your room."

A long instant, her words, monstrous, betraying, hung naked in the silence between them; while, very slowly once more, Sherry's eyes came open, and he looked full at Helen. And for a lost, cold, hollow instant—watching the heavy lids lift inexorably from over the steady gray eyes that now looked, straight and hard, into hers—Helen sought desperately for other words with which to cover her quick words' nakedness, and could find for herself none.

Sherry found them for her.

The reprieve—sudden, unmerited, when she believed everything lost—left Helen shaken. She had blundered, appallingly, stupidly—how could she longer trust her tongue and brain? She thought, as she had thought before that night: I am getting old. . . .

"What do you mean by that, Helen?" Sherry's eyes probed hers: the reprieve was not yet. Now it came: "You don't understand. . . ." he sounded faintly puzzled now because she didn't, nothing more. "Molly was there tonight on the cliff. The headlights caught her as I came round the corner of the house, and, just for a second, I saw her there. . . . She was all in white—wearing something white with long full skirts. She looked tall, and familiar, and unreal. Like . . . like a ghost in my memory. And then, out of the blue, it happened to me— In the flash of a moment that I saw her there, she flung up her arms and . . . I remembered."

Again Sherry's eyes found Helen's.

Again, as though it must stand alone, rounded and apart from all else: "I *remembered*, Helen," Sherry repeated.

Helen was brave. For another long, cold, emptied instant, she held her eyes steady to his—suffering in her own, the knowledge that she saw in them; and leaving unanswered, but for that, the reproachful challenge of his words.

She had, queerly, a sort of victory. It was Sherry who looked away.

He turned his head from her, and once more his eyes closed— shutting themselves against the pity that he would not feel. He knew, then, that through all the bitterness his new knowledge had brought him—his sad certainty of what Helen was—he had clung on to hope: the hope that by some merciful ingenuity of his own, he might persuade himself that she was not to blame. That hope had died before the barren defiance in her eyes. Helen was guilty— of how much, or how far-reachingly, Sherry was not sure. But of this he was—he was going to find out. Helen was guilty, and he would not pity her. . . . He spoke again now, his voice slow and weary with disillusion.

"Why have you lied to me, Helen? . . . all my life."

"Lied to you, dear boy . . . ?"

"Please, Helen, don't. . . . I've remembered. It's no use any more. . . . Answer me, Helen. Why?"

"I . . . I believed you had forgotten. I thought it was better that way."

"Nell . . . Nell. . . ." Pity, forbidden, was there, close to him. "You can't be sincere in that."

"I am!" Helen cried. "How could I bear—"

"For over twenty years, denying me the truth. . . ."

"How could you expect me to tell it to you! How could I bear for you to know that your mother was— That your mother had killed herself?"

"Better that I should believe myself mad?"

"Sherry . . . !"

"Oh yes, Helen!—isn't it odd that you should wince, Nell, because . . . at last . . . I've said the words? Isn't it that, that you've let me believe? Growing up through the years . . . haunted by old terrors . . . tormented by half-memories. . . . Plagued and bedeviled by things in my mind that I couldn't explain? Tortured. Until— Until there was only one explanation that would fit, only one ugly truth left for me to find? 'Better that way,' you said. God in heaven, Helen! Tell me? Do you know a 'better' route through Hell?"

Helen didn't answer. A small silence took the violence of Sherry's words and dropped them into quiet.

After a moment, Helen said primly:

"That was a most uncharitable thing to say." Her tone softened, became warm with urgency, "I never knew. . . . Can you suppose," she pleaded, "that had I ever dreamed that you—"

"You're lying, Helen," Sherry said bluntly. "Why don't you stop? How often must I tell you that's no use? . . . But if it's any consolation, let me assure you that it failed to work. I married Molly, there's your proof. I couldn't have done that, if I hadn't been sure. God knows how, but I was. Yes, in spite of everything—the whole bag of bogy tricks: headaches and bells and what besides— I've always known that I wasn't off my rocker. There've been bad patches, I'll admit. But straight through the whole rotten hell of it—down underneath I've never been convinced for a single second that I wasn't perfectly sane." He paused and added almost apologetically, "I must be super-tough mentally, Helen, for, as you see, it didn't work."

"You speak," began Helen plaintively, "as though you actually believed that I—" She stopped abruptly, thinking better of this. She grew wary—here was dangerous ground. Implications, no matter how obvious, were best left unchallenged. The whole thing was going very badly: getting dreadfully out of hand. But in the morning it would all be different. . . . She said brightly.

"I'm so glad. Then everything's all right, isn't it?"

She got up and tucked in a corner of the blanket; she made brisk patting movements indicative of settling Sherry down to sleep. Still Sherry did not open his eyes.

"Sit down, Helen," he commanded quietly.

"Dear boy, you've really got to get to sleep. . . . I'll sit down, but you must promise not to talk. You've been very ill tonight, and you must be feeling—"

"I am. I feel damn-awful," Sherry agreed. "What can you expect? It's been like all the hangovers ever perpetrated, rolled into one. For hours—is it hours?—I've been whirling down tunnels stood on end, and whooshing up out of them again. *Tant pis*, I've grown quite accustomed to it by now; and the tunnels are getting much shorter and they've lost all their pretty, jagged lights. They're merely an uninteresting gray. What a pity! . . . Sorry Helen, but I'm not going to sleep. Not until you've told me my bedtime story. Sit down, Nell, the sooner you begin, the sooner it'll be over."

"Sherry!" Helen gasped. "You can't mean—?"

"Yes, I do, Helen. Just that."

"But Sherry, dear, of course. I'll tell you all about it, just as it happened— Only not, darling boy, tonight. In the morning . . . some other time. . . ."

"No, Helen. Now. Tonight."

Sherry's voice left her no escape.

"Sherry!" Unutterable weariness surged over Helen—the old story, the old words, now when she was so tired? So completely spent? . . . But, if she must, she would buy with it the safety that she had to have. "Well, if I do—" Helen spread it before him like a peddler showing his wares— "If I consent to go into all that at this time of night, will you promise, after I've finished, to go straight to sleep? Will you give up any foolish notion you may still entertain of—"

"Of waking Molly?" Sherry ended for her. "God damn it, Helen," he said angrily, "I'm not a child, to be wheedled with bargains! Yes, probably I will, for on second thought, Molly's undoubtedly had all she can stomach of me tonight—she was in here, I'm almost sure, just before Clytie came. Still, Clytie will have explained for me. . . . 'Your husband's hopped to the eyeballs, my dear.' . . . Nice, isn't it! I'm not likely to find courage to wake Molly tonight if, as you say, she's fast asleep. But I'll be damned," Sherry said, returning to where he started, "if I'll promise you like a two-year-old. Have you no conception of what has happened to me tonight? Never mind—" he brushed aside her protest—"let it ride. . . . Sit down, Nell, and tell me—slowly and in all its details, so that I can check it, bit by bit, with my memory—the story that for twenty long years you've refused to tell. Give it to me now, Helen. The Story of my Mother's Death. And—" said Sherry harshly, with a kind of sad and driven flippancy—"make it good."

The room was very quiet as, at long last, Helen's gentle voice took up once more the old story of Janet's death . . . so polished, so well-worn with repetition, that she was hardly conscious of the words she said. Sherry lay perfectly still upon the bed; the curve of his closed eyelids, the little shadows under his cheekbones and along the line of his jaw, molded his face into an appearance of utter repose—he looked as if now, indeed, he slept. . . .

A sense of peace wrapped Helen. Turbulence and fear flowed away on the drowsy tide of Sherry's quiet breathing. The hushed, tender sound rose and fell under the muted cadence of her voice, until, listening to it alone, Helen no longer even heard the words that she was saying. . . . Unheeded, she sent them out, memorized, obedient, into the shadowed lamplight—to where, remote and still upon the big bed, Sherry lay in his waking sleep.

Lulled by somnolent peace, Helen's mind forgot its wariness. She saw, not a scene grown dim through the passing of many years, but another, vivid and near to her, with no more than an hour's going. Her lips told Janet's story, but her treacherous mind told Molly's. She saw, instead of Janet's motionless dark head, Molly's fair one; and, as she spoke, watched once again a sheen of glinting light shift along the sleek fall of Molly's hair, as ever so slowly, her head began to move in time with the tolling of the bell.

Slyly, so smoothly that Helen was unaware that it had happened, the new story wove itself into the old:

"Moving her head," Helen said aloud, "ever so little in rhythm with the ringing of the bell. . . ."

Unnoticed, out of the vivid picture in her mind, the new words inserted themselves into the old; and Helen never knew that she

had said them. A little phrase . . . insignificant, unrevealing, carrying in itself no danger . . . it sounded, nonetheless, the danger
ahead. But, secure in a sleepy peace, grown falsely confident, Helen
failed to hear its warning. . . . And yet, already she had blundered
and been reprieved, when truth slipped into speech.

Perhaps had Sherry not lain so still upon the bed—if, just then,
he had looked at her—had he, too, not seemed wholly unconscious
of the words that she was saying, Helen might have realized her
danger. But the little phrase that did not belong, like a tiny warning signal, slid by unnoticed; and the remembered words went on,
telling a story that she did not see; while before her eyes, Molly
ran and moved and spoke in Janet's stead. . . . And, where a sentry
should have stood guard between her thoughts and her words,
Helen posted none. . . .

She brought it out . . . that well-worn story . . . shaping it in her
gentle voice, as she had for Clytie and Nona . . . for Malcolm . . .
and, so short a time ago, for Molly herself. . . . She told it again
now . . . automatically, unthinkingly, for the last time . . . to the
remote, still figure that lay, seemingly unhearing, upon the bed.
And . . . telling it, Helen had never felt more safe.

And never before, with any listener, had she been in like danger.

Sherry lay perfectly still, every nerve alert—all his senses focused on the single act of listening. He had closed his eyes because,
without the distraction of sight, his hearing always seemed to him to
be more acute. He could hear nuances, subtleties of sound, that he
might otherwise have missed; he could detect the delicate shade of
falseness in a voice, the faint overtone of emphasis that betrayed a lie.

He heard every word that Helen spoke, testing it for accuracy,
as a musician might test with his tuning fork a note struck slightly
off key. He recognized the 'absolute pitch' of truth in the vivid little
phrase that was Helen's unheeded danger signal: and, although he
could not remember that his mother had moved her head to the
bell's ringing, he thought then that it must be so.

At first he had been satisfied. In the beginning the story had
been true: answering to the test of his hearing; checking, in all
that mattered, with his memory. But now— Now it was all a lie.

"She had become more quiet," Helen said, "and I thought I had succeeded in calming her fears. She said something about being able to sleep, took you by the hand, and left the room. . . ."

No, said Sherry's memory, no: feeling again the trembling of his mother's body as, sensing her terror, he pressed his own close to hers; seeing, once more, through a window that was not there, a little boat, pitching and tossing, trailing from its mast a pennant of blue fire. . . . No, said his memory, no. It was not that way. . . . You have left out the boat, Helen . . . and your story is no longer true.

"She left the room," Helen said. "And a moment later I heard her footsteps running down the stairs. I snatched up a coat and followed "

That was not what happened, corrected Sherry's memory. You still are lying, Helen, his memory said. You were with us on the stairs. . . .

It had all come back to him now—it lived, vivid and real, through each remembering nerve of his body, held stretched and motionless upon the bed.

The stairs were very steep, and he was frightened. . . . They had him by the hands— Helen on one side, his mother on the other. They were half-carrying, half-dragging him, because he could not go as fast as they were going. They tugged at him, uncaring. . . . And that frightened him even more than the stairs; for he knew by their remote and terrifying indifference to him—their terrible, adult preoccupation—that in that vast, grown-up world of theirs, some-thing was dreadfully wrong. . . .

He heard the sharp urgency in Helen's voice, and his child's instinct linked it with his mother's cold, shaking fingers, that, tightly as she held to his, could not stop their trembling. Around his other hand Helen's grip was hot and firm; and with instant cer-tainty, he knew that he hated Helen. . . . Hated her fiercely for making his mother afraid . . . for the cruel, sharp thing in her voice that was making his mother tremble. . . . She would not stop. In that strange, shrill voice that he had never heard, she kept crying to his mother to hurry—to go faster, faster. . . . And they tugged and pulled at him and did not know how much it was hurting. . . .

Then they were out of doors, in the rain and the darkness . . . running, dragging him between them, running. . . . Until the cliff was there and the sea. . . .

Helen's voice cried louder than ever before— "Run, Janet, run! . . . Get to the light, quickly, quickly. . . ."

And suddenly, when she had said it, Helen stopped. She did not run any more. She stood still, all at once, where she was; yanking him back by his arm, stopping him, too. So that trying to follow his mother . . . trying to hold on to her . . . he couldn't, he stumbled and fell, hitting his head. . . . Unable to get up . . . unable to stop his mother running away from him. . . . (Not toward the point of the cliff, as he had remembered it first. . . . No, that was wrong.) Running across the dark lawn toward the post where the deep crevice was. . . . Only the post wasn't there . . . for afterward, just before Helen picked him up, he had seen it lying on the ground, level with his eyes. . . .

He had cried to his mother to stop . . . to come back to him hurt and frightened. . . . But Helen had cried out again, drowning his voice . . . so that his mother did not listen . . . so that she could not even hear him. . . . "Run, Janet, run," Helen cried, standing stockstill there behind him. "Faster, faster! Go on, hurry, hurry—"

And . . . helpless, watching, then he had seen it happen. . . . The swift, forward flight. . . . The tiptoed pause . . . the upflung arms, the whole body poised, white and glimmering. . . . That, for an instant, and suddenly there was only black emptiness to see . . . his mother was gone. And, tall and terrible, standing over him, as though, even now she could not find it enough, once more Helen cried: "Run, Janet, run!" and, low in her throat, she laughed.

That was how it was, said Sherry's memory. That was what happened, Helen.

The true story was finished—he had remembered it all. He felt tranquil and sleepy. Tomorrow, freed of old terrors, he could go to Molly. "Happy ever after" . . . the end of the story. . . . He lay very still, only half-listening now, while Helen's gentle voice flowed on— tenderly, persuasively, fashioning its lies. . . .

"I cried to her to stop," said Helen. And she, too, was living it again—forgetting wariness, absorbed, unmindful of her words. Telling one story . . . thinking another . . . until it was too late, and by a fatal slip of the tongue, the mistake had been made.

"I called to her," Helen said, thinking to say Janet's name, but watching Molly running . . . watching Molly falling. . . . Seeing Molly . . . only Molly.

"I cried out to her," Helen said. "I cried: 'Stop, Molly, stop! Molly . . . Molly. . . .'"

The wrong name had been said; and in an instant's forgetting, everything was lost. . . . From this blunder there would be no reprieve. Even as she spoke it, hearing at last, too late, her words, Helen knew herself condemned.

Sherry's eyes came open.

"Nell . . . what have you said?" he whispered slowly. "Do you know what you have said?"

His eyes found hers.

"Why! . . ." Instinctively she tried to tuck it away. "Just a . . . break in speech."

In his eyes she saw no mercy. They were hard and cold. He stared at her, unbelieving. Yet, when he spoke, his voice was soft . . . and somehow, that seemed to her worse.

"You've made your second slip, Helen," Sherry said in an oddly conversational tone that frightened her more than anything had ever frightened her in her life. "And now I believe I understand the first. I think I know what made you say I could not have seen Molly on the cliff because I was here in my room. . . . Where is Molly?" Sherry asked, still in that empty, curiously social way—it was as though he had said: "Isn't Molly joining us for tea?" But mercilessly, the stern eyes that belied his careless tone kept searching in hers. Suddenly he sat up. "WHAT," he thundered all at once in a terrible voice, "HAVE YOU DONE TO MOLLY!"

Helen giggled. She shook her curls gaily.

"Done to Molly, darling boy? Why nothing . . . nothing at all."

Things waited.

"If you're lying," Sherry remarked, speaking once more with bland, deadly casualness, "I shall kill you, Helen. Get out of my way, Nell," he said.

Helen caught him by the arm.

"Sherry, where are you going? Get back into bed. . . . Oh," she cried angrily, "you've hurt me!"

"I told you to get out of my way," Sherry said. "I'm going to Molly."

"Please, Sherry . . . not yet," Helen begged. She caught hold of him again. "No, Sherry. No!" Helen screamed.

She clung to him, trying to stop him. He shook her roughly off; staggering a little, for the drug made his movements uncertain. She ran in front of him—a small, squat, desperate figure; her rosy face as white and stricken now as his. She wrapped her arms about him as he came toward her, throwing her weight against his tall lean body. Horribly, they jostled together.

It was a painful scene—brutal and without dignity.

Sherry pushed her before him relentlessly. Above her white curls pressed against his chest . . . her small round head, which butted him, every now and again, like a furious and demented little goat . . . his eyes stared straight ahead, blank and unseeing.

Their progress down the hall was noisy.

Neither of them paid the slightest attention to Nona and Clytie standing, amazed in horror, together on the threshold of Clytie's room. Very possibly, they did not even see them.

They reached Molly's door.

Sherry stopped. He stooped, placing his hands one on either side of Helen's waist. He braced himself. And then, with a single, strong, swift movement, he had lifted Helen clear of the floor— tossing her (there is no other word for it) to one side out of his way. He jerked open Molly's door and disappeared into the bed- room.

Helen stood in the dark doorway and jeered at him. She was beside herself with anger.

"You won't find her," she taunted, "you won't find her. She thought you were mad, and she's run away—"

Clytie spoke.

"That's a lie, Helen," Clytie said quietly.

Sherry came out again, side-stepping Helen. He seemed to see Clytie for the first time.

"Of course it's a lie," he agreed fiercely. "Every word she's uttered has been a lie. . . . I want the truth," he said to Clytie. "Clytie, you will tell me the truth. Where is Molly?"

For an instant Clytie shut her eyes. Then:

"She's drowned," Clytie answered. "Molly's dead."

"How dare you say that!" screamed Helen. "You stupid, inter-fering fool! . . . I'll fix you—"

She ran at Clytie, but Nona blocked her way. Her wiry, red-dened hands seized Helen's raised, clawing fingers in a tight grip—forcing them impotently down. For a dreadful moment, looking at them, it might have seemed to be some curious kind of parlor game that they were playing.

"Now, Miss Helen . . . now " Nana said reprovingly.

She looked over Helen's shoulder at Sherry. From the instant of Clytie's words he had not moved. She addressed a dead man:

"It's true, Mr. Sherry." She pushed Helen away from her, still holding her by the wrists. In a strange way she appeared to offer her to Sherry. Or perhaps it was merely that she wished to point to Helen, and could not, because her hands were not free. "She did it, Mr. Sherry," Nona said. "She killed Miss Molly."

The dead do not hear: Sherry made no reply.

"Liar . . . liar. . . ." Imprisoned in Nona's grip, Helen swiveled her head round at Sherry. "I did not! I did not! I never laid a finger on her!"

With a sudden, violent twist of her wrists, Helen broke away from Nona. She flung herself on Sherry, circling him with her arms; throwing her head back to look beseechingly up at the white death mask of his face. She pleaded with him, pressing herself against his rigid, unresponsive body.

"You believe me, darling boy, don't you?" she implored. "I couldn't bear to tell you. . . . I did everything I could. I cried to her to stop . . . I called to her. That's why, don't you see? Oh, you must see, that's why I made that funny break in speech— I cried, "Stop, Molly, stop!" just as you heard me do. . . . But she wouldn't listen because she thought you were mad. She killed herself . . . and I was too late to prevent it. She flung herself over the cliff and— I never laid a finger on her. I swear it. Oh, you do believe me, darling boy . . . tell me that you do!"

Not once had Sherry looked at her. Over Helen's head, he spoke again to Clytie.

"How long?"

"Three quarters of an hour, perhaps a little more," Clytie answered him.

Nona said softly, "It's no use, Mr. Sherry. The currents. . . ."

"No use!" Sherry shouted, and it was as though somewhere inside him something had, all of a sudden, begun to live again. "No use? You don't know Molly!"

After empty despair, hope is a heady thing. Sherry was drunk with it. Molly wasn't dead: Molly could be trusted: Molly wouldn't fail him by dying.

"Molly's not dead," he exulted. "She's a fighter. A rip-snorting, never-give-up fighter. . . . And how she can swim! She's got a chance . . . a good chance, and she'll win. But God! what am I doing standing here!"

Helen closed her arms tighter.

"Darling boy," she whispered, "please look at me. . . . Won't you tell me that you believe me?"

Sherry's voice went stilled and slow once more. He said:

"Take your hands from me, Helen. . . . Never touch me with yourself again so long as either of us lives." A sort of fastidious loathing spaced his words. "Because," he said, "if you do, I know that I shall surely kill you. . . ."

Then, at the very last, he looked at her, down into her upturned, waiting face.

"Strange. . . ." he murmured, "that any flesh so pink-and-white, smelling still so sweet, should seem to me noisome with corruption. . . . Take your hands from me, Nell," Sherry said. "I am going to find Molly."

CHAPTER TWENTY-TWO

A shaft of bright spring sunshine crept slowly upwards across the wide double bed, reached the man's outflung arm and touched with its tip the sleeping eyelids of the girl.

Molly stirred and moaned a little for she was dreaming.

It was dark and cold and all about her was the lapping, heaving whisper of the sea. She was drowned and dead, her body laved smooth and cold and heavy with the waves. She reached out, and against her arm and hand something moved, sea-slimy yet crisp, like the gigantic fin of a fish. In her nostrils was the decayed, dank smell of sea-weed. Her fingers closed and then, all at once, she knew what it was that she touched. She wasn't dead. She was lying naked on the boathouse floor, and the substance that her hand touched was rubber—the rubber of a heavy slicker hanging on the boathouse door. She hadn't drowned. But now—

Once more into Molly's dream came the riven terror which had flooded through her with returning consciousness on that bitter February night nearly three months ago.

She hadn't drowned. She was alive. But now, gentle and smiling, up there in the house Helen was waiting. Helen who—

Molly's eyes flew open and with a little sobbing jerk she awoke. She raised herself on one elbow; and slowly out of the turbulence of her dream, her senses found reality for her in the bright spring sunshine that promised a perfect May day, the loved, familiar objects of their bedroom, the warmth of Sherry's body beside her own. She turned, looking down at his sleeping profile outlined against the pillow, remote and calm as the head on a coin. Then, very gently, she put out her hand and touched the soft ends of his hair with her fingertips.

It was all over—behind her. Helen was dead. Dreams shattered in sunlight and terror could not stay. The events of that terrible night, the anxious days that followed—her illness, the inquest—all were back there in the past, and never again could they reach her. She was alive and well. It was a beautiful spring morning. And beside her, her husband was sleeping. It was all over. . . .

From Sherry's sitting room came the sound of a padded thud: Matilda jumping down from his chair. Molly reached for her dressing gown flung across the bottom of the bed. She had better get up and let him out. It was very early still, but there was lots to do— flowers to arrange, meals to plan with Nona, the house to be made especially bright and gay. . . . For today Clytie and Derwent were coming to see them on their way home from their honeymoon.

Molly paused in her gesture, holding her dressing gown slackly between her hands, while her eyebrows drew together in a frown. Clytie. . . . Was that the reason she had had that bad dream, started thinking about it all, all over again? Because she knew that today she would see Clytie? Oh, why couldn't she let it alone? Why must that hateful suspicion remain, down underneath everything she could do, staying there to torment her? Why must she always want to *know?* She had no right to that knowledge. Even if it was true, she should be ready to accept it since through it had come her happiness. . . . Impatiently, Molly completed her gesture, and pulling her dressing gown about her shoulders, slipped out of bed. Banish it, forget it, that was what she must do. . . .

But she was dream-haunted still; and when she had let the black cat out into the hall, impelled by an impulse she no longer tried to check, she followed him to where he stopped as always outside the closed door of Helen's room. She recognized the symptoms of her mind and knew that it was no use. As she would have expressed it, she was 'for it': on this perfect May morning she was going to hash. . . . Better get on with it then—moil it all over as she had not allowed herself to do. . . . Look at it, take it apart, and then perhaps it would go. . . .

"Come on, Matilda," Molly said, "you and I are going to hold a wake."

With her hand on the knob Molly looked down for an instant at the black cat, arching and rubbing himself against her legs, then with something like despair she pushed open the door and walked in.

She had dreaded the moment when she would see Helen's room again; the idea of this second had both fascinated and repelled her, but now that it was there she felt nothing. The room, unaltered, was changed into another by the bright sunlight streaming through the windows. Gone was its shadowed mystery, its impalpable air of evil. It was humdrum, a little shabby, and above all, staid. Molly let out the breath she had unconsciously been holding, sat down in the chair where she had sat before, put her elbows on her knees and her chin in her hands.

Helen was gone. Helen was dead. . . . And that had changed the room far more than the sunlight. . . . Just as it had changed Matilda . . . not a black familiar, merely a cat, ordinary and quite nice. . . . Helen, alive, had distorted everyone and everything she touched— twisting them, animate or inanimate, by some malignant power into a facet of herself, until they, too, wore the taint of her corruption. She had done it by charm, for Helen had been charming. . . .

And thinking of her, sitting there in the early morning sunshine, Molly was aware of how much, in spite of it all, she had liked Helen. It had seemed to her then, and it still seemed to her now, that a curious bond had existed between them—something that in other circumstances might have been called friendship. And she wondered if Helen, too, had liked her. . . . If she had wanted to kill her, or had only been driven by fear. Had Helen hated her for herself alone, or only for what, inadvertently, she knew? Molly would never be sure. She had heard the bell and Helen dared not let her live.

Molly smiled, a little ruefully. Guilt made truth seem always near at hand: Helen had thought her far cleverer than she was. Almost at the very beginning, her second night at Prescott Point, standing in Sherry's room, running past Helen's door, she had heard the bell buoy ringing. And yet, later, leaning from her window, she had noticed, but hardly questioned, that in all the ocean speech the bell was silent. She had said that to herself like a line of poetry, pleased with it, but she had not asked how that could be. . . . She had held in her hands the key to it all and for the want of a little thought—the elementary adding of one plus one to make two—she had let it drop. Submerged somewhere in her mind, the discrepancy of a bell buoy never to be heard out of doors, remained a formless oddity and that was all.

But even if she had worked it out, Molly decided, determined to be quite fair to herself, even if she had arrived at the obvious—that the 'bell buoy' was merely a bell ringing in Helen's room—even then, she could never have grasped its significance. How could one's imagination reach to so strange a goal?

And suddenly, in asking herself this, Molly realized that she need not have been thought clever, after all. She saw quite clearly, all at once, that it had not been necessary for her to understand to have become a mortal danger to Helen. She had only to hear, and having heard to speak of hearing, and all that Helen had successfully hidden—the mental torturing of Sherry, the murder of Janet—would be disclosed. For the moment that Sherry's ghost-bell (which Helen had made him believe he alone could hear) was heard by another, Helen was doomed—murder became her one way out.

Yes . . . Helen may have hated her as, more terribly, she had hated Janet: from jealousy, from a thwarted sense of power, for any number of reasons—but she had tried to kill her out of fear.

Fear . . . Was that the explanation behind all that had happened since Janet's death? The primary motive back of the monstrous thing which she had done to Sherry? Had Helen been hagridden by the haunting dread of disclosure through all the smug safety of twenty long years? A memory in a child's mind—had Helen feared it so much that, by a simple and yet effective means, she had sought to destroy it? Even though, by so doing, she risked the destruction of that very mind itself? *Fear* . . . the start of it all. . . .

Only later, perhaps, had come the cruel satisfaction of power . . . the wicked joy in the absolute domination of another's soul. . . .

The exoneration was shoddy and yet, out of scrupulous justice, Molly offered it to Helen.

She got up, crossing the room to where the tapestry curtain hung over the sill-less window. Her fingers found a switch, and the sun-lit room once more was filled with the mournful sound of the bell's low tolling. Behind her she heard Matilda jump down from Helen's chair and the pad of his paws as he trotted to her feet, to sit upright with alert pricked ears and eyes fixed expectantly. With a little shudder of anticipation, Molly put up her hands and jerked back the curtain.

But what she saw was tawdry and childish only. Like the room, bright sunlight had dispelled its mystery. Behind the false window-pane the shallow cupboard showed as no more than a few feet deep. The black velvet hanging against its back wall was seamed and dusty and limp with age. Only the cunningly arranged lamplight glinting across the pane had transformed it into the depth and blackness of night. Before it, a crude silhouette of cardboard waves stretched from side to side, while dingy billows of gray gauze completed the foreground of the sea.

Again Molly touched a switch and, listening carefully, heard below the bell's monotonous tolling the tiny whirring sound of some simple sort of machinery, revolving on the cupboard floor behind the masking screen of painted waves. A moment passed and then, rather jerkily, the little toy boat rose into sight to begin its patient rocking. Pallid in the sunshine, once more a blue light flashed. . . . And once more, from deep in his throat, the black cat growled.

"Hush, Matilda," Molly said gently.

Out of what seemed a very long time ago, she remembered Nona—dear Nona, whom she had called The Ghost—standing there on that first morning of all, at the foot of the bed, holding a tray in her hands. "Always making things," Nona had said. "Although, mind you, they weren't all sensible like this tray. . . . Some of them were plumb foolish."

Plumb foolish . . . A boy's innocent plaything, turned by adult ingenuity into a bizarre implement of death and the means of a child's torturing. Malcolm's wife and Malcolm's son. . . . Had he ever dreamed that through a creation of his own hands—

"But he never knew," Molly whispered to herself, "in mercy, he never knew. . . ." Anymore than he had sensed, she thought, the consuming and incestuous love which Helen had borne for him. He had been spared that too. Just as, until the very end, Sherry had been spared. . . . For until that moment in the hall, the last time he was ever to see Helen, Sherry had not known that to himself in turn had been transferred the dark, tormented longing of Helen's forbidden love. And only for that one moment was he to suffer the revulsion and horror which this knowledge had brought to him. Helen had died . . . and with her death had come cleanness and peace and forgetting. . . .

It was all over.

She reached out, silencing the bell, bringing the little toy boat once more to rest. Then, as it began slowly to sink behind its painted waves, she drew the tapestry curtain close over the sill-less window. She turned away but not to leave the room. She knew that for her it was not over. It would never be over until she had banished forever the suspicion which troubled her, or, accepting it as true, had come to terms with it.

From whence had it sprung? How pertinent were the reasons for her suspicion? Had she more than intangibilities—a look, a tone of voice—to make her believe that it was Clytie who was guilty of Helen's death?

Molly leaned forward in her chair to touch the black cat curled at her feet, letting her fingers slip for a moment over the warm, plushy fur between his ears.

"Are you really the one, Matilda?" she murmured softly. "Was it you, after all?"

Why couldn't she believe the story that Clytie had told them? Wasn't it in the bizarre key of all the rest? And hadn't it, too, its own retaliative justice? For who but Helen, had taught the black cat his dangerous trick?— Teasing him, awakening his savagery when he was only a tiny kitten, as if through it she had found vicarious appeasement for the cruelty which lay hidden behind her gentleness. Wasn't it plausible, part of the pattern, that, springing suddenly upon her as she stood on the very edge of the cleft, it had been the black cat and not Clytie who had sent Helen hurtling to her death? And yet—

The facts leading up to that instant Molly did not question. And once more it had been Helen's fear of disclosure which had brought them about. Or, in this case, it would be truer to say her fear of its consequences. For she had known, as Clytie and Nona did, that the only *proof* of her crime was to be found in the crooked post and her footprints in the loosened soil around it; and that if she could obliterate all concrete evidence of her guilt, she would be safe—neither Clytie nor Sherry would be foolhardy enough to call in the police. She must have realized, of course, that she had lost them. It would have become very plain to her during the sordid scene in the upstairs hall that she had forfeited their allegiance. . . . She must have been, Molly thought with a quick twist of unreasoning pity, very lonely and very frightened.

So she had gone to fix the post. . . .

And while Molly lay unconscious on the boathouse floor, where only later had it occurred to Sherry to look for her—and while Sherry himself was frantically searching along the shore of the farther cove—Clytie, keeping watch at her bedroom window, had seen Helen as she stealthily crossed the dark lawn below. Knowing what she was going to do and determined to prevent her, Clytie had followed.

"My duty was plain before me," Clytie, telling them, had said sadly. "Whatever was to happen, I knew that this time I must not shirk it. My cowardice had caused enough pain. . . . Now, when it was too late for all but the cold meting out of justice, I had found at length the strength to be brave. I went down to Helen there on the cliff. . . ."

Helen had not heard Clytie coming for the noise of the waves drowned the sound of her footsteps. She was, besides, wholly absorbed in what she was doing—tugging and pulling on the heavy chain to gain enough slack so that the post would be straight. Oblivious of her danger, she stood on the very edge of the cleft where a single step backwards would carry her over. . . .

And then, just as Clytie was about to speak to her—quietly so as not to startle her, so close was she to the edge—the black cat appeared out of the darkness, crouched for an instant and sprang, hurling himself violently against Helen's knees. Before Clytie could change her words to a cry, Helen was gone. . . . That was the story Clytie told.

Molly's memory went back to the vivid and unforgettable moments of its telling. She closed her eyes, shutting off the present, the sun-lit room—seeing again a look on Clytie's face . . . hearing again the controlled emptiness of her voice, as though by an indomitable effort of the will, each word were being drained of the emotion it might betray.

That was it, that was one of her reasons: Clytie had been so taut, so careful. . . .

And forgetting nothing, living it again, Molly's searching mind began now with the first instant of it all, when, shivering with shock and cold, once more Sherry had carried her over the threshold. . . . Once more the door had opened as though of itself and Nona was there . . . and, this time, behind her, Clytie. . . .

"Helen is dead," Clytie had said.

She waited for them there in the bright hall, erect and rigid under the garish lights, in her cruel mauve wrapper, her braid of iron-gray hair lying over her shoulder. And for all the incongruity—of wrapper and pigtail and middle-aged spinsterhood—so might, Molly thought, an executioner have stood—tortured and yet unswervingly bound by his bitter duty. . . .

And watching her, as in her flat voice, her lips scarcely moving, she had told her story, Molly had shivered again, though not from cold.

"I saw Helen there," Clytie had said, "standing on the very spot from where twenty years ago she had sent Janet plunging to her death. And where, only tonight, another young girl had known safety still beneath her feet in that last awful instant, before she, too, had gone hurling downward into the blackness. . . . She stood there," Clytie said. "And I thought: In that tiny stretch of earth . . . that little span of ground between her feet and the black emptiness beyond . . . lies all justice and retribution."

Clytie had stopped. And it had seemed as though for her, in those final words, the end of the story had been reached.

Sherry spoke into the silence. Pity and horror mingled in his voice. "Clytie . . . Are you telling us that *you*. . . ?"

And it had been then that Clytie had looked at her—that look, that in remembering, had made Molly so sure. . . . A long look, searching and yet beseeching, as though Clytie had asked of her an assurance and a pledge.

Before her closed eyes she saw once more the little smile, bitter and curiously tender, which had twisted Clytie's lips as at last, turning from her, she had answered Sherry.

"No, Sherman, no," Clytie had said. "You have not that to face too. Right as it was that she should die, I did not kill Helen."

And Molly had known, by the relaxed pressure of his hand upon her arm, that Sherry had believed her. . . .

"'You have not that to face too'"—In the sunlight, remembering, Molly's head moved nodding, just as it had moved on a winter night three months ago. "I promised you, Clytie," Molly said. "I shall not forget. . . ."

She got up, crossing to the window, to stare with unseeing eyes out at the bright May morning. There it was, the sum of her intangibilities: A smile, a tone of voice, a look that passed between them. . . . And yet now, more than ever, she was sure.

Remembering it all again had not brought her what she'd hoped for, but it had brought her this: she knew at last what troubled her. And, queerly, it had not to do with Clytie but with her. What Clytie had done, belonged to Clytie only—looking into herself, Molly knew her feeling for Clytie to be untouched by what she believed. That feeling had grown, during the days of her illness, into a vital and warm affection, upon which her secret suspicion had left neither embarrassment nor constraint. Like Matilda, like Nona, like the very house itself, Clytie had altered since Helen's death.

Or perhaps it was, thought Molly, only that she had come to know and understand her. Yes . . . if it were only for Clytie, Molly could say that it was truly over. She could forget, and it would be as though it had never been. . . . But there was Sherry. . . . And so long as anything lay hidden between them, Molly could not be at peace.

They had come so close together. All she had dreamed, all that she had believed of her "sweet infallible remedy," had come true. All that she had been, or was, or would be, was a part of Sherry now, as all that he had been, or was, or would be, was a part of her. And yet, because he must never know, all her life she must go on carrying within her this one thing which she must never show him. Spoiling by it alone the completeness of their sharing. . . .

A little sense of resentment moved in Molly. And leaning her head against the window frame, she knew with surprise that what she felt was disappointment. Because they were so close, she asked of their closeness a miracle. She was hurt, she was disappointed that, although she could never tell him, Sherry had not known what it was that she hid. Perhaps some day, Molly acknowledged to herself with a sudden burst of realistic common sense, she might be glad that it couldn't be so—but now, right then, she wanted to think that Sherry could always read her mind. She wanted to believe that he would always know exactly what she was feeling and thinking. "For I want to feel that Sherry *is* me—that's all," Molly whispered.

Sherry's voice reached her from the doorway.

"Darling . . . I missed you and woke up."

He crossed the room and kissed her, throwing his arm companionably around her shoulders. He looked down at her and smiled. "It's a beautiful morning. . . . Brooding, dear?"

"I had a bad dream." Molly reached up and touched his cheek. "I dreamed that I was back in the boathouse. . . . And somehow when I woke up I couldn't throw it off, I began thinking about it all again. I don't know why."

"Don't you, darling?—" Sherry asked. "Isn't it, perhaps, because you are going to see Clytie today?"

"But why should—" Molly stopped.

"You're such a poor liar," Sherry said gently. "You think, don't you, my dearest, that Clytie killed Helen? What's more this notion of yours has been troubling you quite a lot."

"Sherry!" Molly gasped. Now that her miracle was working she was immensely startled. "How did you know?"

Sherry laughed. "Because I was there, as the boys say. I saw it happen."

"There?" Molly felt a little confused.

"At the birth of your idea, darling." Sherry's tone sobered. "For a split second I had had the same idea myself. Don't you remember?—I practically accused poor Clytie. But even while I was doing it, I realized that of course it wasn't so. . . . You, my darling, didn't say a word, but how you looked! Your expression was a prosecuting attorney's opening address all in itself."

"Oh dear. . . ." murmured Molly, chagrined. "Did Clytie—?"

"Perhaps. I saw her look at you somewhat questioningly and she did give you a very peculiar smile just before she answered me."

Molly felt her cheeks go pink—her intangibilities!

"Oh, Sherry, I'm so sorry. I must have hurt her."

"No, dear, don't worry. For the moment maybe, but underneath all her stiffness she's very understanding, and besides which she's extremely fond of you." Sherry paused ruminatively. "I suppose, quite unconsciously, her sense of drama rather got the best of her. She did build up to it a bit, didn't she?"

"Yes," Molly agreed absently. She took a little breath. "Even so— Sherry, how can you be so sure?"

"That she didn't? Well, first of all I know Clytie. And when you know someone well you can usually predict pretty accurately how they will act in any given set of circumstances." He broke off, and tightening his arm around her, drew her closer against him. "I've been stupid not to realize how much this was worrying you. I'd thought if it were, you would have told me. . . . I see now that that was even stupider of me. Of course you couldn't. I wish with all my heart that I'd said something about it long ago. Will you forgive me, Molly?"

"Of course, Sherry dear. It's I who's been the stupid one. If you only *knew!*" But unaware of her illogicality, she hoped, quite fervently, he never would. She sighed contentedly. It didn't matter now which of them was right. . . . Everything was lovely. Marriage really worked—all the way.

"So you see," Sherry was saying, having returned to the place where he left off, "although I don't suppose it would be safe to say that any one of us is incapable of murder given enough provocation, it's reasonably safe to predict how we will behave if we are guilty. And that's my point about Clytie. If," Sherry said in a Q.E.D. sort of tone, "under terrific stress of emotion, she had conceived for one mad moment that it was her duty to kill Helen, she might have gone through with it. *But* after it was over, she would have done penance. She would have been ruthless in her punishment of herself for, no matter how righteous might have been her motives, she would have seen the act itself for what it was—a heinous crime. And there, in a nutshell, it is, darling."

"Yes . . . You mean, don't you, Sherry," Molly said, putting it really in the nutshell, "that if Clytie had done it, she would never have married Derwent?"

"Exactly. Don't you see, we have her own pattern of behavior twenty years ago to prove my point? She suspected Helen then, but because, as she's expressed it, she was a coward, she denied her suspicions. But she punished herself for her cowardice—she broke off her engagement to the brother of the girl whom she suspected her twin sister of murdering. She felt herself, because she did not speak, implicated in Helen's crime. So she refused to marry Derwent and lived a lonely old maid—loving him and wanting him still for twenty long years."

"Twenty long years," repeated Molly. "Do you remember how radiantly happy she looked the day of her wedding? So much younger—almost as if all those years had been wiped away? . . . Oh, what an idiot, I've been, darling," cried Molly contritely. "Going back to that terrible night for the proof that I might be wrong, when I should have gone to the lovely present, as you did, and found it right away!"

"You're sincerely convinced now, Molly? No more reason to brood? No more secret notions?" Sherry put his hand under chin, tilting up her head to look into her eyes. "Let's look at you. . . ."

Her eyes met his, candid and steady. Sherry kissed her. "Good morning, dearest," he said, beginning their real day there, "it's a beautiful morning. . . ."

"It's all over, darling," Molly assured him, happily. "It's all over."

They stood for a moment, quietly side by side, and then, moved by a common impulse, together they flung open the window and leaned forward into the warm spring sunshine.

COACHWHIP PUBLICATIONS

COACHWHIPBOOKS.COM

LOUIS F. BOOTH

THE BANK VAULT MYSTERY
BROKERS' END

ISBN 978-1-61646-326-7

MYSTERY AT
LYNDEN SANDS

J. J. CONNINGTON

ISBN 978-1-61646-320-5

COACHWHIP PUBLICATIONS

COACHWHIPBOOKS.COM

THE
DARTMOUTH
MURDERS

THE
WAILING ROCK
MURDERS

CLIFFORD
ORR

ISBN 978-1-61646-323-6

THE MUMMY
CASE MYSTERY

DERMOT
MORRAH

ISBN 978-1-61646-250-5

COACHWHIP PUBLICATIONS

COACHWHIPBOOKS.COM

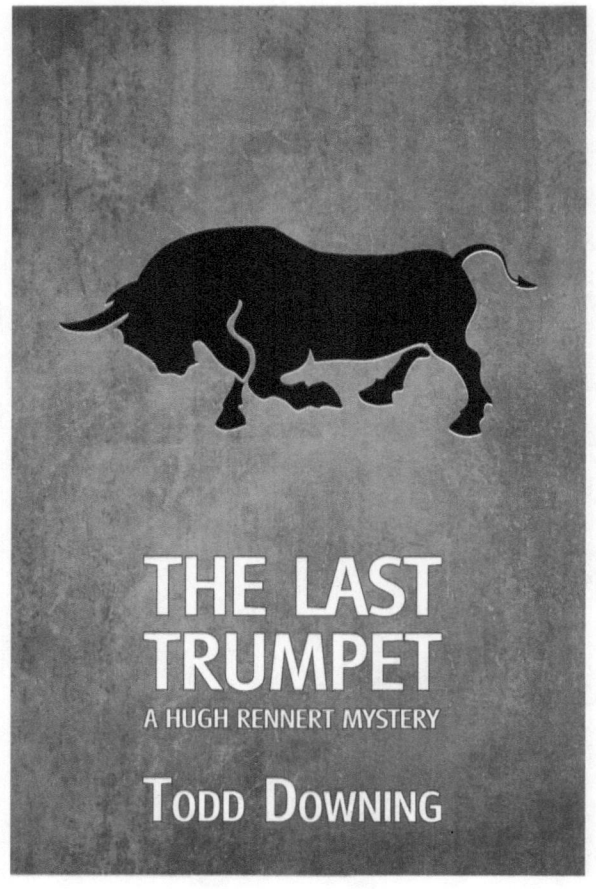

THE LAST
TRUMPET

A HUGH RENNERT MYSTERY

TODD DOWNING

ISBN 978-1-61646-152-2

COACHWHIP PUBLICATIONS

COACHWHIPBOOKS.COM

ISBN 978-1-61646-332-8

www.ingramcontent.com/pod-product-compliance
Lightning Source LLC
Chambersburg PA
CBHW021845010726
47493CB00005B/1562